I0614889

A HARD WINTER RAIN

John Inman

Dreamspinner Press

Published by
Dreamspinner Press
382 NE 191st Street #88329
Miami, FL 33179-3899, USA
http://www.dreamspinnerpress.com/

This is a work of fiction. Names, characters, places, and incidents either are the product of the author's imagination or are used fictitiously, and any resemblance to actual persons, living or dead, business establishments, events, or locales is entirely coincidental.

A Hard Winter Rain
Copyright © 2012 by John Inman

Cover Art by Reese Dante   http://www.reesedante.com

All rights reserved. No part of this book may be reproduced or transmitted in any form or by any means, electronic or mechanical, including photocopying, recording, or by any information storage and retrieval system without the written permission of the Publisher, except where permitted by law. To request permission and all other inquiries, contact Dreamspinner Press, 382 NE 191st Street #88329, Miami, FL 33179-3899, USA
http://www.dreamspinnerpress.com/

ISBN: 978-1-61372-382-1

Printed in the United States of America
First Edition
March 2012

eBook edition available
eBook ISBN: 978-1-61372-383-8

For John B., who never stopped believing.

PROLOGUE

THE man was young, still in his twenties. His skin was pale and his hair so blond as to look almost white in a certain light. His eyes were the palest blue. And cold. As cold and unforgiving as this winter night he was driving through. But for those expressionless blue eyes and the cruel way they looked out at the world, he would have been handsome.

His body was tall and lean but well-muscled, and many women had noticed the way he filled out a pair of jeans. Men, too, if the truth were known. But the pale man ignored them all. His body, his seed, had never been shared, except by one. And even then, only once. And that had happened almost a decade ago.

He drove down a rutted gravel road with graded snow piled high on either side. The snow looked dirty and stained as it reflected off the headlights of his car. The night was bitter cold, and he had the car heater cranked up as high as it would go. The hot air blowing through the heater vents made the blood on his hands feel sticky against the steering wheel.

Minutes before, he had left the farmhouse that sat at the end of this road. The farmhouse he had known all his life. The man he had grown to become was a direct result of events that had occurred inside that farmhouse. The memories that had flooded over him when he stepped back inside that house tonight after years of absence had shamed him and made him angry. And excited him. His cock was hard even now. It had been an exhilarating night. At long last, after only a few minutes of work, he had severed all links to that house. All links but one. And that final link would be severed soon enough.

After several miles, the gravel road came to an end, and the man pulled onto a highway that would eventually lead him to his home. But it would not be his home much longer. Tonight he would sever that link as well, and his mission would truly begin. The mission God had set for him. The mission that would reconcile him with the weakness of his past and give him absolution for his sin. His one sin. The one flaw in a perfectly lived life. A life he had devoted to God even in his childhood. Upon completion of this mission, his one sin would be, at long last, forgiven.

He would know redemption.

But he had to be smart. And he had to be strong. The mission was not an easy one. God did not set easy tasks. And the man was not ready to be welcomed into heaven just yet. He had enjoyed the things he did inside that farmhouse tonight. It had been a new experience for him, but it did not seem new. It seemed like something he had been waiting for his entire life. It had unleashed a power inside him that he had always known was there but had never dared to express. Not until God told him to let that power go, to set it free, did he understand. It was like a light going on in a shuttered room. Suddenly, he could see everything.

He had known, long before entering that farmhouse tonight and beginning his mission to set things right with God, that he was indeed flawed. He was human, with human frailties and human desires. And he had come to know that it was those desires that flawed him. They made him less than perfect in God's eyes, and he would not settle for less than perfect. His faith was too precious to him to be brought down by sins of the flesh. Even now, he longed for a release from the torment of those desires. They lived in him at this very moment, even after all he had accomplished this night. The farmhouse, and the memories it stirred inside him, had brought those longings rushing back to him, angering him, feeding the hatred that gave him the strength to do what he had just done.

Tonight was only the beginning of the cleansing process. There was much more for him to do. More blood would be shed for his salvation. It had to be that way. Especially the blood of one. The one who had brought him down in the beginning, the one whose death would resurrect him from this imperfect life he found himself mired in.

His one desire. The desire that never left his body, like an ache that could not be healed.

His one sin.

He spotted the hitchhiker two miles from his home. The boy looked to be no more than seventeen. What he was doing here on this empty highway on such a bitterly cold night was anybody's guess. Perhaps his car had broken down somewhere, or perhaps he was just wandering.

If it was a future the boy sought, the pale man knew he would soon find it. With him. This night would be the only future the boy would ever know.

The boy was tall and lanky and built very much like him. When the man realized this, he knew that God had sent the boy to him. To find this young man here, on this icy, wind-swept highway, was nothing short of a miracle. A gift.

As he pulled the car over to the side of the highway and watched the young man jog toward him in his rearview mirror, he thought, *Thank you, my Savior.*

With a smile that felt alien upon his face, he pushed open the passenger door, patted the seat beside him with a bloodied hand, and beckoned the boy to his death.

CHAPTER ONE

OUTSIDE the west terminal of Lindbergh Field, a man stood clutching a new Samsonite travel bag. The bulky trench coat draped across his other arm told the skycap on duty that this man was an arrival and not a departure; therefore, his services would not be required.

The skycap, a black man named Charles Warren MacCauley, or Mac to his friends, studied the arrival with the eye of one who had seen a lot of humanity come and go over the years as he stood at his station outside the airport's main entrance. Consequently, he considered himself a pretty fair judge of human character. Since he had nothing better to do at the moment, Mac studied the arrival more closely. This was a ritual of his—a hobby, almost—which he had developed over the years to help him pass the slow times, what few slow times there were in this business.

Mac figured the man with the trench coat was on his first visit to San Diego because he looked kind of lost. Well, not lost exactly. Just… indecisive. And unhurried. The man was eyeing the sky and the palm trees that skirted the parking lot across the street like he had seen neither sky nor palm tree before in his life. And Mac also guessed the man was an infrequent traveler. The pristine Samsonite suitcase told him that much. Very few luggage items, Samsonite or otherwise, survived many trips on the airways unscathed. Mac knew that for a truism if he knew nothing else.

Luggage got chewed up around here on a regular basis.

Mac also came to the conclusion that the man was traveling for pleasure, not business. He was too unhurried for business. Business travelers didn't just stand around looking at palm trees; they whistled for cabs and checked itineraries and griped about the service. This guy didn't look as if he had ever griped about anything in his life. A very mellow fellow, Mac thought, chuckling inwardly at his own poetic phrasing.

He figured the man to be about thirty years old, if that. Clean profile. Light colored hair, so blond as to be almost white, thinning on top. By the time the guy hit forty Mac figured the ladies would be calling him Baldy behind his back. And the guy had a baby's complexion. Smooth skin. Not just smooth, but *smooth*. Unlined. Fragile looking. A real baby face, as if a safety razor would just peel the skin right off with the whiskers. December was a good month for this man to be visiting San Diego, Mac decided, because a summer California sun would not be kind to that pale skin.

Despite the baby-soft skin, Mac had to admit the guy looked like he could take care of himself. Solidly built, broad shoulders. Well over six feet tall. And big hands. Curled into fists, they would probably look like hams. But there was nothing menacing about the man. Or so he thought at first.

Mac thought he might have been staring a bit too long because suddenly the man turned. They made eye contact.

Mac responded with his standard noncommittal humble-nigger smile, the one that usually sat so well with most nonblack travelers. But this time his smile was not returned. The man's pale blue eyes, almost as pale as the skin around them, gave Mac nothing back in return, as if Mac were just another palm tree the guy had spotted.

Embarrassed, Mac flipped through a stack of luggage labels, trying to look busy. Trying, in fact, to look as if he had not been staring at this guy with the ice-blue eyes. For to tell the truth, the cold eyes that were now aimed in his direction made him more than embarrassed. More than uncomfortable, even. What they did, really, was scare the crap out of him.

How could he have ever thought this guy was mellow?

Those ice-blue eyes continued to burrow into Mac until Mac couldn't take it any longer. He made a pretense of checking his watch, as if it were time for his break or something, and then he got the hell out of there. He hurried into the terminal while trying not to *look* like he was hurrying. And for one second, as he waited for the automatic doors to whisk open, he turned to see if the pale traveler was still staring at him.

What he saw sent a shiver of fear shooting up his spine.

The man was grinning. And with the finger and thumb of his right hand, he formed the semblance of a gun, aiming the imaginary barrel straight at Mac's startled face.

Softly, but loudly enough for Mac to hear, the man said, "Bang."

THE man with the pale blue eyes blew invisible smoke from the barrel of his imaginary gun and turned away from the retreating skycap. The smile died from his lips, but inside his mind, *deep* inside, he still laughed at the comic figure of that frightened black man. They were such animals, really, he thought. So primitive. Perhaps he would seek a remedy for that particular abomination on his next crusade. But for now, he had more important fish to fry.

He retrieved his suitcase from the curb, stepped into the crosswalk, and headed for a string of Yellow Cabs parked along the opposite side of the street.

The man tossed his suitcase into the backseat of the first cab in line and climbed in after it.

"Downtown," he said to the back of the driver's head.

The driver checked him out in the rearview mirror.

"Downtown where, please?"

The man bristled at the cabbie's accent. Iranian bastard. Should be out in the desert somewhere watering his camel instead of trying to communicate with an honest-to-God American. But he held his tongue. No sense getting worked up. Things tended to get complicated and messy when he did.

"Just downtown," he repeated. "Drive around. Show me the sights. When I see a hotel I like, I'll let you know."

"Yes, *sir*," the cabbie said, squeezing out into traffic, happy to have lucked into a better than average fare. "I show you everything."

The pale man settled back and relaxed. He could afford to waste some time. It would be good to get a general picture of the city in his mind. And though such things rarely affected him, he had to admit that San Diego appeared to be an uncommonly attractive place. Ignoring the cabbie's broken-English tourist spiel, he looked over at the bay. Far across the water, an aircraft carrier was berthed; on this side, sailboats gently swayed at their moorings. The air smelled of fish and salt water. Towering palm trees lined the roadway. Joggers were a rare commodity in the middle of December where this man came from, but here they were everywhere, futilely trying to outrun their own mortality. The man in the backseat of the cab had seen people trying to outrun death before and knew it to be a hopeless undertaking. People were such amusing fools.

Harbor Drive, clogged with traffic at this evening hour, followed the graceful curve of the bay. Soon, the man saw before him the San Diego skyline. Not as grandiose as some, perhaps, but commanding, the lines of it clean and precise in the smog-free air. Farther south, the Coronado Bridge, a graceful blue ribbon of concrete and steel, arched its tall back across the water, connecting the city to Coronado Island. A Navy destroyer with the number "13" stamped across its bow passed slowly beneath the bridge. Sailors in winter blues flanked the rail of the ship, they, too, watching the city skyline as they made their way out to sea.

A dark band of clouds on the horizon promised them a stormy reception. As yet, the rain had not drifted inland, but the smell of it threatened the air. It would arrive before morning if it did not veer south toward the Mexican coast.

The cabbie turned left, leaving the bay behind to cruise up Broadway. This was the heart of San Diego. Bustling. Crowded. It was rush hour and cars were everywhere. Roaring city buses cleaved their way through traffic. A red trolley clanged a warning to pedestrians standing too close to the tracks. Fountains sparkled pink in the setting sun. As he watched, someone somewhere in the bowels of the city flipped a switch and yellow streetlights came on. Their poles were decorated for Christmas, angels and stars on stiff red banners that did not move in the wind whipping inland from the ocean.

And people. People everywhere. Most well dressed, many lugging their Christmas shopping in colorful bags from Nordstrom's, F.A.O. Schwartz, and smaller specialty shops. A young man awkwardly pushed a new bicycle with training wheels along the sidewalk. A bag lady with scabby legs reached for a handout with one hand while the other clutched a shopping bag from Neiman-Marcus filled to overflowing with what looked to be rags. San Diego, the man knew, was a haven for the homeless. Here the rats and vermin clustered. It wasn't only tourists who came for the balmy weather. Here the homeless could sleep, unmolested, on street corners and under freeway overpasses, without fear of freezing to death even in the midst of winter. This city cared for them. Fed them. Clothed them. Tolerated them. Treated the scum of the earth like royalty. This was another crusade the man might launch one day. Even now, his fingers tingled with the anticipation of it.

But first things first.

He tapped the cabbie on the shoulder, interrupting the man's endless prattle, and handed him a slip of paper.

"Find this address for me," he said. "Just drive by it. Don't stop. After that, you can bring me back to that hotel there." He pointed to an imposing gray structure straight ahead, one with flags flying from its front edifice and a top-hatted doorman looking ridiculously out of place on the sidewalk outside. Across the street from the hotel a gazebo-shaped fountain spewed water under a blue light. Holiday music could be heard coming from speakers hidden somewhere at the base of it.

The driver nodded. "U.S. Grant. Very fine hotel."

"Good," the man said. "Now find that address for me before it gets dark."

The cabbie nodded again. "Yes, sir. It's not far. Just up the hill."

Five minutes later, the cabbie slowed in front of an aging apartment building on Walnut Street. Untrimmed palms stood like fat sentinels in the yard outside. With a coat of paint and a half hour of labor with chainsaw and axe to get rid of those ugly trees, the place wouldn't look so bad, the man thought. Still, it would be nothing more than he had expected. A hovel. A fitting home for the person he had come these many miles to administer his particular brand of justice to.

The sky was almost fully dark now. A light switched on in one of the upstairs apartments. The man's heart quickened as he leaned closer to the taxi window, peering out. He wondered if his quarry was there, puttering around the kitchen, perhaps, or feeding his fucking cat, if he had one.

The pale man's fingers commenced to tingle again. He felt a tightness in the crotch of his slacks as his cock stirred. God's work was beginning.

He could hardly wait.

Fat raindrops began to pepper the cabbie's windshield. And just like that, the man thought, the storm begins. A cleansing was about to take place in this city. He wondered just how many souls would be swept away in the rain of God's wrath.

And his own.

CHAPTER TWO

UPON entering his forty-fifth year on this planet, two weeks ago today as a matter of fact, Harry Connors figured his chances for excitement, adventure, and true love were pretty well shot. From this point on, it would all be downhill, a slow, ungraceful slide into the toothless oblivion of old age. And he could think of few things more pathetic than an aging hairdresser reliving the thrill of his youth over cocktails at the Cailiff Lounge, studying his collapsing reflection in the grimy mirror behind the bar and getting slobberingly shit-faced as he recounted his past exploits to some equally shit-faced acquaintance who couldn't have cared less and who was also casting surreptitious glances at that goddamn dirty mirror as *he* tried to figured out when *his* face had lost *its* battle with gravity.

Harry had figured the best gift he could give himself for his forty-fifth birthday was to stay the hell away from the Cailiff Lounge.

But that was two weeks ago.

So now, as he opened the red enamel door which led into the shadowy interior of that very same bar on this cold and drizzling San Diego night (two weeks to the day after swearing never to darken its doorway again), it occurred to Harry that he had never had much luck sticking to New Year's resolutions either. After all, he must have stopped smoking on the first day of January from his twelfth birthday onward. By January 2nd he was always back at it, puffing away, trying desperately to bring the nicotine level in his body back up to one he could live with—until the damn cigarettes killed him dead, anyway. Quite a balancing act. One he felt certain would do him in some day, but God, that first cigarette every January 2nd always tasted so *good.* He looked forward to it like Christmas, which, by the way, was just around the corner. He supposed his five cats would destroy the tree again. Maybe that was what *they* looked forward to. They could certainly tear the shit out of a Christmas tree with enough gleeful abandon to make one *think* they had been looking forward to it all year. And what the hell. If all it took to make those five pampered pusses believe they were rampaging felines back in the wilderness was a forty-dollar Scotch pine from Ralph's parking lot, which had already been dead for six weeks but was too dumb to know it, then who was he to deprive them of that enjoyment? Christmas didn't mean crap to Harry anyway. Not this year, since he had no one to share it with. He would only do it for the cats.

Stepping into the Cailiff was like stepping into a cave. A cold, black cave. The lights were too dim, and the air conditioning was set low enough to preserve meat. But by the look of most of the patrons hunched around the horseshoe at the end of the bar, the act of preservation was a matter of too little and too late. The under-thirties gay set called this the Wrinkle Room. Or was that Wrinkle "Wroom"? And they had pegged it right. Unfortunately for Harry, he could think of nothing more depressing than gazing around a bar only to discover that he was the oldest patron there. So, a few years ago, he had decided to donate his liver exclusively to the Cailiff. Here, at least, he could occasionally look around and make the pleasant discovery that he was actually the *youngest* sheep in the fold. Quite an ego booster, that. After several Miller Lites at least. In the cold, gray dawn of the morning after, he could see how pathetic it really was, but that came later. For the moment, it always seemed to be enough to perk up his spirits just knowing that, at that particular point in time, he was the youngest flaming old fart on the premises, no matter how feeble and decrepit the other old farts around him were. It simply cheered him up no end.

And everything being relative, the old farts looked at Harry in the same way Harry looked at himself in those moments. Like he was a fresh-faced kid just off the farm in Minnesota who had somehow found himself transported hundreds of miles to the southwesternmost point in the continental United States for no other purpose than to cheer up these aging faggots who were too far away from their own youth to ever see it again in their own reflections no matter how dark the bar was kept.

Harry knew that when the day came that he started looking at some forty-five-year-old hairdresser in the same way these guys were looking at him, it would be time to move along and relocate his aging ass to another bar. Or a nursing home.

In his usual self-deprecating manner, of course, Harry was being a good deal harder on himself than was actually called for. For truth be told, studying his reflection now in the mirror behind the bar, Harry had to admit he still looked pretty darned good for forty-five. He maintained the 32-inch waist he had had when he was twenty. He worked out on a fairly regular basis at his health club, and he still jogged three times a week, although lately his forty-five-year-old knees had begun to complain about it afterward. But for the smoking and perhaps a few too many beers, he lived a reasonably healthy life. And a reasonably happy one too. All that was missing was someone to share his life with.

He had had three lovers during his lifetime, and all three of those relationships had lasted several years. His last, Ben, had died of leukemia during their fifth year together. It was four years ago that Ben had died, and Harry still missed him. But he knew it was time to share his life with someone again. The time had come to move on. Eventually, he knew, the right person would show up on his doorstep, and on that day, Harry's life would change again. And it would be a change for the better. When not in a relationship, Harry always felt adrift. Not quite lost, but disconnected. He functioned much better with a lover, and he was always happier than when he was alone.

Yes, it was time.

And he knew who it was he would like to fill that position. Unfortunately, his prospective lover didn't have a clue that he was at the top of Harry's list of prospects. In fact, the young man would probably have laughed his Reeboks off if he even suspected as much.

Harry scanned the crowded bar, looking for a seat. Then he chuckled to himself. He hadn't seen a polyester leisure suit in thirty years, but there was one now, in mauve no less, holding together a delicate specimen of manhood with a stringy neck poking out the top and skinny hands poking out the sleeves. The head perched on top of that stringy neck looked like a ragged eraser on a battered pencil. Thin hair, dyed a little too dark to be natural, and a mouthful of teeth that seemed far too white and far too numerous for reality. Tijuana dentures, Harry supposed. They were cheaper down there. Harry figured he would rather go toothless than wear Tijuana dentures that could be spotted like a beacon from twenty feet away in a bar as dark as this one. What in God's name did they look like in broad daylight?

The smiling beacon's name was Biff Sullivan. Who but a Biff would wear that leisure suit and those teeth?

The odd thing was, Harry liked Biff, who was now motioning Harry forward like a man directing traffic.

"Over here! I saved you a pew!"

Every head at the horseshoe turned to study Harry as he was sucked into the dark and noisy womb of the Cailiff. Upon recognition (or non-recognition), the heads swiveled back to their drinks like so many cows at a trough.

Garth Brooks spewed out a countrified jazz riff from the jukebox in the corner as Harry settled himself self-consciously onto the barstool Biff had so graciously commandeered for him.

Or perhaps Biff had brought this particular barstool with him from home, since it stood at least a foot shorter than any other barstool in the place. After settling in and propping his elbows on the bar at about chin level, Harry felt like the one stunted stalk in a row of corn.

"Hey, Biff. Nice suit."

Biff sweetly flushed, or Harry thought he did; he couldn't be certain since it was so goddamn dark in here.

Biff's false teeth clattered like wet castanets as he whispered, "Wiseass."

Biff was a great fan of Gilbert and Sullivan, and his conversation, especially when fueled by a generous supply of martinis, was liberally sprinkled with quotes and quippets from their librettos.

"And how is our love-blighted fool this fine December evening?"

"Wet," Harry replied, signaling to the bartender, Jonah, for his usual bottle of Miller Lite and a glass. Jonah fetched them before Harry could shrug out of his coat.

Biff made a big production of looking around for anyone Harry might be with. "And where is young Sean?"

The constant ragging he had received from Biff lately about the young man he was currently enamored of had begun to wear a bit thin. "Working, I suppose. Just as I've been working. Just as *everyone's* been working, aside from yourself, of course."

Biff made a pouty face and wagged his jowls at Harry. "I'm merely enjoying the fruits of a well-earned retirement after my half century on the boards."

In Biff's case, the "boards" he referred to was the drywall business he had operated until alcohol and old age had made it all but impossible for him to continue working. He had been a rogue in his day, Harry didn't doubt, but now Biff spent most of his time drinking himself into a coma at the Cailiff, where he was looked upon with a certain amount of good-natured tolerance, not unlike a favored old dog who has grown arthritic and senile and sometimes poops in the corners but is too fondly thought of to be put down.

"Ah, the fruits of your labor," Harry said.

"Precisely, dear boy. With particular emphasis on the fruits."

He suddenly hauled himself back and studied Harry from head to toe. "You're all wet, sir."

"I know. It's raining outside."

"Is it?"

"It's been raining for hours. What time did you start downing those martinis?"

Biff thought about that for a moment. "I'm not quite sure. The last thing I seem to recall with any lucidity is Queen Elizabeth's coronation. When was that?"

"A while back."

"Then it's time for dinner." With that, Biff delicately clamped his gigantic dentures around the olive on his toothpick.

Chewing with gusto, he added, "To quote the inimitable Yum Yum, 'How time flies when one is thoroughly enjoying one's self.'"

Harry grinned, then, and clapped old Biff on the back. He really did like the guy. Go figure.

SEAN ANDROS stood naked before the bathroom mirror in a sixth-floor luxury condominium on Albatross Avenue and wiped the splash of semen from his chest. The semen came from the guy sprawled contentedly on the bed in the next room. He had deposited it on Sean's chest only because Sean had had the foresight to pull his lips away in the nick of time, even though the guy had promised faithfully to warn him before THE BIG MOMENT came. Sean elicited that promise from all of them, but very few could be trusted to follow through in the clinch. Sean supposed that was his fault. He was very good at his job.

He tossed the soiled towel into a hamper by the shower stall and studied his reflection. Running his fingers through his short, strawberry-blond hair made it poof up enough to look a little better. It was very erotic, seeing one's naked body in new surroundings. It gave one an entirely different perspective. And Sean had to admit he looked good. A little chest hair, not much. Slim waist. Round ass. Nice fuzzy legs. Good definition, but not overly done. His cock nestled comfortably in a pillow of reddish pubic hair, asleep now. Waiting....

Very few johns got THE BIG TREAT. They all wanted it in the beginning, but ultimately it was their own orgasm that carried them past the point of really caring about anyone else's. Mostly, they wanted the excitement of touch. The feel of his body. The feel of his hands on *their* bodies. The wet caress of his lips as he burrowed himself between their legs. The freedom that can only come from making love to a complete stranger and knowing the relationship will end at the point of orgasm. Then a few soft words, an appreciative kiss, the rustle of money changing hands, and the closing of a door. It was all very civilized, really, and Sean could think of worse ways to make a living.

He had never had any trouble. No drunken johns wanting to get rough or refusing to pay. No sudden surprises like a third party popping out of the closet (no pun intended) or an irate lover storming through the bedroom door to pound him to a pulp. He had been lucky so far and he knew it.

Still, more and more lately, Sean's thoughts had been turning of their own accord, unbidden by him, to a more normal, more acceptable lifestyle. One that wouldn't take him into harm's way as often as this lifestyle did. The money wasn't bad, and he did sort of enjoy the control he wielded over his customers. His youth and good looks made that an easy thing to do. But he longed for stability, and he longed for a life that wasn't permeated with the sense of shame this one was. And the sense of fear. For always, hanging over him like a dark cloud, was the threat of AIDS.

He enjoyed the sex, usually, but he would enjoy it more with a person he loved. A person he trusted and knew to be healthy. A person who wasn't a stranger. And in this business it was almost always a *flawed* stranger. For ordinarily, only the flawed would seek out a prostitute. Especially in the gay world. They were either shy or felt themselves inferior in some way. More and more, their flaws made Sean sad. And a little impatient. They could screw but they couldn't talk.

Sean feared that someday, after too many couplings with too many flawed strangers, he might end up just like them.

He knew, deep down and with no sense of conceit, that he was better than this.

He splashed water on his face and grabbed another towel from the rack. He held the towel against his face and savored the richness of it. He hoped he would live like this someday. A gorgeous condo overlooking San Diego Bay. A nice car. Designer duds. And rich, luxurious towels to press against his face.

And maybe he would. Maybe, just maybe, he could make it happen. Maybe he could open the door. Not just the door to another john, but the door to a whole new life. A life he could see himself living just as clearly as he could see his reflection now in the mirror.

His cock slowly raised its head as if awakening from its slumber, and he felt the cool marble of the countertop brush against it.

This john was a fairly good-looking guy. Maybe thirty-five or so. But shy. That, Sean knew, was why his services had been required. The guy probably had trouble meeting people. But there had been nothing shy about him in the bedroom. As usual, that level of communication had been no problem for the guy at all. Maybe the drinks Sean shared with him had helped. He was, in fact, a very considerate lover, of sorts. Not condescending like some. Fair body. Warm and responsive to Sean's touch. And rich. That didn't hurt either.

Sean dropped the second towel to the floor, flicked off the bathroom light, and headed down the hall toward the bedroom, enjoying the feel of cool air against his naked skin and the sensation of his semi-hard cock bouncing along in front of him like a seeing-eye dog, leading the way.

Maybe Sean would give this guy THE BIG TREAT after all, whether the john really wanted it or not. And in the end, Sean knew, he would want it a lot. Sean would see to that.

THAT morning the pale man had rented a gray Taurus from an Avis lot not far from his hotel and driven it directly to the UPS office on Miramar Drive, which he was finally able to locate after studying the San Diego map given him by the clerk at Avis. The heavy package he had mailed a week ago to general delivery was waiting for him, just as he knew it would be.

He had returned to his hotel, parked in a loading zone for five minutes while he carried the package up to his room, and then driven to Walnut Street where he parked at a corner near his prey's apartment and waited. And watched.

In the early part of the afternoon, it began to rain, and as the afternoon wore on, the rain came down harder until it was nothing short of a deluge.

At three o'clock, for the first time, he saw his quarry. The young man he had come these many miles to kill poked his head through the front door of his apartment building just long enough to assess the rain, then jogged to a crappy little blue car that stood at the curb and took off up Fifth Avenue with the pale man following not fifty feet behind.

The sight of his prey, after all these years, had caused a storm of conflicting emotions in the pale man that he had not expected to feel. Hatred, of course. But something else. Something deeper and more disturbing. Memories he had long tried to suppress came raging back into his mind. Painful memories of sins once committed and long regretted. Sins of his youth that still tortured him every minute of his adult life. Sins he had come here to expunge. But now, seeing his quarry again after all these years, he realized the longings of his youth were still alive inside him. More alive, perhaps, than ever before. And that angered him. He felt dirty and ashamed, but above all, angry. And as always, with anger, came the need to strike out.

The blue car stopped in front of a luxury condominium tower, and his quarry once again parked on the street. A well-dressed man stood at the entryway of the building, protected from the rain beneath an awning that hung above the front door. His quarry ran to the building, and he and the man hugged before stepping inside.

So the whore was still at it. Selling his body. Selling his soul.

The man flipped up the collar of his raincoat and quickly walked to the doorway that the two had just entered. He watched them step into an elevator at the back of the lobby and disappear. He could clearly see the numbered lights above the elevator door flash one-two-three until they stopped at six.

He returned to his car to escape the rain. A half hour later, the garage door off to the side of the entryway rumbled up into the ceiling, and a white car pulled out onto the street and drove away. Before the car had reached the corner, the pale man was out of his own car and ducking through the garage door just as it began to slide down.

At the rear of the parking area below the building, he found an unlocked door. He stepped through it and began to climb the stairway inside. He took the stairs two at a time until he reached the sixth floor, meeting no one on the way. On six, he pulled the stairway door ajar just far enough to peer down the hallway. There he waited.

For twenty minutes, he saw not one person either leave or enter their apartment. Then, three doors down, he saw the boy he had followed here step out into the hall and, shrugging into his leather jacket, walk toward the elevator. He had not latched the apartment door behind him, merely pulled it almost closed, as if he meant to return quickly.

The man in the stairwell waited, fingering the knife in his coat pocket. A smile spread across his face as he thought of the surprise the boy would find waiting for him upon his return.

An elderly gentleman entered the hallway from a doorway farther down. The pale man watched through the slit in the stairway door as the man pressed the elevator button and waited. When the elevator arrived and the doors rang open, the elderly gentleman stepped inside. The elevator rumbled away. Before it reached the first floor, the pale man was through the stairway door and standing outside the apartment his quarry had just left. He listened for sounds coming from within and, hearing nothing, stepped quickly inside, reclosing the door to its original position, almost latched but not quite.

The condo was dark but for a light that burned at the end of a hallway to his right. Eager now, and unafraid, the man walked through the living room past a white piano that looked like something Liberace might have had in *his* fucking living room and entered the hallway.

A man's voice called out, "Sean, is that you?"

"Afraid not," the pale man said as he stepped through the bedroom door.

The man he had seen earlier at the entryway to the building was lying naked on the bed. At the sight of the knife in the stranger's hand, the naked man grabbed for the phone beside the bed. By the time he punched in 911, the stranger was beside him. As the telephone rang at the other end of the line, the naked man watched with surprise that quickly turned to horror as the stranger reached out, grasped his flaccid penis, and with one swift motion of the knife, sliced it from his body.

Stanley Baker screamed and dropped the phone onto the bed. The stranger stood over him smiling, the bloody penis still clutched in his hand. He dangled it in front of Stanley's face and said, "Lose something?"

Weak with fear and pain, Stanley fumbled for the phone and heard a woman's voice on the other end.

Already slipping into shock, Stanley said into the mouthpiece, "Help me. I'm being murdered."

The stranger laughed and pulled the phone from his hand, dropping it to the floor beside the bed.

"Don't cut me anymore, please."

But again, Stanley screamed as the stranger pressed the tip of the knife beneath his chin and pushed the blade deep inside his head. With death, Stanley Baker's eyes went blank, and all traces of fear fell away from his face as if it was only sleep that had overtaken him. His scream faded quickly to silence.

The pale man pulled the knife away and Stanley's head slipped back onto the pillow—at rest, like a man who has dozed off in the middle of a good book. With a grin, the pale man placed the severed penis between Stanley's lips and stepped back to study his work.

Satisfied, he turned away and heard a sound in the other room. Immediately, he heard the rattle of the apartment door bang against the wall as it was flung out of the way, then heavy footsteps running down the hallway outside.

The boy.

The pale man raced from the condo just as the stairway door closed. He ran to it and chased the footsteps down the stairs. Two floors behind, the pale man heard the boy slam through the door that connected to the lobby, and seconds later, he heard him push his way through the entryway and into the rain.

By the time the pale man reached the front doors and flung himself outside, the boy was almost a block away. He gave chase but knew it was hopeless. The boy, in his fear, was just too fast.

A block farther up the street, he watched the boy rush through the lighted doorway of a bar.

He let the boy go. There was no hurry. He had all the time in the world. He smiled to himself as he felt the cold rain wash the blood from his hands.

IT WAS a busy night for Emergency Services. The heavy wind and rain that had descended upon the California coast a few hours earlier had all but guaranteed this would be the case. On the freeways, automobiles were plowing into each other like bumper cars, creating injury accidents from one end of San Diego County to the other.

Shirlene Johnson, a large black woman with three-inch acrylic nails painted candy apple red and cinnamon-colored hair extensions that had set her back two hundred dollars but looked hot enough to warrant the cost, sat at her cubicle in Emergency Services, fielding calls from desperate San Diego citizens with the aplomb that can only come from years of practice. With twelve years on the job, she thought she had pretty well heard it all at one time or another.

Still, she treated her job and her callers with the respect they deserved. Once, years ago, she had been at the other end of a 911 call. She would never forget the heart-stopping fear of watching her mother collapse onto the kitchen floor like a bag of wet cement after a heart attack she had incurred while standing at the kitchen sink, washing up the dirty dishes after one of their crowded Sunday family dinners.

Shirlene came from a large family. Large in every respect. Large in size. Large in numbers. Large in love and laughter. Her mother's house on that evening twelve years earlier had been a cacophony of laughter and singing and cheerful racket until the sound of her mother's body dropping to the kitchen floor had brought the noise to a sudden, heart-wrenching stop. Shirlene's frantic call for an ambulance was answered promptly and professionally by Emergency Services and Shirlene had never forgotten how quickly the EMTs had arrived on her mother's doorstep. Never forgotten the efficiency of their movements as they carried her mother away and saved her life. Her mother would live to reign over many more Sunday dinners in her little house on Arbison Street, and Shirlene had always known who to thank for that blessing.

Later, when she herself applied, and was accepted, to work at Emergency Services, she made a private pact with herself to never forget that it was people like her mother who were asking for help every time those headphones rang. It was a matter of respect. Respect for the EMTs, respect for herself, and respect for each and every desperate caller whose voice came through the phone lines pleading for assistance.

Shirlene was damned good at her job and she knew it. The job demanded nothing less.

Every shift was a busy one for Shirlene, but on this rainy December evening, the calls never stopped. Not for a moment. Beneath her two-hundred-dollar extensions, a sprinkling of sweat had formed on Shirlene's brow when she was no more than thirty minutes into her night.

Frantic calls were coming in from one end of the county to the other. All desperate. A collision on Highway 5, phoned in from a callbox. A frightened man whose wife had suddenly gone into labor after slipping on the front steps of their home. A child, tearful, explaining to Shirlene between frightened hiccups that her mother would not wake up.

Usually when the calls came in, people would pounce on her as quickly as the connection was made. Immediately asking for help. Not wasting a precious second.

So, when her headphones rang and only silence greeted her from the other end of the line, she was taken aback for a moment. With the tip of her cherry red fingernail. she pressed the earpiece closer to her head.

"This is 911," she repeated. "Go ahead, please."

Shirlene thought she heard laughter but she wasn't sure. Laughter in the background.

"Can I help you?" she said again.

A man's voice, soft, unhurried, already stunted by shock, came through the line.

"Help me," he said. "I'm being murdered."

Shirlene knew that the call would be automatically traced. But that took time. "Where are you?" she asked. "Can you give me your location?" She heard a clatter at the other end, like the phone had been dropped to the floor. "Sir? Stay on the line, sir. Help is on the way. Stay with me, sir."

Then she heard the scream. The man's scream. And a dial tone. The call was terminated.

"Shit!" Shirlene muttered.

She flagged down her supervisor, explained the situation to him, and he scurried off to contact the police. Shirlene had little time to think about the call before the next one came in. An elderly woman with chest pains. And after that, another automobile accident in North County. But that man's seemingly disinterested voice, almost casually explaining to her that he was being murdered, would return to haunt her throughout the remainder of her shift.

Later that night, lying in bed with her husband nestled comfortably beside her, she would remember that voice again, and it would be several hours before sleep overtook her.

JIMMY SMITH had been with Homicide for eight years. He figured a person would have to be a sick son of a bitch to really like the job, but it did have its finer moments. Like when some scumbag who had poked forty-eight air holes in his wife with an ice pick because he didn't like the way she fricasseed the chicken finally got thrown into the slammer for a good long time and then some. Or better yet, when society decided to do away with the bastard altogether and vaccinated his little ass against further criminal activity with what is commonly referred to as a lethal injection. That could certainly be one of the finer moments, especially if you were the one who had worked days, nights, weekends, and holidays to set the bastard on that final journey to Needletown.

Jimmy Smith was pureblood Indian. Sycuan Indian. And looked it. Roman nose, black hair, lean. Before marrying Carol, he had been quite popular with the ladies. He had a knack for flashing those pearly whites of his at just the right moment, and you could almost bet that the unsuspecting target of that easy smile was greasing up down below. Women seemed to love everything about him, from the rich chestnut color of his skin to the way he wore his wristwatch with the dial facing in instead of out. Smith was tall for an Indian, and the ladies loved that too. What they didn't like was the way he earned his living. His relationships usually lasted only a few short weeks, and then they tended to self-destruct when the female half of the relationship began to consider what it would mean to be married to a man who might or might not come home in one piece at the end of his shift.

He could usually tell when the self-destruct mechanism was about to be activated. Suddenly, there would be serious conversations, and even more serious questions, where before there had only been laughter and good times. Sometimes after sex, when they both lay sweating on the sheets, he would feel her hand stealing toward the scar beside his left nipple where a kid on PCP had once popped him at point blank range with his father's revolver because he didn't want to take a ride downtown like the nice police officer had requested. Smith barely survived that one. And the naked lady lying next to him on the sheets with her leg comfortably draped over his abdomen would begin to wonder how many more of those surprises this nice police officer would survive. And if he didn't, what would happen to *her*? When she ran her fingertips across his scar and thought these private thoughts, Smith would always know.

Then Carol came along. Carol didn't like Jimmy's job any better than all the other women he had known, but there was one major difference with her. From the beginning, Carol had loved him enough to accept the risk. And now, five years and two kids later, she *still* loved him enough to accept that risk. They had a good marriage. And Jimmy Smith tried very hard every day to come home in one piece at the end of his shift.

On this rainy San Diego evening, that shift would be ending no time soon. He could tell that by the naked stiff on the bed with the bloody stump of his own dick poking out of his mouth like a mushroom.

The 911 call came in at 5:36 p.m. Twenty-four minutes before Smith's shift would have ended. When the paramedics arrived, Smith was hot on their heels, his wet shoes squeaking across the tiled lobby of Brittany Towers Condominiums like two damp rats getting the shit punched out of them by bigger and meaner rats.

Smith hated the rain. It muddied up crime scenes and wrinkled his suits.

The door to 6B was ajar when they arrived. The paramedics hesitated at the entryway but Smith waved them on in.

"Just don't touch anything," he said. "Not until we see what we see."

They trundled their gurney through the door, and Smith shadowed along right behind. His initial reaction was that the white baby grand piano with the silver candelabra on top was a bit much even for this place. If a concert pianist didn't live here, then the tenant had to be a fruit. Not that Smith had anything against fruits. At parties, they were probably lots more fun than concert pianists. He just hated the way they decorated their apartments.

Smith and the two paramedics scattered in different directions, looking for whomever it might have been who placed the 911 call.

"Help me," the caller had said, in an oddly disinterested tone of voice. "I'm being murdered."

If *he* were the one being murdered, Smith thought he most likely would have sounded a bit more upset about it than this guy had. He would have been downright pissed off, as a matter of fact.

The blond-headed paramedic who looked to Smith to be a little fruity himself was the one who found the body.

"In here, guys," he called from the master bedroom.

Smith passed him in the hallway. Him coming out, Smith going in.

"You won't need us," the blond kid said. "He's got no pulse and he's not apt to get one. We're outta here."

"Thanks, guys," Smith muttered, as he peered through the doorway and saw the dead stiff with the even deader pecker poking out of his mouth.

"Lorena Bobbitt live here, or what?" Smith asked the stiff, but the stiff didn't answer.

Smith's partner arrived twenty minutes later. The techs were all over the bedroom, dusting for prints, raking the carpet, poking around and photographing everything that didn't move, especially the body, which certainly wouldn't be moving any time in the near future. Not of its own volition, anyway.

Jefferson McCray and Jimmy Smith had been partners even before Smith had happily settled into his marriage five years ago. Jeff had played linebacker for the San Diego Chargers for two seasons, until a knee injury knocked him out of that line of work. And the murder of his parents at the hands of a gang of assholes from Logan Heights over a matter of some twenty-six dollars had pushed him into police work.

Smith liked having Jefferson McCray as a partner. One look at the six foot four, two-hundred-pound black man with the mean eyes made most perps melt into little quivering piles of cowardly mooseshit well before any physical acts of force were made necessary. But then, most perps were stupid. They tended to take things at face value. They weren't smart enough to realize just because a guy is black and big and towers over them like a tree and looks like nothing would make him happier than to rip off their head and piss down their neck that maybe, just maybe, the guy is really a sweetheart in disguise.

"Hello, sweetheart," Smith said as Detective Jefferson McCray poked his head through the doorway to make sure he was in the right place. "You look lovely."

McCray was wearing a very spiffy tux, patent leather shoes, and a little red AIDS Awareness ribbon on his lapel. His spongy, black hair glistened from the rain, which had transformed itself from a drizzle to a regular monsoon outside.

"Yo, redman. How's it hanging?"

McCray filled the doorway as he came through it like a very large truck squeezing through a very narrow alley.

Smith shrugged. "For the guy in the other room there, it isn't hanging at all. Take a peek."

Smith led him down the hall toward the crowd of technicians in the master bedroom.

"Love your suit," Smith mentioned in passing. "How was your sister's wedding reception?"

Jefferson McCray's voice was like a rumble of distant thunder. Soft, but menacing. "Just great, thanks. And kiss my black ass."

Smith looked stunned. "You mean your ass is black, too?"

"Yeah. Yours is red. Mine's black. It's all part of the natural order."

Smith bowed McCray into the bedroom like the prince consort leading the queen to dinner.

McCray took it all in, did a double take that Jimmy Smith found highly entertaining, then moved closer to the bed to convince himself he was really seeing what he thought he had seen.

"Um, excuse me, Detective Smith, but does this man have a pecker in his mouth?"

Smith crossed his arms and studied the corpse for a long moment before nodding. "Looks like a pecker to me. Could be a mushroom, I suppose. " He squinted and bent closer to the body. "Nope. Definitely a pecker."

McCray nodded in unison with his partner, as if he suspected as much. He took an even closer look.

"I've got to tell you, man. I've been around the block a few times and I've seen a few peckers in mouths before, my own not excluded, but doesn't it seem to you that it's usually the head that goes in first? Not the tail."

Smith gave an agreeable grin. "Yes. Almost always when you see a pecker in someone's mouth, it's the head of said pecker that enters the orifice first. Now oddly enough, this pecker is *protruding* from this man's mouth headfirst."

"Like a snake coming out of a hole."

"Well, yes," Smith agreed. "But I think you're missing the big picture here."

Jefferson McCray cupped his chin between thumb and forefinger like a big black Sherlock Holmes, only Sherlock Holmes never dressed this well. He twirled an imaginary goatee.

"I suppose you're referring to the fact that the particular pecker protruding from this man's mouth happens to be his own."

Smith slapped him on the back. "Yes. That's exactly what I'm referring to. Now, I suppose that in an especially nimble individual it might be possible, even enjoyable, to pop one's own pecker into one's mouth, as long as one did not do it with any great regularity or at public functions. However, it is very rare indeed to see that same said pecker protruding *out* from said mouth headfirst."

"Practically impossible."

"No, Jeff. It *is* impossible. *Completely* impossible."

A sixty-year-old crime technician with white hair and a paunch, who looked like he should be doing anything but crawling around on the carpet gathering fiber samples, gazed up at these two comedians and chuckled. "You guys kill me."

Both detectives ignored him.

"Got a name?" McCray asked.

Smith pulled a rumpled notebook from his back pocket and flipped it open.

"Guy's name is Stanley Baker."

"Oh, Stanley."

"Thirty-seven years old. Owns a chain of coin-operated laundries. Must be a lucrative business, my friend. You're standing in the middle of a $900,000 condominium that he paid for with cash."

"Quarters?"

"Well, no. He actually paid for it with a check, but the goddamn thing was good."

"Huh!"

Smith continued. "Single. Never married. Actually goes to church on Sundays. Imagine that. Ever see a churchgoer end up with his pecker in his mouth before?"

McCray considered this. "Only the big ones, actually. Churchgoers, I mean, not peckers. Televangelists and others of that ilk."

"Well, of course, that ilk would."

"Yes, of course. Highly understandable."

Smith wondered aloud. "You don't suppose God did this, do you? I mean, suppose this guy hadn't been dropping every tenth quarter he made from his laundromats into the collection plate and God got a little ticked off about it and…."

McCray shook his head. "No. God doesn't work that way. Well, not American gods. Maybe one of your *Aztec* gods might be inclined to de-pecker a man and serve it to him as an appetizer, but American gods simply don't work that way."

Smith looked hurt. "I'm not Aztec. I'm Sycuan. My maternal grandmother always told us our gods were sweet and cuddly."

"Well, there you go."

The gray-haired techie chuckled again from the floor by the dresser where he was lifting something from the carpet with tweezers. "You guys really kill me."

Smith bent closer to see what the object was. "What you got there?"

The techie placed the object in a clear evidence bag and groaned to his feet. "A pubic hair."

"Yours?" Smith asked.

The technician smiled like a guy humoring a four-year-old kid. "No. It's red. Must be yours."

Smith whirled on his partner with mock severity. "You told him!"

Smith took another glance at the body. At the junction of those hairy legs splayed out across the bed was a circular patch of bloody meat where Stanley Baker's penis had once resided, and surrounding that bloody hole was a thatch of brown, tangled pubic hair. Not a red one in the bunch, if you discounted the blood.

"This guy gay?" McCray asked.

"Judging by the baby grand piano in the living room, I'd have to say yes."

For the second time, McCray looked offended. "But I've got a baby grand piano in *my* living room."

The techie grinned. "Well, there you go."

Smith and McCray both told the guy to shut up and he did just that, going on about his business.

"Losing a pecker might break a guy's heart," McCray said, "but I don't think it would kill him. What did? That?" He indicated what appeared to be a stab wound directly beneath the victim's chin.

Smith nodded. "We think so. It's deep. Won't know for sure until after the autopsy."

"All the way into the brain?"

"Looks like it."

"Find the weapon?"

"No. The killer must have taken it with him when he left."

McCray popped a rubber glove onto his right hand and gently eased the victim's head to the side, hoping all the while that the man's penis wouldn't dislodge from his lips and go rolling across the bed. McCray wasn't sure he could handle that.

"There's semen in his hair. If it isn't his own, that might be the break we need. Don't forget to analyze it," he said to the tech. "Don't lose it in the shuffle."

The tech only frowned. "What am I? New on the job?"

"So what do you think?" McCray asked the tech. "A natural death?"

"Oh, yeah. Looks natural to me."

"Hmm. That would explain why you aren't a detective."

"Check out the phone," Smith said. It was lying on the floor beside the bed. The victim's arm trailed off the side of the bed, as if the phone had just fallen from his hand.

"Poor bastard called in his own murder. The killer must have let him do it."

McCray watched with fascination as one last drop of blood trickled off the end of the victim's finger, adding to the small pool coagulating in the carpet next to the phone where it had traversed the downhill slope of the arm from the neck wound above.

Smith nodded. "The 911 operator said she heard laughter in the background. Just before the victim screamed."

"You can bet it wasn't Stanley laughing."

"No shit."

"We're going to have to canvas this building," Smith said. He checked his watch. It was a few minutes past eight. "Bit late to do it now."

McCray sighed. "Thank Christ. First thing in the morning then. We should catch most of the residents at home if we get an early start."

Smith agreed. "Okay. Seven o'clock sharp. We'll do this floor first, and after that, I'll start on the ground floor and you start at the top. When we're finished we'll meet in the lobby and compare notes."

"Gotcha."

They took one last look at the body on the bed, the one unmoving human in this milling mass of crime technicians and detectives.

Flashbulbs popped.

Jefferson McCray gave a comforting pat to Stanley Baker's cold knee.

"Don't worry, Stan, my man," he said. "We'll get 'em. Nobody deserves to go out of this world looking as ridiculous as you do."

Jimmy Smith, serious for a change, said, "Amen to that."

HARRY CONNORS sucked on his fifth Miller Lite. He was at that pleasant stage of a gentle inebriation where everything begins to look not only possible, but totally reasonable as well. One more beer and he thought he might even ask Biff Sullivan just where the *fuck* he had purchased those teeth. Not that he could expect an answer. Biff Sullivan was in the final stages of a different sort of inebriation. The sort where one's tongue seems to cleave to one's forehead like a fat leech on a rock, leaving one not only incapable of coherent speech but damn near blind as well. A serious doubt had recently formed in Harry's mind as to whether Biff's brain was actually functioning at all. A brain scan at this point would probably reveal nothing. *Absolutely nothing.* Indeed, old Biff's gray matter might be floating free inside his melon in a puddle of Beefeater martinis, like a big, gray, wrinkled olive. Biff still sat upright on his barstool and his drink still made its way to his lips occasionally, but other than that, life as we know it had ceased to exist as far as Biff Sullivan was concerned.

So Harry left him to it.

Since tomorrow was a workday and Harry had early appointments, he thought it might not be such a bad idea to toddle on home. There were few things more dangerous than a hungover hairdresser with a pair of scissors in his hand. He was just about to reach into his trouser pocket for the car keys when the kid rushed into the bar.

Harry recognized him right away, of course. He had, in fact, been with the kid on three separate occasions. On Harry's forty-fourth birthday, Biff and a handful of the other old farts who frequented the Cailiff had presented this kid to Harry as a birthday gift. And a lovely gift it was too. So lovely that Harry had given himself an encore engagement with the kid a few months later, and then again a few months after that. Harry had a limited acquaintance with the hustling element of gay life in San Diego, but he thought that perhaps Sean Andros was several steps above the average. If not, then he was a wonderful little actor. And why should the straights have a monopoly on hookers with hearts of gold?

He had liked the kid a lot, in every way, from the very beginning, so Harry received a pleasant jolt of surprise when the kid spotted him and made a beeline in his direction.

"Hi, Harry."

Sean rested a cold hand on the back of Harry's neck and used his other hand to wave at the bartender. "Hey, Jonah, bring me a Bud!"

Harry spun around on his munchkin barstool and found his face at tummy level to the boy. A nice place to be. He felt absurdly flattered that the young man even remembered his name.

"Hey, Sean. Good to see you."

Sean looked down at him with an innocent but preoccupied smile. "Is it?"

"Well, yeah, actually it is."

Sean's cool fingers applied gentle pressure to the back of Harry's neck. He felt a cold drop of rain dribble down the inside of his collar. The kid was soaking wet.

"Ooh, you're soaking wet," the bartender cooed as he delicately placed the Bud and a glass on a napkin in front of Harry. He took the money for the beer out of Harry's little pile of cash on the bar. Harry didn't mind at all.

Jonah then handed Sean a stack of napkins and told him to wipe himself off before he made water spots on the furniture, referring to Biff, who was still sitting comatose next to Harry.

Jonah hurried off at the behest of a thirsty patron at the other end of the bar, and Harry watched Sean wipe down his leather jacket with the fistful of napkins. With his eyes casting nervous glances at the door every few seconds, he did a poor job of it. Harry finally reached across the bar, grabbed his own stack of napkins, and finished wiping the kid down.

"Your hands are shaking," Harry said. "Must be cold out there."

"It is," Sean said. "Scrunch over, Harry. Let me share your barstool. My knees are shaking too. If I don't sit down real soon, I'm gonna fall flat on my face."

Harry accommodated Sean as best he could and the kid plopped down beside him, one arm wrapped tightly around Harry's waist to keep them both in place. He took a long pull from his beer and almost dropped the bottle placing it back on the bar.

"What the hell's the matter?" Harry asked, loudly enough to be heard over the jukebox but still softly enough not to be heard by the nosy old farts surrounding them on the horseshoe.

For the first time, Harry detected a tremor in the boy's voice. "Jesus, Harry, I think I'm in big trouble. I don't know what the hell to do."

Sean's blue eyes suddenly clouded in a film of tears. One tear slid down his cheek like a wayward raindrop. He tightened his grip on Harry's waist.

Harry was reminded that Sean Andros really wasn't much more than a kid, after all. Twenty-one, tops. He was also reminded that this was the young man he had had such an all-consuming crush on for the past year.

"What can I do to help you?" Harry asked. "Just tell me what's the problem. Maybe we can work it out."

Sean looked at him, his young face inches away from Harry's. Any sneaky little thoughts of sex that Harry might have been harboring throughout this discourse were blown away like leaves in a gale when he saw the look of fear so plainly evident in the boy's eyes.

Harry had met Sean only three times, but on each of those occasions Sean had been in complete control of the situations. He had led Harry gently but confidently through very enjoyable sexual encounters that had left Harry wondering why relationships couldn't be like this.

Now, Harry realized it was he who was being given the reins to control whatever this encounter was leading up to. And except for the kid's obvious pain, it was not an unpleasant sensation. Harry could think of nothing he would rather do than offer his aid to this kid who had not once, but three times, charged him for sex. That was business, Harry supposed. But this wasn't. This was real life. And Harry wanted to help.

"Do you need a place to stay?" he asked.

Sean gave him a sidelong glance, and Harry wondered if the kid could see him at all with all those tears in his eyes.

"Don't worry," he added. "I won't molest you." He crossed his heart and smiled. "Scout's honor."

Sean gave him a sad smile back. "I don't know why you'd want to. After… you know."

"Don't be ashamed of that," Harry said. "I'm the one who paid and I'm not ashamed. It would have been a deal at twice the price for the confidence you sold me. Not to mention the flat-out enjoyment of the whole thing."

Sean wiped a tear from his cheek with the cuff of his jacket.

"What do you mean… confidence?"

Harry touched Sean's knee beneath the bar. "That's your big commodity, kid. Didn't you know that? You're not just selling your body. You're giving your customer confidence in his body too. And you do it very well."

Sean's fingers gave a squeeze to Harry's ribcage. "If I remember right, Harry, there's not a damn thing wrong with your body. I don't go out with customers more than once if I think they're dogs."

Harry grinned. "Well, thanks… I think. But answer my question. Do you need a place to stay?"

Sean nodded. Once more the tears threatened to spill from his eyes. "Yeah, I think I do. I'm afraid to go home. And I don't want to be alone tonight. Can I really stay with you?"

Harry cupped the back of the boy's head and gave him a fatherly pat. "For as long as you want, kid. For as long as you want."

"You still got a hairy chest and five cats?" Sean asked.

"Last time I checked."

"Good," the boy said. "I can use all the fuzz therapy I can get."

"I'm glad that's settled," Harry said. "Now finish your beer. You look like you need it."

With the pressure of Sean's hip against his own, Harry studied the young man's face. The kid was so beautiful that it took Harry's breath away, just as it had the first time Harry laid eyes on him that night a year ago when Biff and Jonah and some others in the bar had presented Sean to Harry as his birthday gift. That night the boy had worn a huge bow around his neck and a gigantic birthday card pinned to his chest that read, "FOR HARRY FROM THE GUYS". He had stood on Harry's doorstep, after ringing the bell, and sang out "Happy Birthday!" when Harry opened the door.

Shocked, Harry had pulled the kid inside, away from prying neighborhood eyes, and after a few awkward moments of getting to know each other, the two had settled onto the sofa with drinks in their hands and before long Sean had reached out and begun unbuttoning Harry's shirt. There was no shyness in the boy, Harry realized immediately. He was not coy or phony or conceited. He was, Harry saw at once, just very, very sure of himself. And incredibly sexy.

After the boy had stripped the last piece of clothing from Harry's body, Sean had stood at Harry's feet and undressed himself, his eyes never leaving Harry's face. When he was naked before him, Harry reached out and brushed his hand along the hair on the boy's thigh, then reached up to knead the tight skin of his stomach and run his fingertips through the thin sprinkling of blond hair across the boy's chest. Like a child, Sean had climbed into Harry's lap and pressed his face to Harry's neck. Harry breathed in the sweet scent of the young man and held his body to him until the hardness of their cocks became too much for either of them to ignore.

Sean's lips moved down along Harry's chest, the boy's fingers caressing the hair there, and to Harry's stomach where his teeth nipped at Harry's skin. Sean's tongue traced a line along the shaft of Harry's penis until his mouth opened up and took Harry inside.

He had spent the night, nestled against Harry in the bed, and not once did Harry close his eyes to sleep. Before the sun came up, Harry knew his heart was gone. He also knew that what to him had been a life-changing experience, had been to the young man beside him nothing more than another night of work.

He had obsessed over the boy for a year, had paid for his company two more times during the course of that year, and now here the boy sat beside him once again. And for the first time, Harry felt needed. There had been no mention of money. Sean wanted only comfort and safety, and Harry was more than prepared to give them to him.

He would give the boy anything he wanted.

And at the moment, Harry had to admit, Sean Andros looked like he could use all the help he could get.

Two beers later, Harry ushered Sean through the red enamel door and outside into the sort of near-freezing rain that only hits San Diego every fifth winter or so. The rain swooped down at a forty-five degree angle, buffeted by the wind that whipped up the hill from the bay.

It felt like a spray of cold needles hitting Harry squarely in the face.

Pointing to his green Boxster convertible, he made a crazy dash for the tiny sportscar with Sean right beside him, both of them vaulting puddles and clutching their jackets tightly about their necks. After an uncomfortable few seconds while Harry fumbled with the car keys to open the door, they dove inside the car as if the rain was a deadly thing that might melt the meat from their bones before they could get away from it.

Once inside, hair streaming, they listened to the rain hit the canvas roof like BBs poured from a bucket.

"Christ!" Harry sputtered. "What a night!"

Sean wiped the film of moisture from the windows with the sleeve of his jacket in frantic little swipes and looked out into the rain in first one direction, then another, as if he thought the bogeyman might be after him. And for all Harry knew, maybe the bogeyman was.

"Come on, kid. Tell me what's wrong?" Harry said, turning the engine over and pressing the DOOR LOCK button. The kid was making him nervous.

"Someone followed me when I went to the bar," Sean breathed, twisting his neck around to look back in the direction of the Cailiff. "For all I know, he might still be out there."

"Followed you from where?"

"From there." Sean pointed to a tower of lights that loomed up from the hillside two blocks away.

"Brittany Towers?"

"Yeah."

"What were you doing there?" Harry asked.

"Working."

"Oh."

The kid put a hand out and rested it on Harry's thigh.

"Come on, Harry. Let's get out of here. I'm scared and I gotta pee."

"Don't worry," Harry said. "We're gone."

The Boxster roared to life and they pulled away from the tiny river rushing along the curb, which had been invisible until Harry flicked on the headlights. Sean's grip on his leg relaxed as the little car moved away into the night. They were all alone on the empty street.

Harry tried to sound casual as he steered the Porsche around a fallen palm frond that had landed smack in the middle of Fourth Avenue.

"You can relax now. You're safe."

Sean's voice was a small, weak thing, barely audible above the engine noise and the lashing of the storm around them.

"I know, Harry. Thanks." No sarcasm there. The kid sounded truly appreciative.

I'm glad *you* know it, Harry found himself thinking. Funny thing, though. *I* don't feel safe at all. He was, in fact, beginning to wonder what he had gotten himself into. Maybe the cold rain slapping him in the face like a wet sock had taken the mellow edge off those five beers he had consumed and now reality was kicking in. But one glance at the boy sitting next to him, nervously hunched over, eyes straight ahead, made Harry feel a little better. And braver.

Such an innocent young face, Harry thought. And what a life the kid was leading.

For the first time, he began to wonder if Sean Andros had many friends.

SLEDGEHAMMER WILLIE huddled against the rain in the doorway of The Nature Store in Seaport Village, an aesthetic tangle of seventy-five restaurants and touristy open-air specialty shops that generally catered to downtown office workers and those travelers intent on spending their last vacation dollar before flying back to wherever the hell it was they were vacationing from. The cobblestoned mall, perched at the very edge of the bay, was perfect for both, being a few minutes from downtown for the 80,000 yuppies who worked there, and a couple of bucks' cab fare from the airport for the tourists. Cruise ships, too, berthed here.

Seaport Village was also Sledgehammer Willie's home. At night, anyway, when the sunburned vacationers and trendily dressed shoppers were gone. The roving security guards could be relied upon to turn a blind eye along about 11:00 p.m. every night when Willie came rattling down the Embarcadero wearing a collection of rags befitting the season and pushing his old shopping cart full of aluminum cans and bottles and everything else Willie could claim to own in this world, which wasn't much.

Where Willie spent his days was a mystery to everyone but Willie himself, but at night he could always be found here, settled into whichever doorway took his fancy. Willie laid claim to all of Seaport Village. Other transients were not tolerated.

Because Willie was special. A good soul. He had lived on the streets of San Diego long before Seaport Village was even dreamed of. People who had lived in this city all their lives might pass the mayor on the street and never recognize her, but they knew Sledgehammer Willie.

He was well into his sixties now and the rescue mission he had founded when he was a young, passionate minister of thirty was a place only in memory. Undoubtedly, some of the other career homeless, men and women who had chosen a life on the streets in perpetuity, as it were, remembered it fondly. It was at the mission that a hot meal could always be had for anyone who needed it. Those were the days when sailors still wore their uniforms off the ships, and the streets of downtown San Diego were alive and bustling with Navy men in their starched white sailor suits.

Touts for massage parlors and tattoo emporiums hawked their services on every street corner. And a lot of people were hungry.

The price of a meal at Willie's Rescue Mission was low for some and entirely too high for others, depending on how they felt about religion, because no one was fed until all were subjected to Willie's particular brand of ministry. And Willie really let them have it. Almost literally, he pounded the word of God into their heads, holding nothing back. Thus he came to be known as Sledgehammer.

Sledgehammer Willie.

His ministry and his mission came to an abrupt end one stifling August night when four Hispanics came through the door for food and Willie laid into them with such gusto and promised them such a feeble chance of salvation that the four men rose up as one in front of the entire congregation and beat Sledgehammer Willie to a bloody pulp, leaving him forever with a dragging leg and a mind that could no longer put two and two together and come up with four.

So Willie became what he had tried so hard to raise the others above.

A bum.

But a bum with heart. A nice bum. Conversationally, Willie now made about as much sense as a politician: one never really knew what the fuck he was getting at, but his eyes were kind.

And now from his dry doorway he watched the night. The lights on the Coronado Bridge were indistinct in the storm, like smears of yellow paint splashed across a black canvas. None of the security guards had come around to wave a polite hello or to offer him a cigarette. They were huddled somewhere just like him, away from the rain and the cold and waiting impatiently for this miserable night to end.

Although to Willie, it wasn't such a miserable night at all. The wind was cold, but that could be tolerated. Being dry was the main thing. As long as Willie was dry, he was content. His gimpy leg burned with the pain of the arthritis that the storm had reawakened, but pain was something he could sometimes bury in the muddy recesses of his mind.

"Stayin' dry, old Willie. Just stayin' dry." It was a litany that he mumbled to himself over and over. The words comforted him. They made him drier.

Along the cobblestoned walkway beside the water, he spotted a figure. A man. Just standing there, looking out over the bay. Willie thought the man's trench coat looked like a flag, flapping in the wind about his legs. Something sparkled in the man's hand. A slash of light that riveted Willie's attention and made him cower deeper into his doorway.

"Oh, lordy," he muttered. "Oh, lordy."

At the sound of the voice behind him the man turned and that slash of bright light turned with him. It was a knife, dripping with the rain and catching reflections from the streetlamp overhead. A long knife. Long and menacingly thin. It looked to Willie like it might be sharp enough to cut the night.

"Oh, lordy Lord," he muttered again as the man moved toward him.

"I was just about to stab me a fish, old hoss," the man said, looking down at Willie where he hunkered in the shadows.

Willie couldn't raise his eyes to look at the man's face; he could only stare at the knife hanging casually from the man's hand, drops of rain forming at its gleaming tip and falling to the cobblestones in slow motion to splatter at Willie's feet.

"You've been fishing?" Willie asked, unbelieving. Even though his mind was usually running on empty, he still knew there were right ways and wrong ways to catch a fish, and he had never heard of anyone catching a fish with a knife before.

"Oh, yes, old hoss. I've been fishing. Fishing for sinners."

Willie shuddered, suddenly colder than he could ever remember being. He tore his gaze from the knife's crystal edge and, for the first time, let his eyes wander upward to the man's face. He thought he saw a smile there, but it might have been the movement of shadow and wind.

"You're the Fisher of Men, then, ain't ya?" Willie whispered. "You finally found me, I guess."

"You a sinner?" the smile in the shadows asked.

"Everybody's a sinner," Willie replied. "Everybody."

"No," the man said. "Not everybody. And probably not you. What *you* are, my friend, is a witness. I'm afraid you bedded down in the wrong doorway tonight."

And with that, Willie felt the sharpness of the knife press into the tender skin beneath his chin. But only for the briefest of moments. After that, as the knife slid deeper, through the base of his tongue and past his palate into his already damaged brain, Willie felt nothing. Even as his body flailed like a puppet on the end of a stick, he felt no real discomfort. Only a painless falling of darkness. A curtain being drawn on his life at last.

It was time for Willie to learn what heaven was all about.

The man shifted his grip on the knife and pulled it from Willie's chin. He stepped quickly back to avoid the gush of blood, then turned away. He retraced his steps over the cobblestoned walkway that rimmed the bay.

"Now for that fish," he said to the storm and flung the knife out into the water. Faintly, over the wind and rain, he heard a distant splash.

A security guard found Willie the next morning. Even in death, Willie's open eyes were kind and forgiving.

And maybe even thankful.

HARRY forked out his prettiest martini glasses from the top shelf and stirred up enough gin martinis to fell an ox. He figured the kid needed a drink. A real drink. And so did he. When Harry was upset, a simple beer just didn't seem to fill the void. He needed something pissy.

Something nice. Something that looked good in a glass. So he scrounged around the kitchen until he found a small box of silver toothpicks, extracted two, and daintily stabbed an olive onto each one.

By the time the kid had finished his shower and donned a pair of pajamas Harry had laid out for him, Harry was perched on the edge of the sofa, martini in hand, like Laurence Olivier. He held a glass out to Sean and watched the boy squat down at his feet. Harry's pajamas hung all over the kid like a forty-foot flag on a twelve-foot pole.

"Feel better?" Harry asked.

"Yeah," Sean said and sipped his martini. The way he screwed up his face immediately afterward indicated to Harry that martinis might be a new experience for the boy.

But then Sean tilted his head back and poured half the drink down his throat like it was a diet Coke instead of one-hundred-proof gin. And he almost carried it off. Only the tears that came to his eyes gave him away.

Harry laughed. "Sip it, kid, or you'll be dead by morning."

Sean carefully placed his glass on the coffee table and rested his chin on Harry's knee.

"I don't know how to thank you for... you know... everything."

"Then don't," Harry said.

A comfortable silence fell over them as they listened to the rain through the patio door.

One by one, Harry's five cats crept into the living room, cautiously at first, their bodies slung low in their wariness, scoping out this new human being who had so unexpectedly infiltrated their domain. After carefully circling the perimeter of the room a couple of times, they finally settled down. Charlie, the bravest of the lot, promptly sprawled out alongside Sean's leg and fell asleep.

Harry lit a cigarette.

"You smoke too much," Sean said. "It's not good for you."

"That's right, my son," Harry countered. "And you're playing Russian roulette with your dick. Haven't you ever heard of a little thing called AIDS?"

When Sean grinned, Harry felt the kid's chin dig into his knee. "Sorry I spoke."

Harry grinned back and they let that comfortable silence return. But not for long.

"So tell me what happened," Harry said. "I can't help you if I don't know what's going on."

Sean pushed himself up from the floor, scaring the bejesus out of Charlie who went flying out of the room like the hounds of hell were chasing him. The other four cats followed suit, creating a tiny stampede that rattled the lamp on the end table.

Sean positioned himself in front of the patio door, looking out, his back to Harry, his face to the night.

"Maybe I shouldn't drag you into this. Maybe… maybe I should just go to the police."

"Is it that bad?" Harry asked.

"Yeah, it is."

Harry set his drink aside and went to the boy. He took Sean's hand and gently pulled him back to the sofa.

"Now, look," he said. "I want you to tell me what's going on. There's not a goddamn thing I can do to help you if I don't know what it's all about. I know what you do for a living, Sean. Did someone try to hurt you?" Harry finally lost patience. "What the hell *happened*?"

Sean reached for his drink, then stopped.

"I don't think anyone's going to believe me, Harry. Maybe not even you."

"Try me."

Sean rubbed his scalp, hard, as if trying to create enough friction to get his little gray cells working. He looked at his hands and frowned. "Not like this, Harry. Let's go to bed first. I'm scared, and I'd like it if you would just sort of… hold me. Can we do that?"

How can this sweet kid sell his body for a living, Harry asked himself. But what he *said* was, "Sure. I can't think of anything I'd rather be doing."

SEAN practically fell out of Harry's pajamas, they were so big on him. He slid beneath the covers while Harry flicked off the lamp on the nightstand and undressed. Before coming to bed, Harry went to the window and opened it a crack so they could hear the rain. He slid into bed beside Sean, and the boy felt Harry's arm slide under his head. Sean burrowed next to this man who had been so kind to him all evening and rested his head on Harry's chest. The downy pelt of hair felt comforting against his cheek. His cock stirred against Harry's leg, but he ignored it, and he hoped the man would do the same. He really did want to talk. He *needed* to talk.

He listened to Harry's breathing, then to Harry's voice, husky in the darkness. "This better?"

Sean burrowed closer, clutched tighter. He figured that would be answer enough and it was.

Their bodies melded together, a warm cocoon beneath the blankets. The feel of Harry's body against his own gave the boy the courage he needed to talk about what had happened. As he spoke, he listened to Harry's heartbeat and it eased his fear. He had never felt so vulnerable in his life.

"The guy's name was Stanley. I don't know his last name. They don't usually tell me. I guess maybe they figure I'll come back at them later and cause trouble. You know, call them up and ask for money or something. I don't even know *your* last name."

"Connors," Harry said, his lips brushing the kid's hair. It smelled of his own shampoo. He liked that. "Go on."

Sean closed his eyes, thinking back. "I've partied with him before. Five or six times, I guess. A real shy dude, but loaded. Really rich, I guess. Brittany Towers isn't cheap, and this guy's place was on the sixth floor. Hell of a view. Things like that cost money. I don't know what he did for a living. He never talked about himself much. He was so shy, he never really talked about *anything* much. It was always the same. He'd meet me at the entrance to the building. Then we'd go up to his condo. He'd have drinks ready for both of us, and we'd take the drinks into the bedroom. The lights were always off. Maybe he wasn't so shy that way, or maybe he thought the view looked more… you know… romantic with the lights off."

Sean felt Harry's hand stroke his back, lazily, undemanding.

"We got it on. Twice. I don't usually cum with the johns, but this time I did." He suddenly looked up into Harry's face. "I did with you, though, didn't I?"

"Yeah." Harry said. "You did. Stop stalling. Tell me what happened."

Sean nestled his face against Harry's chest again, the only place he felt safe.

"The guy was never kinky or nothing. Just nice, straight sex, if you'll pardon the expression. It seemed to really do something to the guy when I shot my rocks. I had never done that with him before. I don't know if he was appreciative or turned on or what, but he asked me to spend the night. I told him that cost extra and he said okay. It was a shitty night outside, as you know, so I figured what the hell. We lay in the dark and talked, and I came to the conclusion that Stanley really was a nice enough guy. I honestly started liking him. I wondered how anyone could make that much money and still be so insecure. Anyway, we decided to have a few more drinks, but wouldn't you know it, he was out of booze, so I offered to go out and get some. I had parked on the street, but Stanley gave me his garage door opener so that when I came back, I could park in the underground lot since I was planning to spend the night anyway. Stanley had two spaces but only one car. A Mercedes convertible. Red. A real beauty. It was funny seeing my old clunker parked next to it. Sort of put me in my place, you know? Anyway, I went. There's a liquor store about four blocks away, and it only took a few minutes."

Here, Harry felt the boy tense up. His hand moved to Harry's waist, pulling him closer.

Harry responded in kind, holding the boy, offering himself for comfort if that was what the boy needed. Dampness touched his chest and he realized Sean was crying again.

"After the liquor store, I went back to Brittany Towers. I buzzed myself into the garage. I still have the garage door opener in my jacket pocket. I took the elevator to six, and when I got to Stanley's door, I just walked on in 'cause I'd left it ajar when I left. I put the bag with the booze in it on the kitchen counter and started for the bedroom. That's when I heard it."

"Heard what?" Harry asked, trying to sound calm but knowing all along that the kid must be listening to his heart racing inside his chest like an internal combustion engine badly in need of a tune-up.

Sean took a deep shuddering breath. He pressed his lips, his damp cheek, into Harry's neck. His body trembled.

"The scream. It was Stanley. Screaming. Something crashed. A mirror. Or maybe the lamp beside the bed. I don't know. Then Stanley was pleading, 'Don't cut me again! Please, don't cut me again!' And whoever was in there with him laughed. I swear to God, Harry, he laughed. And then there was nothing. No sounds at all. Just… silence."

The boy laid his hand across his face, as if trying to block out the memory, but the words kept spilling out. "I was still in the living room. There were no lights on anywhere in the condo except for the bedroom. I didn't know what to do. I saw a shadow on the hallway floor. Like someone was moving around in there, in the bedroom, doing… something. I figured Stanley must be dead or why did he stop screaming? Why didn't he say something? I panicked, Harry. I didn't know what else to do, so I just flung the door open and ran. And when I did, I heard the man running after me. I didn't dare wait for the elevator, so I took the stairs. I ran down those stairs like I've never run before. I flew. And all the time I'm running, I'm thinking, he'll get me when I try to start my car. I could hear his footsteps pounding down the stairs behind me. It sounded like he was gaining, but still he must have been a couple of flights behind me. When I got to the lobby, I just split through the front door. I didn't even try to make it to the garage because I knew that's where he would get me. That's where he would do to me whatever it was he did to poor Stanley. He would… cut me. Jesus, Harry!"

"He followed you outside?"

"Yeah. It was so damn dark. And the rain. The sidewalks were slippery. I was afraid I'd fall and then he'd have my guts for garters. I headed for the only place I knew where there were people around. Where I thought I'd be safe. The Cailiff. Surely to Christ he wouldn't kill me in front of witnesses. And *you*, you poor bastard! There you sat, half drunk, I guess, or you wouldn't have gotten yourself involved in all this, but I gotta tell you, Harry, when I ran through that door, you were the best looking thing I'd ever seen in my life. Thank God you were there."

Harry listened to the rain outside. He breathed in the cold air from the open window.

He shook his head. "I don't know what to say."

"It's true, Harry. Every word of it."

"I believe you," Harry heard himself saying, and he realized in that instant that he did believe the boy. Why, he didn't know. Maybe just because he wanted to.

For the first time, the boy's tears did not simply spill out silently. He could no longer hold back the sobs. And he cried. Like a child. Holding onto Harry like an injured youngster might clutch a caring father. Harry rocked him. Whispered soothing words into his ear. Tried to calm him with gentle kisses. This was more emotion than Harry had seen spent in twenty years, and it scared him more than the boy's story. He had to do something. Something….

He gently pulled away, easing himself out of bed.

"Where… going?"

"Stay there," Harry said.

He padded to the bathroom and dug through the medicine cabinet until he found a prescription bottle of Valium. The kid needed sleep.

He returned to the bedroom with a glass of tap water and two capsules. He hooked an arm behind Sean's back and coaxed him to a sitting position.

"Take these," he said. "You need to get some rest. We'll figure out what to do in the morning."

Sean choked down the Valium with a sip of water and collapsed onto the pillows. Harry sat beside him, stroking his hair while the pills took effect. Gradually, the boy calmed. His sobbing ceased.

And just before drifting into sleep, he raised his hand to touch Harry's cheek.

"Can I stay here with you?" he asked. "Please, Harry, let me stay. I'm afraid... he'll cut me."

Harry pressed his lips to Sean's forehead and tucked the covers snugly beneath his chin.

"You can stay here as long as you like," Harry whispered. "You'll be safe. Don't worry."

Only then did the boy sleep.

HARRY triple locked the front door on the way out. Door knob, dead bolt, security screen. Three locks, three keys. No way anyone could get inside. And the kid wouldn't be waking up for hours, not if the martinis and the Valium knocked the boy ass over teakettle as Harry suspected they would.

It was still raining. Harry clutched his car keys in one hand and the garage door opener he had swiped from Sean's jacket in the other. A third set of keys, Sean's car keys, were stashed in his trouser pocket. He knew he was crazy for even contemplating doing what he was about to do, but he knew he had to do it. For Sean. Or maybe for himself. It didn't really matter which.

It was all Harry could do to keep from laughing at himself. Here he was, forty-five years old. Certainly old enough to know better. But it didn't matter. His feelings had gone far beyond the "crush" phase. He was falling in love with the kid. Jesus, falling in love with a male prostitute. But if this wasn't love, then what the hell else could it be? He was long, long past puberty, so it couldn't be a matter of raging hormones. Face the facts, he told himself, you fell in love with Sean the first time you laid eyes on him. And nothing has changed since then.

Great. And when it's all over, he thought, the kid'll probably charge you for the night.

Pissed off at his own stupidity, he almost lost control of his little sports car by pulling out too quickly onto the rain-washed street. He took a deep breath, forcing himself to calm down and slow down at the same time.

Brittany Towers was twelve blocks up and two blocks over from his house. When he reached it, he circled the block twice, looking for squad cars. He saw one black and white and also a gray sedan that looked like it might be an unmarked car, but there were no policemen standing around outside the building. Two blocks from the Towers, he found a parking space, well hidden in the shade of overhanging branches from the glare of the streetlight.

He hunched his shoulders and ducked his head against the wind and rain and started walking. By the time he was back at the Towers, he was soaked. His hands shook from the cold and from his own rattled nerves as he extracted the garage door opener from his pocket and gave it a try. The metal grating at the bottom of the steep incline leading from the street into the underground parking clattered right up into the ceiling. He breathed a sigh of relief. He thought maybe the police would have it locked or something. He didn't know what the hell to expect, actually, but at least he was inside.

He hurried in out of the rain and began his search for a red Mercedes convertible. A real beauty, the kid had said. Well, there were a lot of real beauties here. A vintage Rolls Royce. A '56 Thunderbird in lemon yellow. A couple of tuna boat Caddys and more Mercedes-Benzes than he could shake a stick at. He found the red convertible in the last row, against the wall. Sitting next to it, looking like a poor relation, was a blue Yugo. Who knew what year it was and who cared? It was a piece of shit. Harry could almost hear the other automobiles around him clucking their grillwork and muttering something along the lines of "there goes the neighborhood."

The Yugo's door was unlocked. Harry gave Sean credit for having the good sense to know that if any respectable car thief had broken into this garage to help himself to a bit of last minute Christmas shopping, then his piece of shit Yugo would have been the safest vehicle on the lot.

Still shaking from the cold and a bad case of nerves, he fumbled with Sean's car keys until he found the one to the ignition, and much to his surprise, the Yugo roared to life immediately. It sounded like a barrel of tin cans rolling down a hill, but at least it ran. He backed quickly out of the parking space, reopened the garage door with Stanley's clicker, and roared up the incline to the street with the image going through his head of everyone in the building, including the cops, jumping up and wondering what the fuck that *racket* was.

Before pulling onto the street, Harry thoroughly wiped off any vestiges of fingerprints from the garage door opener and flung it out the window. It landed in a stand of shrubbery by the front walk and disappeared.

That much accomplished, Harry took off, leaving nothing of himself or Sean behind, he hoped, but a dense cloud of blue exhaust smoke. Now he and the boy could figure out what to do without having to worry about the police knocking down his door—for a while, at least. Harry could only hope Sean had left no evidence of himself behind in the apartment. He supposed there would be fingerprints, but that would take a while. At least it took a while in the movies. Any DNA Sean might have left behind would take even longer.

Back at the house, Harry parked the Yugo in his driveway and covered it with the car cover he had bought for the Porsche. Then he set off walking through the rain once more to retrieve his own car.

CHAPTER THREE

LEAH SILVER, the Jewish widow who lived in 6E, just down the hall from Stanley Baker, was without a doubt the shortest Jewish widow Detective Jimmy Smith had ever seen. She stood perhaps four foot eleven. In heels. Spiked heels. And he calculated her weight at about one eighty.

She looked amazingly similar to one of his daughter's Weebles.

Detectives Smith and McCray had been at it for two hours now, and they were still on the sixth floor. They had learned absolutely nothing of value since commencing their canvas of the building at precisely 7:00 a.m. as they had planned. Not until they humbly pecked at the door to 6E and found themselves face to with the little Jewish Weeble did they learn anything at all that might benefit their investigation.

She had ushered them inside, *way* inside, all the way to a back bedroom that had been converted to a sewing/hobby/reading and (due to the season) gift wrapping room. The detectives had parked themselves on the edge of a frilly daybed, which was covered with stuffed animals. They both looked extremely uncomfortable being surrounded by so much fluffy cuteness. They also looked a little greedy, for they were being fed some very good and very satisfying information.

Mrs. Silver wore half-specs perched low on the end of her nose, for while she spoke she was also wrapping gifts. Obviously, her being Jewish had in no way curtailed her gift-giving spirit. Presents, wrapped, unwrapped, and half-wrapped were scattered all over the room.

"Mr. Baker was what my late husband, Cecil, used to call a queerboy. No disrespect meant, of course. He was a nice enough man, I suppose. Stanley, I mean. Quiet. You never heard a peep from his apartment. Not a peep. Very considerate of his neighbors was Mr. Baker. But still… that lifestyle. Tsk. Not healthy at all."

Mrs. Silver looked up from her gift wrapping and peered over her glasses at Detective McCray with a disapproving glare. "AIDS, you know."

McCray looked taken aback. "Pardon?"

She snipped off a piece of ribbon with a large pair of scissors in such a robust fashion that the black detective felt an uncontrollable urge to cross his legs. Especially after seeing what he had seen down the hall in 6B.

"AIDS! I said, AIDS!" Again the woman looked directly at McCray. "It came from Africa, you know. All those natives. Nothing better to do, I suppose. But still, it's so hot there."

Smith cleared his throat, hoping he wouldn't laugh out loud at his partner's look of surprise. "Hot where?" he asked, purposely fueling the fire under McCray's embarrassment.

She fluffed up a gaudy bow that was twice as large as the box it decorated.

"Africa! Africa! What have we been talking about? All those natives, excuse my French, but… well… copulating! In that heat! And they never have enough to eat. You'd think they would be too weak."

McCray considered picking up the little fat woman by her shoulder pads and pitching her off the balcony, just to hear her squeak like a rat going down. But then he thought better of it. It would be counterproductive to the investigation.

He sighed instead. "About Mr. Baker…."

"What about him?" she asked sweetly, scraping a length of ribbon along the blade of her scissors to make it curl.

"What can you tell us about him?"

She gathered up a fistful of these curled strips of ribbon, daintily placed them at the very center of the foil-wrapped package, and with the other hand, nailed them down with the blast of a staple gun.

Both detectives jumped.

McCray hoped there was nothing fragile inside that box.

"He was lonely, I think," she said. "The poor man. But good with money. Oh, yes. Stanley certainly knew how to make money."

Jimmy Smith tried a change of tack. "One can't help but wonder if he also didn't have a knack for making enemies."

Once again, she studied them over her glasses.

"Who? Stanley? Don't be ridiculous."

"Someone must have had it in for him, ma'am."

"Why?" she asked. "Because he's dead? I think not. It might be just a matter of associating with the wrong sort of people, you know. The wrong *element*."

"What element are you referring to? The gay element? Being gay isn't a crime, Mrs. Silver. And it is certainly no excuse for doing to someone what was so heartlessly done to Mr. Baker."

Mrs. Silver slapped a diamond-studded hand to her pudgy breast with enough force to kill a cat. "Why, I never implied it was. I certainly did not. But no matter what sort of lifestyle one leads, it would be wise to pick your associates with a bit of prudence, don't you think?"

"Spell it out, Mrs. Silver. What associates, exactly, are you talking about? Did Mr. Baker have unscrupulous friends? Did he hang out with the Mob?"

His weak attempt at humor sailed directly over the Weeble's head and splattered dead against the wall.

"I'm referring to sex, Detective McCray. Prostitutes. *Male* prostitutes, if that's what they are called. Mr. Baker had a very unsavory taste for such practices. I suspected all along that it would kill him one day."

Here, she relented a bit in her testimony.

"Well, of course, I never expected it to kill him *immediately*. I merely meant I thought he was flirting with death from AIDS. But still, he was actually quite a nice-looking boy. One wouldn't think him capable of violence at all."

"Who? Baker?" Smith asked.

Mrs. Silver commenced tearing off little pieces of scotch tape and plastering them to the back of her hand for easy access.

"No, no, no. I mean the little blond boy. The one with the pleasant smile."

Smith wondered if there was anything like a Tylenol about the place. "Which boy is that?"

"The boy who visited Stanley yesterday evening about five o'clock."

Detective McCray felt the exhilaration that in his experience only comes from two things: the tug of a salmon on a fishing line, and the sudden appearance of an honest-to-God witness in a murder investigation.

"Are you implying you saw someone entering Mr. Baker's apartment yesterday evening?"

"I didn't imply it. I said it. Shouldn't you be taking notes?"

Both detectives guiltily reached for their notepads.

Mrs. Silver unrolled a length of wrapping paper and gave it a critical eye. "Is this gauche?"

Jimmy Smith poised pencil over notepad. The wrapping paper was gauche indeed. Downright ugly, in fact. "No, ma'am, it's lovely. Can you describe him for us?"

Mrs. Silver set the paper aside and, for the first time during the interview, honestly seemed to be considering her answer carefully.

"He was very young. Twenty. Twenty-one. Reddish blond hair cut rather short. Most gay men seem to wear their hair quite short these days, don't they? I wonder why that is? He wore faded jeans and a leather jacket. Big on leather, too, are the gayboys. Black leather. It was dry."

McCray stopped writing. "What was dry? You mean the jacket?"

She nodded. "Yes. The jacket."

"I don't understand...."

"It means, Detective, that the young man must have come from the garage. He must have driven his own car here and parked it downstairs in the garage."

Smith considered this. "I don't know. He might have cabbed it."

Mrs. Silver shook her head. "Oh, I don't think so, dear. Even running from a cab to the front door, the young man would have gotten a bit wet, don't you think? That was no light shower we had last night, gentlemen. It was raining to beat the band. And he was carrying a bag."

"A bag?"

"Yes. A paper shopping bag. Not a very large one. It was dry, too."

This, Smith knew, was the bag the techs discovered on the kitchen counter containing a liter of Tanqueray, a roll of Certs, and a sales slip from Cottage Liquor, just up the street. They had interviewed the clerk on duty by telephone this morning, but the man did not specifically remember the transaction.

"I don't understand exactly what it is you're driving at, Mrs. Silver. Spell it out for me. I'm not too bright."

Mrs. Silver eyed the big black detective with an air of complete disbelief. "Don't play dumb with me, sir. The way I've been egging you on, I'm surprised you haven't pulled your piece, as they say in the movies, and blown me away. I believe that's the correct terminology, is it not?"

McCray had to agree with her. "It certainly is."

Smith laughed. He couldn't stop himself. "So tell us, Mrs. Silver. Why do *you* think the boy was dry?"

The woman pushed the wrapping debris away from her and rested her heavy arms on the tabletop.

"Simply put, I think the boy was here earlier. Mr. Baker must have needed something at the store and sent the boy out to get it. He loaned him his garage clicker, and the boy parked in the garage when he returned from the store. That's why he wasn't wet from the rain."

McCray turned to Smith. "There was no garage door opener found in the condo, was there?"

"No," Smith said.

"Then the boy still has it," Mrs. Silver stated unequivocally. "And that really is about all I can tell you. I know the boy reentered the apartment at five o'clock but I have no idea what time he left. He nodded and smiled at me when he arrived because I just happened to hear footsteps in the hall and I was peeking out my doorway at the time to see who it was. Unfortunately, at five o'clock Wheel of Fortune comes on and I never miss it. I simply adore Vanna White. Did either of you ever notice what a large head she has?"

"Uh, no," Smith said. "I don't believe we ever did."

Mrs. Silver once again began puttering with her packages.

"I suppose you'll be sending one of those police artists here for me to help him with a composite sketch of the suspect?"

"Most likely, ma'am, if that would be all right."

"Oh, certainly," she replied. "I adore making new friends."

She coolly snipped another length of ribbon.

THE former two-hundred-pound linebacker for the San Diego Chargers simpered down the hallway in his rendition of a short Jewish Weeble in stiletto heels. "I simply *adore* making new friends! I simply *adore* that large-headed Vanna White! But, oh, those *queerboys*! And *Africa*!"

"She was pulling your big black leg, my friend," Smith chuckled. "But she's a very good witness. We might even get a decent composite sketch out of her."

McCray frowned. "I never trust composite sketches."

"Neither do I."

An elderly gentleman in jogging pants and sweatshirt watched them from a bench by the elevator. As they approached, he stood.

"Excuse me, officers. Might I have a word with you?"

"You can have a word with my partner here," McCray said and slipped away. He wanted to check out Baker's car. Maybe the errant garage door opener was inside the vehicle.

"How can I help you?" Smith asked.

The man had a thick head of snow-white hair and a small portable oxygen tank on wheels resting at his feet like an obedient dog. Plastic tubing snaked from the machine up under the man's sweatshirt and over his ears. From there the tubing hugged either side of his face and clipped to his nose. The jogging outfit was for comfort, Smith decided, nothing more. Emphysema was not conducive to running down the street for your health.

"Shall we sit?" Smith asked, indicating the bench.

The man's breathing could be heard in tiny gasps, reminding Detective Smith of his father just before he died of the same affliction.

Detective Smith didn't smoke.

"Thank you," the man said, gratefully taking a seat. "My name is Howard Mikulski. My wife and I live on the ninth floor."

Condos that high up in this particular building, Smith knew, sold for more than a million five, thus proving the old axiom that money couldn't buy good health. Jimmy didn't doubt for a minute that this man would give up his million five condo and every nickel he had squirreled away over the past fifty years and everything else he owned for one deep, fulfilling breath of air.

"Yes, sir?"

Mr. Mikulski was a very courteous man. "Please excuse this contraption here," he said, pulling the oxygen tank away from Smith's feet and out of the way. "But it is literally my lifeline. Can't do without it."

"Of course," Smith said politely, still trying to block out memories of his father; an inordinately happy man who had tried to cope valiantly with an inordinately unhappy ending to his life. "Do you have some information for us?"

"My wife thinks so," Mr. Mikulski said. "You see, our parking space is next to Mr. Baker's. Mr. Baker has two spaces, you see, but only one car, and my wife is an invalid. She had a leg amputated last summer due to complications arising from diabetes. Mr. Baker always left the empty parking space between my car and his so that my wife's wheelchair could be pushed right up to the car door. Mr. Baker was a fine young man. We're very sorry this terrible thing has happened to him."

"I don't quite understand, Mr. Mikulski...."

The old man adjusted the plastic tubing beneath his nose.

"You see, last night my wife and I were returning from a dinner party at my daughter's home in Point Loma, and when we arrived here, that space was no longer empty. There was a car in it. An old car."

"Yes," Smith said. "We think Mr. Baker had a guest and that he let this guest use his extra space."

Mr. Mikulski looked relieved. "Then you already know about it." He started to rise. "I hope I haven't taken up too much of your valuable time. It's only that my wife thought...."

Jimmy Smith laid a hand on Mr. Mikulski's arm. "Wait, sir. Can you identify the car?"

"Well, no, I'm afraid I didn't look at the license plate, if that's what you mean."

"But in general," Smith said. "What did the car look like?"

Mr. Mikulski thought for a moment, the oxygen tank whirring softly at his feet.

"It was an *old* car. No, wait. Not old, exactly. Just... well worn, if you know what I mean." He chuckled, creating a sibilant hiss of oxygen from the tubing above his lip. "I'm afraid it looked rather out of place in our garage, to tell the truth. A rather unsavory blue, if I remember correctly. And small. Tiny, actually. We were still able to push my wife's wheelchair between it and my own."

"What make?" Smith asked. "Do you remember?"

"Yes, sir. A Hugo."

"You mean Yugo?"

Mikulski nodded. "Yes, that's it. Yugo. Rather an odd name for an automobile, isn't it?"

"I believe they are made in Yugoslavia."

"Ah," Mikulski said. "That would explain it."

Smith jotted notes onto his pad. "And what time did you return from your daughter's dinner party? About five o'clock?"

"Oh, no, sir," Mikulski explained. "It was a rather formal affair, and no one can drag out a dinner party like our daughter. We didn't return home until almost midnight. My wife was exhausted."

Smith stopped jotting. "*Midnight*?"

"That's right. It might even have been a wee bit later. I didn't really check the time precisely. Why? Is that important? You seem surprised."

"Let me just say, Mr. Mikulski, that you've certainly given us something to chew on."

With that, Smith thanked his informant and headed for the garage.

HE FOUND Jefferson McCray rummaging through the trunk of Stanley Baker's Mercedes convertible. The parking space to the left of it was, as he suspected it would be, empty.

"Jesus Christ, Jeff, what moron forgot to seal off this garage yesterday?" Smith pointed to the empty space as if it were personally responsible for all his problems. "There was a car parked *right there* for as long as seven hours after the murder took place! Where is it?"

"Beats me, Massah. Are you sure?"

"Yes. Did you find the clicker?"

"No."

"Shit."

"I believe *I* did, gentlemen," said a voice from behind them.

They both turned to see the gray-headed crime tech with the paunch approaching them from between the next row of cars. He triumphantly held up a plastic evidence bag. Inside it rested a damp and dirty garage door opener approximately the size of a cigarette lighter.

"Found it in the shrubbery outside," the tech explained.

"Prints?"

"I doubt it. It's covered with mud."

"Great."

THE man, his thinning blond hair still damp from the shower, rolled the room service tray to the edge of his unmade bed and quickly devoured a late breakfast of eggs, sausage, toast, and oatmeal swimming in cream.

God's work made him hungry.

His hotel room window looked out upon a gazebo-like fountain across the street. He could occasionally discern the sound of its cascading water, but only during lulls in the street noise.

Somewhere down below, the piping voice of a street-corner preacher raved on and on about the coming of the Lord, as if the Lord could be expected to speak through the lips of a gibbering fool such as that.

God, the man knew, only worked through the strong and the sane.

And that fact did not displease him in the least.

Having eaten, he stood naked at the open window. The morning breeze felt cool against his pale skin. He was sorry to note that the rain had stopped with the dawn. Last night the rain, like God, had been his ally. It had covered him as darkness alone could not have done.

His quarry, the whore, had escaped. The pale man had chased him through the rain last night, but the whore, spurred on by fear, had been uncatchable. This had infuriated the man at first. But on later consideration, he figured it would only serve to prolong the game. Not a bad thing at all. He had stood outside the bar, two doorways down, protected from the rain, and waited for the boy to reemerge. And in less than half an hour, he had done just that. With another of his perverted kind. An older man. Together they sped off in a green sports car.

The pale man, on foot, could not follow. But he would not need to.

Beneath a streetlight, he had checked himself for any signs of blood from the man he had punished only minutes earlier, and seeing none, stepped casually inside the Cailiff. The switchblade knife rested securely in his trouser pocket.

The bar was packed. As he entered, everyone sitting at the horseshoe by the door turned to gaze at him. Appraising him. What a freak show, he thought, ignoring the lecherous old bastards who were eyeing him like they were picking out a steak at the meat counter.

He moved deeper into the dark room and squeezed himself up to the bar. When the bartender came, an old queer with earrings and a ponytail, the pale man tried not to laugh. Instead, he gave the bastard a sweet smile and ordered a coke.

"A *coke*?" The bartender asked, batting innocent eyes at him like fucking Heidi of the Alps.

The pale man merely stared back at him, friendly-like, until the bartender swished off to fill his order.

On his return, the pale man paid the bartender but would not allow himself to touch the glass.

"I'm looking for Sean," he said.

The bartender leaned forward and rested his elbows on the bar, giving the pale man his undivided attention. New faces, and handsome ones at that, were a welcome change of pace around here. The bartender thought the man before him looked sexy as hell. He liked tall men. He liked everything about them. This man also looked dangerous. The bartender liked that, too.

"Sean?" he repeated. "You mean the little hustler who just left with Harry?"

"Yes. We were just at my apartment and I'm afraid he left something behind. I'd like to return it to him."

The bartender smiled. "A customer of his, are you?"

The pale man was tempted to pull the switchblade from his pocket and stick it in the old faggot's eyeball, but he knew that wouldn't do. Wouldn't be polite.

"That's right," he said. "I'm a customer of his. Can you tell me where Harry lives? I saw them go, but I was too late to catch them."

"Sorry. Can't help you," the bartender simpered. "It would be a little too much like tattling."

Someone from the other end of the bar called out for a Coors and the bartender reluctantly moved away, hoping later to come back and try to get to know the guy a little better. He really did like the tall ones. And blond to boot.

The pale man jerked away as a hand came down on his shoulder. He grimaced as a very drunken Biff Sullivan breathed gin in his face and grinned.

"He went with Harry," Biff mumbled, his eyes not quite focusing on the man he was speaking to.

"So I heard."

"Yeah, Harry. Harry Connors. Lives on Eagle Street in Mission Hills. That's where they were going. Old Harry got lucky tonight."

The pale man watched with disgust as a thread of drool traveled down the old drunk's chin and dribbled onto his shirt.

"Say," Biff cooed. "How would you like to come up to my place for a drink?"

"Nothing could make me happier," the pale man intoned, his eyes cold. But the look was lost on Biff who was about one drink away from a martini-induced near-death experience.

"You say he left with Harry Connors, huh? I thought the guy looked familiar."

Biff belched and damn near puked. "Yeah, good old Harry. A nice guy, Harry. Owns that big beauty salon up the street. Harry's For Hair. Clever, huh?"

The pale man didn't bother looking interested. The old fool was so drunk that he wouldn't have recognized interest if it crawled up his pant leg and bit him on the ass.

"You said he lives on Eagle Street?"

"Yep. Went to a bash at old Harry's house one time. He knows how to throw a party."

"That's good to know."

The pale man leaned into Biff's ear and whispered, "How would you like those ugly fucking false teeth crammed up your ass? Would you like that?"

Biff didn't quite gather the gist of what his new friend was saying, but it didn't matter, because in two seconds the blond guy was gone and old Biff was once again sitting all alone in a crowded room. A couple of minutes later, he had forgotten where he was, who he had just been talking to, and what the hell he was supposed to be doing.

Biff took one more sip of his martini, sloshing most of it into his lap, before his brain shut down altogether and his head came down plop onto the bar. Tomorrow he wouldn't remember a thing.

The man left the bar and walked two blocks back to where he had parked his car. From there, he drove to Seaport Village, where he intended to dispose of the switchblade, unaware of the fact that more fun would be waiting for him there in the guise of a homeless, crazy old man who had chosen the wrong doorway to sleep in.

It had been quite a night all around.

The pale man turned away from the hotel window, gathered up the dishes and tablecloth from the room service tray, and placed them neatly along the wall beside the door. He dampened a wash cloth in the bathroom sink and painstakingly wiped the top of the cart clean. Then he wiped it down again. From a box in the closet, he removed several innocent looking items that, when joined together, would no longer be innocent at all. He neatly placed them on the cart.

Perched naked on the edge of the bed, he worked for two hours. Sweat beaded his forehead, although the room was cool. He stared, almost with awe, at the precise movements of his fingers. At the delicate positioning of the separate components of the device he was creating. God was doing the work. He was merely providing the body through which the work could be done.

When he was finished, the bomb was small, but size could be deceiving. It had the capacity to make a great deal of difference in a great many lives.

The awareness of his own power excited him, sending torrents of strength to every part of the man's body. His cock was erect and throbbing with blood, aching for the release that he knew would only come when his work at the table was done.

He carefully pushed the room service tray aside. The device that now rested on its surface was a dangerous thing. It must be delicately handled.

The man's head lolled back as he stood, the muscles in his neck straining. He moved to the open window, eyes closed, feeling the air against his body. He touched the smooth skin of his chest, felt his heart, alive inside him. He floated above himself and, like a voyeur, watched his hand slide down across his stomach and lower, cupping his balls with wonder at the miracles they held. Slowly, his body trembling, he felt his fingers glide up the length of his cock. It hummed in his hand like living iron. He grasped it gently, letting the strength of it overwhelm him. His hand began to move, to stroke this living animal that could create such incredible wonders.

He leaned into the window, stroking harder, arching his back into the cool morning air, into the emptiness of the open window. He cared for nothing but the heavy ache building in his groin until at last, his brain dead to everything but this climbing passion, he released his sperm into the air. It sailed like liquid stars into the morning, dispersing in the wind. He cried out with the pain and the pleasure of it.

Then, looking down, the pale man pointed to the street and laughed.

AT A bus stop, sixty feet below and directly across the street, Yolanda Esposito tried to control her four children, all under the age of seven, and keep an eye out for the San Ysidro bus at the same time. It was not an easy task.

Beneath her cheap flannel coat, her belly was swollen with the partially developed fetus of her fifth child, a boy, who, unbeknownst to her on this December morning, would be christened Steven and who, even now, was inflicted with Down Syndrome, his brain cavity bulging with liquid inside the placental sac. At Steven's birth, in February of the following year, she would blame the child's disfigurement on the events that were about to transpire on this day. And later, in the summer of that year, as she placed the barrel of her husband's rifle between her lips and pulled the trigger, blowing brain matter into Steven's crib, her last thought would be of this cool December morning.

The end of her life began with Miguel Esposito, six, tugging at the sleeve of his mother's flannel coat.

"Look, Mama, an angel."

Yolanda's back ached with fire. None of her other pregnancies had been like this. She imagined the fetus she carried inside her body to be a viscous mass of pain, nothing more.

"Please, Miguelito, don't pull on me. Mama's tired."

The child tugged harder.

"But, Mama, look! An angel!"

She let her eyes travel upward to where the boy was pointing, at a window high up in the hotel across the street.

There she saw a man, naked, his white skin radiating light in the morning sun. To a child's eyes, he might indeed look like a shimmering angel, she thought. The man's head was thrown back as if in pain, but the hand at his genitals told Yolanda another story.

"My God...."

Her first impulse was to laugh. She glanced around her to see if anyone else at the bus stop had noticed the man masturbating at the hotel window, but apparently no one else had. Only she and Miguel.

She made a move to turn the boy away from the man. He should not be watching this. But then she froze.

The man seemed to be gazing directly at her, a grimace of ecstasy transforming his face into something ugly, leering. His body tensed. His hips strained toward her.

Then he came, violently. Yolanda gasped as she saw his passion spill out of his body, sailing out into the air like a string of light, cascading down to the street below.

Miguel pulled away from her but she barely noticed.

"Mama...?"

She did not answer because even now she felt the man's eyes burning into her. She watched his hand release the withering thing at his groin and come through the open window. A long, slender finger pointed downward to the street at a movement she could now see from the corner of her eye.

A child....

It was Miguel, running toward the angel, face upward as if seeking a blessing.

Yolanda screamed. Images assailed her. The screech of braking tires on asphalt. Her son's small body being flung into the air like a doll. Limp little arms flailing. Car horns. The boy's head striking the centerline with the homey sound of a melon being dropped to the kitchen floor.

Miguel's tiny shoe, a red sneaker, came to rest at Yolanda's feet, the knot still neatly in place where she had tied it that morning. There was a smear of blood across the heel.

Yolanda screamed and screamed.

She looked up.

The man smiled at her. Once again he let his hand wander down to his genitals. His movements told her that even now he was squeezing the final drops of semen onto his fingertips. He brought those fingers to his lips and closed his eyes. Like a child, savoring. Feeding.

Then his body drifted back into the shadowy interior of the hotel room and disappeared.

Yolanda fainted. She did not hear his laughter, nor did she see the window slowly close.

WITH the commotion down on the street muted by the closing of the window, the pale man strode across the hotel room. His sated penis bounced around at half-mast as he flung himself across the bed, laced his fingers behind his head, and stared up at the ceiling.

He giggled.

Then he reached for the phone.

CHAPTER FOUR

"MAYBE if we lay low and keep you hidden long enough, the police will find the real killer."

"Jesus, Harry! What makes you think the police are looking for the real killer! It's *me* they're looking for and you know it. They think *I'm* the killer! They've probably got the dogs out right now. God, what a mess!"

"We don't know anything of the—"

"Come on, Harry! I practically kissed that woman hello, the one who lives down the hall from Stanley. Do you think she won't remember me?"

"Not like this," Harry said.

He switched off the blow dryer and handed the kid a small mirror.

Sean was seated at Harry's dining room table, wearing only Harry's baggy pajama bottoms, and behind him, like a proper hairdresser, stood Harry, giving his most recent creation a critical eye.

Sean's hair spiked up from his head like a new stand of grass. What had once been strawberry blond was now a deep chestnut brown.

"Clairol 46," Harry said. "What do you think?"

Sean's eyes widened. "I look like Freddie Prinze Jr."

"Who?"

Sean rolled his eyes. "Never mind."

The boy turned his head from left to right, studying his reflection. It might work, he thought. For a while.

He sprang to his feet and gave Harry an enthusiastic hug, almost losing his pajama bottoms in the process. Harry awkwardly hugged the boy in return. He noticed now that every time he touched the boy, his movements were tempered with a restraint that he didn't fully understand. Or maybe he did.

One-sided love was a real pain in the ass.

Sean hiked up the pajama bottoms to an acceptable level, although their trip south, he knew, certainly hadn't disturbed Harry any. He laced his arms around Harry's neck and looked deep into his eyes. At that moment, he began to understand a lot of things. He began to see Harry as more than just… a john. A friend, maybe. He knew that it could go beyond even that if he let it, and he wasn't so sure he wouldn't.

Maybe it was time.

"Why are you doing this, Harry? Why would you risk yourself for me?" He thought he knew the answer to that, but he wanted to hear it from Harry's lips. All the while, in the back of his mind, he wondered if he was manipulating the man. No one in Sean's life had ever done as much for him as Harry had done in this one short night and day. The mere fact that he was young and good looking made manipulation an easy process when dealing with someone like Harry. He sensed the older man's longing for him. He sensed it in every move the man made. Every word he spoke. But Sean didn't want to manipulate him. Not this time. Not now.

"Why, Harry? Tell me."

Harry pulled away from the boy and began gathering up the tools of his trade. Should he tell the boy? Tell him how he felt? He knew before he asked himself the question that the answer would be no.

"Can't I help you without an ulterior motive? Does there have to be some big cosmic reason for it?"

But he knew he could be more honest than that. The boy deserved that much.

"Maybe it's an adventure for me," he said, knowing even as he spoke that his words held no ring of truth. "Or maybe I just feel sorry for you. Maybe I believe your story. And I do. Maybe I think you've got a lot of cards stacked against you and there's no one else to help you try to deal yourself a better hand. If you had friends, Sean, you would have gone to them. Not me. I don't feel that I've really risked myself because I truly think you're safe here. From the police and from the man who killed your... trick. They might be able to trace you to me but I think it will take some time. Maybe even enough time for the real killer to do something stupid enough to get himself nabbed. That's really what we're hoping for, isn't it? I can't see any other way out of this for you. Right?"

Harry stopped fiddling with his blow dryer and combs and scissors and scooped the boy into his arms.

"Maybe I *want* to help you. Isn't that enough?"

Sean closed his eyes, allowing Harry's arms to hold him, enjoying the same sense of security he had felt the night before when lying in Harry's bed with the pounding of Harry's heart plucking at his cheek.

Harry brushed his lips against Sean's hair, smelling the chemicals.

He felt the boy's hands beneath his shirt, warm hands snaking across his back, holding him in return.

"Where's your family?" Harry asked. "Do they live here?"

"Indiana," Sean said. "I... don't see them much."

"Why's that?"

Sean eased himself out of Harry's arms and began to gather up the mess on the dining room table.

"We don't get along that well. They're really religious. They think I'm the original sinner. I get a Christmas card from my mom, but that's about it. Even then, she has to send it without my dad knowing. And my brother...."

"You have a brother?"

"Yeah, I have a brother. But he's worse than they are. He's been thumping a Bible since he was ten years old. I think the word is 'obsessed'."

"No sisters?"

"No. No sisters."

"I suppose going back to Indiana to lay low would be out of the question."

"It's beyond being out of the question. Aside from the fact that I wouldn't exactly be welcomed with open arms, it's also stupid. If the cops get an ID on me, wouldn't that be the first place they'd check?"

"Yeah," Harry admitted. "I suppose it would."

Sean carried all of Harry's beauty paraphernalia into the bathroom and, for lack of a better place, tossed it under the sink. He glanced in the mirror and pulled himself up short when a stranger with brown hair stared back at him. With no thought beforehand as to what he was about to do, he unsnapped the top button of Harry's pajama bottoms and watched in the mirror as they slid past his hips to the floor.

Later, surrounded by cats, he and Harry lay catlike, too, on the living room floor, enjoying the sensation of a warm wedge of sunlight that slowly crawled across their bodies. Idling there in the warmth, Sean wondered again at the incredible softness of Harry's skin beneath his hands and the amazing gentleness of Harry's touch when they made love.

"It's stopped raining," he mumbled, drowsing.

"I know," Harry said, pulling the boy closer.

With his cheek against Harry's chest and the taste of Harry's passion still on his lips, Sean felt safe and content, able to forget, for a while at least, everything that was happening outside this room. Soon he drifted into sleep.

Beside him, adrift in wonders of his own, Harry could feel the boy relax as sleep overtook him. The fragrance of their lovemaking lay over him like a blanket. He breathed it in, relishing the scent.

Outside, the morning sun climbed its way across the sky to afternoon, burning away the clouds as it went. But even now, Harry knew, another storm was moving in from the ocean. The sun would not be with them long.

Harry tried to put his fears for Sean aside, just long enough to enjoy this one perfect moment. The fears, he knew, would still be there when they awoke. He would deal with them then.

With his arms wrapped tightly around this boy who had come to mean so much to him, Harry, too, soon dozed, a smile of contentment playing at his lips.

DETECTIVES Smith and McCray were interrupted in their investigation of the Stanley Baker murder by a phone call from Deputy Coroner John Martin. After what amounted to a tactical assault through chaotic downtown traffic, made all the more impossible by mobs of holiday shoppers and what appeared to be an injury accident in front of the U.S. Grant Hotel at Fourth and Broadway that pretty well shut down traffic in two directions, they finally arrived at City Morgue.

Deputy Coroner Martin, who looked more like a middle-aged accountant than someone who cut up cadavers for a living, was waiting for them in the autopsy room.

As usual, all twelve autopsy tables were occupied. Recessions be damned, there was never a shortage of business at City Morgue. Approximately one percent of the population in any given city dies each year, and about one-fourth of those deaths are investigated by the coroner's office. San Diego had a population approaching two million people. It made for a lot of autopsies.

Coroner Martin had the weary look of a man who couldn't be shocked by a cattle prod, let alone any possible manifestation of death. He had seen its many faces time and again.

He led the detectives to the last two autopsy tables, facilitating a trip past the other ten tables, which neither Smith nor McCray found enjoyable at all.

Jimmy Smith, whose sense of humor actually underscored the mental workings of a very good detective, inevitably lost all desire for any light-hearted prattle when inside the four walls of the autopsy room.

And ditto for McCray.

They worked well together. They even had fun sometimes. But not here.

Stanley Baker's remains rested comfortably on the last autopsy table, his eyes finally closed. Smith was relieved to see that Stanley's penis no longer protruded from his lips but resided in a clear plastic bag taped to his hip. Unlike most of the other bodies around them, Stanley was still pretty much intact. His autopsy had yet to begin.

The same could not be said for Stanley's neighbor on table eleven. The man, for man it was, more closely resembled a side of beef on a butcher's block. The Y incision extending across the man's emaciated chest from shoulder to shoulder and continuing down to his pubis was still wide open. The ribs were broken out of the way, and his internal organs, previously removed, were now haphazardly piled inside the gaping wound, not at all the way nature intended them to be. An intermastoid incision had been made across the top of the man's head from ear to ear and the scalp peeled down to cover the face. A small electric saw (a macabre device which sometimes made a cameo appearance in some of Jimmy Smith's more disquieting nightmares) had been used to remove that section of the skull. The brain was nowhere to be seen, probably tossed into the chest cavity with the other organs after being weighed and sectioned. The resultant hole in the top of the man's head looked like a silent screaming mouth. Dr. Sardonicus, sans teeth and tongue.

"So what have you got for us?" Smith asked.

Deputy Coroner Martin got right down to business. He was a busy man, but fortunately for the San Diego Police Department, he was also very good at his job.

"I know you've already met Mr. Baker here," he said, "so I'll introduce you to what may very well be his companion case."

"Companion case?"

"Yes." Martin took hold of number eleven's hairline, which at the moment was tucked inside out beneath his chin, and smoothed the flap of skin back over the hole in the skull, exposing the face of a man in his sixties. "Say hello to William Earl Guest."

"Jesus Christ," McCray said. "I know that guy. That's Sledgehammer Willie. The bum with the gimpy leg."

"That I didn't know," Martin intoned. "But I do know a couple of other things about the gentleman that you might find interesting."

"Give it to us, Doc," Smith said, hoping his churning stomach would not be heard above the sound of his voice. "We're just as busy as you are."

"Very well." Dr. Martin indicated a patch of skin beneath Willie's otherwise hairy chin that had recently been shaved. "There is a stab wound here, as you can see, that perfectly corresponds with the stab wound in Mr. Baker. Both caused death. Both penetrated upward from below the chin, through the mouth and into the brain. And both were made by, if not the same instrument, then certainly the same *type* of instrument. A knife with a very thin, and probably a very long, blade. Stab wounds are fairly common, as you know, but not in this particular area, and not, ordinarily, with such depth. It's a very good way to kill somebody. A brain wound is almost always fatal, and from this angle, upward from the soft area beneath the chin and through the tongue and palate, there is very little resistance to the weapon's path. No bone to speak of. Nothing to deflect the knife. Pretty efficient."

"Where did they find him?" McCray asked. "And when?"

"They found him this morning in Seaport Village in the doorway of The Nature Store. Twenty feet from the sea wall."

Smith considered this. "The sea wall, huh?"

Martin nodded. "Yeah. The sea wall. Just across from the best place in town to dispose of a murder weapon. The sea."

Smith knew from experience that murders usually occurred within definite boundaries of social status. Due to association, the rich killed the rich and the poor killed the poor, although as horse races go, the poor were way out ahead of their rich counterparts. On the surface, one could discount any connection between a homeless old man who slept in doorways and a successful thirty-five-year-old businessman who turned down his sheets each night in a $900,000 condominium. But sometimes paths such as theirs did meet. Randomly or otherwise.

This looked random.

"The way I see it," Martin continued, "we have one of two choices here. Either you have a maniac out there who doesn't care *who* he kills, or you have this man, Mr. Guest, who unintentionally saw something he shouldn't have seen. And that seems the most likely, don't you think? It's only an educated guess, I admit, but I don't believe there is any other reason for these two men to come together like this at the tail end of such divergent lifestyles. And even now, the only common trait they share is the manner in which they died. Discounting Mr. Baker's wayward penis, their autopsy reports will confirm identical causes of death. To within an inch in entry point and depth of insertion, their stab wounds are the same. And I don't believe in coincidence."

"Looks like we have a very efficient killer on our hands," McCray said.

Martin agreed. "Oh, yes. Very efficient, indeed. Death from this type of wound is instantaneous and requires no great physical strength. And it's a lot cleaner than simply slicing across the throat. Less mess."

"So," Jimmy Smith said, "considering where Willie's body was discovered, it would be highly unlikely that he witnessed Mr. Baker's murder. But what he might have seen was the murderer trying to dispose of the murder weapon."

"In the great Pacific," McCray added. "Deep sixing the fucking thing."

Smith agreed. "Feeding it to the fishies."

"Poor Sledgehammer Willie," he added, in what would probably be the poor bastard's only eulogy. "Wrong place, wrong time. The story of his life."

DRESSED casually in faded jeans and a tan cable knit sweater, penny loafers without the pennies on his feet, the man in 725 sat leisurely at the hotel room desk and read. The tabloid-style magazine laid out before him was the December issue of the Update, San Diego's most widely distributed gay publication.

Across the entire front cover was a grainy photograph of a well-muscled young man wearing Santa Claus hat and boots and nothing else. The model's private parts were tactfully hidden behind the festively wrapped Christmas package he held in his hands.

"Here COMES Santa Claus," the caption read.

Cute.

On page three, the man carefully studied the quarter-page ad for the annual Christmas On The Prado celebration, which according to the Update, was San Diego's ultimate party for gays and straights alike. A delicate blend of religious fervor and Christmas music and goodies, as well as untold pick-up opportunities, since every gay soul in San Diego would undoubtedly be attending.

The man glanced toward the cylindrical bomb resting securely in the open drawer beside him and smiled, showing small white teeth that gave his face a somewhat childlike aspect. But that childlike aspect did not reach the eyes. They remained, as always, cold and unforgiving.

"Maybe I should make another one," he said quietly to the empty room.

Turning back to the Update, he neatly tore out the quarter-page ad and tucked it into his pocket.

On page six, in the "Personal Services" column, he found an ad which read:

YOUNG MIDWEST FARMBOY
Handsome, trim, auburn-haired pup with blue
eyes and a great smile. Offering erotic massage
and more. Try me. Safe and discreet. Call
Sean at 555-3202.

Auburn my ass. The man smirked, reaching for the phone.

WHEN Sean awoke, the wedge of sunlight that had warmed him earlier, lulling him into sleep with his head on Harry's arm, was gone. And so was Harry. The sky outside had darkened, and the house was cold. A woolen lap robe had been laid over him as he slept, and he shared it now with two of Harry's five cats. The house was silent, and he knew instinctively that, but for the cats, he was alone.

He wondered where Harry had gone. And when he would return.

The silence and the chill in the room unnerved him.

Gently easing the cats aside, he scooped up the lap robe to cover his nakedness and moved to the patio window, where he closed the vertical blinds, shutting out the gray day.

He found the clothes he had worn the night before still in a heap on the bedroom floor. Putting them on, he felt more at ease. Less vulnerable. Vulnerable to what, he wasn't sure. He was certainly safe here. The police would not find him, not for a while at least. And Harry, he knew, would do everything he could to protect him. Sean still did not know how he knew this to be true, or why Harry would be willing to go to such lengths for him. Removing his car from the parking garage at Brittany Towers had taken some guts. Sean didn't think he would have been able to go back there. The memory of the killer's footsteps chasing him down the stairway was still too real for him. Without Harry, his car would have been discovered and the police would know who he was.

He froze for a moment with one sock on and the other dangling forgotten in his hand. It dawned on him that maybe it wasn't the police he should be worrying about. What if the killer thought Sean had seen his face? What if he thought Sean could identify him? If so, the killer could have easily learned Sean's identity after following him to the Cailiff. He might even have backtracked and found Sean's car. The door was left unlocked and there were papers inside that would have told the killer who he was. Registration. Receipts in the glove box. Mail on the seat. *The killer could easily know where Sean lived!* Until matters were resolved, one way or the other, Sean would not go back to his apartment again.

But the killer could not know where he was now. Could he? Sean tried to remember if any cars had followed Harry's green sports car through the rain last night. He didn't think so. Surely to God he would have noticed, considering the state he was in.

From across the room, he heard the familiar ring of his cell phone.

It took him a minute to locate the phone. He found it in the pocket of his leather jacket, which hung on the coat rack by the front door. Sean tugged it out and looked at the numbers on the digital readout.

The telephone number was not familiar to him. Usually, only johns answering the ad in the gay rags used his cell number. The last thing Sean intended doing was going out to pound the pud on some lonely faggot. Not today. The killer was out there somewhere. But the biggest reason, Sean knew, was that he didn't want to hurt Harry. Harry had done so much for him. It would feel like betrayal. Sean would not repay Harry that way, no matter how much he needed the money. Which he did.

The phone, which had gone silent, now rang again. Whoever wanted to reach him was being persistent about it. He rummaged through the clutter on Harry's rolltop desk until he found a pen and scrap of paper and jotted down the number displayed on the readout.

He agonized over whether to return the call. It could be anyone. Even the cops. He had almost decided to ignore it completely when it rang for the third time and he thought, *fuck it*, and grabbing the phone, flipped it open.

"Yeah?" Sean said.

The voice on the other end sounded muffled, indistinct.

"Hello, Farmboy."

Before Harry's Regulator clock above the desk could tick three ticks, Sean knew he had made a mistake.

"May I help you?" he heard himself say, like the waitress at the corner IHOP patiently waiting for an order. He wished he felt as calm as he sounded. But he didn't. His legs were suddenly weak with fear.

"I saw you," the voice said.

Sean had to reach out and grab the desk to steady himself.

"Saw me what?"

"I saw you," the voice said again. "I saw what you did."

Sean dragged the chair out from in front of Harry's desk and all but fell into it.

"But I didn't do anything," he said. A burning in his eyes told him tears were on the way. "I *didn't*."

A chuckle at the other end of the line caused the little hairs at the nape of Sean's neck to do a cakewalk. Memories plucked at him, but he was too afraid to follow where they led.

"Who is this?"

"A friend."

"Do I know y—"

"A friend who can save your little ass."

"But I didn't *do* anything."

Sean could almost feel the man smile. Imagining that unseen smile frightened him even more. It was a crooked smile with sharp teeth and chunks of flesh between them. He had seen it in a hundred horror movies. The smile of someone who relished pain. A smile that Sean could only imagine, now, but imagining was enough.

The voice mumbled something Sean could not understand.

"I'm sorry. I didn't...." He hated himself for sounding weak. But he was scared. His hands shook so badly that the cell phone tap danced against his ear.

The voice bellowed out of the phone like a cannon going off. Sean jumped, dislodging a tear that rolled down his cheek to his lips. It tasted like the ocean.

"I know you didn't do it, you stupid fuck! Do you want my help or not?"

Sean brushed a forearm across his face, wiping the tear away. The words soaked in. The man was trying to help him.

"I… yes. But where were you? How do you know?"

Breathing. The man was calming himself.

"I'm sorry," Sean said, "but…."

"You like organs, don't you, Fruit Loop?"

"What? I…."

"Organs! Cocks!"

Sean squeezed his eyes shut as the fear welled up in him again. He tried to hide in the darkness behind his eyelids. A weariness surged through him. The words reverberated through his head like angry echoes bouncing back and forth from canyon walls. He felt dirty. Shamed.

"Yes," he said, subdued. Whatever it took to end this, Sean was resolved to do. He would tolerate this man's taunts. He had no choice. The man owned him. Whatever knowledge the man possessed might save him from a murder charge.

"What do you want me to do?"

The man chuckled again, a sound like vicious static on the line. "Since you like organs so much, you can meet me at the Organ Pavilion in Balboa Park. Tonight. Eight o'clock. By the nativity. We'll celebrate Christmas On The Prado together. I'll give you a gift."

"A… gift?"

"Your innocence. As relates to poor dickless Stanley, anyway. It's much too late for any other kind of innocence where you're concerned, I'm afraid. Too many spurting cocks up the old wazoo, you know. Too many…."

Sean raked his arm over Harry's desk, scattering papers halfway across the room. "All right, you son of a bitch! I'll be there! Just shut the fuck up!"

"Testy," the voice said. "Better watch that pretty mouth of yours, or I might change my mind."

Sean's anger drained out of him as quickly as it had risen.

"I'm sorry. I'm... upset."

The man exploded in a booming laugh. "*You're* upset? I haven't even started my Christmas cards yet! I've been so wrapped up in your little melodrama that I haven't had time to bake or shop or *anything*. So, is it a date?"

"Yes," Sean said. "I'll be there."

Mocking, wheedling, the man said, "You won't charge me, will you? I know you usually charge for dates. An auburn-haired pup like you...."

Sean swallowed bile. He knew if he didn't get off of this phone soon he would either throw up or pass out or both. He forced a calmness into his voice that was the hardest thing he had ever done in his life.

"No, I won't charge you."

"Good. And bring your buddy."

"My buddy?"

"Is there an echo in here? Yes, your buddy. Do as I say, my fairy friend, or *I* might be the one who charges *you*."

With that, the line went dead in his hand.

Sean jumped at the sound of someone coming through the door behind him. He whirled, pale, the blood all but drained from his face.

At the sight of Harry, in gloves and scarf, awkwardly struggling to drag a fat Christmas tree through the front door, he broke into sobs.

And that final release of fear made Sean realize how much he cared for Harry. How much he relied on him.

And how much he hated himself.

THE fat California spruce, still bound in twine, lay forgotten in the entryway.

"How do you know he's not the killer?"

"Come on, Harry. If he was the killer, why would he try to help me? It must be someone who lives at the Towers. Someone who saw me. Someone who knows I didn't do it."

Harry was unconvinced. "How could anyone possibly know you didn't do it unless they were right inside the condo?"

"The window! The drapes were open in the window. He must have seen me through the window. Or seen the killer. It must be someone I know, Harry. The voice was… familiar. I think. I'm not sure. But if he didn't know me, how could he know how to get in touch with me?"

Even as the words were spilling out of him, Sean knew he wasn't making much sense. But Jesus, there had to be an explanation. He chose to ignore the undercurrent of hatred, the blatant animosity that underscored every word from that faceless voice on the phone. The viciousness. He could not deal with that now. It was beyond his realm of understanding. He didn't want to think about it. It scared him too badly.

His statement came out flat and toneless. A weary conviction. "We have to meet with him, Harry."

Harry nodded. "I know."

They were interrupted by the yowling of the old mother cat. Her inner clock had just informed her it was time for her dinner and she wanted it *now*.

The clock above the desk gave a creak, then chimed the hour. Five bongs. It would soon be dark.

Harry feared it would be almost impossible to find this man on the Prado. Or, more accurately, for the man to find them. Especially tonight. Half the city would be there.

And he shared little of Sean's faith that this man, whoever he was, was actually trying to help the boy. A darker perception had come to him as he listened to Sean relate to him all that had transpired over the phone.

He feared for the boy's safety.

It did not once occur to him to fear for his own.

LOOKING like a Roman viaduct, Laurel Street Bridge connected Balboa Park from east to west. Two hundred feet below the bridge, along a twisted canyon that bisected the park, lay Cabrillo Freeway, a major artery connecting downtown San Diego to the south and Mission Valley to the north. Tonight the highway was packed, bumper to bumper. Looking down from the bridge above, Harry knew that most of those cars were headed here to the Christmas festival on the Prado. Where they would find to park all those automobiles was anybody's guess, Harry thought. The park was jammed already.

The bridge, arched high above the sounds of all that traffic below, was ablaze with Christmas lights. Carillon bells high in the tower above the Museum of Man resonated with metallic clarity in the crisp night air as they chimed the hour. Eight o'clock. Following the eighth stroke, the bells, programmed by computer, chimed their way through "Oh, Come All Ye Faithful," giving the familiar carol a reverence and dignity, a *grandness*, that simple human voices could never have rendered.

It was cold. Harry could see his breath puffing out of him as he walked. That simple act of condensation, so common in other parts of the world, was a novelty here, reminding Harry of childhood winters in Minnesota. It was ironic, he thought, that he left the Midwest to escape the winters, and now he found himself missing those dramatic changes of season. In San Diego, the seasons were beautiful yet bleak in their sameness. Years unbroken by autumn colors and snowball fights were empty things, recipes without a key ingredient, leaving the finished product bland and tasteless.

Not unlike his own life, he thought, until these past two days when Sean had dropped into it like an anvil crashing through a barn roof. Having been raised on a farm, as indeed they both were, Harry smiled at the analogy.

As concerned as he was for the boy, and as uncertain as he felt about any future they might have together, he still had to admit that his life was no longer dull. Whatever came out of this whole sorry mess, he would at least have one solid adventure under his belt. Something to drag out and chew on in his old age.

Which wasn't that far away, dammit.

"What?" Sean asked, walking beside him. "You clucked."

Harry tried to laugh. "Just thinking about old age. Something you don't have to worry about for a while."

Sean clucked back. "Jesus, Harry, you got that right. The way my life is going I'll be lucky to reach *middle* age. Hell, I'll be lucky to reach twenty-two."

Harry rested his hand on the boy's shoulder. "You have a point."

Sean burrowed his hand into Harry's coat pocket for warmth, the small gesture of familiarity causing the older man to smile.

The bridge, awash with Christmas lights, was packed with humanity. Families. Gay couples. People with dogs and kids. All headed toward Balboa Park. Christmas On The Prado was a big event in San Diego. It always drew a crowd of thousands.

The park, built for some long-forgotten Exposition of umpty-aught-six or thereabouts, was a collection of towers and promenades and museums built in a sort of fussy architectural hybrid that was a cross between gothic and Moorish and which drew millions of tourists to it every year. The locals, too, loved the old park. It also housed the Old Globe Theater, the San Diego Zoo, a Japanese rose garden, an arboretum, five separate museums, and more. It was a gathering place for the rich and poor alike. Scores of homeless lived here year round in the wooded areas on its verge. There, stately pines and eucalyptus trees sheltered them from disapproving eyes and horse-mounted policemen who constantly tried to roust them out, shooing them and all their belongings off to some other, more appropriate, section of the city. Where, exactly, they were supposed to go, the homeless never quite understood. Anywhere *else*, seemed to be the general consensus.

As they walked, Harry left a proprietary arm draped across the boy's shoulder. This was, after all, Hillcrest. The gay center of San Diego. If two guys, or girls, could show affection anywhere in the city without fear of reprisals, it was here. The straight religious crowd who came for the Christmas celebration every year had either learned to live with it or ignore it. Total acceptance, Harry knew by the occasional glance or whisper from someone in the crowd, was something the straights were not quite ready to commit to. But Harry figured it would come sooner or later. Maybe not in his lifetime, but eventually.

"Poor guy," Sean said.

"Who?" Harry asked, torn from his thoughts.

"Stanley. The guy at Brittany Towers."

"Oh. Yeah, I know."

He glanced at Sean. The boy's cheeks were splotched with color from the cold.

"How did you ever get into this business you're in? You're a smart kid. You could be doing *anything*."

Sean's look was resigned. "I wondered when you'd ask me that. Everybody does sometime or other."

"Well?"

Sean ran a hand through his newly dyed hair. "To tell you the truth, I'm not exactly sure. Just sort of fell into it, I guess. The money's good. I don't have any formal training in anything, Harry. How else could I make as much money as I do? I'm sure not getting rich, but I'm not on minimum wage either. To tell you the truth, it's not as bad as most people think. And I've been lucky. No one has ever so much as raised a hand to me in anger. I treat the johns like I would want to be treated, and they respond to me in the same way. Most of my customers are just lonely. They're not bad people. Like you. You were always decent to me, Harry. Why was that?"

Harry shrugged. "I guess because you never made me feel like I was buying sex. You seemed to enjoy being with me." He laughed. "And the fact that you're young and gorgeous didn't hurt. I always felt lucky to be with you."

Sean frowned. "Even now? With all this shit I've dragged you into?"

Harry smiled at the boy. "Even now. Especially now. Now, I feel like a friend."

"What you're doing for me, Harry, has gone way beyond friendship. I'm a suspect in a murder…."

Harry shook his head. "You don't know that."

"Yes, I do. And so do you. You could get in a lot of trouble for helping me. It's called abetting a criminal. You could wind up in prison yourself."

Harry grinned. "I hear the sex is good."

"Yeah, right. Maybe in the fuck flicks."

"Besides," Harry said, "I'm not abetting a criminal. You didn't kill the man. You're innocent. I figure if we keep you out of sight for a while, the cops will come to realize that."

"Maybe I should turn myself in."

"Why? So they'll stop looking for the real killer? I don't think so."

They were swept along with the flow of the crowd, and soon they passed beneath the archway at the end of the bridge. The Museum of Man was to their left. To their right, on a makeshift stage, carolers in choir robes sang. Between the carolers and the crowd, the noise was deafening.

Sean leaned closer to Harry, trying to be heard but not *overheard*. "But why, Harry? Why are you helping me?"

"I don't know. I…."

"Tell me."

Harry pulled Sean up the museum steps. Here, they stood a little above the crowd and the din was less overwhelming. Here, they were also more visible to anyone who might be looking for them. Harry wasn't sure this was a good thing. He didn't see any policemen, but then it wasn't really the police he was worried about. What was the caller's real motive for luring them into this mob of people? Did he really intend to help the boy? Sean seemed to think so. Harry wasn't so sure. If the man really wanted to help, why was he being so damned clandestine about it?

"I don't like this."

Sean took a look at the crowd. "What?"

Harry pulled the boy around so that their eyes met. "I don't like this whole 'meet me in the park' routine. What the hell are we doing here? Do you really think this guy wants to help you?"

"Answer my question, Harry. Why are *you* helping me?"

Harry groaned. "Jesus, kid, I've never in my life seen anyone as scared as you were when you ran into that bar last night. You were like a rabbit going underground with a coyote on its ass. Who wouldn't have tried to help you? And I knew you. Well, in the biblical sense."

"Oh, please."

Harry laughed. "Okay, maybe not biblically. But I knew you well enough to know you're a nice person, regardless of what you do to earn a buck, and I just figured that if you had any real friends, you would have called them from the bar. But you didn't. You latched onto me like a sinking man grabs a lifeboat. Maybe I was flattered. Maybe I wanted you to realize that all the good men aren't just the ones under twenty five—"

"I already knew tha—"

"Don't interrupt. Maybe I've thought about you a lot over the past few months. But maybe I didn't want to just see you on a paying basis. Maybe I wanted us to see each other as friends. But I'm twice your age. In the gay world, that's equivalent to a kiss of death. You would have branded me a dirty old lech and that would have been the end of it. Or worse, you would have thought I was a dirty old lech who was too cheap to pay for your company."

"No, I—"

"Shut up, Sean. You want to know the real reason I'm doing this? Because it's exciting. And I like you. And if anyone ever needed help, it's you. I'm glad you came to me because I think I *can* help you. I think together we can get through this, if we keep our heads and just give the police time to do their job."

Sean hunched his shoulders against the wind. "You really think it's going to be all right?"

"Yeah, I do."

Sean glanced over the crowd for a moment, then back to Harry. "You're right, you know. About me not having any friends. I guess hustlers aren't too popular with most people."

Harry smiled. "You're popular with me."

"Am I?"

Harry laughed out loud. "Don't be coy. I figure you know damn well how I feel about you."

Sean gave the older man a lopsided grin. "Yeah, I guess I do. But I don't know why."

Harry pulled the boy into a quick hug. The kid's poor frozen ear felt like a popsicle against his cheek. "Actually, that makes two of us."

Harry pushed him away and straightened the boy's collar. "Let's talk about this later, okay?"

"In bed?"

"God, I hope so," Harry answered, pulling the boy down the museum steps and back onto the promenade. In seconds they were lost, just two more faces in a mob of thousands.

Or so Harry hoped. He had never felt more uneasy in his life. Like he was being stalked.

Sean walked close beside him and once again buried his hand in Harry's pocket. He felt safe with Harry. And it came as a bit of a shock to him that he also felt loved. If this nightmare ever ended, he wondered what it would be like to commit himself to one person. To Harry. It wasn't the age difference that made him hesitate. Harry might be twenty-five years older, but he was still handsome. And sex with Harry was always a sweet experience. Even now, in this crowd of people, the thought of Harry's body against his made his young cock swell. And the memory of Harry's arms holding him close after sex, their bodies cupped together with Harry's breath brushing the nape of his neck, made Sean smile.

The memory of Stanley screaming in fear wiped the smile from his face in an instant.

Harry seemed to know what the boy was thinking. He tucked his hand into his pocket alongside Sean's and wrapped his hand protectively around the boy's cool fingers.

"Don't worry," he said. "We'll get through this."

He watched, startled, as a tear slid down Sean's cheek.

"You're not alone," he added, squeezing the boy's hand. "I won't let anything happen to you." It was a promise he hoped he could keep.

Sean nodded and brushed the tear away with his other hand.

They walked between kiosks erected on both sides of the promenade, with vendors hawking everything from roasted chestnuts to fudge to handmade Christmas decorations, some beautiful, some just plain tacky. A dozen different smells bombarded them. Freshly baked pies. Wreaths of newly cut pine. Charcoal burning in braziers, the smoke all but suffocating. Children squealed in delight, cutting in and out of the crowd. People jostled for position in lines waiting to buy the vendors' wares. And above it all, inundating them, the sound of Christmas music and carillon bells, and somewhere off in the distance, the somber tones of a massive pipe organ playing an excerpt from *The Nutcracker*.

At the end of the promenade, the crowd thinned a bit, and by a fountain in front of the Museum of Modern Art, they turned right toward the Organ Pavilion. With a lesser sea of humanity to wade through, they reached it quickly.

The Pavilion was an arched outdoor stage with rows of wooden benches in front of it. On stage, a tuxedo-clad man played the massive organ, the notes issuing from tall brass pipes behind him that reached as high as twenty feet. Encircling the area, thatched huts had been built for the celebration, open at the front, each one depicting a scene from the life of Christ. The first hut as they entered held the nativity, with life-sized figures of Mary and Joseph and the Magi and some rather weather-beaten plastic livestock standing around what might very well have been a Chatty Cathy doll nestled in a bed of straw at their feet.

"Time for the city to put our tax dollars to work and spring for some new decorations," Harry muttered in Sean's ear.

Sean didn't respond. He was eyeing the crowd around them. "Where do you suppose he is? And how is he going to find us with all these people milling around?"

Harry, too, cast nervous glances at all the faces surrounding them. "To tell you the truth, I'm sort of hoping he *doesn't* find us. I have a really bad feeling about this."

Sean seemed suddenly unsure. "But he said he wanted to help."

"Yeah, right. He also said he knew you didn't kill that man. How do you suppose he knew that, Sean? Do you really think he was watching through a window in the middle of a thunderstorm? You were on the sixth floor, for God's sake, and it was raining cats and dogs. How much would he have been able to see? How could he know it wasn't you that killed the guy?"

"Well, I—"

"He couldn't, Sean. That's how. He couldn't know it. Not unless he killed the man himself."

This was a possibility Sean had tried really hard not to face. But hearing Harry say the words, it stopped him dead in his tracks.

"Jesus, Harry, how could he know who I was? How could he know how to reach me?"

Harry frowned, shaking his head. "I don't know. You must have left something behind. A business card. Something."

"Come on, Harry, you really think I have business cards?"

"Well, *something* anyway. I don't know."

Harry watched the boy shiver, and he didn't think it was from the cold.

"Let's get out of here, Sean. Please. There's something going on that we don't understand. If this guy really wants to help you, then I'm the Queen of England."

Sean looked uncertain. "Maybe you're right."

Harry took Sean firmly by the arm, tugged him around and back through the crowd toward the bridge and home.

"I *know* I'm right," Harry said. "Let's get out of here."

Sean practically had to gallop, pulled along in the man's wake.

"Harry, wait."

Harry looked back over his shoulder at the boy. "What is it?" His pace never slowed.

"Can we get some of that fudge on the way out?"

Harry groaned. "Jesus, kid. Where's your sense of priorities? Let's just get our asses home and I'll *make* you some fucking fudge."

"With walnuts?"

Harry just shook his head. "Shut up, Sean."

TWICE since the two had entered the park, the pale man could have reached out and touched them. Just like Ma Bell. He could have killed them fifty times over, but what would have been the fun in that? He was in no hurry. In fact, the more he played with them, the more he enjoyed himself.

He stood now, not more than a dozen feet away, the hood of his brown parka pulled snug around his face. They had stopped in front of the cheesy nativity scene. The man couldn't hear what they said to each other but he knew when they decided to run.

"Shit!"

A woman passing beside him looked up in surprise. When he aimed his cold eyes at her, she drew back as if slapped.

He ignored her. Unless she got her fat ass out of here pretty damned fast she was as good as dead anyway.

He glanced at his wristwatch. Less than ten minutes. He had better get himself out of here as well. Too bad about his prey, but what the hell. A little postponement wouldn't make much difference. The end result would still be the same. Only the timeline had changed. He knew where they were going. He could reach out and touch them any time he wished.

In the meantime, he might as well find a vantage point and watch the fireworks. Even with his intended stars a no-show, it promised to be good entertainment.

The thought made him smile.

THE backpack lay beneath the last bench, fifteen feet from the nativity scene where Harry and Sean had stood only a few moments earlier. It held two twelve-inch lengths of plastic plumber's tubing, packed with gunpowder. A simple alarm clock detonator had been rigged to ignite the tubes simultaneously. Two pounds of one-inch roofing nails had been poured into the bag as well. For oomph.

Standing next to the bag, with the toe of his dirty sneaker pressed against it, Dwayne Childers studied the crowd. This had been a profitable night for Dwayne. Already, beneath the ratty plastic poncho he was wearing, he had six wallets and two cell phones. A trickle of snot dribbled off the end of Dwayne's nose, but he didn't know it. He was too excited about the backpack. He supposed it belonged to the young couple with the howling brats who were sitting on the bench above it, but he wasn't sure. If it did belong to them, they were certainly paying it no nevermind, the dumb shits. People should take care of their belongings. No one knew that better than Dwayne.

The goddamn screeching organ up on the stage was giving him a headache, so he thought, *fuck it*. He bent down and grabbed the shoulder strap of the backpack, and when he stood again the bag was all safe and snug beneath the folds of his poncho. Dwayne was surprised by the weight of the thing. Must be ten pounds if it's an ounce, he thought. Dwayne sucked the snot back up into his nose and headed for the parking lot behind the Pavilion, dying to get his hands inside that backpack and those six wallets. He might just have a merry Christmas after all.

His beat-up old pickup truck, surrounded as it was by some pretty respectable automobiles, looked like a turd on a tray of hors d'oeuvres. He knew he'd never make enough money tonight to buy a new set of wheels, but hell, a guy could dream. He was sick of driving this piece of crap. Romance wasn't really Dwayne's long suit, but he did sort of figure that with a nice car maybe his ratty little face and brown teeth wouldn't be quite so appalling to some simple-minded cunt who treasured transportation over looks. Maybe he could actually get laid without having to pay for it. That would be a novel experience for Dwayne.

He reached his truck nine seconds before the bomb was scheduled to detonate. Nine seconds to manhandle his creaking door open, fling himself inside the truck, and pull the backpack out from under his poncho. He just had time to unzip the thing and stick his ugly face inside it when it blew, sending most of Dwayne's ugly face, along with the rest of his head and his dreams, out through the pick-up's back window. Glass and roofing nails shot out in every direction, lifting the truck a good six inches off the asphalt before dropping it back in place with a thud, the cab all but disintegrated into fairy dust.

Back at the Organ Pavilion, voices were momentarily hushed by the sound of the bomb, and several expectant faces scanned the night sky, looking for fireworks. Only one man, the man in the parka, seemed to know what that echoing report signified, but he wasn't about to share his knowledge with anyone else. From a distance, he had watched in disbelief as the greasy guy in the poncho walked off with the device he had labored for hours over, shaking his head in wonder and marveling once again at the stupidity of people and the vagaries of dumb, blind luck.

You had to laugh.

Curiosity certainly killed that cat.

CHAPTER FIVE

THE new police headquarters at Broadway and 15th Street was a marvel of architectural incompetence, or so Detective Jefferson McCray constantly complained. Doors to the Homicide Division didn't close properly, elevators broke down on a regular basis, and the air conditioning sucked, but not in a good way. In that respect, it shared a lot of similarities to McCray's ex-wife, Denice the Bitch. She, too, was always out of order in some aspect or other, and the only thing Denice could suck with any sense of ardor was fun from a relationship and money from a bank account. McCray's sisters, of which he had four, had warned him against her, but he had allowed his hormones to lead him straight down the aisle of Freedom Baptist Church and into six long months of marital misery. Now, when his sisters offered an opinion, he listened.

Which is more than Smith did when his partner started grousing about their office conditions.

This particular morning began in typical fashion.

"The goddamn thing ate my quarters!"

Detective Jimmy Smith rolled his eyes so far back into his head that he almost toppled backward off his chair. The vending machines again.

"Jesus, Jeff. The city's falling apart and you're worried about Snickers and Ding Dongs. Give it a rest."

"Hhnnh!"

"And stop growling." Smith waved a rap sheet in his face. "Remember this guy? Dwayne Childers?"

McCray snatched the paper out of his partner's hand and glared at it. "The pickpocket."

"Right."

"Looked like a weasel with acne."

"Right again."

"Don't tell me…."

Smith poured himself a third cup of coffee from the pot in the corner, which was about two cups too many. His body was starting to vibrate like a tuning fork.

"Yep. He's the one who grabbed the bomb. God knows how many lives he saved."

"Well, certainly not his own."

Smith grimaced. "You got that right. What's left of him is down in the morgue right now in a bucket."

"Did they ID him from the vehicle?"

Smith sipped the coffee and made a face. Jesus, you could strip furniture with this shit.

"Naw. He was being tailed. Jamison from vice was working undercover on the Prado. Saw Childers lift a wallet and was moving in to apprehend when the moron snagged the bag with the bomb in it and took off for his truck. Jamison was two rows away in the parking lot when the bomb went off. We don't know yet if it was on a timer or rigged to explode when the bag was opened. Popped Jamison's eardrum when it blew."

McCray studied the paper. "Look at the rap sheet on this guy. Must be three feet long." He tossed it onto his desk. "Guess it won't be getting any longer."

Smith concurred. "Nope. The weasel's career in crime is over. He's retired."

"In a bucket."

"Our hero. Probably the only decent thing the little rat bastard ever did in his life. And he didn't even know it."

McCray studied his partner with a suspicious glint in his eyes. "Why are you showing me this? Don't tell me we've got this case on top of the six others we're working."

Smith pulled a roll of Tums from his shirt pocket and tossed a couple in his mouth.

"Not just us. Everybody's on this one. Could have been a major disaster."

McCray squeezed the bridge of his nose. "Yeah. Thank God that didn't happen."

"So we'll concentrate on this case and the gay murder in Hillcrest. I've got patrolmen and a couple of loaner detectives from Robbery pounding the streets on the other four. That'll free us up. Right now we're waiting on Stanley Baker's phone records."

"Peckerboy."

"If he did have a hustler in his condo that night, he must have contacted the guy by phone to set it up. If we get the phone number he called, we'll get the guy and that might very well be the end of it."

"When are we ever that lucky?"

"Never. But who says this can't be a first?"

McCray checked a ragged slip of paper tucked beneath his phone. "I sent a sketch artist over to work with Baker's neighbor. The little Jewish troll woman. I also sent along all the local gay mags. A lot of the hustler ads have photos. Maybe she'll spot the guy she saw in the hallway. It's worth a shot."

They were interrupted by a young patrolman who looked like he was about two weeks out of high school. They seemed to be getting younger all the time, Smith thought, or maybe he was just getting older. A depressing, but pretty standard, thought for this early in the morning.

"Here's the security tape from Cottage Liquor. Just came in."

Smith snatched it from the youngster's hand, mumbled a thank you, and slipped the tape into the VCR that rested on a stand by the window.

"Let's see what we got."

He switched on the 14-inch TV above the VCR and he and McCray pulled their desk chairs up to the screen like a couple of kids watching Saturday morning cartoons.

Hours, minutes, and seconds ticked away on a digital readout in the lower right hand corner of the tape. Smith fast-forwarded to the approximate time they figured the transaction was made. They found it almost immediately.

"Cancel the sketch artist. We don't need him anymore."

"Gotcha." McCray reached for the phone and did just that.

On the screen, an older couple could be seen buying a case of Corona beer. Behind them stood a young man with a bottle of Tanqueray gin cradled in his arm. The older couple received their change from the guy behind the counter, and the young man stepped forward, placing the bottle in front of the clerk.

For a security tape, it had unusual clarity. The young man, in his black leather jacket, jeans, and high-topped tennis shoes, looked like a kid. They watched him reach for something in a display stand and place it beside the bottle of Tanqueray. It looked like a packet of breath mints. The clerk said something and the boy laughed, pulling out his wallet and handing the clerk an ID He seemed utterly relaxed, his smile easy and natural. The clerk scanned the ID and handed it back to the boy. The silent tape showed the boy then reaching into his pocket and pulling out two bills. He handed them to the clerk who placed them in the register and gave the boy back his change. The clerk bagged the Tanqueray and dropped the breath mints into the bag after it. The boy smiled at the clerk, retrieved the bag from the counter and sauntered casually from the store.

The two detectives looked at each other.

"Does that kid look like a butcher to you?" Smith asked.

McCray switched off the VCR, ejected the tape, and slipped it into an evidence bag he had pulled from his desk.

"I don't know, Hoss. If he is, he seems pretty relaxed about it."

"Yeah. *Too* relaxed," Smith said. "If that boy offered to babysit my kids I'd probably let him."

McCray considered. "Well, you never know. Maybe Mr. Baker said something to piss him off later, after the kid returned to the condo. He's a hustler, after all. How many morals can he have?"

"Being a hustler is a long way from being a murderer. I don't buy it. I'll grant you that anybody's capable of murder, but everybody isn't capable of doing what was done to poor old Stanley."

McCray wasn't convinced. "Penis mutilation is fairly common in gay murders. Cut off the penis, cut off the power. That's the mind-set."

Smith rocked back in his chair, eyeing his partner.

"Jeez, Jeff, I know the theories. I studied Criminology 101 just like you did. But did you see that kid? He looked like he should be singing tenor in a fucking boys' choir somewhere instead of peddling his ass on the street. *My* kids aren't as likable as he is."

"I doubt if Carol would agree with you."

"Probably not," Smith conceded. "But if Carol got a good look at that young man, she'd probably be drawing up adoption papers right now."

McCray sighed. "All I'm saying is, looks can be deceiving."

"That's profound."

"Don't be peevish, Chief. You know how it upsets me."

Smith snagged his coat off the back of his chair.

"Come on. Let's get out of here. By the way, we're taking your car this morning."

"*My* car? Why are we taking *my* car?"

"Ours is in the shop."

McCray was grousing again. "What the hell is wrong with it? It ran perfectly fine yesterday."

"Jamison checked it out last night when he was working the park."

"So?"

"So he parked it behind the Organ Pavilion. Close to Childers's truck."

"And?"

"And now it's down in maintenance. They're removing the nails."

"Oh."

They took the stairs two at a time down to the parking level. McCray had parked his vintage '59 Chrysler 300F convertible in the safest spot he could find that morning, behind the dumpsters way in the back.

"I'm surprised you didn't shrink-wrap it," Smith grumbled, trudging across the wide expanse of the parking lot.

When they reached the car, McCray looked on the maroon beast with pride. Flicking a speck of nonexistent dust from one of the tail fins, he said, "Hey, this fine automobile represents two years of hard work playing for the Chargers. Denice the Bitch gobbled up the rest of the money. This is all I have left to show for my career in the NFL."

Smith laughed. "That, a ruined knee, a twitchy rotator cuff, and an overactive ego."

"Jealousy is very unattractive."

"So tell me, my man. What do you have left to show for your six months with Denice?"

McCray straightened his tie. "An abject fear of women and all things feminine."

Smith nodded sagely. "That's what I thought."

McCray settled himself behind the gigantic steering wheel and popped the passenger door lock for Smith.

"But now there's Janeane."

Smith flung himself inside the Chrysler. It smelled of Polo. "Janeane? I've got shoes that are smarter than Janeane."

McCray smiled. "Yeah, but you ain't got no shoes that *feel* like Janeane when you're slipping into them."

"Don't get pornographic."

They pulled out into traffic.

"She is a fox," Smith conceded.

McCray nodded. "She's buff."

Smith agreed. "And best of all, she ain't Denice!"

Both men waggled admonitory fingers at a jaywalker who scuttled across their path.

McCray's cell phone chirped on his belt. It chirped to the tune of "'Deck The Halls'."

"Jesus God!" Smith bellowed. "I'm sick of that stupid song. Reprogram that fucker, will you?"

"To play what, Chief? 'The Indian Love Call'?"

"Blow me."

McCray pressed the phone to his ear. "McCray here," he said. He listened for about thirty seconds, then flipped the phone closed and dropped it in his lap. He jotted something down on a notepad attached to the dash.

"That was Laurie in Judge Kavner's office. The techs learned the phone numbers Baker called on the day he died. One of them didn't pertain to either his family or his small circle of friends or his business. They think it's the hustler. They got the guy's address, too, from billing records."

Smith looked at the address on the notepad. The guy's name was Sean Andros, and he lived on Walnut Street in Hillcrest. They had a name to go with the face on the security tape. Maybe.

"Has anyone tried the number?"

McCray shook his head. "Naw. No sense spooking the guy. Don't want him rabbiting before we get there. Laurie's sending a courier to meet us there with the search warrant."

"They must really want this case wrapped up in a hurry to save us the footwork of getting the warrant ourselves."

"No shit. The judge was standing by. He approved the warrant as soon as the phone records came through."

Smith eyed the handsome black man beside him.

"You dated Laurie once, didn't you?"

McCray nodded. "Yeah. More than once, actually."

"And still she's willing to go out of her way to help us? I'm amazed. Guess she didn't hold a grudge."

McCray smiled. "Women love me, what can I say? I probably left a very pleasant taste in her mouth."

"God, I hope you're speaking metaphorically."

This time it was Smith's phone that chirped, to the tune of absolutely nothing. A simple fucking chirp. He glanced at McCray to see if his partner had registered that fact, then tugged the phone from the inside pocket of his blazer.

"Smith," he said into the mouthpiece, sticking a finger into his other ear to block out the siren of a passing ambulance.

This call was considerably longer than the one McCray took a moment earlier. Smith offered nothing in the way of conversation aside from an occasional grunt or a pointless nod now and then. He hung up with a curt, "Thanks, Joe," and stuffed the phone back into his blazer pocket.

"Well," he said, "your information on the phone records was correct. They ID'd the right guy. We've got fingerprints from your Mr. Andros all over Baker's condo. The prints matched with BMV records, so we've got the make and model of his car, too. The old guy with the oxygen tank was right. Andros drives a Yugo. Don't ask me why. They're crap."

McCray grinned. "That's a superfluous observation."

"Thanks. Funny thing about the prints, though. Only two of them are mixed with Baker's blood and those two have no print signatures. They are only smudges made by rubber gloves. They figure the killer was wearing gloves at the time of the murder. Why would Andros leave his prints all over the place and then slip on a pair of rubber gloves to do the actual killing? Doesn't make a lot of sense."

"Maybe the guy's fastidious. A neat freak. Didn't want to get all messy."

"Gee, Jeff. I don't know. Most fastidious neat freaks who like to avoid getting messy don't usually go around chopping off peckers and poking them in people's mouths. That's just about the epitome of messy, if you ask me."

"Well, maybe he didn't want to come into contact with the blood. Maybe he was afraid of AIDS."

Smith rolled his eyes. "A street hustler? Afraid of AIDS? Don't forget that our Mr. Andros was probably giving lip service to that very pecker just prior to cutting the damn thing off. How afraid of AIDS can he be?"

McCray shrugged. "We've seen a lot of things over the years that didn't make any sense."

Smith had to agree. "Yeah, but this is just plain stupid."

"We've seen a lot of that, too."

"I suppose," Smith said, unconvinced. Something wasn't right. He'd have to think on this a while. He squeezed off a couple more Tums from the roll in his pocket and sucked on them while he did just that.

McCray turned left off Broadway onto Fourth Avenue and headed up the hill. The cross streets in Hillcrest were all named for trees, alphabetically. Ash, Beech, Cedar, Date, all the way up to Walnut. Their destination.

"Think he's home?" Smith wondered aloud.

"We'll soon find out. Like you said, maybe we'll get lucky on this one."

"I don't believe in luck."

"Me either. But we can hope."

"I don't believe in hope."

McCray just shook his head and drove.

THE squat apartment building stood at the corner of Walnut and Second. It was surrounded by jacaranda trees that, in the springtime, would lay a sprinkling of blue blossoms on the ground around the building like the hem of a crouching woman's skirt. The building was built in the early fifties. Like a lot of structures in San Diego it smacked of Spanish influence. Low arches arced across the front of it with a long veranda over that stretching from one end of the building to the other. Hanging baskets of trailing bougainvillea added splashes of color, but the general impression one got from a first glance at the building was that of a former *grande dona* fallen upon hard times. Paint peeled, the lawn was unkempt, and the two palm trees flanking the entrance were in desperate need of pruning. Several dead fronds hung limply around the trunks, and several others had been torn loose by the wind and rain of the night before and lay scattered across the yard.

Smith and McCray had both been inside this building once before on the case of a domestic squabble that had gotten out of hand and ended with the death of an abusive husband at the hands of his unfortunate wife who quite justifiably, they believed, had stabbed the bastard in the liver with a four-inch paring knife. Both Smith and McCray figured the city should have given the woman a parade and the keys to the city, but the powers that be thought it best to give her twelve years in Chino for manslaughter. That was several years ago. With time off for good behavior, Smith figured she was probably out by now. He hoped she was. He hoped she had survived incarceration. It was a simple fact that many didn't.

It had been a long time since he thought of that woman. A sad case. Many of the cases he and McCray investigated were sad. Many times they felt more empathy for the perpetrator than they did for the victim. The case they were working now was different. He felt no empathy at all for this perp. This fucker was crazy. Crazy and reckless and mean. And deep down, in some sublevel basement of his mind, he had a nagging suspicion that the answers they were seeking were not to be found inside this apartment building.

Smith hoped he was wrong, but his gut feeling, which he had learned long ago to heed, told him he was not. If this Sean Andros guy was the one who de-peckered Stanley Baker, then poked a hole in

Sledgehammer Willie's brain pan for some obscure reason, Smith was going to be very, very surprised.

The building was a four-plex. Two up, two down. Through the front door, which was unlocked, was a small foyer. Two of the apartments could be entered here. The other two could be accessed by a flight of stairs leading to the second floor. At the foot of the stairway were four mailboxes. On the third box they saw the name they were looking for, Sean Andros. They headed up the stairs.

Both Smith and McCray opened their jackets for easy access to the guns in their shoulder holsters before knocking on the door to 2B. They knew there were no back doors to these apartments. And no fire escapes. If Andros was inside, this was his only means of escape, short of leaping from a second story balcony.

McCray rapped sharply on the door, then stepped aside on the off chance that Mr. Andros should decide to answer their knock with a blast of gunfire from the other side.

The apartment was silent. No TV noise. No barking dog. No little scuffling sounds like someone was sneaking around inside.

McCray rapped again, waited perhaps five seconds, then tried the knob. It was unlocked.

He gave Smith a questioning look. "Should we wait for the warrant?"

"Naw, it's been issued. We're legal."

They pulled their guns, just to be on the safe side, and stepped through the door. Ten seconds later the guns were back in their holsters. The apartment was empty.

"Well, shit on a stick," Smith muttered to no one in particular.

The apartment was fairly large for a one bedroom, furnished with unmatched pieces of furniture that were neat and tidy but obviously culled from garage sales and Salvation Army outlets. The bathroom was spotless. The kitchen clean. No dirty dishes in the sink. The bed was made. An old dinosaur of a Compaq computer stood on a marred desk in the corner of the living room, video game cases stacked neatly at its side. A small TV rested on a metal stand in front of a sofa that had been covered with a flax-colored throw in a failed attempt to make it appear less battered than it was.

It reminded Smith of *his* first apartment, that thought bringing with it a twinge of nostalgia.

Two French doors, badly in need of paint, led to the balcony, which overlooked the front of the building. Here Smith found well-tended plants, a bicycle hanging from a bracket on the wall, and a Nautilus machine. The guy obviously took care of himself.

Smith supposed that in this guy's line of work that would be a prerequisite. Who would pay to screw the Pillsbury Doughboy?

McCray called him back inside the apartment.

"The closet's full of clothes but I don't see any luggage anywhere."

"Maybe he doesn't have any."

"Maybe."

"If he chose to take a powder, I can see about a dozen things here he would have taken with him. A wrist watch and ring on the dresser. About sixty dollars in cash in a drawer by the bed. About five hundred dollars worth of video games."

Smith agreed. "No, the kid didn't run. But where the hell is he?"

From his shirt pocket, McCray pulled the slip of paper he had taken from the car. "Should we try the number?"

"Yeah, go ahead. Wherever he is, he probably has his cell phone with him. See what happens."

As McCray punched in the numbers, Smith pulled out a stack of mail from the desk. Bills, mostly, and a couple of Christmas card envelopes, one with a return address from some one-horse town in Indiana that Smith had never heard of. Then he pulled something else from the desk drawer that caused his breath to catch.

"Hold it," Smith said. "Hang up."

McCray pressed disconnect. "What?"

Smith held in his hand a large zip lock bag. Inside it were snips of wire, several empty shotgun cartridges—dismantled, not fired—a pair of needle-nosed pliers, and a computer printout with step-by-step instructions on the making of a pipe bomb, compliments of a website called Anarchist International.

McCray stared at the bag with a dumb expression on his face.

"What the fuck?"

Smith couldn't have expressed his thoughts more succinctly himself. It looked like their two separate cases were suddenly one.

He laid the bag of bomb remnants on the desk and once again pulled out the stack of mail from the drawer, separating the greeting card envelopes with the Indiana postmark from the pile.

He studied the address. It was in a town called Nine Mile. It had the name of Andros on the return label. The kid's family.

If a young street hustler should suddenly decide to hightail it from a shitload of trouble, Smith could only think of one place he would try to run *to*. Back to his roots. Back to where he felt safe. Back home.

ON SUNDAY morning, Sean and Harry stood side by side, frozen to immobility, staring at the television set in Harry's living room. Bacon sizzled in a skillet in the kitchen, forgotten until the house began to fill with smoke. Only then did Harry think to turn off the stove.

On the screen, Steve Fiorina, a local newsman, stood next to the thatched shack that housed the nativity scene at the Organ Pavilion.

"Police tell us this is where the bomb was meant to be detonated." He pointed to the last row of benches in front of the stage. "The bomb was left there. Beneath that bench. Thankfully, it was removed to the parking lot just prior to detonation by a man…," here the newsman checked his notes, "… by a man named Dwayne Childers. Mr. Childers was killed in the blast. It is unclear at this time whether Mr. Childers was the person who left the bomb or if he was doing a good deed by removing the bomb to a safer location. Either way, San Diegans were very lucky last night. At the time of the blast, this location, the entire park in fact, was a sea of humanity with the estimated attendance at these Christmas festivities at well over fifty thousand. Unfortunately, since a large section of Balboa Park is now a crime scene, the Christmas On The Prado celebration for this evening has been canceled."

"My God," Harry said. "We couldn't have been out of there more than a few minutes when that thing went off." He clicked off the TV when the newscast ended. "That's a little too coincidental for me."

Sean's eyes were still puffed with sleep. "What do you mean?"

"Wake up, Sean. That bomb was right where that man told us to meet him. Do you think that was a fluke?"

"You mean he was trying to kill us?"

"Either one of us or both of us, yes, that's exactly what I mean."

Sean collapsed onto the sofa. He ran a hand through his newly dyed hair, causing it to pook up in a way that made him look about twelve years old. The innocent expression on his face made Harry's heart give a little tug. This kid was into something way over his head. They both were. And unless they figured out what was going on, Harry had a horrible suspicion they were both going to find themselves dead.

"I think someone is after you. I mean, besides the police. I think someone is either trying to kill you or set you up for things you didn't do. I don't think you stumbled onto a random murder when you went back to that trick's condo. I think that man was killed for no other reason than to lay the blame on *you*. Who would do that, Sean? Who would hate you enough to do that?"

Sean picked up his cell phone from the coffee table where he had dropped it the night before and idly flipped it over and over in his trembling hands.

"Jesus, Harry, I've never done anything to make anyone hate me that much. I know I'm not a saint, but I don't go around intentionally trying to hurt people or make enemies."

He carefully laid the cell phone back on the table, as if afraid it might explode like the bomb in the park, and picked up a pack of Harry's cigarettes. He clumsily shook one out and stuck it in his mouth.

Harry almost smiled as he plucked the cigarette from between Sean's lips. "This is no time to start smoking, kid. You've got enough problems."

Sean looked up at Harry standing over him. He reached out and pulled Harry to him, pressing his face into Harry's stomach and breathing in Harry's smell, inhaling the sense of security that Harry's mere presence gave him. He had never felt more scared in his life. Or more protected.

"What are we going to do?" he whispered, gazing up into Harry's face. "Tell me what I should do."

Harry ran a hand across Sean's hair, smoothing it down, then pulled the boy into him, holding him close.

"We have to think."

Sean's cell phone rang, causing them both to jump. Sean reached out to pick it up but Harry stopped him.

"No," he said. "Give me that."

He took the cell phone from Sean's hand and flung it against the wall, where it shattered into silent bits of plastic and metal.

"Jesus, Harry…!"

"It's time we broke this fucker's line of communication. If he wants to talk with us he'll have to do it in person. Plus, who knows what the police are capable of? Can they trace your location by the cell phone signal? Better safe than sorry. They can't trace it now for sure."

He stepped to the antique rolltop desk in the corner and rolled back the cover. From a small drawer behind a stack of old letters, he pulled out a handgun. A Colt .38 Commando Special with a six-shot cylinder and a stubby two-inch barrel that fit snugly into a coat pocket. Harry aimed the gun at the floor and swung out the cylinder, making sure it was loaded.

"Souvenir from Afghanistan," he said. "Might come in handy now."

Sean eyed the gun nervously then gave Harry a baleful look. "God, I'm being protected by an armed hairdresser."

Harry laughed. "Yeah, but this armed hairdresser was also once an armed Marine. I can handle more than spit curls and blow dryers."

I hope, he thought, staring at the gun in his hand, the weight and feel of it bringing back long-buried memories from a time in his life that he tried never to think about.

Sean appeared doubtful. "Guns make me nervous."

"Well, that's pretty much a gun's purpose, isn't it? To make the bad guy nervous."

"But I'm the good guy."

"Yeah, well…."

Harry laid the gun atop the desk and crossed the living room. He pushed aside the sliding door and stepped out onto his deck.

He breathed in the morning air and, as he had done every morning since purchasing the house in Mission Hills more than five years ago, drank in the view. The terrace, braced up by stilts, overhung a steep cliff, and from it he could see all the way to the horizon. The ocean was flat and gray in the distance. Dark clouds were forming in the northwest. More rain was coming. You could smell it in the air. Maybe by tonight. Good.

Sean came up behind him and leaned out over the rail, staring down at the cliff face of boulders and sagebrush that led to a canyon far below where other homes sat nestled against the base of the hillside.

"Quite a drop," he said.

Three of Harry's cats had followed the boy outside. Two of them began sniffing beneath the birds of paradise that grew in planters lining the side of the house. The third cat, Charlie, leaped onto the railing beside Sean and, as he had done, peered down along the cliff face.

Sean put a protective arm around the cat.

"Aren't you afraid he'll fall or jump?"

"No. He's not stupid. Cats can measure distance better than we can. He knows where it's safe for him to sit."

The two enjoyed the view for a few moments until finally Sean asked, "So, what are we doing?"

Harry pointed to the clouds. "We're going to wait for the rain. Then we're going to get rid of your car. Park it somewhere that won't lead the police to you here if they find it."

"But what about the guy? The guy with the bomb?"

Harry sighed. "I figure he already knows where you are. If he doesn't, that's even better. But if he does, and if he wants you as bad as we think he does, then I guess sooner or later, he'll come to us."

Sean burrowed beneath Harry's arm. "I'm scared."

The boy stood about six inches shorter than Harry. Harry squeezed the boy against him and kissed the top of his head. Sean could feel the stubble on Harry's chin when he did. He hadn't shaved yet.

"I'm scared, too. We just have to make sure we're ready for him when he comes."

Sean stepped back and studied Harry's face. "You're going to kill him, aren't you?"

Harry watched the old mother cat sniffing at what looked to be a cricket on the redwood deck. Her tail twitched with excitement as she prepared to pounce.

"Only if he tries to kill us first."

Then a more mundane thought struck Harry. This was a work day. He had appointments at his salon. Well, they would just have to get along without him for once. The other stylists who worked for him could cover. Or cancel. He didn't much care what they did. What sort of moron worked on Sunday anyway? It was a practice he had meant to stop long ago. Funny how things had changed in the span of two days. Before, his salon had been the driving force in his life. He had carved it from nothing and now it was a damn fine business. Suddenly it seemed unimportant. Amazing what a little perspective could do. A little murder, a little mayhem, and a little falling in love, and your priorities changed real quickly.

Harry looked at the young man at his side. This is what's important, he thought. Saving this boy's life. Not boy. Man. Saving Sean was the only thing that mattered. He wanted to pull Sean into him. Surround him. Protect him.

What a fool I am, he thought. I've fallen hopelessly in love with a twenty-one-year-old hustler who looks like a school kid and who probably knows more about the seedier side of life than I will ever learn if I live to be a hundred. And I don't care. It doesn't matter. Was he being a fool to think the kid could ever love him back? Was the kid using him just for protection and nothing else? He didn't think so. He *wouldn't* think so.

A cloud slipped across the morning sun, and the air turned chill in an instant.

"Harry," Sean said, still pressed tight to his side. "When this is over, do you think I could stay with you?"

"What do you mean?" Harry asked, his pulse quickening. "What are you saying?"

Sean faced him, pressing his lips into Harry's neck.

"I mean I want to be with you, Harry. I… love you."

Harry's heart stopped. "You do?"

The boy faltered. "Yeah… but I don't know if you would want somebody like me. You know, the way I am. The way I've been."

A tear spilled down Harry's cheek and fell into the boy's hair. "Jesus, Sean, there's absolutely nothing wrong with the way you are. There isn't a single thing I would change about you."

"Really?"

There was such hope in the boy's voice that Harry had to swallow back the emotions that suddenly flooded through him. He hooked a finger under Sean's chin and lifted his face to look into the boy's eyes. He brushed his lips across Sean's forehead. "You can stay with me as long as you want."

Sean snaked his arms around Harry's waist. His eyes were as bright as diamonds. "As lovers?"

"If that's what you want," Harry said, his tears flowing freely now. "I love you, too, you know. I've loved you since the first time I saw you."

As their lips met, Sean muttered, "I know."

Later, with Harry spilling his seed deep inside him, and with Harry's labored breath hot against the back of his neck, Sean cried. His own sexual release, held back to coincide with Harry's, seemed to be the floodgate that unleashed a flurry of thoughts and emotions that assailed him and left him sobbing like a kid. Poor Stanley, pleading for his life. That mocking voice on the phone saying, "You won't charge me, will you?" And Harry. Harry admitting his love for him.

When he felt Harry begin to pull away, thinking perhaps he had driven too hard and hurt the boy, Sean clutched Harry's hip, pulling the man deeper into himself, holding him in place.

"Stay inside me," he managed to say. "Please, Harry."

Harry let himself be drawn back into the boy, as deep as his cock would take him, the length of his body covering Sean's, caressing him, holding the boy close and safe, feeling the velvet heat of the boy surround his hard flesh, and feeling, too, Sean's tears spilling across his arm. Slowly, Harry began to move again, exploring the boy, possessing him. Using him. When he came a second time, he cried out with the intensity of it.

Only then was Sean calmed.

Afterward, they slept, breakfast forgotten, the cats purring on the bed beside them.

FOR the second time that morning, the pale man strode past the house on Eagle Street. It hadn't taken him long to find the house thanks to the drunk at the bar. It was a short street, and the green Boxster parked at the curb had drawn him like a beacon. In the short driveway, another automobile sat hidden beneath a canvas car cover. A glimpse of a battered blue fender peeking out from where the wind had lifted a corner of the canvas told the man that they were both inside the house at this very moment. Probably sucking each other's cocks. Sinning. Abominating. He chuckled to himself. Enjoy it now, he thought. There won't be many more opportunities.

From a safe distance, he had watched the detectives enter the boy's apartment building earlier that morning. They were in there a long time. He suspected they must have found the little gift he had left for them inside the boy's desk. His prey's desk. That must have given them food for thought. Pretty much confused the issue, hey what? God, it was so funny. He was just so much smarter than they were. Than they *all* were. If he weren't having such a darn good time with it all, his power would be downright frightening.

Maybe he would let the boy and the man live a little longer. This was like eating your vegetables first so you could save the good stuff for last. He was having too much fun to let it end.

On the sidewalk, a young woman approached, walking her dog.

As they passed, he smiled at her, "A beautiful morning," he said.

She returned his smile but didn't speak. They walked on in opposite directions.

It is a beautiful morning, he thought to himself. I wonder what the rest of the day will bring.

As he walked to the rental car he had parked two blocks over in the lot of a radiology clinic, closed since the day was Sunday, he noticed the dark bank of thunderclouds creeping up the Mexican coast toward the city. They only told him what he already knew.

The storm was far from over. It was, in fact, just beginning.

Chapter Six

HOMICIDE Detective Leroy Jamison and Detective Sergeant Alan Beers, on loan from Robbery Division, sat in an AT&T van parked across the street and half a block down from Sean Andros's apartment.

As if nature liked to keep things neat and orderly, it started to rain just as night began. Like fucking Camelot. No sooner had the darkness fallen than fat drops began pelting the windshield and roof of the van. Within minutes, the rain became a torrent, insulating the two policemen in a wall of sound.

When Jamison placed his hand over his left ear, he couldn't hear the rain at all. He wondered when, or if, the hearing would return to his right ear. That fucking pipe bomb had really done a number on it. Doc said the hearing would return. Probably. Jamison wasn't convinced.

This was the first time Jamison had worked with Sergeant Beers. They had been sitting inside this van for two hours now, and Jamison had already learned two very annoying facts about his new partner. First, Beers always spoke so low that even people with *two* ears wouldn't be able to hear him, and second, whenever he *did* mumble whatever the fuck he was mumbling, you could bet your ass that he would be bitching about something.

He was bitching now.

"Surveillance sucks."

Jamison had heard this sentiment four times already, on an average about once every thirty minutes. Sergeant Beers was like a goddamn cuckoo clock.

"Do you chime on the hour?" Jamison asked.

"What?"

"Never mind."

Surveillance wasn't Jamison's favorite pastime either, but there was no point bitching about it. He *could* bitch about the rain, however. The sound of it was putting him to sleep.

He reached behind the seat for the thermos of coffee he had stashed there when their surveillance began and poured out another dollop into the Styrofoam cup he had brought along for that purpose. He offered some to Beers, who shook his head and said, "Ulcers."

What Jamison *thought* he said was, "No sir."

He liked that.

They settled into a truce-like silence that Jamison found much more enjoyable than trying to milk conversation out of this depressing asshole sitting beside him and then trying to decipher it.

In the past two hours, they had seen three people enter the apartment building and one person exit it. None of them was Andros.

Jamison would happily have killed his partner, his family, and the Holy Pope himself for a cigarette right then, but he was trying to quit. He rubbed the nicotine patch he had stuck on his upper arm that morning, hoping to kick-start it and get a little more nicotine coursing through his system. All he managed to do was make the fucking thing itch.

Jamison had been with the department for fourteen years, a homicide detective for six. He was forty-seven years old and looked sixty. He had two divorces under his belt already, and it looked like number three was in the works. He had loved all three of his wives. Couldn't get enough of them. And they had loved him too, at first. Or maybe they had loved him all the way to the end. He wasn't sure. But he did know they didn't love being the wives of a cop. At first it probably seemed exciting to them, but soon the excitement palled, he knew, and that excitement turned to fear. Fear for their husband. Fear for themselves—being left alone, widowed, another statistical decimal point. Police work, Jamison knew, had not only the highest death rate for any profession, it also had the highest divorce rate. Those numbers were not conducive to secure, stable relationships. He was a living testament to that fact.

The rain was falling harder now, and the wind had picked up, rocking the van and blasting sheets of water against the windshield like the spray from a carwash. Andros could return to his apartment in a clown costume leading three elephants on a leash and they wouldn't be able to see him.

"We need to pull up," he said to Beers. "I can't see the building."

"Building, hell. I can't even see the hood."

"This is a van, you moron. It doesn't have a hood."

"Figure of speech."

But Beers obligingly cranked up the engine and pulled the van a few feet closer to the nearest car parked on their side of the street. This would have to do. There were no more spaces they could see where the van might park. The street had filled up continually over the past two hours as people came home from wherever they had been, and with weather like this, Jamison figured they were apt to *stay* home.

Jamison used his sleeve to remove some of the condensation from the windshield. That helped a little. He sipped his coffee, watched, and waited. They wouldn't be relieved until twelve o'clock. It was going to be a long night.

Of course, nights on surveillance were always long. The only thing Jamison liked about surveillance was it gave a person time to ponder life's imponderables. Like fast food. Jamison had a pretty good start on a gut, and it was all due to fast food, the curse of every homicide detective, because homicide detectives seldom made it home in time for dinner. The scumbags of the world had a really bad habit of offing their acquaintances, or sometimes total strangers, just before the homicide detective's shift was about to end. Ergo, homicide detectives rarely made it home for dinner, another facet of the job that pissed off their wives or significant others to no end. There's the little woman, or the little significant other, sitting alone at the dining room table watching the pot roast she had lovingly prepared turn into a lump of vulcanized rubber before her very eyes, and on the other side of town, we see the homicide detective, for whom that pot roast had been lovingly prepared, standing in line at a Jack in the Box ordering fries and greasy tacos because he doesn't have time to fly home and eat the goddamn pot roast. This scenario always ended later, when the poor hapless detective did finally make it home, with tears and recriminations from the little woman and promises to do better next time by the poor detective, who would most likely turn around the very next day and do the same thing all over again. Not purposely, of course, but just because that was the nature of the beast which is homicide. An imponderable if there ever was one.

Another imponderable that Detective Jamison liked to ponder on these long nights of surveillance was why, dear God, did he always have to be teamed up in some stale-smelling van that reeked of smoke and farts and cold Chinese food with someone he would most assuredly try to avoid completely in any other sort of *social* situation. If he were to meet Detective Sergeant Beers at a cocktail party, he would break a leg trying to get far away from the fucker as quickly as possible.

He looked over at Beers now, just as Beers looked back at him.

Beers wiggled his ass around in the seat and said, "My hemorrhoids are killing me."

Jamison sighed and placed his hand over his left ear again.

Much better.

He checked his watch. Five minutes had passed.

Jesus Christ.

ONE imponderable that Jamison failed to contemplate on this rainy December night was, arguably, the most important of all. This being, that when one is on surveillance and one's powers of observation should be at their peak, in reality, the sheer boredom of surveillance creates an opposing effect. After a few soporific hours of doing absolutely nothing, the human eye begins to look inward, to inconsequential things such as pot roasts and fast food and ever-widening waistlines. Powers of outward observation drop to their lowest ebb. A clown with three elephants on a leash could very easily walk right past you and you wouldn't notice a thing.

Thus, when the tall man with pale skin and a revolver in his right hand walked up to the passenger door of the van and fired three bullets through the glass, Jamison barely had time to register the fact that the man was there before one bullet caught him just below the chin, shattering his Adam's apple going in, and tearing out a baseball-sized chunk of flesh at the back of his neck going out. Jamison was dead before his coffee cup hit the floorboard.

Beers had time to scrabble around for his service revolver, never quite reaching it before the second and third bullets pierced his chest. One entered his heart and the other severed the spinal cord as it ricocheted merrily through his body. The ricocheting bullet was found a few hours later by a crime tech with the unlikely name of Mary Tripp, where it had finally come to rest deep inside the blood-soaked seat cushion.

No one witnessed the scene. No one heard the shots. The darkness and the windblown rain that hammered against the windows of surrounding houses had blanketed the murders as effectively as if they had been committed in another dimension.

No one saw the man in the parka, its hood pulled close around his face to ward off the pelting rain, unhurriedly walk away. No one knew he had come this way at all.

Not until later, when radio calls to the two men on stakeout went unanswered for too long a period of time to be acceptable, was a squad car sent round to check on them.

By then, Detective Jamison's head, which lay exposed to the elements as it rested lifeless beside the shattered van window, had been washed clean of blood by the cold rain. But for his open eyes, flooded with raindrops, he might have been asleep.

AS DETECTIVES Jamison and Beers lay dead in a blood- and rain-soaked AT&T van less than twenty blocks away, Harry stood at his patio door and watched the storm gather momentum outside. Between the darkness and the rain, any sort of visibility was almost nonexistent. This was what Harry had been waiting for.

The Christmas tree he had purchased earlier now stood tall and plump in the corner of the living room, filling the house with its Christmasy fragrance. Sean, for lack of anything better to do, was sorting through boxes of ornaments Harry had dug from a closet. Carefully, because his hands were shaking, he began hanging the ornaments on the tree.

Sean hated himself for being so afraid, but he didn't want Harry to leave.

"Let me go with you, Harry."

Earlier, on the evening news, they had seen Sean's BMV photo splayed across the TV screen with a request for any information concerning his whereabouts. The reporter did not say that Sean was a suspect in either the murder at Brittany Towers or the bombing in Balboa Park, only that he was wanted for questioning. But both Harry and Sean knew that now the boy was definitely a suspect in either one or both of the crimes. And Harry had refused to let him leave the house.

"I want you to stay here," Harry said for the third or fourth time. "Every cop in the city is probably looking for you. This is the only place you're safe. I'll dump the car and be back as quickly as I can. I can't leave it in the driveway any longer. If I had a garage where I could hide it, we wouldn't be having this discussion, but I don't."

He watched the boy's hand tremble as he hung yet another ornament, this one crystal, on the tree.

"I'm leaving the gun. It's ready to fire so don't even touch it unless you have to. But it won't come to that. I'll be back before you're finished with the tree." He tried to cheer the boy up. "It's looking pretty good, by the way. In typical gay fashion, you're hanging all those nellie little doodads with quite an eye for artistic flair. Now that you've retired from your current line of work, and when all this misery is over, maybe we'll think about sending you to beauty school."

Sean smirked. "My folks would be so proud. Finding out I was gay almost killed them. If they learned I was a hairdresser, it would probably finish them off."

"Well," Harry said, pulling on his coat and scooping up Sean's car keys from the kitchen counter. "Thanks for putting me in my place."

Sean looked repentant. "I didn't mean that the way it sounded."

"I know."

"It's an honorable profession."

"Oh, shut up."

With a Marvin the Martian ornament still dangling from his fingertips, Sean crossed the room and slipped his arms around Harry's waist. Putting on a brave face, or so he hoped, he pecked Harry on the cheek. "Hurry back then," he said, his eyes wide with worry.

Harry cupped the boy's face in his hands and kissed him on the nose. "I will. And don't fret. The house is all locked up. You'll be safe."

He stepped back a pace and grinned. Sean was once again wearing Harry's pajamas, and they didn't fit him any better than they had the first time the boy had put them on.

"You need some clothes. I put the stuff you were wearing in the washer, so even if you want to go out, you can't. There's nothing for you to wear."

"I know," Sean said. "I'll stay here. Just please hurry."

"I promise."

With another hug, and another reminder to Sean not to handle the gun unless he absolutely had to, Harry left.

He hunched his shoulders against the wind and rain and jogged to the Yugo, ripping off the car cover and practically diving into the car to escape the weather. The Yugo was without a doubt a piece of shit to look at, but remarkably, once again, it started right up.

Not for the first time, Harry figured he really must be out of his mind. Abetting the boy could land him in some serious shit with the law. But he also knew that Sean was innocent. He had believed the boy's story of what transpired at Stanley Baker's condominium because he wanted to believe it, but after the bombing in the park, he knew without a doubt that Sean's innocence was beyond question. If he needed a rationale for helping the boy, it was that it couldn't be a crime to help someone *wrongly* accused of a crime. Could it? But if he went to the police, would they believe him? He had his doubts. Other high profile cases in San Diego's recent past, where the police had tried to push convictions when evidence had either been sorely mishandled, or completely nonexistent, left him with very little faith in the legal system. No, if Sean's innocence was to be proven, he would have to do it himself, or at least give the police time to do it properly on their own. The real murderer had killed twice already. Mr. Baker and the man in the park were dead because of him. But Sean, for some reason, was obviously the man's real target.

Maybe he shouldn't leave the boy by himself, but it was far too risky to take him along. What if the police recognized Sean's car and pulled him over? Both he and the boy would then be at the mercy of the cops, and that was no place Harry wanted to be right now. Outside the system, on their own, they had a chance. Maybe.

Harry let the car idle for a minute to get the kinks out, then backed out of the driveway. The streets were all but empty. What little traffic there was crept along as if in slow motion. This storm, much worse than the last, had struck with a savage force that was rarely seen in San Diego. In the backcountry, Harry knew, there would be mudslides where recent brush fires had left the ground unprotected by foliage. People who had been lucky enough to survive the forest fires of the summer with their homes intact would now be facing a new threat as the rain-soaked ground began to slip away beneath them. Hillsides would shift, and sinkholes were not uncommon. Even in Southern California, which ordinarily enjoyed one of the most temperate climates in the world, Mother Nature could occasionally be a nasty adversary. At these rare times when she did rear up in sudden anger, many people suffered. Homes were lost and lives shattered. And in the end, Mother Nature always won.

He hunched into the wheel, chuckling to himself about what a fool he was, and tried without much success to see where the hell he was going. The first thing Harry would do for the boy would be to buy him new wiper blades. Or better yet, a new car. He was freezing to death because the heater didn't work, but he was too nervous to worry about that. Between trying to maneuver through the rain-swept streets and keeping an eye to the rearview mirror for police cars, Harry was a nervous wreck by the time he reached Fashion Valley Mall.

He parked the car in shadow at the farthest corner of the lot and, pulling his coat sleeve down over his hand, proceeded to wipe his fingerprints from any surface he thought he might have touched. Their only chance for success, he knew, was to keep the boy hidden, and he didn't want to lead the police to himself by leaving prints in the car. For the car would be found soon enough. There was no getting around that, short of driving it into the ocean, and Harry wasn't quite prepared to go to that extreme. He left the keys in the ignition on the off chance that some idiot would actually steal the thing, but he didn't hold out much hope for that scenario. Who would want it? Even car thieves had their standards.

Harry climbed from the car and, with a final swipe of the outside door handle, took off running through the pouring rain to Macy's. There he spent twenty precious minutes in the men's department picking out a few items of clothing he thought might fit Sean, and after paying for the items with a credit card because he forgot to bring any cash, he asked the clerk to call him a cab.

As he waited for the taxi, sheltered in Macy's doorway, he could see the Yugo still sitting there, way off in the corner of the lot. At least this was preferable to having it sit in his driveway. It would buy them time, he hoped. And Harry figured that was pretty much the name of the game. Bide time. Stay hidden. Let the police do their work. And with any luck at all, give the real murderer time to make a mistake.

Oh, and one other thing.

Try not to get killed in the meanwhile.

SEAN watched from inside the front door as Harry backed the Yugo out of the driveway and disappeared into the rain. He immediately closed the door, blocking out the night, and made sure the latch clicked. From there, methodically, he went to every window and every door, testing them, making sure they were securely locked.

When he felt satisfied that he was safely locked in, he returned to the living room and turned off the stereo. He had found some of Harry's old Christmas LPs and had been playing them as he decorated the tree. But now he craved silence. If anyone should try to break into the house, he wanted to be able to hear them.

The house stood silent and protective around him. Only the occasional sound of one of the cats crunching on dry cat food from a large bowl that Harry kept on a tray on the kitchen floor could be heard. That, and the constant sweep of wind and rain against the windows, which never seemed to let up for a moment. Like white noise in the background of a poorly laid soundtrack, it was always there, cocooning the house in sound. It comforted Sean. He felt somehow protected by it.

He was reminded of nights as a child in the old farmhouse, a place that from his very first memory had always been his home.

He recalled the old iron bedstead in which he had always slept, with its high head and foot boards, painted rather unconvincingly to look like brass. He smiled, remembering the many times his mother had coaxed him from that bed in the middle of the night and hustled him off to sleep on the sofa in the living room whenever lightning was near. Her fear was that the iron bed would attract the lightning and electrocute the boy as he slept. Sean laughed at the memory but wondered none the less whether her fears might not have been justified.

The storm he listened to now reminded him of those summer storms he had known as a child before she pulled him from his bed. They had never frightened him. They were like acquaintances who came to visit once in a while. As long as he was inside, away from the lightning, away from the hard rain and the piercing wind and the smell of ozone, those storms had comforted Sean. His childhood was not without fear, but that fear did not come from nature. It did not come from outside the walls that protected him. It came from within the house.

He shuddered now, remembering, and glanced at the rolltop desk in the corner of Harry's living room and the gun that rested on top of it. He moved closer and looked at it, but he didn't pick it up to test its weight or to see how it would feel in his hand. He knew how it would feel. And he knew he could use it if he had to. But he did not like guns. He had never liked them, even though they were common where he came from. In Indiana, everyone hunted. Everyone owned as many guns as they could afford, it seemed. Even his father. And Sean had used guns as a child. Shot birds from the trees. Hunted rabbits in the snow-covered fields in winter. But looking back at that period in his life, it was as if he had been going through the motions of living a life that he should not have been born into.

He had always known he was different. Different from the children he went to school with. Different from his family. Different from the people he met at the church that his parents made him attend every Sunday.

But he never knew what the source of that difference was until his thirteenth summer, when his sexuality began to awaken and childhood suddenly fell behind him. It was not only his body that began to change. The sprouting of hair beneath his arms and around his penis and on his legs told him he was becoming a man. It seemed his body changed with each and every passing day. And his thoughts changed as well. Dark, hungry thoughts that scared him and made him confused. Fantasies. The tightness of a friend's blue jeans as he bent to pet the dog. The odor of young bodies in the locker room after gym class at school. The dusty torso of a young man who worked shirtless in the sun that summer, helping his father put up hay in the barn loft. The smell of that young man and the looks the young man had given Sean when he knew that Sean had been watching him made him uneasy. Made him ashamed. The young man knew what Sean was thinking. Knew it better than Sean did himself. For with all the hungry thoughts, all the longing and sexual awakening going on inside his mind and body, Sean never actually understood what it was he was hungering for. The practice of sex was still pretty much a mystery to him.

He had heard, many times, the squeak of bedsprings in his parent's bedroom at night. And he knew, vaguely, what that sound meant. But mostly, it was just a reassuring noise to the young boy who lay alone in the darkness in the next room, cradled in his big iron bed, listening to it. He did not think of the actual act taking place in that room next to his; he could only comprehend what it signified. It signified love. His parents loved each other. And in loving each other, it also meant they loved him.

Not until that night in his thirteenth year, when his parents were gone to a meeting at the church, did Sean suddenly come to know why he was so different from everyone else.

That night, his brother, Jackson, five years older than Sean and grown tall now like their father, came into Sean's room as Sean lay reading on his bed. Sean still remembered the book he was reading. It was *Swiss Family Robinson*. Jackson stood at the foot of Sean's bed, looking down at him, his face twisted with disgust.

"I saw you today," he said.

Sean did not look up from his book.

"Saw me what?"

Jackson hooked his thumbs in the rear pockets of his jeans and smiled. "I saw you watching the kid in the barn. Saw you slobbering like a dog every time he flexed a muscle. You're a queer, ain't ya?"

Sean's heart began hammering in his chest. Still, he did not look up from his book. He was afraid to. He was afraid of what he would see on his brother's face. The hatred he would see. The revulsion.

"You're crazy," Sean said. "You're crazy as a goddamn loon."

Jackson grabbed the footboard of Sean's bed and gave it a vicious shake. "Don't you take God's name in vain, you little faggot! Don't you do it! I'll bleed you out like a butchered hog if you ever do it again."

He gave the bed another shake and straightened his back, the nasty smile returning to his face.

"You know what a cocksucker is?" Jackson asked, one hand beginning to rub the crotch of his jeans, the other still firmly grasping the footboard. "*Do* you?" he asked again.

"Yes," Sean said, beginning to tremble.

"'Cause you've done it, ain't you? You've already done it."

"No!" Sean yelled. "I ain't no queer!"

Sean's breath caught as he stared at his brother's crotch. Jackson's dick was growing, stretching the denim. His brother continued to rub himself, and with his other hand, he stripped off his T-shirt, standing now half naked at the foot of Sean's bed. His free hand slid across his chest, touching his nipples, running down the flat stomach until both hands now caressed his own crotch.

He unsnapped the button of his jeans and slowly began pulling the zipper down, watching Sean's face as he did it, smiling that nasty smile, exposing his pubic hair to the boy.

Sean's own cock was moving now. He could feel it swelling beneath the underpants he always wore to bed. Thank God the sheet kept his brother from seeing it. Sean was really trembling now. And not just with fear. He hated himself for getting excited. And he hated his brother even more for making him feel that way.

Jackson let his hands fall away from his crotch, his dick still hidden beneath the denim, and stepped around to the side of the bed.

"Get out of here!" Sean screamed. "Just get the hell out of here!"

Jackson stood over him, less than a foot away, looking down at the boy, still smiling his evil smile.

"You're hard, ain't you?"

"No!"

"Really? Let's see." Jackson grabbed the sheet and ripped it from the bed, throwing it to the floor. Sean sat in the center of the bed, rigid with fear, wearing only his white BVDs, his hands trying to hide from his brother the swelling beneath them. He looked up at his brother looming over him, smelling him now. The clean smell of soap and talc. And something else. Something hot and musky and wild. A scent he had unknowingly been hungering for. A scent that had haunted his imagination.

Jackson pulled the boy's hands away and smiled at what he saw.

Tears began to well up in Sean's eyes. Tears of shame.

"Leave me alone," he said, but his voice was little more than a whisper. He knew now that his brother was right. He was queer. He looked again at the length of Jackson's cock outlined beneath the denim. The tangle of blond pubic hair above it. The white skin of his stomach. The sprinkling of blond hair across his young chest. And up into his brother's eyes. His brother's accusing eyes.

Jackson dipped his fingers into the waistband of his jeans and slowly pushed the Levis down to his thighs. His cock, long and sleek, sprang out, a drop of moisture glistening at its tip.

Jackson slid his hand along its length, pulling back the foreskin, exposing himself completely.

"Open your mouth, boy."

Sean looked up into his brother's face grinning down at him, mocking him, the image distorted through his tears.

Sean began to cry.

"Please, Jackson...."

"Please what? Please give you this?"

He roughly grabbed a handful of Sean's hair and pushed his head back. Stepping closer to the bed, Jackson laid his hard cock across the boy's face.

"Open your mouth," he said again.

Sean could feel the velvet warmth of his brother's penis against his cheek. Could smell the clean smell of his brother's pubic hair brushing his face. He closed his eyes for a moment, then opened them and stared up into his brother's face as he stretched his mouth wide and took Jackson's cock between his lips.

Jackson gasped and clutched both sides of the boy's head. Slowly, he moved his hips closer, sliding himself deeper into the boy's mouth.

Sean continued to watch his brother's face as he finally let himself go. Let himself do what he wanted to do. He slid his hands around Jackson's legs and pulled him nearer. Sean closed his eyes and really tasted his brother's cock for the first time.

Yes, he thought, this is who I am.

Jackson came then, without warning, a long shuddering climax that startled him as much as Sean, that filled the boy's mouth and made him choke. But not once did Sean take his mouth from his brother's cock. Not once did he stop clutching his brother's strong legs and reveling in the feel of his brother's body beneath his hands, lost in the sweet smell and taste of him. Not because he was his brother, but because he was male.

Because, he now knew, this was what he was born to be.

With a moan, Jackson pulled free from the boy's mouth, feeling the eager heat of it slide away from him, and pushed the boy down hard on the bed. His hands circled Sean's throat and he saw Sean's young dick standing rigid beneath his shorts. He stared at it for long seconds, then reached back and slapped Sean across the face with as much strength as he could muster. The boy's head bounced back against the headboard and his eyes flew open in pain.

Jackson looked down at him with pure hatred, his body still trembling from the intensity of his orgasm.

"Swallow it," he said, his voice harsh, breathless.

Sean swallowed the thick mass of semen in his mouth, blinking at the feel of it, the musky taste.

"If you ever tell anybody about this, I'll kill you, do you understand?"

Sean managed to say, "Yes," before the sobs began.

Jackson slapped him again, harder than the first time, jarring the boy so badly that he bit his tongue, the taste of blood now mixing with the taste of his brother's semen.

"This will never happen again," Jackson hissed, his face so close that Sean could feel his brother's hot breath against his skin. "Do you understand? Never talk to me again. Never look at me again. You will not exist for me from this day on. God will take care of you some day. You're going to burn in hell, boy. Faggots burn in hell. It's a sin against God."

Sean squeezed his eyes closed, trying to block out the hatred he saw on his brother's face. Ashamed now of what he had done. Of the secrets he had just exposed. Exposed to himself and, worse, exposed to Jackson.

He tried to twist away, and after a moment, Jackson's hands released him. Sean buried his face into the bed and cried. His face still stung where Jackson had slapped him, and his tongue hurt where he had bitten it. But most of all, he cried for what he now knew he was.

Jackson scooped his T-shirt off the floor and turned the bedroom light out as he left the room, slamming the door closed behind him. The boy laid in the darkness for more than an hour, sobbing as if his heart had died inside him. When he heard his parents come home, he pulled the pillow over his head and continued to cry as quietly as he could.

They left him alone, thinking he was asleep, he guessed. But it was hours before he finally dozed. And his last thought before he fell into an exhausted sleep was the feel of his brother's cock between his lips. The taste of his brother's sperm shooting into his mouth as Jackson gasped with the pleasure and the shock of it, whether his brother would ever admit to the pleasure or not. Sean supposed he never would. But the truth was out now. The truth that Sean had managed to hide even from himself. Now he understood so many things that had only confused him before. Now he understood himself. And in understanding himself, a new pain began.

For two years following the incident on that hot summer night so long ago, his brother had made each and every day of the young boy's life a misery. Jackson had held to his word. He barely spoke to the boy again. The only time he acknowledged his existence was when he beat him. And the beatings were frequent and vicious, and although Sean was young, barely in his teens, he understood why the beatings took place. Jackson, like Sean, was also ashamed of what had transpired that night.

But it was Sean who accepted the blame for that incident, which he knew, even at thirteen, would tear the brothers apart forever. Somehow, the longings inside himself had brought it about. Perhaps, unknowingly, he had always wanted it to happen. Regret for what he had done on that warm summer night would return every time he saw the hatred on his brother's face, eat into him like a cancer every time

Jackson snubbed him or struck him or spat cruel words at him in passing as they attended to their chores around the farm.

What to Sean had been an enlightening, a realization of his own sexuality, one that he eventually came to accept, to Jackson had been a moment of weakness. A weakness of his flesh. A failing of the religion that he had embraced as a young child, embraced with a passion that was almost sexual itself in its intensity. Sean instinctively knew this, and he was sorry, every day, for causing his brother such pain.

It wasn't until years later that Sean began to wonder if perhaps his brother might not be afflicted with the same longings as himself. If so, Jackson had managed to bury those feelings deep inside himself, never letting them out again, drowning them in the fervor of a faith in God that was almost frightening in its depth. An affliction in itself.

On the morning of his twentieth birthday, Jackson packed up his clothes and left the farm, saying good-by to neither Sean nor his parents. Sean remembered his mother crying at the kitchen table and his father trying to soothe her. But for Sean, Jackson's leaving was a relief. It meant he would no longer have to live in fear of the constant beatings, the hateful glares, and the sullen silences. The release from fear was a blessing to the boy.

Idly, as he stared out at the storm through Harry's patio door, locked up tight like the rest of the house, Sean wondered where his brother was now. But that thought did not occupy his mind for more than a few seconds. He had more important things to worry about. It crossed his mind that maybe his brother's prophecy had finally come true. Maybe this was hell. His punishment for being gay. The payback for the sin of being born this way.

But that was ridiculous. This was not hell. Finding Harry was not hell. Finding Harry was the best thing that had ever happened to him.

Wherever his brother was now, it had nothing to do with Sean. His brother was lost to him, and Sean still felt guilty about that, but just the same he was happy to be as far away from him as he was.

This was his life now. It had nothing to do with his past. Not with his brother or his parents or anyone else from his childhood. And if he was in trouble now, as he most certainly was, then he would sort it out himself. With Harry's help. And when this nightmare was over, he would prove to Harry that he loved him. He would make Harry happy. And in doing that, he would make himself happy too.

No, this was not hell. Hell was back in Indiana. Hell was behind him, and he would leave it there with his brother, dead in his past where it belonged.

The sudden sound of a tree limb brushing the side of the house brought Sean back to the present. He picked up the old mother cat that was purring against his leg and pressed his face into her warm fur. Come on, Harry. Hurry home. It was more a prayer than a thought. He needed Harry with him. He needed Harry's strength. He wanted Harry to hold him. To make love to him. To make the fear go away, as only Harry seemed able to do.

DETECTIVES Smith and McCray sat in a secluded booth at the Star and Garters, a one-time strip joint on University Avenue that had several years earlier lost its license for nude dancing, thanks to a prostitution sting that sent the owner to prison for pandering and the girls scattering to the four winds to ply their trade elsewhere. Since that time, the new owner, a retired police captain who wasn't cut out for the inactivity of retirement, had bought the establishment and turned it into a beer bar that, over the years, had evolved into a hangout for off-duty cops. On this miserably wet night, there were only a handful of patrons in the place, two playing pool and a couple more chatting over Buds at the bar.

The drone and occasional roar of a Browns and Forty-Niners football game played softly on the TV. Smith and McCray sipped their icy beers and ignored the game. The awning over the front door could be heard, like gunfire, snapping and popping in the wind. Their coats, wet and dripping, hung on a rack beside their booth.

"This Andros guy wasn't even hooked up to the Internet," Smith was saying. "Apparently he just used his computer for video games. How do you suppose he got that computer printout for making bombs if he wasn't on the Net? Even the paper it was printed on was different from the ream of paper we found in his desk."

McCray wasn't buying his partner's logic. "The kid could have got that printout anywhere. There's about twenty Internet cafes spread around the county where he could have gone online while sipping a latte, for Christ's sake. I can't believe you're being so obtuse."

"Obtuse? Why was the kid's door unlocked? Why would he leave incriminating evidence sitting in an unlocked apartment if he decided to make a run for it? Why would he leave cash and his wristwatch behind?"

McCray tapped his knuckles on the table top for emphasis. "Why would he run at all? If he's innocent, just why the hell would he run?"

"Jeff, this kid is twenty-one years old. Do you remember what it was like being twenty-one? I don't know about you, but I was pretty fucking naïve back then."

"This kid is a hustler. There's nothing naïve about him."

"Well, yeah. But he has no record. He's never been in trouble with the law. And he looks like a fucking cherub."

"Those kids that blew away their classmates at Columbine looked pretty innocent, too. It didn't slow them down any."

Smith conceded the point but all he could think of to say in support of his theory that the kid might be innocent was, "I've just got a feeling about this. Something's not adding up. Let's say it's possible that Andros and this Stanley Baker guy got into an altercation over money for services rendered and Andros offed him. Why, then, would he cut off the guy's pecker and cram it down his throat? And why, after doing all that, would he decide to plant a bomb in a crowd of innocent people risking God knows how many lives? Why would he do that, Jeff? Explain it to me."

"Maybe he's just plain crazy. It happens, you know."

"I know it happens. But I don't think it's happening here. Don't ask me why, 'cause I really can't tell you. It's just a gut feeling."

McCray was starting to come around. He had worked with Smith for enough years to trust his partner's instincts. Those instincts had, in fact, saved their asses and their reputations more than once. If Smith felt so strongly about this, then he would have to at least humor the guy. And what if he *was* right? It wouldn't be the first time gut feeling took precedence over evidence.

"So what are you suggesting we do?" McCray asked. "For the sake of argument, let's say the kid isn't guilty. Where does that lead us? What do we do about it?"

"Well, willingly or unwillingly, he's obviously in the middle of whatever is going on. And there must be a reason for it. I think we need to learn more about Sean Andros."

Smith pulled a wrinkled envelope from his blazer pocket and laid it on the table, pushing it toward McCray.

"This is where the kid hails from. Some pissant town in Indiana. We need to contact the parents and whatever other family members the kid has and try to learn more about him. In fact, I already did. Or at least I tried to."

He tapped his finger against the return address label on the envelope. "I tried to contact these people right here. His parents. But I couldn't reach them. So then I made a call to the county sheriff who oversees this pissant neck of Indiana and asked him to take a run out to this address and see if he could find them. Maybe get them to call me back. He said he would, although they're having some weather problems of their own right now, I gathered. Up to their shitkicking asses in snow, according to the Sheriff. But anyway, we'll see what we find out. Maybe nothing. Maybe a lot. Just have to wait and see."

McCray's cell phone rang. He had indeed reprogrammed it. Now it played the theme song to Dragnet. Smith groaned.

"McCray here."

As he listened to the voice on the phone, his eyes widened like a 1920s caricature of a surprised black man. Round white eyes against black skin, mouth stupidly agape. Then the eyes narrowed in anger.

"Fuck!"

He terminated the call and, for a moment, sat speechless, staring at his partner.

"Well, what is it?" Smith asked, knowing even as he said it that the answer wouldn't be anything he wanted to hear.

McCray ran a hand across his face and tossed the phone onto the table in disgust.

"It's Jamison and Beers. On stakeout at the Andros apartment. Somebody's shot them."

"Are they dead?" Smith asked, feeling a sudden loosening in his bowels.

"Yeah," McCray said, reaching for his coat. "They're dead."

They both knew the investigation had just been ratcheted up several notches. It didn't get much more serious than killing a cop. Not for fellow cops. And these were detectives who were killed. The elite. The cream. Usually it was the lowly patrolman on the street who died in the line of duty. A mundane traffic stop that turns deadly or, as Smith knew all too well, a kid on PCP who panics while holding up a 7-11 and aims his father's gun at the cop who answers the call. Through his coat, Smith touched the scar on his chest, remembering.

Now there would be a shitstorm of activity. The brass would hold press conferences, thrilled at getting the air time. Patrolmen would be itching for a fight, their guns always at the ready. Citizen's groups would be outraged, holding meetings and forming new neighborhood watch programs and getting in the way as often as they helped. The local media, always a pain in the ass even at the best of times, would try to outdo each other in their eagerness to get a story. A byline. And the funerals. Another media event.

And both Smith and McCray knew that in the middle of all this mess would be themselves. It was their case. Their responsibility. All eyes would be on them.

"Still think the kid is innocent?" McCray asked as they headed out the door.

Smith flipped his collar up against the rain but didn't answer.

EARLIER, the pale man had watched from the shadows as a black and white cruised past the van on Walnut Street, made a U-turn, and returned to park alongside it. A patrolman in a yellow rain slicker stepped out of the squad car and approached the van, tapping the driver side window, amused, perhaps, to think the two detectives had fallen asleep on the job. The pale man knew better, and soon the cop would know better as well. He had to smile, imagining how the cop would react to the bloody mess he was about to find inside the van.

There had really been no reason to kill the two detectives. At first, he hadn't known they were there. He had been watching the apartment from his vantage point in the shadows, huddled against the weather, thinking maybe his prey would return here to pick up some of his belongings. From the corner of his eye, he had caught a movement, a tiny flicker of light that he recognized as the phosphorescence on a wristwatch inside the van. Looking closer, he could make out someone pouring something from a thermos into a cup. Then he knew the police were staking out the apartment. At first he was angry, thinking perhaps they might have spotted him. But then he figured that with the storm at its peak, and with the rain coming down in buckets, no one farther than five feet away would be able to see him. Not without a night scope and a snorkle.

His gun, a Redhawk, bored to handle .44 Magnum rounds, lay heavy in his coat pocket. It was a comforting presence there in the dark, and on a sudden whim, he pulled it out. The feel of it in his hand caused his heart to quicken, and he walked toward the van, the parka pulled close around his face, the gun nestled hidden in the crook of his arm. He could now see there were two men inside the van, and neither had turned to look at him. Only at the last moment, when he pressed the Redhawk to the window, did the man nearest to him turn and register surprise. Seconds later, they were both dead, their lives punched out by the lethal Magnum rounds, and the echoes of the gunshots had melted into the wailing of the storm.

The pale man saw no movement of curtains in the houses around him, no indication at all that anyone had seen or heard anything out of the ordinary. He slipped the gun back into his pocket and strolled casually back to his place in the shadows. There he waited.

And only now, at the approach of the black and white, did he slip away into the night. Soon the street would be teeming with activity, with cops crawling all over the area like maggots on a carcass. The boy would not come. But the boy, he knew, would be blamed. And that amused him.

He whistled as he walked, and the wind pulled the tune from his lips and carried it away into oblivion even before the sound of it reached his own ears.

CHAPTER SEVEN

DARKNESS had not yet settled over the secluded farmhouse in the southwestern corner of Indiana. What *had* settled over the farmhouse, the surrounding fields, and every square inch of land in this and three other states, was nine inches of snow. Drifts reached as high as four feet. The temperature hovered around ten degrees, and during the night, which was fast approaching, it would plummet to well below zero. Snot would freeze on the end of your nose before you knew it was there. You had to chip it away like paint.

Boyd Lucas, Greene County Sheriff, could think of many things he would rather be doing than sitting in his Bronco out here in the middle of nowhere on this godforsaken gravel road, which was all but impassable thanks to the drifting snow, and running down a lead for some citified detective in San Diego, California who was probably too busy getting a suntan to run down the lead himself.

The farmhouse belonged to Evelyn and Walter Andros. They had lived in it for as long as Boyd could remember. He didn't know them well. Only by sight. Didn't think he had ever spoken two words to them in his life, but most people in this farming community knew just about everybody around, at least by sight. They met in the stores, the banks, the churches, and on street corners in the little town of Nine Mile where they swapped stories and griped about the weather, an all-time favorite pastime of farmers everywhere.

Boyd had known something was wrong the minute he topped the rise a quarter mile from the farm. He noted two automobiles parked in the cinder driveway at the side of the house, which would indicate that people were home. But no smoke rose from the chimney. And as he pulled up into the driveway, he saw that the front door to the farmhouse was standing wide open. In a side lot, where a dilapidated old barn stood, he spotted a brown and white milk cow standing by the fence, her udders swollen and red for need of milking, lowing in pain. He hated to see an animal suffer. He was tempted to hop the fence and milk the poor thing himself just to quiet her down and ease her pain, but he had an unpleasant feeling that there were worse things waiting for him inside the house.

Boyd prided himself on being a pretty stoic fellow. Not much fazed him, aside from a suffering beast, but something wasn't right here. He knew it in his bones. He pulled his revolver from the holster at his hip and made sure there was a round in the chamber before slipping it back into the holster, leaving the restraining strap undone, an act which pretty much amazed even him.

He stepped from the patrol car and immediately felt the mind-numbing cold begin to permeate his clothes, like it would reach into the very heart of a man if he stayed out in it long enough, which undoubtedly it would. He walked behind a late model Ford pickup with high wooden standards around the bed that was parked there and approached the front porch. The steps leading up to it were coated with ice, another indication that no one had been doing much work around here lately. He clutched the hand rail, just in case, as he carefully climbed the steps. Didn't need to fall on his ass and break something.

All he could see through the open front door was darkness. There were no lights on anywhere that he could see.

He called out, "Anybody home?" He thought he heard sounds of movement inside and that heartened him a little. He rapped hard on the door frame and called out again, "Hello?"

Four or five barn cats came flying through the front door, one shooting right between his legs, and he damned near had a coronary infarction right there on the spot. His heart started hopping around inside his chest like a basketball bouncing down a flight of stairs. He pulled his revolver and, for a moment, seriously thought about blowing every one of the little bastards into the next cosmic level of existence. Then he calmed down. But not much.

"What the *fuck!*"

He could think of no reason to put it off any longer, so he stepped inside the house, his pistol leading the way. If he scared poor Mrs. Andros to death, so be it. He'd apologize to her later. Right now he didn't feel like taking any chances.

It didn't take him long to realize that he wouldn't be needing to apologize to *anyone*, except maybe that detective in San Diego who was waiting for a call from these nice people. Boyd was pretty sure they wouldn't be calling anybody any time soon.

The furnace had either been turned off days ago or shut down on its own after running out of fuel. The air inside the house was just as mind-numbingly cold as the air outside. Colder, maybe. Like the cold had really seeped into the walls and furniture and meant to stay a while.

Walter Andros, a mild-looking man with thinning blond hair maybe a few years short of sixty, was sitting in a recliner, his feet propped up for all the world like he had just come in from the field and was taking a breather before getting up and going in to have his dinner. There were a few things wrong with the picture, however. First of all, it was obvious that Mr. Andros was frozen as solid as a tray of ice cubes. Frost had settled into his open eyes. Boyd took a couple of steps closer to him, not exactly sure of what he was seeing in the dim light. It looked like the man was grinning at him. Then, with an almost audible click, it registered with Boyd what he was truly seeing. He felt hot bile burn in his throat as he quickly looked away. Mr. Andros had no lips. They had been eaten away, along with most of one cheek. The cats. The goddamn cats. They must have run out of Friskies and field mice and decided to supplement their diet with frozen farmer for a change. Mr. Andros' teeth, obviously none too lovely when the man was alive, looked a hell of a lot worse now, all exposed as they were. They reminded Boyd of some long forgotten horror movie he had seen as a child. Lord, those movies use to give him the fantods. He wasn't too sure he wouldn't be having a few fantods after today either.

Tired of squinting in the dark room, and figuring there wasn't anything worse to see, he flipped on the overhead light and immediately regretted it after getting a *really* good look at Mr. Andros for the first time.

Now he could see the cause of death. He didn't know how he had missed it before. The yellow handle of a Craftsman screwdriver protruded from the farmer's ear like the hand grip on an old fashioned butter churn. It had been driven deep into the man's head. Death must have been instantaneous. Thank God for that, at least.

With the overhead light now burning brightly from the ceiling, Boyd finally turned his attention to the other figure in the room. Mrs. Andros. Evelyn, Boyd remembered her name was. She was sitting with her back to him on one of those round stools that you spin to adjust the height, in front of a cherrywood sewing cabinet, the kind that opens up like a flower when in use. A black dress she had been hemming was still draped over the side of it, held there by the needle of the sewing machine. The spool of thread, which should have been perched on top of the machine, now dangled over the edge as well. Evelyn's hands had been tied in front of her with yards and yards of the black thread, all tangled and snarled about her wrists. Moving closer, Boyd realized that her hands and arms were bloody where the tightly bound thread had sliced into her skin in a dozen places. From her wrists, the matted thread had been looped around the arm of the sewing machine, holding the woman upright on the stool.

She was younger than her husband. No more than fifty, Boyd figured. Her waist was still trim, her hair neatly curled at the nape of her neck. Where her head had fallen backward, the tendons in her neck stretched taut. A paisley head scarf was wrapped so tightly around her throat that parts of it were buried in her flesh. A cheerful bow had been painstakingly tied in it at the side of her neck. A perfect bow, looking coquettish and perky and altogether out of place. Her eyes stared up at the ceiling, the mouth open in a silent scream. She had not died easily, the agony of it evident on her face. In the twisted mouth. The pain-haunted eyes.

She, too, was frozen. The white skin, like marble, contrasted with the black slip and taupe stockings she wore. She had obviously been preparing to go somewhere, into town or to the church perhaps, and was doing a last-minute repair job on the hem of her dress.

The only hint of color in her skin was on her legs, where the nylons had been shredded when the ankles and calves of both legs had also drawn the interest of the barn cats. Here, they had feasted well. Red meat had been stripped from white bone by claws and teeth.

Boyd made a quick check into every other room in the house but found nothing more out of the ordinary, thank God. All the horrors were centered in the living room.

He scanned the walls until he found the thermostat for the basement furnace. It was set to zero, turned off intentionally. Boyd decided to leave it that way. He didn't want Mr. and Mrs. Andros thawing out just yet.

He flipped off the light as he left the house and closed the front door behind him. If I do nothing else, he thought, I have to keep those goddamn cats out.

From his car, he radioed for a deputy to join him at the Andros farm with crime scene equipment and told the deputy to notify the coroner that two hearses would be needed.

While he waited, he climbed the fence at the side of the yard and quietly approached the old milk cow. He needn't have worried about her being jumpy. She came to him and stood stock-still as he squatted down and began to drain her bulging udders. The steaming milk shot into the snow at his feet, some of it already beginning to freeze even before he had finished.

At dawn of the following morning, after the crime scene had been gone over to Sheriff Lucas's satisfaction, and as the bodies were being removed from the house, he saw the barn cats again. He heard them actually. Heard them growling deep in their throats as they fought over those chunks of frozen milk lying in the snow. Just as they had no doubt fought over the meat inside the house.

He wondered what would happen to them now. Now that the master and mistress of the farm were no longer in residence. He found he didn't much care.

For these beasts, he felt no sympathy whatsoever. Let the damnable things starve.

SHERIFF Boyd Lucas put in a long distance call to Detective Smith of San Diego Homicide after guzzling two Red Bulls and a cup of day-old coffee he found languishing in the bottom of the Mr. Coffee machine in his office. He had been awake and active since the morning before and he needed a buzz. He got it. He was so wired by the time he picked up the phone that he could barely dial.

Detective Smith picked up on the second ring.

Boyd didn't bother with pleasantries. He wasn't in the mood. "What sort of case are you working on, Detective?"

"Murders," Smith answered, recognizing the Sheriff's Midwestern drawl.

"Duh. You're Homicide. I didn't figure it was hog rustling. How many murders?"

"Four."

"Make it six."

"You're joking."

"I don't joke."

"Mr. and Mrs. Andros?"

"Bingo."

"How?"

"You know, I *heard* you were Indian."

"Very funny. How did they die?"

"The man had a screwdriver poked into his ear and the woman was tied to her sewing machine and strangled."

"You're joking."

"I told you I don't joke."

"How long have they been dead?"

"Hard to say. They're still defrosting."

"Do I want to know why that is?"

"Probably not, but I'll tell you anyway."

Sheriff Lucas proceeded to relate what he had found at the farmhouse on the outskirts of Nine Mile, including the open door and the lack of heat inside the house which had resulted in the bodies being frozen like ice sculptures. He also told Smith about the mutilation by the barn cats.

"*Barn* cats? What the hell are *barn* cats?"

"You *are* a city boy."

"Actually, I grew up on a reservation."

"You didn't have cats?"

"Yeah. Mountain lions."

Boyd chuckled. "These are smaller. Regular size house cats, except they don't live in the house. They live in the barn. They're wild. Farmers use them to keep down the rodents."

"And they eat people?"

"They're scavengers. They eat pretty much anything that comes along that doesn't eat them first. Just like mountain lions, so I hear. But like I said, smaller."

"One of my victims was mutilated, too," Smith said conversationally, a happy lilt to his voice. Phony as hell.

"Gnawed on?"

"In a sense. He was nibbling on his own pecker which somebody had snipped off and stuck in his mouth."

"Jesus, I'm glad I don't work in the city."

"Yeah, we get it all. So, what's next?"

"We'll get the bodies thawed out enough to do an autopsy. Try to figure out when they died. But it's been a while. Maybe as long as a week or ten days. And there's another son I need to track down."

"There are two sons?"

"Yep. Two. The one you've got there, who I'm assuming is your suspect, and one who lives here."

"What's his name?"

"Jackson Andros."

"Do you know where to find him?"

"Yeah. He lives in a trailer over on Buck Creek Road. As soon as I go home and shower, I'll take a run out there. Can't raise him on the phone. He may be working."

"What does he do?"

"I don't have a clue."

"I want to talk to him."

"I figured."

Boyd cleared his throat, a little uncomfortable with what he was about to say.

"Tell me, Detective Smith. You got a tan?"

"Do I *what*?"

"Do you have a tan? I thought maybe you were lying on the beach right now working on a tan while I'm over here in four feet of snow, running down your leads."

"In the first place, Sheriff, unless they're partial to monsoons, *nobody* in California is lying on the beach today. It's pouring down rain here."

"A real frog strangler, huh?"

"That's quaint. Yeah, Pa, it's a real frog strangler. And in the second place, I don't need to get a tan. I'm a fucking Indian, remember?"

"Sorry. Forgot about that."

"And in the third place, you won't be running down my leads much longer. I'm flying into Indianapolis tomorrow morning at ten and would appreciate you arranging for someone to pick me up at the airport. I think I need to be there."

This wasn't exactly the direction Boyd had intended for the conversation to go. "I can handle it, you know."

"I know, Sheriff. This has nothing to do with your capabilities.

I'm sure you have all the admirable qualities of a fine county sheriff. I just need to see some things for myself. Won't stay long. Won't step on any toes. I just need to get some background on this Andros kid. I think he's being framed."

"You're shitting me."

"That's what my partner said."

"I'll bet he did."

"Anyway. Send someone to pick me up."

"Gotcha. You know, I've always sort of fancied myself a lone ranger kind of guy. Now I'll have my very own Tonto."

"Screw you, Sheriff."

IN INDIANA, the major highways were clear of snow, but the smaller byroads were still iffy. The cold was so intense it brought tears to Smith's eyes the moment he stepped outside the Indianapolis terminal. He had expected to be met by someone from the Greene County Sheriff Department, but instead he got Jesse, a tall, lanky youth of seventeen who turned out to be the Sheriff's son. The young man sirred Smith up one side and down the other as he took the detective's carry-on bag and tossed it in the back of a tan-colored Jeep Sahara. Jesse paid the attendant at the exit to the terminal parking lot, and in seconds they were on the freeway.

"Sorry, sir," Jesse was saying as he expertly merged onto the off-ramp that would take them south to Greene County. "Dad's pretty tied up with the murders and couldn't spare any of his men to pick you up, so I volunteered."

"I appreciate it, son. Thanks."

"My pleasure."

Smith liked the boy immediately. Obviously, a nice kid. And Smith liked him even more when he reached around to the back floorboard and hauled out a thermos of coffee and a bag of Wenchell's doughnuts.

"I figured you've been up most of the night, so I thought you might like some breakfast."

And the kid was exactly right. He was starving. He rooted around in the bag and pulled out a bear claw the size of home plate, wrapped it in a napkin and handed it to the boy, then grabbed another for himself. They settled into a companionable silence as they worked on their bear claws, the boy driving and Smith watching the countryside—which consisted mostly of stark leafless trees surrounding snow-blanketed fields—unfold.

At the moment, the sky was clear, giving Smith hope that maybe it wouldn't start snowing again. He'd hate to be stranded here, snowbound.

An hour later, they passed a sign that indicated they were entering Greene County. If he'd had a dollar for every cow they passed along the way, Smith figured he could retire. At one point, he was even shocked to see a herd of llamas. Now that was a surprise. Dining opportunities seemed to be limited to truck stops and fast-food franchises.

He really *would* hate to be stranded here. He might be American Indian, but he had developed a taste for sushi, and Greene County didn't exactly look to be a Mecca for sushi restaurants. In fact, it didn't look much like a Mecca for anything but grain elevators and silos. The silos reminded him of egg rolls, and that reminded him he hadn't seen any Chinese restaurants either.

How did these people live?

Smith dug beneath the layers of clothing he wore and hauled out his cell phone. He punched in some numbers. Two thousand miles away, McCray answered the call.

"Yo, black man. I'm here."

"How's the weather, Chief?"

"Don't ask. Anything new there?"

"Yeah. We found the kid's car parked by Macy's in Fashion Valley. Seems to have been abandoned. The steering wheel and door handles had been wiped clean so we didn't get any prints."

Smith considered this. "Why would the kid wipe his fingerprints off of his own car? We *know* who it belongs to."

McCray agreed. "I know. Think someone's helping him?"

"Maybe. But why would they?"

"Who knows?"

"Okay," Smith said. "Keep me posted. I'll try to be back by Wednesday."

"Thank God. I'm so lonely."

"Piss off."

As soon as Smith terminated the call, Jesse's cell phone rang.

The kid pressed it to his ear and said, "Hello?"

Then after a pause. "Okay, Dad. We'll meet you there. We're almost to Nine Mile now. Won't be long."

Jesse laid his phone on the dashboard and said, "Dad's at the trailer where Jackson Andros lives. Wants us to meet him there. He said to tell you not to expect any answers from the older brother."

"Why's that?"

"He didn't say."

Smith pondered this as the boy pulled off the main highway and proceeded to take him through a circuitous route of potholed back roads and unpaved lanes that left Smith lost in a matter of minutes. After a bone-jarring twenty minutes, they pulled into the driveway of a double-wide trailer parked on a hillside in a stand of bare and frozen oak trees. The place would probably be quite beautiful in the summer but looked sere and lifeless now in the dead of winter.

Two Ford Broncos with Greene County Sheriff insignias on their doors were parked at the side of the trailer. Behind them sat a black hearse from the Coroner's office.

"Shit," Smith muttered. "This can't be good."

As he stepped out of the Jeep, he told the boy, "You stay here, son. I imagine there are things in there that your father wouldn't want you to see."

Jesse looked disappointed, but nodded. "Yessir."

There are probably things in there that I don't want to see either, Smith thought, as he trudged through the snow to the small porch that had been built onto the front of the trailer.

HARRY paid the cab driver, awkwardly gathered up his shopping bags, and ran for the house, leaping puddles along the way. He used his keys to unlock the front door and found Sean sprawled on the floor beside the Christmas tree, now fully decorated and smothered in little white lights.

Sean jumped at the sound of the door opening, but quickly relaxed when he saw Harry shaking the rain off himself like a wet dog in the entryway.

"What are you doing?" Harry asked, moving into the room and rubbing the rain from his hair with a dish towel he had snagged from the kitchen counter.

"Bonding," Sean said.

Only then did Harry realize that Sean was reaching under the tree, petting, in turn, each and every one of Harry's cats, who were all hunkered down beneath the lowest limbs of the tree as if they had dredged up genetic memories from their long forgotten past and were envisioning themselves as wild forest beasts lying in wait for some unsuspecting prey to amble innocently along and provide them with a late-night snack. Harry could hear a combination of purrs and low growls, each of the cats, apparently, enjoying the imaginary hunt at different levels of seriousness.

"Everything all right?"

Sean rolled over onto his back, looked up at Harry and grinned. "I'm still alive."

"Good."

"I'm glad you're back."

"Me too."

"Does the tree look okay?"

"It's beautiful," Harry said. "And the cats seem to like it too."

Sean laughed. "I know. They're lying in wait. For what, I'm not sure."

Harry dropped the store bags on the floor beside the boy.

"I bought you some things. As much as I enjoy seeing you continually falling out of my pajamas, I thought you might be a little more comfortable in clothes that fit."

Sean started rummaging through the bags, hauling out sweatpants and a San Diego Chargers sweatshirt, which made him groan, some T's and two pair of drawstring pants that Harry thought might fit the boy.

"Wasn't too sure of your size. Extra small, I figured."

Sean continued to pull things out of the bags. Packs of underwear. Several pairs of white socks. A tube of strawberry flavored massage oil.

Sean looked up at Harry, one eyebrow arched and a lascivious leer in his eyes.

"Thought it might come in handy," Harry said.

"I'm sure it will."

Sean got to his feet and started stuffing everything back inside the shopping bags.

"Thanks, Harry. I appreciate the clothes."

"Don't you want to try them on?"

"Maybe later. Right now I kind of like being in your pajamas. We aren't going anywhere, are we?"

"No," Harry said. "We aren't going anywhere."

Sean opened the bottle of massage oil, sniffed it, and squeezed a drop onto his finger. He pressed the finger to Harry's lips.

"How does it taste?"

Harry took the boy's hand and pulled the finger into his mouth. He held it there for a moment, tasting the lotion.

"Just like strawberries," he said. "And you."

Sean smiled. He grabbed Harry's belt buckle and led him toward the bedroom. Harry had done so much for him, and all Sean had to repay him with was his youth. His body. It was a commodity he knew how to use. He could make Harry happy with it, and he could make Harry know he loved him. Harry might not honestly believe it yet, but he would in time. Sean would see to that.

WHILE his partner slogged through snowdrifts in Indiana, Detective Jefferson McCray had not been idle. His morning began, as most mornings did, with a quick perusal of the Union Tribune. A front page headline proclaiming "POLICE BAFFLED" did not set too well with him, to say the least. Considering some of their past cases that had left the Department with a less than exemplary reputation in the eyes of the average Joe on the street, he supposed that now the public would think they were assholing their way through another bungled investigation.

But he knew better. They were far from "baffled." A bit confused, perhaps, but never "baffled." They had leads, and they were working those leads as quickly as they could. What the press thought or printed was of little consequence to McCray. They were like wolves, always homing in on any perceived weakness in the herd. And if that weakness happened to be in the San Diego Police Department, McCray knew the press would eat it up with a spoon. They loved that shit. They lived for it. It sold papers, and that was, of course, their major goal. Truth be damned.

McCray took scissors from his desk drawer, snipped out the offending headline, and taped it to Smith's computer monitor. Smith had an even lower opinion of the *Trib* than McCray did, and McCray never missed an opportunity to set the Chief on the warpath. It was always good for a few chuckles.

More and more, McCray was thinking that Smith might be

correct in thinking Sean Andros was being framed. And just as it was with his partner, McCray couldn't really put his finger on why he felt that way. It wasn't a matter of evidence, certainly. More a gut feeling.

McCray must have watched the security tape from Cottage Liquor more than a dozen times that morning. When he finally gave it up and returned the tape to the evidence bag, he could only agree with his partner that this kid was not a killer. In fact, McCray could barely believe the kid was a hustler. Even in those few minutes on tape, while he paid for his purchases, McCray could sense an innocence about the young man that was totally contrary to the violence of the crimes.

But why would anyone want to set the kid up? What could he have done in his short life that would make someone want to bring him down like this, to pin these horrendous crimes on him? It couldn't be random. The killer had to know who the kid was. Had to know everything about him. Had to know he was meeting Mr. Baker. Had to know where the kid lived to plant the bomb-making evidence in his apartment, for McCray was certain now, just like Smith, that the evidence was planted. And just like his partner, he couldn't tell you why he felt that way. Not in so many words. It was just a hunch. But a strong one.

Now, also, after a thirty-minute records search, McCray knew that the kid had never purchased a firearm in his life, not through legal channels at least. Not in California. Not anywhere. The Magnum rounds found in the bodies of Jamison and Beers didn't just come out of the blue. But what bothered McCray most about the murder of the two detectives was the sheer pointlessness of it. *Why* were they killed? For what purpose? The only reason he could comprehend was simply to lay the blame, once again, on the kid. And only a fucking maniac would go to that extreme. A maniac with an agenda. And agendas, in the criminal world especially, always made McCray nervous. There were few things more dangerous than a lunatic with a mission.

Was it a vendetta against gays? Couldn't be. Only one of the victims was gay. Poor Stanley Baker. Just because the crimes were somehow centered around a gay street hustler did not mean the killings were directed at gays. It only meant they were executed in such a way as to direct the blame toward Andros.

And where *was* Andros? Did he know he was being targeted? He must. Why else would he have flown the coop? And where the hell did he go? Was he still hiding in the city, or was he long gone? Was he soaking up rays on some Mexican beach somewhere, or was he being protected by someone here in San Diego? And if he was being protected, who would take such a risk? They had done background checks on the kid and had found many acquaintances but not anyone you could actually call a true friend. Aside from his clients, the kid was pretty much a loner. And aside from peddling his ass for a living, he really didn't seem to be much more than a regular kid. Playing video games. Reading books on archeology. There had been dozens of each in his apartment. He rode his bike. He worked out on his Nautilus. He watered his house plants. He made his bed. Just a seemingly normal young man who looked more like a child than a man and who happened to be a prostitute. And who, by all the evidence they could unearth, appeared to be nothing but nice. There were no sinister undertones about him. No police record that would indicate a history of violent behavior. No police record at all. The kid didn't have so much as a jaywalking ticket on the books. And now, all of a sudden, he was mutilating faggots, planting bombs, and shooting policemen?

Nope. Smith was right. The kid was being framed. McCray had just convinced himself of that fact, and now he was faced with wondering what he should do about it? What *could* he do?

McCray felt sure the kid was hiding in the city. And to be hiding, he had to have an accomplice. Someone had dumped the car in Fashion Valley. And it hadn't been Andros. There would have been no reason for Andros to wipe prints from his own car. Someone had dumped the car for the boy. And that person knew that leaving his prints in the car would lead the police to him, and if the police found him, they would also find the boy.

But why had a bomb been planted on the Prado? Why were so many lives jeopardized? Was Andros supposed to have been there? Had the killer set up a meeting with the kid with the intent of murdering him there, and with a complete lack of concern for any others who might be killed or injured in the process? If that were the case, then the man who had planted the bomb truly was a maniac.

They had to find the boy, that much was obvious, if for no other reason than to protect him. McCray had tried the kid's cell phone number the day before with no result. It no longer worked.

It was time for some old-fashioned footwork. McCray had to hit the bars. The gay bars. There were almost thirty gay bars in the San Diego area. And the kid would certainly be known in at least one of them.

At two o'clock in the afternoon, McCray cranked up his Chrysler 300F and set off. A third storm in as many days was lashing the California coast, the rain so intense that driving was almost impossible. But McCray, intent on making some headway into the investigation while Smith was gone, stubbornly ignored the weather and began the task he had set for himself, to interview every bartender in every gay bar in the city, if need be, until he got a lead on where Andros might be hiding. Somebody knew something, of that he was certain. Somebody always did.

Two-and-a-half hours later, he was soaking wet, pissed off at the lack of results, but determined to persevere. He had been to eight bars, and unless his luck changed, he would have to visit more than twenty more before the night ended. He was certain this was still the fastest way to track down Andros. It had to be. The hustler could have gone into any one of these bars after leaving Brittany Towers that night. For a calming drink. To pick up more business. Who knew for what reason? But if he had, then this was the time to check. It was only forty-eight hours after the fact, and it was likely that the same bartenders would be on duty as were on two nights before. They might remember the boy. He was a good-looking kid. He figured the gay bartenders would remember him quite well.

Indeed, two bartenders he had already spoken to recognized Andros from his BMV photo. But neither had seen him on the night in question or any time since.

The Cailiff was next on McCray's list of bars. It catered to an older crowd, he knew. But maybe that was a good thing. The kid was a hustler, after all. Most of his clientele would probably be older men. Looking at it that way, he probably should have visited this bar first.

Also, it was located closest to Brittany Towers. Only a couple of blocks away. Duh.

Two minutes into his interview with the pony-tailed bartender with the hoop earrings and suede vest, he knew he was right. The bartender's name was Jonah. He eyed McCray's six-foot-four frame with an undisguised lust that simultaneously set McCray's teeth on edge and amused him. Jonah was a likeable enough guy, as long as he didn't try to grab McCray's crotch or make too overt a pass, McCray figured he could put up with him. Of course, as soon as the detective flashed his badge, poor Jonah deflated a bit and answered McCray's questions with a minimum of suggestive references to his physique. Although McCray did still catch him eyeing his crotch once in a while, it was with a look of resigned forbearance that didn't bother McCray at all. Everybody to their own bag. No pun intended. What other people did, didn't really bother him, so long as they weren't doing it to him. And they weren't doing it with deadly weapons.

"You're sure he was in here that night?"

"Dead sure."

"Early in the evening?"

"Yep. Sitting right about where you're sitting now."

"Was he alone?"

"He was when he came in. But kids as cute as that one don't stay alone long, if you know what I mean."

McCray sighed. The bartender's eyes were roving over his body again. "Yeah, I know what you mean. So how long was he here?"

Jonah shrugged. "I don't know exactly. It was pretty busy. Happy hour, you know. I was running my tits off. But he wasn't here long. Maybe thirty minutes tops."

"Did you see him leave?"

"Naw, I just turned around and he was gone. Him and the guy he was sitting with. Harry."

"Do you know Harry's last name?"

Jonah eyed the handsome black man before him, weighing his

options, considering just how far he wanted to go to help him. Not quite all the way, he decided. There were other factors to consider.

Jonah had been a bartender for twenty years, and for twenty years he had kept his customer's secrets. He was good at keeping secrets. He had been HIV positive for the past eight years, and that secret he had also kept. He carried his positive status with a profound sense of responsibility. His sex life now consisted of little more than flirting, which was pretty much required by the job anyway. Customers always got the hots for their bartender, just as patients did for their doctors. Keep them interested and they keep ordering drinks. But Jonah never let the flirting move on to the next level. Not anymore. Not since that doctor visit eight years ago, which had changed his life forever. But he could still look and he looked with alacrity.

This cop was a good-looking hunk of manhood all right, and he probably sported a nice-sized cock. Jonah had enjoyed putting the guy a bit off balance by flirting with him. But he was still a cop, and Jonah had had enough run-ins with the law in his younger years not to let that impress him too much.

He knew Harry's last name as well as he knew his own. But Harry was a good customer and a damn good tipper, and HIV meds were expensive. He wasn't about to risk losing Harry's business for this cop who, if he didn't need information, wouldn't be giving Jonah the time of day.

"Nope," he lied. "I don't know his last name. He don't come in that often."

What a joke. Harry came in four or five times a week. But this guy didn't need to know that either. Maybe he'd give Harry a little surprise present, seeing as how he was such a good customer and it was almost Christmas and all, and send this guy off into a different direction of pursuit.

He leaned across the bar conspiratorially, close enough to smell the detective's cologne, which made his pecker tingle, and said, "I think I'd be more interested in the other guy, if I were you."

McCray, who was stashing the photo of Andros back in his shirt pocket, looked up sharply.

"What other guy is that?"

"The blond guy. The one who came in asking about the kid as soon as he left."

"Somebody was asking about Andros?"

"Yeah. Called him Sean. Wanted to know who he left with."

"And what did you tell him?"

"Same thing I told you. He left with Harry."

McCray considered this new information. A slight quickening of his pulse told him he was finally onto something.

"Tell me what he looked like."

"Good-looking. Tall. Maybe not as tall as you, but tall. Well built but on the thin side. Nice ass. But that's probably more than you want to know."

"What else?"

"Blond hair. Thinning. Or at least I think it was thinning. It was wet so it's kind of hard to say. The guy had really light skin, like he could use a few hours under a sunlamp."

"How long did you talk to him?"

"Not long. Couple of minutes. The guy was a little intense. Spooky, almost. And I don't think he was gay. I can spot 'em, you know."

He gave McCray a little flick of the eyebrow, as if to say, "And what's your story?"

McCray ignored him.

"What makes you say he was intense? Spooky?"

Jonah thought back to that night. "Well… like I said, he was wet. All wet. Like he'd been standing out in the rain a while. And he was all keyed up. This was not a mellow sort of guy. Looked a little too bright-eyed, if you know what I mean. Like maybe he was on drugs or something. But I don't think that was it, really. I think he was just, you know, keyed up about something. On an adrenaline high. Said he was one of the kid's customers and the kid had left something at his house, but I could tell he was lying. Don't ask me how. I just knew."

McCray studied the bartender's face as if wondering whether the man was pulling his leg or not. He decided to trust him.

"If I should find a picture of this guy, do you think you would recognize him again?"

"Oh, yeah. No doubt about it." And Jonah meant it. He would recognize the guy in a line-up of fifty people. The guy was way too scary and way too sexy to be forgotten.

McCray got Jonah's home phone and address and promised to call him in a couple of days if a picture of the man should be forthcoming.

Jonah said that would be fine. As the detective left the Cailiff, Jonah hoped he hadn't opened himself up to a barrel of grief, like a court appearance or something. He didn't need that shit. Everyday life was hassle enough. Good-looking cop, though, Jonah thought, with more than a twinge of regret.

HE HAD paid for his room at the Grant with cash. Four days in advance. Almost four hundred bucks. He still had a day to go, but the pale man knew it was time to move on to different digs. Some place a little less conspicuous.

As he returned to the hotel that morning, after breakfasting at a greasy spoon on the wrong side of Broadway, he had overheard a policeman asking questions of the woman at the front desk. Questions concerning rooms that faced Broadway. No doubt it had something to do with that unfortunate incident a couple of days ago when the poor little Mexican child had ended up dead in the street, squashed flat like a day-old burrito. The pale man knew the mother of that child had seen him standing at the window. She had been looking right at him as he squeezed the last drops of semen from his cock and flung them in her direction. Seemed like a good idea at the time.

He chuckled to himself as he gathered up his stuff from the bathroom, dropped it all into his shaving kit, and then tossed the kit into the suitcase on the bed. The way the pregnant señora had keeled over, like a breaching whale falling back into the sea, at the sight of her little niño lying dead in the street, he'd thought that maybe she wouldn't remember. But apparently she had.

Oh, well, it was time to move on anyway.

He had seen a hotel, if you wanted to call it that, on Market Street that morning. It would suit his purpose nicely, thank you very much. He would be lost to prying eyes amid the swirl of scum that no doubt resided in the place, and that would *exactly* suit his purpose. If it was filthy and infested with roaches, and he had no doubt it was, then so be it. Mustn't be prissy in times of trial.

It was time to finish his mission and move on to bigger and better things. The whore had apparently disconnected his cell phone, but he now knew where the whore was, and he knew who was sheltering him. Harry the hairdresser was in for a big surprise. He would teach him that some things were meant to be left alone. His prey in particular. Never come between a hunter and his prey. Rule number one.

Rule number two? Always try to die like a man. He would give Harry that opportunity and see how he measured up. Unless he was sorely mistaken, he didn't think Harry would measure up very well at all. And as for the kid? He already knew the fears that lurked in that mind. Knew them well. Had, indeed, planted many of them there himself. The smile of anticipation died from his lips as he recalled a night long ago, and as always, he tried to block that memory from his mind. But it kept returning. It had taken him years to finally realize there was only one way to kill that memory forever. To kill the guilt. To erase the sin. It had festered in his mind too long. It was time to cleanse the wound.

He left the "Do Not Disturb" sign hanging from the doorknob and didn't bother checking out with the front desk. They would know he was gone soon enough. But he knew they would do nothing. His bill was paid.

And he always paid his bills. Always settled his debts. After all, why else was he here, so many miles from home, if not to settle debts?

To pay the piper, so to speak.

He didn't bother hailing a cab. The Stevens Hotel was only a few blocks away, and it was a beautiful morning. Later, he knew, the night would be stormy and wild, but right now, it was pleasant enough.

A nice morning for a stroll.

THE balding clerk at the front desk of the Stevens Hotel, with patches of dry skin sprinkled across his scalp like dirty snow, welcomed the new arrival less than enthusiastically, just as he did everything else. The clerk filled out the required paperwork for a check-in by asking questions. He didn't bother verifying any of the information given him, and he didn't ask for a credit card.

The pale man paid for a week in advance with cash, the only way this establishment did business, apparently, and signed a swirl of gibberish that was supposed to be his signature in a logbook the clerk had pushed toward him. He signed with a flourish that amused himself but seemed to impress the clerk not a whit. When the pale man had finished scribbling, the clerk spun the logbook around on the counter and looked at it, then he spun it 180 degrees and looked at it upside down.

"Umm, my eyes ain't what they used to be. What am I supposed to call you?"

"Sir."

"Gotcha." He tossed the logbook beneath the counter and turned to retrieve a room key from a wall of hooks behind him. He handed the key to the man and said by rote, "No visitors after ten o'clock. Vending machines are in the basement. No phones in the rooms, so you'll have to use the pay phone over there in the corner of the lobby if you want to make an outside call. And keep it quiet. We have respectable people here."

The pale man smiled. "Oh, I'm sure you do. You won't hear a peep from me."

He didn't bother waiting for a bellhop—only a fool would think they had one—but set off with his suitcase in hand to find his room. He headed for a dilapidated elevator with a folding grill across the front of it. Before he reached it, the clerk yelled out behind him.

"The elevator's temporarily out of order. You'll have to use the stairs."

The clerk smiled to himself. He loved saying that to the new arrivals. And he always waited until they were halfway across the lobby before he did so. Temporarily out of order, my ass, he thought. The elevator hadn't worked for two years.

The man looked at his room key. 314. Third floor.

"No problem!" he yelled back over his shoulder as he veered toward a stairway. "I love to walk."

"Yeah, whatever," the clerk mumbled. He reached beneath the counter and hauled out a grimy porno magazine he had borrowed from one of the rooms when he knew the tenant, a real character study in himself, was out of the hotel. On the magazine's cover was a picture of two fat black broads and a white dwarf with stringy red hair and a boner doing the nasty. Piled one on top the other, they looked like a sweaty Oreo cookie. You had to laugh. The dwarf, stuck in the middle, looked like he could barely breathe, much less hump. Respectable boner, though. For a dwarf.

The clerk tore his eyes away from the magazine long enough to watch the new arrival disappear up the staircase. That was pretty nice luggage the man was carrying. Might be worth his while to keep an eye on the guy, and when he was sure he would be out of the hotel for a spell, sneak up to his room and take a gander inside the suitcase. You never knew what you might find if you took the trouble to look. He sure couldn't live on tips in this dump, since tips were damn near nonexistent.

The pale man found his room at the end of a dark and dingy hallway on the third floor that smelled like piss and greasy hot-plate cooking. It was right next to the fire escape. Before checking out his room, he stepped out onto the fire escape and looked down. It ended with a retractable ladder that dropped to an alley behind the hotel. He liked that. Could come in handy. A person never knew when they might need an escape route. Or a way to get back in without being seen.

When he finally entered his room, he wasn't disappointed. He had expected a hole and that's what he got. A week in this place had cost him only a few dollars more than a *day* at the Grant. But he wasn't paying for amenities, after all. He was paying for anonymity. And he figured this shithole was about as anonymous as it gets. A perfect place to disappear. At least for a while.

He checked his suitcase, made sure it was locked, and slid it under the dingy-looking bed. Then he left the room, relocking the door behind him and stuffing the key in his pocket.

He gave the clerk at the front desk an ingratiating smile and a little finger wiggle of farewell as he left the hotel, whistling. The clerk, startled, tossed the porno rag under the desk and watched the man go out the door.

Back on the street, the man looked around for the nearest drugstore and spotted a Rite Aid one block up across the trolley tracks. He needed a few things for the room. A can of Lysol, a can of Raid, and a can of air freshener.

After making his purchases, he spotted a pay phone on the street corner. One more thing to do. He hadn't had a haircut in a while. Thought he might be needing a trim. Rumor had it that Harry's for Hair was a fine tonsorial establishment. The pale man thought he might give it a try. Just for the heck of it.

He found the number in the damp phone book that hung from a filthy chain below the phone and dialed the number.

"Harry's for Hair. Stella speaking."

"Hello, Stella. What are my chances of getting a haircut with Harry today?"

"Oh, I'm sorry, sir. Harry's out for a few days. Could I book you with someone else?"

The man wasn't surprised to learn that Harry wasn't in. A little too busy with private matters right now was poor old Harry.

"I guess that would be all right. But it has to be a late appointment. As late as you've got."

A short pause, and then, "Kimo can take you at 9:00 p.m. Would that be okay with you?"

"That would be fine."

"We'll see you then, sir. Have a nice day."

"And you have a nice day, too, Stella."

"Oh, sir, wait. Can I get your name?"

He hung up the phone as if he hadn't heard her, picked up his bag from Rite Aid, and began a leisurely stroll back to the hotel.

Idly, he wondered what one was expected to tip a California hairstylist. Seeing as how the proprietor was a particular friend of his, he thought he might have a few ideas on what would be appropriate.

CHAPTER EIGHT

THE body of Jackson Andros, or what little was left of it, lay half buried in a pile of burnt timbers and other assorted junk in the backyard of the double-wide trailer on Buck Creek Road. What had apparently once been a small tool shed had gone up in smoke with Mr. Andros inside. He had been handcuffed to a wall at the time of the fire, so accidental death pretty well ruled itself out, or so Sheriff Lucas informed Detective Smith as they both stood off to the side in six inches of snow looking down at the blackened mess. They were flanked by Boyd's two deputies, Carter and Lawson.

"Left him in situ for you," Lucas said.

Smith stared at a charbroiled forearm poking up from the ashes, the handcuff still holding it in place against a wooden corner beam that had not burned all the way through.

"So I see," Smith said. "This happened a while back, didn't it, Sheriff?" He was referring to the dusting of snow over the top of a blackened power mower that had been parked in the shed at the time of the fire. "When was the last time it snowed?"

"It's been snowing off and on for weeks. But I figure it would have taken this fire a couple of days to cool down enough not to melt any new snow that landed on it."

"And no one reported the fire?"

The Sheriff pointed to the tall trees surrounding the lot. "Naw. Smoke pretty much disappears in a snowy sky. You know that. Or maybe you don't. But anyway, we're out in the middle of nowhere here. The closest house is half a mile away. And people burn trash all the time in these parts. Even if someone had seen the smoke, they might not have thought anything about it."

Smith leaned closer to the body. There was a ring on the second finger of the blackened hand that had been cuffed to the wall. What sort of ring it was, was anybody's guess. It was misshapen from the heat and seemed to have sunk into the flesh it once rested on, fused with the black residue that had once been skin. Smith was sorry now that he had eaten that humungous bear claw. If he should toss it up in front of this Hoosier sheriff, he knew he would never hear the end of it.

"Looks like somebody's got it in for your suspect, Detective. His whole family's been wiped out. Are you sure he didn't do it himself? Has he traveled lately? Like in an easterly direction?"

Smith tried to shrug but it turned into a tremble. He was freezing to death. "We can't be sure. There were no records of any flights with his name on the manifest, but he might have traveled on an assumed."

"That's unlikely, with the political climate the way it is. You have to do everything but give a sperm sample to fly these days. There are other modes of transportation, however. I don't know what your timeline looks like back there with the other crimes you're investigating, but *could* he have been here a week or ten days ago and got back to San Diego in time to do whatever it is he's supposed to have done?"

Smith shook his head. "Anything's possible, but I still don't believe it. Not after seeing him. It's not like he's a career criminal or a professional hit man. Sean Andros is a kid. A hustler."

"You mean a pool hustler?"

"No, Sheriff. The other kind. Of the gay variety."

Carter interjected himself into the conversation.

"A wienie wolfer, huh?"

Smith eyed Deputy Carter, who must have weighed in at close to three hundred pounds but had the happy, honest face of an inquisitive, but obese, ten-year-old.

"That's wight, Deputy," Smith said. "A wienie wolfer who works for wages."

Deputy Lawson, weighing all of 140 pounds and looking like he was no more than one missed meal away from starvation, chimed in with, "That's iwwegal."

Carter nodded sagely, fingering an imaginary goatee, "Wight as wain, wabbit."

Sheriff Lucas rested a hand on his gun butt.

"If you two idiots don't shut the fuck up, I'm going to shoot you both right here in front of God and everybody. Go find the coroner and tell him he can have the body now."

Crestfallen, the two deputies trudged off through the snow in search of the coroner who was waiting inside the trailer in an attempt to avoid frostbite as the lawmen chewed everything over in the interminable way always did. He wished that, just once, they would call him only after the chewing was over, but that never seemed to happen.

The Sheriff kicked his foot in the snow. "Jesus, those two. Like having Stan and Ollie on the force."

Smith laughed. "Don't worry about it, Sheriff. My partner and I have done a few comedy routines in our time. Sometimes you have to or the gore and the horror just gets to be overwhelming."

The Sheriff looked again at the charred hand poking up from the ashes. "You're probably more used to this shit than I am, Detective. We don't get much violent crime out here. I've found three murdered bodies in the last two days, and I've got to tell you, it's taken my breath away. And you're right, those two deputies are just as wrung out about it as I am. Joking around is their only means of coping, I guess. Their way of fighting back."

"That's why humor's a good thing, Sheriff. Let them use it. Might help them keep their sanity."

They both stood silently for a moment, lost in their own private thoughts as they stared at the charbroiled hand. Smith stomped his feet a couple of times to ward off the cold.

"Sheriff, I'd like the coroner to do a DNA test on this body."

"That could take a while, you know. A few weeks, probably. And it's expensive. Is it that important to you?"

"Yeah, it might be. I just want to be sure that's Jackson Andros laying there. Circumstantially, it's him, I know. But we can't absolutely confirm it without DNA. All right?"

The Sheriff conceded. "You're the expert on murder, Detective. I'm more used to chasing speeders and refereeing marital squabbles. Whatever you say, we'll do."

"Thanks. Now, I'd like to get in out of this cold before my nuts snap off and go rolling down my pantleg. Show me the trailer. Let's see if we can learn anything about my boy in San Diego. The wienie wolfer."

As they headed toward the trailer Smith asked, "Did you know them, Sheriff?"

"The two sons? Sorry, no. Not really. But I might be able to track down a few people who did. I know where Jackson went to church. That oughta help."

They met the coroner coming out of the trailer as they went in.

"Thanks for waiting, Bill," Sheriff Lucas said, patting him on the shoulder. "We want samples sent to Terre Haute for DNA testing and ask them if they can rush it."

"Like that's gonna happen."

"I know. But ask them anyway."

"Will do."

"And take care handling those cuffs and the ring on the right hand," Smith said. "I'll be by your office later to look at them."

The coroner rolled his eyes. "Gee, it'll be an honor."

Smith chose to ignore the sarcasm. "Have a nice day."

"Oh, yeah."

As the coroner walked away shaking his head, Sheriff Lucas said,

"We may be in the asshole of the world, Detective Smith, but we know a few things about evidence."

"Sorry," Smith replied. "Didn't mean to be pushy or step on any toes."

"That's all right, son. Just lighten up a little. We'll give you all the help you need. We only seem inept. Actually, we're pretty good."

Smith laughed. He liked this guy, although he'd probably never ask the coroner to dinner.

"Does that include your deputies?"

"Well, I wouldn't go that far."

The back door of the trailer led into the kitchen. Entering, Smith felt like he had suddenly stepped back into the eighties. Avocado refrigerator. Avocado range. Avocado dishwasher. Even a yellow Happy Face throw rug in front of the sink. Aside from the bile-inducing color scheme, everything looked neat and pristine. The guy obviously kept a clean house. Just like his brother. This one simple fact told Jimmy Smith a lot about how the boys were raised.

As they walked down a narrow hallway carpeted in Harvest Gold, Smith gave perfunctory glances into two bedrooms and a bathroom before entering the living room. Here he stopped short.

"You say this guy attended church, Sheriff? Why am I not surprised?"

Every picture on every wall, and there were many of them, were all of a religious nature. Jesus in Gethsemane. Jesus feeding the masses. Jesus on the cross. Jesus rolling the stone away from the door of his tomb. Jesus ascending into the sky on beams of light. A Bible that must have weighed thirty pounds rested on a cheap oak veneer coffee table. A nativity scene of Wal-Mart-grade crystal was arranged atop the console TV. A cotton throw, meant to warm old legs on cold evenings and sold in every cheap mail order catalog that came down the pike, was thumbtacked to the wall behind the sofa. It showed the Virgin Mary extending a baby Jesus in her arms like a woman presenting a ten-pound ham to a needy neighbor on Easter morning.

"Devout fucker," Sheriff Lucas stated to no one in particular.

Smith nodded. "Or crazy."

The Sheriff agreed. "I suppose that could be an option. Kind of hard to parlay religious fervor into serial murder, though."

"Not that hard."

"Well, maybe not. I guess it's been done before."

"Oh, yeah."

Smith flipped the heavy Bible closed, then reopened it to the flyleaf. Sure enough, a family tree of the Andros family was outlined there, going back to Jackson Andros's great-great-grand-parents, who had migrated to America from Norway, according to the footnote. Smith did not overlook the fact that beneath Evelyn and Walter Andros, dead now and lying in the morgue, only one son was listed as progeny. Jackson Andros, who was en route to join his parents right now, was an only son, if the writing in the Bible was to be believed. Why was Sean Andros not listed beside his brother? Had he been disowned by his family, perhaps because of his lifestyle? He doubted if homosexuality was quite as accepted here in the corn belt as it was in the cities, but was it enough to have the kid plucked from the family tree like a piece of bad fruit, another pun not intended? Or was it only the brother who felt this way? Smith would have to see the parent's farmhouse next. Maybe he could learn more there.

He had a thought and began searching like a man with a purpose.

"Help me, Sheriff. I'd like to see some family photos. Maybe there's an album somewhere."

Sheriff Lucas glanced around the room as if suddenly struck by an oddity. Of all the pictures in the room, not one was of a living human being. Jesus looked down at him from every angle, but that was it. No studio shots from Sears of happy people posing proudly. No school pictures of impish children or graduation ceremonies. No treasured moments of coworkers captured on film, arms slung across each other's shoulders, beaming happily into the camera with self-conscious camaraderie. No people. No actual people.

"Well, I'll be," he muttered, wondering why he had not noticed what had so immediately struck the detective as strange. He began searching alongside Smith. For twenty minutes they probed every drawer, every bookcase, every conceivable place where photographs might be stored, and came up with nothing. Finally, they gave up the search. Not one snapshot had been found.

Sheriff Lucas didn't quite know what to make of it.

"That's damned odd, isn't it?"

While searching, Detective Smith had found the thermostat for the trailer's electric heater and turned it from OFF to eighty. By the end of their search for photographs, the trailer was beginning to warm up, praise Allah. Smith had only been in Indiana for a little over two hours, and he was already sick and tired of being cold. He sucked in the warm air from the wall heater like a fish sucks in water.

"That's better."

"Find something?" the Sheriff asked.

"Oh. No. Just enjoying the heat."

Boyd thought about that for a moment. "Seems a little strange, doesn't it? That someone would murder Andros by setting the poor bastard on fire, and then be polite enough to turn off the heat before he left to save on the power bill?"

Smith stepped even closer to the heater, happily rubbing his hands together. "There are a lot of strange things about this case. Strange things in San Diego. Strange things here. Strange that Andros, the older one, wouldn't have any family photos. No pictures of his parents, even."

Not for the first time, Smith studied the Gateway computer that sat on the bar between the kitchen and the dining area of the mobile home. He moved to it, clicked it on, and watched the sign on message from AOL post itself across the screen. The guy was hooked up to the Internet, unlike his younger brother, who only used his computer for games.

"I'll need somebody to access this computer, Sheriff. Somebody who knows what they're doing. Have them check for a recent visit to a website called Anarchist International. See if this computer downloaded instructions on the making of a pipe bomb."

"All right."

"Also have them check for any visits to travel websites. Especially airline bookings."

"I'll get Judy in here from the office. She can do just about everything with a computer except fuck it."

"Good. And let's search this place one more time. We're looking for evidence of the purchase of weapons, or recent travel, or sudden withdrawals of money from Andros's bank account, or anything else that strikes you as out of the ordinary. And where is this guy's automobile? It wasn't in the driveway."

"Maybe the killer drove off in it."

"Maybe so. But just in case, have one of your deputies put in a call to Indianapolis Airport Security and have them check long-term parking for whatever this guy's automobile happens to be. Okay?"

"Sure. Right away. I get the impression you're pretty well convinced that the poor chap who got barbecued in the back yard isn't Jackson Andros."

Smith continued rubbing his hands together in front of the heater, all but purring with the pleasure of it.

"We'll see what we see, Sheriff. But, yeah, I've got my doubts."

"So tell me then, Detective. If that isn't Jackson Andros out back, just who the hell is it?"

"I don't have the vaguest idea."

"Hmm. Okay." Sheriff Lucas was beginning to look a little skeptical at this citified detective who seemed to have more questions than he had answers. But obviously the guy wasn't sharing everything he knew.

"Anything else you need?"

"Well, Sheriff, if you have no other plans for the evening, I'd like to see the farmhouse where the parents lived. And died. And also, I think we should resurrect your son from his Jeep out front. He's probably frozen solid by now."

Boyd pushed his khaki hat far back on his head and rubbed his scalp as if attempting to stir up his memory.

"Jesus, I forgot all about him."

"So did I. Send the poor kid home, and let's you and me take a run out to the farmhouse. That is, unless you have opera tickets or something."

The Sheriff laughed. "Ballet. But I'll cancel 'em. Let's go."

HARRY lay nude on the bed. Sean was doing something in the kitchen, rattling pans and opening and closing cupboard doors. The bedroom smelled of strawberries. Harry could still feel the massage oil seeping into his muscles, relaxing him, as he lay on his stomach listening to all the sounds around him. The storm outside his bedroom window had reached a level of fury that Harry had never witnessed in San Diego before. This had to be the mother of all storms. For the first time, Harry felt a sense of unease concerning the house, perched as it was on the edge of the cliff. There had been mudslides all over the county due to the unprecedented amount of rain that had fallen in the past three days. The backcountry, where summer brushfires had seared the landscape and left it unprotected by ground cover, had fared the worst. Several homes had already been lost. Many roads were closed, inundated with water. Fashion Valley, where Harry had dumped Sean's car, was now sealed off by flooded streets. He had made it there in the nick of time. A few hours later and he would have been forced to abandon the car somewhere else.

Harry was startled by the ringing of the telephone on his nightstand. He looked at the digital clock beside the phone. It was two a.m. Jesus. Who would be calling at this hour?

Sean was suddenly standing in the bedroom door, barefoot and shirtless, but wearing a pair of the sweat pants Harry had picked up for him at Macy's. He had a big wooden spoon in his hand.

Harry turned on the bedside light and gazed at him. The boy looked scared.

"Don't answer it," Sean said. "It's him."

Harry swung his legs out of bed and reached for his T-shirt and jeans that lay on the floor. He began pulling them on.

The phone continued to ring.

"You don't know that," he said.

Sean took a step closer. "Yes, I do. Don't answer it."

Even if it was him, Harry figured they'd better listen to what the man had to say. They had been in limbo for hours, just waiting for the guy to make his next move. Maybe this was it.

Harry needed to know what they were dealing with.

He picked up the receiver and pressed it to his ear.

"Hello?"

"Harry, is that you?"

Everything in Harry's body seemed to liquefy at the relief he felt on hearing the familiar voice.

"Jonah?"

"Yeah. Is the boy still with you?"

"Wh-what boy?"

"Don't give me that crap, Harry. Sean. The little hustler. Is he still with you?"

"Look, Jonah, I don't know what—"

"Can it, Harry. The cops were here asking about him. They know he left with you."

"When?" Harry asked. "When were they there?"

"A few hours ago."

"You told them?"

"No. I only told them the kid left with someone named Harry. I didn't give them your last name. It took me a while to figure out that maybe I should warn you. Are you all right?"

Sean crossed the bedroom and sat at Harry's side, leaning close, trying to hear what was being said on the other end of the line.

"I'm fine, Jonah. But I don't know what you're talking about. The kid and I might have left the bar at the same time but we went our separate ways after that. I haven't seen him since."

Jonah didn't sound convinced. "Whatever you say. But I think you should know that the big black cop with the real healthy-looking basket isn't the only one who's been asking about the kid. There was a blond guy in the bar not ten minutes after you left looking for him too. The guy looked like trouble to me, Harry. I think you should watch your back."

"What do you mean... trouble?"

"Just trouble. I don't know. He said he was the kid's last client and that Sean had left something at his house that he'd like to return to him. You know anything about that?"

Harry knew enough about it to know that the man had been lying. Sean's last client was dead. But he saw no reason to share that information with Jonah. The bartender might have gotten himself in a bind with the law already, withholding what he knew from the police. If he learned that Sean was wanted for murder, the gravity of the situation might scare him into answering questions more truthfully the *next* time cops came calling.

"No," Harry said. "I don't know anything about anything. Did the policeman say what he wanted with the boy?"

"Not exactly. But the guy was a homicide detective. How good could it be?"

"What did you tell the blond man?"

"More than I told the cops, I'm afraid. The guy caught me off guard. And he talked to Biff for a few minutes. God knows what Biff might have told him."

"Shit."

"Yeah. Shit. So watch yourself, Harry. I don't know what's going on with you and Sean, but there are a lot of people looking for him. The kid has obviously pissed off somebody. Don't let yourself get dragged down with him."

"He hasn't done anything."

"Well… maybe not. But watch your back. The cop said he might come back with a photo of the blond guy. If he does, I'll have to identify him. You know that, right? I can't be lying to the cops. Not any more than I have already."

"I know, Jonah. Thanks. Next time I see you I'll make it right with you."

"I didn't do it for money, Harry."

"I know."

"But you've always been generous with me at the bar. Most of the time these old queens, by the time they stagger out, they're too drunk to remember a tip for the poor old nellie bartender. But not you, Harry. Thought maybe this was the least I could do to return the favor."

"Okay, Jonah. I appreciate it. And you do what you have to do where the police are concerned. But I hope you don't do it too quickly. The kid and I need time to think."

"I thought you said he wasn't with you."

"Well, you know. In case I see him."

Jonah chuckled. "Right, Harry. Amazing what we do for love, isn't it?"

"Amazing," Harry repeated, as he slowly replaced the phone on its cradle. He turned to look at Sean beside him. "Amazing, indeed."

"They've traced me to you, haven't they?" Sean asked.

Harry shook his head. "Not quite. Thanks to my inexplicable penchant for overtipping, we're safe for a while. From the police, anyway. We might not be so lucky with the killer, though."

"He talked to the bartender? The guy who killed Stanley talked to the bartender?"

"Yes. I assume it was him. Right after we left. Some blond guy. Ring a bell?"

Sean absentmindedly licked the wooden spoon he still held in his hand. He had apparently been making fudge.

"I know lots of blond guys, but none that would want to kill me."

"Sorry, Sean, but I think you may be mistaken about that."

He took the wooden spoon from the boy's hand and gave it a lick himself. "Needs more sugar," he said.

They sat in silence for a few moments, each thinking his separate thoughts.

At last, Harry said, "Where's the gun?"

Sean blinked. "On top of the desk where you left it."

"Bring it here."

Sean gave Harry an enquiring look, then heaved himself up off the bed and went to fetch the gun. He returned, holding the revolver out to his side like someone carrying roadkill from the highway. He handed it to Harry.

Harry opened the chamber, checked that it was loaded, then clicked the chamber closed. He patted the bed beside him.

"Sit down."

Sean sat.

"Do you know how to fire a revolver? How to load it? How to handle it?"

"I think so."

"Thinking isn't good enough. Let me show you."

Sean eyed the gun nervously, then looked into Harry's face.

"Why? Are you going somewhere?"

"No," Harry said, giving the boy a reassuring smile. "But who knows what's going to happen? I want you to be able to protect yourself. If somehow I'm taken out of the picture, you'll be on your own. And I don't want anything to happen to you."

"I don't want anything to happen to you, either."

"Good. Then listen and learn."

JIMMY SMITH stood under the steaming shower for fifteen minutes, hoping the hot water would permeate into his bones and linger there long enough to get him through another day of Indiana winter. He wasn't used to this crap. He hadn't had one sexual thought since he stepped outside the Indianapolis terminal the day before. It was just too cold. How did these people procreate? Did they wait for spring? Were their gonads acclimated to the minus degree temperatures? Did their sperm cells don little overcoats and earmuffs, like those morons at the circus who truss themselves up in protective gear before being shot from a cannon?

Was the steam making him hallucinate?

Reluctantly, he stepped out of the shower and dressed. Sheriff Lucas said someone would pick him up at 7:00 a.m. Most likely either Stan or Ollie, one of his two likeable but inept deputies.

It turned out once again to be Jesse, the Sheriff's son, who beeped his horn as he pulled into the motel parking lot in his Jeep Sahara at seven o'clock on the button.

As Smith jogged to the Jeep, he was less than thrilled to find that the morning was actually colder than the night before. He leaped into the Jeep like a Titanic passenger procuring a life boat.

Jesse looked all chipper and alert. A red knit ski cap was pulled down low over his ears, and his hands were encased in bright red mittens.

"Good morning, sir."

"Morning, son. I hope they've put you on the payroll."

Jesse blushed, making his face match his cap. "Naw, I'm on my way to school. Pop thought I might as well kill two birds with one stone." He tossed a paper bag into Smith's lap. "Mom told me to give you these."

Smith peeked inside the bag and hauled out a pair of mittens like the boy wore. His were black, thank God. Not red.

Smith slipped his hands inside the mittens and all but slobbered all over himself with the joy of it. They were nice and soft and toasty.

"Tell your mom that as soon as I get back to San Diego, I'm putting her in my will."

Jesse laughed. "Take a look around while you're working today and you'll see more of them. It's one of Mom's hobbies. She knits mittens and passes them around to everyone she sees. Half the town's probably wearing a pair."

Smith looked proudly at his new mittens, ridiculously touched by the kindness of a woman he had never met. He made a mental note to phone her sometime during the day and thank her personally. He supposed there must be people in San Diego who go around doing nice things for total strangers, but he had yet to meet any of them. Maybe the nature of his work had something to do with that. Murderers and pimps and purveyors of crime weren't usually prone to acts of charity. They had other things on their minds.

It was a blindingly white morning. White snow on the ground. White sky overhead. Little white snowflakes floating through the air.

"It's snowing," Smith said.

"Just a few flurries. Won't amount to anything."

"Good. I'm hoping to fly out tomorrow."

"So soon?" The boy seemed absurdly disappointed by that fact. Smith supposed this was all pretty exciting for the kid.

"So, where are we headed?"

"To the station house. Dad's got some things lined up for you today. And Judy's there, working on the computer they hauled out from the trailer."

"Is she a deputy?"

Jesse laughed. "No, but she thinks she is. She just runs the office. But she can do everything with a computer except—"

"I got the picture, son. Your father already filled me in on her talents with a hard drive."

Jesse grinned. "You'll like Judy. She's a pip."

Smith had never in his entire life heard anyone called a pip. In books they called people pips. In books, and apparently in Indiana. He'd have to remember to try it out on McCray when he got home. He felt fairly certain that the only pip McCray was familiar with would be a back-up singer for Gladys Knight.

The night before, after ducking under the crime scene tape that sealed the front door, Smith and Sheriff Lucas had spent two hours at the farmhouse where the two Andros sons had begun their lives and where the parents had ended theirs. The bodies were long gone, of course, but the bloodstains were still there to show what had occurred inside that house. Smith had taken in the blood-soaked recliner with passionless interest, but he had stared for long seconds at the sewing machine that was also splattered with blood. He had yet to see Evelyn Andros's body where it rested now inside a stainless steel drawer in the Greene County Morgue, but in his mind he saw her as plain as day, smiling as her fingers pushed fabric beneath the needle of the machine, sewing a perfect hem onto the dress she would unknowingly be buried in before the month was ended. Perhaps she would be humming as she worked, the music bringing life back into the house that was now so quiet since her boys had grown up and moved away. In Smith's mind, he saw her as a happy woman, perplexed perhaps by the way her sons had turned out. Was she disappointed that one was gay? Did it bother her that the other was a religious fruitcake who had plastered cheap pictures of Jesus all over his living room? Smith thought of his own two children. What sort of adults would time mold them into? Would he still love them, no matter how they turned out? He supposed he would. And he supposed Evelyn Andros had felt the same. They were her children. They would always be her children. No matter what.

He wondered what her thoughts were as the black thread was slicing through her wrists and the paisley scarf was being wrapped around her throat, cutting off the air, squeezing the life from her, but at least, thank God, releasing her from the pain of that damned thread tearing into her skin. Did she know her killer? Smith suspected she did. Knew him and loved him.

Did she wonder in the last moments of her life, how it had come to this? Did she blame herself? Or did she merely accept it as God's will?

For Smith knew that God also lived in this house. Here, too, a Bible rested on the coffee table. A hymn book stood open on the upright piano that graced the parlor wall. A stack of *Guideposts* lay on the nightstand beside the bed. But the religion didn't scream out at you as it had at the son's trailer. Here it was a benign presence, not a malignancy. Here it was merely a part of this couple's life, not life itself.

Here Smith had found pictures. Family pictures. Not unlike those in his own home. A chronological record of lives spent together. Baby pictures. A second grade school picture of Sean, grinning impishly into the camera, his two front teeth missing and looking cute as hell. The older boy, Jackson, building a model battleship at the kitchen table, concentrating on his work, ignoring whoever held the camera. Another snapshot of Jackson, maybe eight years old, holding a toddler in his arms. High school pictures. Jackson, tall and lanky. A good-looking young man. Sean, looking angelic and sweet, in a white dinner jacket and tie, a pretty girl on his arm at what was obviously a school prom. No prom pictures of Jackson. Smith wondered why. Had he been unpopular in school? Had his religious fervor already set him apart from his classmates? He was a handsome boy. He should have been popular with the girls, at least. But in all the photographs Smith had studied at the farmhouse, there was no suggestion of it.

One picture of Jackson Andros rested in Detective Smith's shirt pocket. He pulled it out now and looked at it once again. It showed a good-looking boy of sixteen or so, shirtless, leaning against the fence that surrounded the yard of the farmhouse. It was one of the few photographs that Smith had discovered in which the boy was actually smiling. In the picture, Jackson looked proud of his physique, one arm flexed in a muscle-builder's pose, the other arm stretched out along the top rail of the fence. His body was pale, untanned, but the abs and muscles across his chest were well defined, his waist trim inside the tattered jeans that hung from his slim hips. A handsome boy. And Smith had no doubt that he would grow to be a handsome man. Would he also grow to become a killer, Smith wondered.

His reverie was broken when Jesse stopped the Jeep in front of a sprawling one-story cinderblock building. The Sheriff's Bronco was parked beside the front door. An American flag flapped in the icy wind atop a pole at the side of the building. The Greene County Sheriff's Office looked open for business.

Smith thanked Jesse once again for carting him around and as the boy drove off toward his high school, Smith ducked into the building, grateful, as usual, to get in out of the cold.

The Sheriff looked up from behind his desk as Smith walked in. He noticed the photograph in Smith's hand.

"If you're looking for the fax machine, it's right through there." He pointed to a doorway to his left.

Smith thanked him and said, "Good morning to you, too."

He found the fax, punched in the numbers of his office in San Diego, and positioned the photograph. With a whirr, the picture was sent. Smith hoped McCray would remember to check for faxes, figured he probably would, and decided not to call him just yet.

For the first time, he noticed that the office was gray with cigarette smoke. If this were California, the nicotine police would be busting heads and burning bodies in effigy. He spotted the source of the smoke at the other end of the large room.

A woman who looked to be in her seventies, with snow-white hair that had been pushed haphazardly into an untidy bun at the back of her head, was punching keys on a computer that Smith recognized as the one they had removed from Jackson Andros's trailer. A cigarette dangled from her lips and another burned in an ashtray beside her. Smith guessed her weight at about ninety pounds, and most of that, he figured, was probably lung tumor.

"You must be Judy," Smith said, approaching the woman and peering over her shoulder at the computer screen.

"And you must be the Indian," Judy said, not looking up from what she was doing. Smoke hovered around her white head like wisps of cloud hovering over the peak of a snow-capped mountain. "Nice mittens," she said. "Mine are blue."

Smith looked down at his mittens, pulled them off, and stuffed them in his coat pocket. He heard the Sheriff snickering in the other room.

Finally, Judy turned to look him over through the curtain of smoke rising from the Marlboro stuck in her mouth. Deep crevices etched her powdered face. A smear of rouge on each wrinkled cheek was meant to denote good health and a rosy complexion. They failed to do either. Her eyes, however, squinting against the smoke, were alight with humor. Smith decided the wrinkles were laugh lines. Regardless of how she looked, this was a happy woman.

"Cold, isn't it? Bet your balls went north when you stepped off that plane yesterday."

Smith was taken aback, but only for a second. He knew when he was being dished.

"They're still north," he said and smiled.

She smiled in return and offered him her hand. He took it and marveled at the delicacy of it. The papery softness of her skin amazed him. He could feel every tiny bone of her hand as it rested in his. But warm. Like a small bird nesting in his palm.

"Judy Fortunato," she said. "*Miss* Judy Fortunato."

"Jimmy Smith."

"You married?"

"Yeah."

"Still happy about it?"

"Yeah, I am."

"Just my luck. Got kids?"

"Yeah. Two."

"I've got five. And it's only a miracle of fortune that none of them has come to the attention of this office. Losers. Each and every one of them. My oldest son is 52. Last week he asked me for grocery money. 52 years old and he can't buy his own goddamn groceries. How many you got?"

"How many what?"

"How many kids? What are we talking about, chickens?"

"Oh. Two."

"That's one too many. Don't have any more. As soon as they hit puberty they're a pain in the ass until the day they die. Or you die. Whichever comes first."

"I'll remember that. Umm… I hear you're a whiz at computers."

"I'm a whiz at a lot of things. Just not raising kids. Never seemed to get the knack."

With that, Judy turned back to the computer and once again started punching keys. She took the cigarette from her mouth, transferred it to the ashtray, and for the first time noticed the other one burning there. She snubbed out the first, and stuck the second between her lips.

"Finding anything?" Smith asked, again peering over her shoulder and staring at the monitor, squinting his eyes against the smoke.

"I've found all kinds of stuff. The guy who owned this machine was about as computer-savvy as our illustrious Sheriff over there. In other words, he didn't know shit."

"Meaning?"

"Meaning, Detective, that he pulled everything from his hard drive and dumped it in the recycle bin to be disposed of but then he just left it all sitting there. Don't you just love stupid people? Makes our job so much easier."

"And what exactly was *in* the recycle bin?"

"Just about everything I was told to look for. This guy didn't have a clue as to how to go about covering his tracks. Not that I couldn't have pulled up the information even if he had dumped the recycle bin, but this way it's just that much easier. No challenge at all."

Smith pulled up a rolling desk chair and plopped his ass down beside the old woman who he was liking more and more with every passing minute.

"We're kind of pressed for time here. Tell me what you've found."

"Okay. We've got an airline reservation for four days ago from Indianapolis to San Diego. Coach. Window seat. Paid for with Visa. No return ticket. No rental car arranged. Probably did that after he got there. I've got a UPS package that was sent two days before that, also to San Diego, to general delivery at the downtown UPS office to be picked up in person. He tracked the package to make sure it got there. God knows what was in it. At some time during the past month he accessed a website called Anarchist International and downloaded schematics on how to build a pipe bomb."

If Smith had had a football in his hand he would have spiked it. "I knew it," he said.

"He also downloaded schematics for building a timing device for *triggering* a bomb."

Smith merely nodded. He had expected as much.

Judy glanced over at him. "Has he used it yet?"

"The pipe bomb? Yes. Killed a man. We were lucky it wasn't more."

"This guy's a real wackjob, huh? Didn't know we grew them like that out here. Usually they're too busy having carnal relations with their livestock to get involved with anything that has moving, explodable parts."

"What else you got?"

"At some time, also in the past month, he downloaded information from a gay travel guide to San Diego. Looks like the guy's a tutti-frutti."

"Maybe not. What else?"

"That's about it. Oh, in case you're interested, the package he shipped with UPS weighed forty-six pounds and cost $82.27 to ship."

"Weapons."

"Weapons? As in guns?"

"Guns. Bomb components. Who knows? How else would he get the stuff out there? Couldn't take it on the plane."

"Don't they X-ray that shit at UPS?"

"Not that I know of. You could probably ship a nuclear device if you told them it was books. How the hell would they know?"

"Shoddy."

"No kidding. What about bank accounts? Any large withdrawals?"

"No banking information at all. No automatic bill payments. Nothing. Guess he didn't do any of that crap online."

"Suppose we'll have to learn about that stuff with good old-fashioned footwork. Anything else?"

"That's about it for the good news, Detective. Are you ready for the bad?"

Smith thought it was awfully early in the morning for bad news but he supposed he would have to hear it sometime.

"Go ahead."

"While I was accessing the airline information I noticed that all flights going into San Diego have been cancelled. Your hometown seems to be asshole-deep in rain and it's still coming down."

"It was knee-deep when I left."

"Well, now it's hit the first orifice."

"How about LAX? Los Angeles."

Judy hit a few keys, then she hit a few more.

"It's socked in too. Looks like the closest airport accepting flights is in Las Vegas."

"Shit." He knew he could drive from Vegas to San Diego in five and a half hours under good conditions. With the rain, who knew how long it would take?

"Maybe I'll stay here another day. Won't kill me."

Judy hocked up a wad of phlegm like a truck driver and folded it daintily inside a Kleenex before tossing it dead center into a wastebasket ten feet away.

"It's not like you'll freeze to death," she said. "You've got mittens."

I've also got McCray, he thought.

He pulled out his cell phone and hit the speed dial for his partner. He wasn't surprised that Jeff didn't answer. With a three hour time difference, it was five in the morning there. McCray was probably entertaining a lady friend, and with her thighs wrapped around his ears, he couldn't hear the phone ring, or play the theme song to Dragnet, or whatever the hell else he had the damn thing doing now.

He left a message. He didn't bother with hellos.

"It's me. Jackson Andros is our man. He flew out there four days ago. I've faxed you the most recent picture I could find of him, which isn't very recent I'm afraid. As soon as I get my hands on an Indiana BMV photo, I'll fax that as well, so watch for it. I didn't get snowed in here, not yet anyway, but I did get rained out of there. I'll try again tomorrow to get a flight. In the meanwhile, I want you to find that son of a bitch before he kills somebody else. In the words of my lovely assistant, Judy, the guy is a real wackjob. He's nuts. As in looney tunes without the humor. Find him and get him off the streets. And while you're at it, find the hustler. I think his brother's coming after him. And next time, answer your fucking phone. Toodles."

"I love a man with a good vocabulary," Judy said.

Sheriff Lucas poured three cups of coffee from a pot on his desk, handed one to Judy, one to Smith, and kept the last one for himself. He cleared his throat, embarrassed.

"I received a missing person report a week ago from a woman over in Bloomfield. Seems her son went missing last Tuesday. Afraid I didn't think too much about it at the time. The kid was nineteen and known to hitchhike all over the place. Now I'm thinking, what if this Andros guy picked him up and decided to barbecue him, figuring he'd throw us off the scent, thinking the dead body was his? I called the coroner, and the ring on the corpse's finger was a school ring. Class of

'04. Andros graduated from high school in '97. The younger brother graduated in '02. And we only have one missing person report, so that pretty well clinches it. The body in the burned-out shed was the hitchhiker. Billy Wallace. Born and raised in Bloomfield. Age nineteen."

"Poor kid," Judy said, sipping her coffee and lighting another Marlboro. "Didn't his mother ever tell him not to hitchhike?"

Chapter Nine

With the dawn came a short respite from the rain, just a brief interlude, as black thunderclouds on the horizon rallied their forces in preparation for one final assault on the California coast. This storm front, moving in from the ocean on the very heels of the last, began a final push toward land, its strength greater than all the storms that came before it, although the citizens of San Diego did not know that yet. This last angry attack would threaten homes up and down the coastline with a fury that Californians had not seen in a generation.

With Sean at his side, Harry stood on the redwood deck at the back of his house and watched the storm approach from the Pacific. The air was cold and laden with moisture. The gusting wind had a bite to it that chilled their skin and drew them closer together.

The cats, more understanding perhaps than their human counterparts of the threat that resonated through the air, remained inside, hunkered down beneath the Christmas tree, the oppressive atmosphere holding them in their places like strong hands pressing them to the floor. Their eyes were wide and alert as they waited for the storm they knew would hit.

Harry looked out across the ocean, the surface of which was steel gray. Swells rolled high as they moved toward the rocks on the beach. When they hit, they exploded in flumes of spray and mist. Harry could hear them hit, every few seconds, like distant artillery fire as they battered the shore.

"What a view," Sean said. In the distance, he, too, watched the waves crashing onto the beach. A couple of miles away, to the left, he saw the rotating observation tower at Sea World, home of Shamu and a whole lot of other unfortunate creatures who would never see the open sea again. Only once had Sean watched Shamu do his tricks in the huge aquarium he now called home, and it had left him with an overpowering sadness for the animal. He had never wanted to go to Sea World again. To Sean, it was not a happy place. To the Tourist Bureau, he supposed, it was heaven on earth.

"Let's hope we still have a view tomorrow," Harry said. "This hillside is soaked with water, and those clouds on the horizon look like they'll be bringing a whole lot more rain before the day is over. Let's pray that by tomorrow morning we won't be sitting at the bottom of this hill instead of on top of it."

Sean leaned out over the railing and looked down at the steep cliff face, most of it covered in ice plant, the rest just scrub and rock. One hundred yards or so below the house the cliff was scarred by a gully of fresh-turned earth that had washed away, the ground cover eroded by cascading water that had swept down the slope, leaving a deep trench that wound a crooked path to the back fence of another house perched far below them.

Harry pointed it out to Sean now. "That wasn't there yesterday."

"Are you sure?"

"I'm sure."

"Jeez, Harry. Are you going to lose your house?"

Harry studied that gouged-out section of cliff face and let his eyes wander upward to where the beams that held up his deck were buried in the hillside. He couldn't see any other places that were washing out.

In the spring, Harry had chipped in with neighbors to have the hillside cleared of brush, spurred on by the fear of fire, not flooding. In hindsight, that might have been a mistake.

"I hope not," he said. "I think I'd be more worried if we were living in that house down there. The gully has washed out right up to the edge of their property. Unless I'm mistaken, their fence will be gone by tomorrow morning. And maybe the house along with it."

"Should we warn them?" Sean asked.

Harry shook his head. "They know. They were in their backyard earlier, looking at it."

"Can we do anything to protect *your* house?"

"No. It's too late for that." Harry watched the threatening clouds on the horizon. Already they looked closer than they had five minutes earlier. "More rain will be here in a couple of hours. Even if there *was* anything to be done, we wouldn't have time to do it. But I think we're safe. The cliff around us looks stable. We'll just have to weather it out and hope for the best. If anything does begin to happen I'm sure we'll have time to get out."

"Besides," he added, brushing at his wind-tossed hair and gazing at the boy beside him. "We have more important things to worry about. It will be dark soon. And your friend is still out there somewhere. He may already know where you are."

The wind was picking up. Sean, too, reached up and brushed the hair from Harry's face where it had tumbled into his eyes. His own hair was too short to be bothered by wind.

"Maybe I should leave. I'm putting you in danger."

Harry smiled. "You aren't going anywhere without me, and I'm not leaving this house. If he wants us he can come for us here. We'll just make sure we're ready for him if he does."

"Aren't you afraid?" Sean asked.

"Scared shitless. You?"

"Ditto. But not as scared as I would be if I were alone. I don't know what I would have done without you these past couple of days, Harry. I guess I'd either be dead or in jail, and I'm not sure which would be worse."

"Trust me. Dead is worse. Dead sucks. I don't like dead. Never did. You, I like very much alive. Alive and with me. Together we can keep you that way. We'll watch each other's backs, and we'll get through this somehow. I won't let anything happen to you, Sean. I love you too much. I don't intend to lose you now."

Sean slipped his arms around Harry's waist and pressed his face into the older man's chest. "I love you too, Harry. I do."

"I mean to kill him, Sean. If he comes here, I mean to kill him."

"I know."

"I always protect what's mine."

"Do you?"

"Yes."

Sean gazed up into Harry's face. "Do I belong to you now?"

Harry cupped the boy's face in his hands. "Yes, you belong to me."

Sean closed his eyes, relishing the feel of Harry's warm hands, absorbing Harry's love for him, and trying, too, to absorb some of Harry's strength.

"Good," he said. "Kill him for both our sakes, Harry. Kill him so we can be together."

"I will," Harry said with his lips pressed against the boy's hair, smelling the clean fragrance of his own shampoo and feeling the boy's arms hold him close.

For you, Harry thought. Not for us, Sean. I'll kill him for you.

DETECTIVE Jefferson McCray was awoken that morning by a lack of sound, a silence that was at odds with what he had come to expect from the world around him. It took him a few moments to realize what it meant. The rain had stopped. If only for a few hours, it seemed, San Diego was being given a reprieve from the pounding it had taken over the past three days. The sky outside his bedroom window was murky gray, promising more rain to come, and there was an ominous feel to the air that told McCray the reprieve would be short-lived. Already, through his bedroom window, he could see dark clouds moving in from the west. The storm would begin again soon. Maybe even before he left for work.

While shaving, he played his voice mail and received Smith's message about Jackson Andros. McCray wasn't surprised to learn that

Smith had been right all along in thinking the hustler was innocent. He had pretty much come to the same conclusion himself, but only because of Smith's urging. McCray considered himself a good homicide detective, but he also knew, without a doubt, that his partner was a better one. The man had a sixth sense about things. McCray often suspected it was due to Smith's Indian heritage and that mystical Indian connection to nature and the universe that screenwriters were so fond of harping on in films. Maybe the screenwriters were right. Maybe there was something supernatural about an Indian's bond with the world he lived in.

Then again, maybe Smith was just a whole lot fucking smarter than he was. Deep down he suspected that explanation came closer to the truth than all the mystical bullshit.

Either way, Smith had found the truth long before McCray had, and that made him a better detective. Period. And McCray was glad to have him for a partner.

When he reached the office, he retrieved the fax photo of Jackson Andros and knew immediately that the snapshot wouldn't help them much. It was taken too long ago. But he needn't have worried. Once again, Smith was on the ball, for less than an hour later another fax came in, this time with an Indiana BMV photo of Andros taken the year before.

The date of birth on the driver's license showed the man to be twenty-seven years old. He stood six foot three and weighed 180 pounds. The snapshot was that of a handsome but stern looking young man with eyes so pale that the color of the irises barely registered in the less than perfectly lighted photograph, giving those eyes a haunting, callous quality. Emotionless and disconnected. The man's hair was blond and as colorless as the eyes, thinning at the hairline.

The bartender at the Cailiff had said the man who came into the bar that night looking for Sean Andros was blond. And intense looking. Spooky. McCray didn't doubt for a moment that this was the man the bartender had seen. Both handsome and frightening. And dangerous. Staring into those cold, faintly blue eyes in the photograph, McCray didn't doubt that for a second either.

Blond hair aside, there was little resemblance to the man in the picture and the young street hustler McCray had watched on the security tape. Hard to believe they were brothers. One so tall and athletically built, the other shorter, with a slighter frame but an open, approachable manner about him. There was nothing approachable about the face McCray now studied in this BMV photo. The first word that popped into McCray's mind was... unfriendly. It was an unfriendly face.

McCray pulled his notebook from a jacket pocket and thumbed through his notes until he found the bartender's home phone number. He doubted if the man would be at the bar yet, and he didn't intend to wait.

Jonah answered on the seventh ring, sounding sleepy and pissed off.

"This better be good," he said in the way of a greeting.

McCray identified himself, verified Jonah's address and told the man he was on the way with a picture for him to look at. Jonah grunted okay, obviously less than thrilled with the news.

Before McCray left the office he rifled through a stack of comparison photos he kept stashed in a desk drawer and picked out a handful that showed men with light-colored hair. He knew never to show a potential witness just one photograph. Show them several. That's why God made line-ups. If the bartender could pick out the Andros photo from all the others, he knew the identification would be reliable.

On his way out of the building, he dropped four quarters into a vending machine and pressed the button for a Kit Kat bar. When nothing happened, he pressed another button, this one for a Snickers. Again, nothing happened. Blood pressure mounting, he hit every button in the array, and the machine just stared back at him. When he pressed the coin return and nothing happened, he kicked the vending machine in what he hoped would be its solar plexus and stormed out to his car.

Another day in paradise.

HE LEFT his shithole of a room at the Stevens Hotel in the early hours of the afternoon, after sleeping through the morning. The rain had started falling at noon, and now, as he strolled out onto the street, he was happy to see that it was coming down as if it had a purpose. Which it did. God had sent the rain to cover his movements. He knew this to be true. God had told him so during the night.

Tomorrow, if all went well, he would leave this city. The mission that had brought him here would be completed by dawn, all the loose ends neatly tied up. After that, he would have to wait and see what God intended him to do next. There would be another mission, he knew. God had told him that during the night as well. But as yet, that second mission was only a dark place in his mind, hidden in shadow, its purpose undisclosed. In good time, God had told him. All in good time.

He breakfasted in a dive on Island Avenue that advertised day-old bakery goods and a menu with nothing over four dollars. It didn't take him long to figure out why. There was nothing on the menu *worth* more than four dollars, but he ate his cold eggs and greasy sausage and two stale doughnuts as if he hadn't eaten for a week. Vacationing was a strenuous business if you put your all into it. And that he had. The thought made him smile.

After paying his bill, complimenting the old oriental woman who stood at the cash register on the five-star quality of the establishment, and asking her to give his regards to the marvelous chef, he laid a penny in her hand and said, "This is for you."

As he walked out the door, the penny went sailing past his head and rolled into the street. The old oriental woman yelled something at him in Chinese that didn't sound like, "Have a nice day!" The man laughed and kept on walking.

He found an upscale cutlery store in the Horton Plaza Shopping Mall that advertised "blades for every purpose" on their front window in bold metallic script. He took his time browsing along the display cases and finally settled on a lovely little knife with a very sharp point and a blade that could be used for anything from filleting fish to sawing the fender off a '63 Buick. He doubted, however, that *his* purpose for purchasing the knife was one of the purposes the proprietors had had in mind when they put up their sign. After leaving the store, he removed the knife from the shopping bag and put it in his overcoat pocket.

His gun waited for him in the hotel room, attached by masking tape to the back of the toilet tank, just in case someone decided to break into his room and sneak around. But he wouldn't need the gun until later.

First, he would need the knife.

From the cutlery store, he took his time meandering through the mall, feeling safe and isolated by the pouring rain that drummed on the sidewalk at his feet. The air was cold, but his coat was warm and well waterproofed. Since you never knew when you might need your hands, he didn't bother with an umbrella. A blue ball cap with "COLTS" stenciled across the front protected his head and hid the color of his hair. Just in case.

The mall was all but deserted due to the rain and didn't offer much in the way of entertainment, so he found the exit onto Broadway and walked four blocks to a concrete parking structure behind the Civic Center where he had parked his rental car the day before. The gray Taurus started right up, and soon he had left downtown behind as he headed north toward Mission Hills. Cars on the street were as sparse as shoppers at the mall. Apparently, the citizenry of San Diego were less than enthralled by the downpour. You'd think they would appreciate the change, he thought. An endless diet of sunshine must get pretty boring after a few months. He wasn't a great fan of sunshine. His skin was too pale for it. It was one of the things that made him special. One of the things that set him apart. White skin was a gift from God. It signified purity.

He found Eagle Street just where he had left it the day before. It was a narrow thoroughfare that wound along the cliff face at the edge of Mission Hills. It was a short street, only a few blocks long, and petered out at a cul de sac where he was forced to turn the car around and head back in the opposite direction.

This time he drove more slowly. The green Boxster had been moved off the street and was now parked in the driveway of the white-stuccoed house. The other car, the little foreign piece of shit, was nowhere to be seen. Did that mean the whore was gone? He didn't think so. Where would he go? No, the whore was still there, inside the house with the other one of his kind. They were waiting for him. And they wouldn't have long to wait.

The house was large. The front lawn well tended but small. He suspected that most of the property extended from the back. That's where the view would be. When the sun went down, and the other job was finished, he would check it out. Perhaps the easiest way into the house was from the back. If not, the front would have to do. One of the windows perhaps. Or maybe he would just knock on the fucking door and let the reunion begin. God would tell him what to do when the time came.

He parked the car at the side of the street two doors down from the whore's hidey-hole, and lowered the brim of his ball cap. He switched off the engine and let the rain engulf the car. He would watch the house for a while. He would watch the house and plan his night. He took the new knife from his pocket and removed the cardboard sheath that covered the blade. He held it to the light and watched it shine. It was beautiful. As sharp as sight, as cold as ice. It would cut through this night. He knew that. He laid the knife on the seat beside him and his hand moved to his cock. Anticipating the excitement of the night to come had made it, too, as hard as steel. He squeezed himself, and through the fabric of his trousers, slid back his foreskin. He closed his eyes, enjoying the sensation.

After a moment, he forced his hand away and again picked up the knife. He laid it flat against his cheek, the blade cold against his skin.

Wait for the night, he told himself. Wait for the night.

It became a litany. A prayer. A promise. Soon the pale man lost himself in it. And all the while, his seed begged for release.

THE knife slid through the twelve-ounce steak like a hand glides through water. It was the most tender piece of meat Smith had ever eaten. He was sitting in a restaurant that was situated four miles outside the burg of Nine Mile, Indiana on Highway 67. With him at the table were Sheriff Lucas and Judy Fortunato. They, too, were chowing down on the steaks they had ordered, sawing away like lumberjacks. It was midafternoon and the restaurant was almost empty. Too late for the lunch crowd and too early for the dinner patrons to begin arriving.

"You say this place is run by Amish people?"

Judy swallowed and took a sip of the bourbon and water she had ordered in spite of her boss's obvious disapproval. Sheriff Lucas had seen her drink before.

"There's a clan of them that live out in the country. They're like a big family. They run this place sort of like a commune. Damn fine cooks though."

Smith agreed with a nod of his head, too busy enjoying his food to actually talk.

Judy was never too busy to talk. "All the men have beards down to their bellies, and the women wear long skirts like frontier women did a hundred years ago. They come to work in a horse and buggy. Right down the middle of the highway, just poking along, taking their time. Pisses off the truckers no end. We get complaints about it all the time."

The Sheriff chuckled. "Yeah, and those same truckers stop in here to eat every time they drive by."

"Assholes," Judy said, taking another sip of bourbon.

Apropos of nothing, Smith asked, "Why Nine Mile?"

Lucas didn't get it. "What do you mean?"

"Why is the town called Nine Mile?"

"Oh. Well, let's see." He laid his knife across the edge of his plate and thought about it for a second before answering. "The town was founded in 1867, and back then we were located nine miles from a bend in White River where supplies were ferried in and crops and livestock were ferried out. Sort of a trading post. There's still a big old chunk of Indiana limestone sitting at the side of a gravel road somewhere west of town that says "NINE MILE" with an arrow that points the way to the ferry landing. The name just stuck, I guess."

"The landing's long gone but the rock's still there," Judy added. "And the town's about as static as the rock. The population of Nine Mile hasn't gone up or down more than a decimal point in a hundred and forty years. A thriving metropolis, we ain't."

"Maybe not," Smith said. "But you serve a hell of a steak."

Judy shook her head. "That's just here. Try the truck stop in town and you'll be shitting blood for a week. Worse damn food in twelve states."

Lucas laughed. "She's exaggerating."

Judy grunted. "Not by much."

After that, their table fell silent while they finished their meals. Finally, when all the food was gone, they pushed their plates away and in less than a minute the table was cleared by a very efficient waitress in a long skirt and bonnet with a name tag on her ample bosom that said "SHIRLEY."

After she was gone, Smith asked, "She Amish?"

Judy gave a loud guffaw and slapped her hand on the table.

"Hell, no. Shirley's one of the biggest sluts in town. The Sheriff here caught her one time trying to have sex with a parking meter."

Lucas lowered his head and groaned. "She wasn't having sex with the parking meter. How many times do I have to tell you? She was bumping it, trying to get her nickel to go down."

Judy narrowed her eyes and glared at him. "She was bumping it with her crotch."

"Well, yeah, but her hands were full of shopping bags. Oh, forget it."

The Sheriff turned away from Judy, dismissing her as a lost cause. He hated it when she drank, and in his eyes, she wasn't much more companionable sober.

To Smith, he said, "You leaving tomorrow?"

"If I can. Depends on the weather."

The Sheriff nodded. "You were right about the bank account.

Andros emptied it out. About $4,300 worth, according to the bank. Didn't leave a sou behind."

"That won't get him far," Smith said.

"It got him far enough to cause you a peck of trouble."

"That it did."

"I don't know what he thinks he's going to do when all this is over. He can't come back here. His family's all dead. He pretty well burned his bridges behind him."

"He pretty well burned that hitchhiker behind him, too," Judy said.

Smith looked at his watch. "I don't think the man is savvy enough to plan that far ahead. He has to be insane."

"Complete wackjob," Judy said, waving her empty glass at the waitress on the other side of the room.

"You aren't ordering another one, are you?"

"Yes, Sheriff snooty pants, I am. You got a problem with that?"

Lucas raised his hands in submission. "Guess not."

"Good." Judy lit a Marlboro and blew smoke rings at the ceiling while she waited for her bourbon to arrive.

Smith tried not to gag on the smoke. "In California they'd keelhaul you for that."

"Wimps. I've smoked for fifty years. Hasn't hurt me yet."

Smith grinned. "It certainly hasn't hurt your appetite for steak."

Judy gave him a secretive smile and said, "It hasn't hurt my appetite for anything."

Smith cringed. "Okay."

A tall, good-looking man in a plaid shirt and blue jeans walked up to their table and rested a hand on the Sheriff's shoulder.

"Hello, Boyd," he said. "Hello, Judy."

The stranger gave the detective a friendly, inquisitive smile.

Smith stood and extended his hand. "Jimmy Smith."

The man took Smith's hand in a firm grip and nodded his greeting. "Brian Lucas," he said. "Pleased to meet you."

Judy patted her hair. "Hello, Reverend. You look good enough to eat. Too bad I'm already full."

Brian looked at the Sheriff. "Is she drinking again?"

"How'd you guess?"

"Just a hunch."

Reverend Brian Lucas pulled out the fourth chair, folded his long legs under the table, and sat down.

"Here's your character witness," the Sheriff said.

Smith gazed from one to the other. "Another Lucas. You two wouldn't be related, would you?"

Brian nodded. "Brothers."

"The Sheriff and the Preacher," Judy said. "Aren't they cute?"

"Cute as hell," Smith said. "Oops, sorry, Padre."

Brian waved off the apology. "It's okay, Detective. I've known Judy here my whole life so nothing *you* say could possibly shock me."

Shirley came with Judy's bourbon and water and the good reverend told the waitress, "I'm afraid there's been a mistake. She meant to order hot chocolate."

Shirley spun on her heel with the drink still in her hand, mumbled, "Thank God," and went to fetch the cocoa.

Judy didn't say a word.

Brian turned to his brother. "I heard about Evelyn and Walter Andros. I still can't believe it."

The Sheriff ran a finger around the rim of his water glass, all the humor gone from his face. "I know. It's a terrible thing."

"And the Wallace boy, too?"

"Yes. Well, we think it's him."

"Good Lord."

Smith had very little use for organized religion, so it came as a surprise to him to find that he actually liked this handsome man who looked to be anything but a preacher. He always imagined preachers as pompous, little, fat guys with too much Brylcreme in their hair who never shut up and who never stopped judging everyone around them. Brian Lucas didn't give that impression at all. In fact, he looked like someone Smith wouldn't mind having a few beers and swapping stories with on a Saturday night. Go figure.

"I understand you knew Jackson Andros," Smith said.

Brian nodded. "Knew him about as well as anybody knew him, I guess. He was a hard person to get close to."

"He was one of your… parishioners?"

The reverend grinned at the detective's choice of words. "He was in my congregation, yes. Came to church every Sunday."

"His parents, too?"

Brian watched Shirley serve Judy her cup of hot chocolate and kept an eye on the older woman until he was sure she was drinking it.

"No. I knew his parents, but they went to the Baptist Church. Mine is Methodist. I don't think it had anything to do with any sort of religious preference, though. I think Jackson Andros came to my church because his parents *didn't*."

"They didn't get along?"

"Not for several years."

"And did you know the younger boy too? Sean?"

"Yes, but not well. I talked to him a few times. He was always very polite and nice. Seemed like a good kid."

"He's a hustler now," Judy said. "A gay prostitute."

"Is he? I'm sorry."

"You don't seem too surprised by that," Smith said.

Brian clasped his hands on the table in front of him and looked at

Smith. "I'm sorry, Detective, I didn't mean to give the impression that it doesn't surprise me. It's just that… well… I never really envisioned a very happy ending for the boy."

"Why's that?"

Brian thought a moment before speaking. "Sean didn't have a very happy childhood, I'm afraid. No. What I mean to say is, he didn't have a very happy childhood after he reached a certain age. When he was a young boy, he was the sweetest kid in the world. But in his teens, Sean Andros sort of pulled into himself. Just like his brother, except that his brother was always like that. I think something happened when Sean reached his teenage years that made a change in his life, and it wasn't a good change. He never became sullen like his brother, but he did change."

Smith considered that. "He was growing up. Hormones were kicking in. Maybe it was the dawning awareness of his sexual orientation that threw him. I've seen it happen before. Learning that one is gay is a lot for a young person to wrap his head around. Some never accept it. Even suicide isn't uncommon."

Smith watched an uncomfortable glance pass between the two brothers, but he didn't have much time to wonder at it before the Reverend said, "I know, Detective. I was a psych major in college. But I don't think Sean's problem was inside himself. I think it was brought on by outside forces."

"Like what?"

"Like Jackson." Brian turned to his brother. "You remember, Boyd. Jackson beat on that kid unmercifully all through Sean's high school years. Half the time the kid was black and blue. I tried speaking to their parents about it once, but they didn't really grasp what I was trying to tell them. They seemed to think their sons were just being boys. I think it was more than that."

Brian turned back to Smith. "Is the boy all right?"

"Sean?"

"Yes."

"As far as I know, he is. We haven't been able to track him down. He's gone to ground somewhere and he's laying low."

"Maybe that's a good thing."

"It is," Smith said. "I think his brother's out to get him for some unknown reason, and he's killing anyone who gets in his way. In fact, I'm sure of it. Excuse me a second, Reverend."

Smith caught Shirley's eye and motioned her over. "Would you mind bringing me a slice of that apple pie that's sitting over there on the counter. Me and that pie have been looking at each other for an hour now and I think I'd like to give it a try."

Shirley batted false eyelashes and said, "Lucky pie."

When she was gone, Judy said, "Told ya. The woman's a slut."

Brian patted her hand. "Drink your cocoa."

"Yes, Reverend."

Smith watched the interchange between the old woman and the young minister, not quite knowing what to make of it. He decided he didn't need to know and said, "It sounds to me like maybe Jackson Andros was a bit off his rocker even when those brothers were kids. Does that sound like a fair assessment, Reverend?"

"Yes, Detective, I think maybe it does. There's no one in my church more devout than Jackson Andros, and there's no one in my church who wears that devotion on his sleeve more than Jackson does either. I'm a religious man, Mr. Smith. I try to live a religious life. Jackson Andros would probably tell you the same thing about himself. But it wouldn't be true. Not really. I think there's something deeply wrong inside Jackson's mind. I've thought it for a long time. Maybe instead of just thinking it, I should have tried to do something about it."

"Let me tell you something, Reverend. For fifteen years I've been a homicide detective. I've seen more terrible crap than any of you ever want to see in a lifetime. And for each one of those terrible occurrences, there's always been somebody who was close to the killer who tried to blame himself. If I had done this. If I had done that. Pardon my French, but it's all bullshit. People do terrible things to each other continually and nothing anybody else does is going to change that. Shit happens.

It's a basic and unflawed philosophy. Shit happens. That's all there is to it."

Judy laid a hand on the reverend's arm as if she didn't give a rat's ass what *anyone* thought about it. She left it there and said, "He's right. You can't blame yourself for any of this. No one could know what that moron was going to do, least of all you. Now get your head out of your ass and order me another hot chocolate. That was pretty good."

Brian blinked in surprise, then laughed. Pretty soon they were all laughing.

"To hell with hot chocolate," Sheriff Lucas said. "Let's all have a drink. I'm buying."

And they all did, even the reverend, who sipped a Pabst Blue Ribbon straight from a bottle as the others nursed cocktails.

Four rounds later, the establishment quietly asked them to leave. They were getting a little too rowdy for Amish sensibilities.

MCCRAY, still driving his vintage Chrysler, cruised along B Street in the Golden Hills district of the city. The area was situated about two miles east of downtown, a straight shot up Broadway from police headquarters. Recently Golden Hills had become popular with Yuppies who worked in the downtown area. Consequently, real estate prices had soared in the past few years, making it one of the priciest parts of the city in which to buy a home. With the infusion of new money into the area, Golden Hills was now a very attractive place to live. Victorian houses, many with widow's walks and ornate turrets, had been refurbished to their former glory. Smaller homes, too, had received a facelift. A tiny one-bedroom cottage had recently made the papers after selling for a record $700,000. Streets that only a decade before had been a canvas for street gang graffiti were now spotlessly maintained. And McCray spotted some very fine automobiles parked along the curb as he studied the house numbers, looking for Jonah's address.

He found it near 27th Street next to a Mexican church.

Jonah lived in a small bungalow that had once been a carriage house behind one of the larger Victorians. McCray approached the carriage house after traversing a flagstone pathway that wended its way around the side of the main house. He rapped at the door and heard the yapping of a small dog coming from inside.

Jonah answered the knock right away. He was wearing a bathrobe and his hair was wet. Unrestricted by its usual pony tail, Jonah's hair framed his face in damp ringlets that looked like they had been recently permed.

He didn't seem overly enthusiastic about finding the detective on his doorstep, but he wasn't rude about it either.

"Come on in," he said, waving McCray inside. To the tiny Chihuahua bouncing and snarling at his feet, he said, "Jose, be nice."

Two seconds after McCray was inside the door, the Chihuahua started humping his leg and rubbing his little Chihuahua pecker against McCray's shin as if he hadn't been laid in a very long time. McCray supposed he hadn't. Short guys always had a hard time getting laid.

"He likes you," Jonah said.

"Yeah," McCray said, "and if he doesn't stop liking me real soon I'm going to shoot the little fucker dead."

Jonah clapped his hands. "Jose, go to your room."

With a couple of farewell humps the little dog finally released McCray's leg and gazed up into his face as if to say, "Was that good for you, too?"

"Scram," McCray said, and the Chihuahua took off running toward the back of the cottage, where McCray figured he would probably pull out a few doggie porno magazines and finish the job of pleasuring himself since he wasn't getting any cooperation in the living room.

"Coffee?" Jonah asked.

"No. I won't keep you. Can we sit down?"

"Sure." Jonah waved him to the sofa. Primly pulling his bathrobe snug around himself so that Jonah Junior wouldn't make a surprise cameo appearance, he settled in beside the detective.

McCray pulled out a handful of snapshots from his coat pocket and spread them across the coffee table.

"Are any of these men the one you spoke to two nights ago at the bar? Take your time."

Jonah didn't need to take his time. He had spotted the man the moment the detective laid down the pictures. Without hesitation, he tapped a perfectly manicured fingernail against the third picture in the array.

"That's the guy."

It was the recently faxed photo of Jackson Andros.

"You're certain?"

"Yes. Positive."

"How can you be so sure? The bar was dark. The man's hair was wet."

"Look at those eyes," Jonah said. "Would you forget those eyes?"

McCray looked again at the picture and said, "No, I guess I wouldn't."

He gathered up the snapshots and returned them to his pocket. He glanced around the room for the first time, at the Parrish prints on the wall and the collection of CDs and DVDs that covered almost an entire wall in stackable shelves of chrome and glass. A framed poster of *Les Miserables* hung over the fireplace. McCray had seen the musical when it was in town the year before. He had the same poster on the wall of his bedroom.

"Maybe I will have that coffee," he said.

Jonah appeared taken aback for a second but then smiled graciously and said, "Certainly."

"Just black," McCray said.

"Black has always been my preference too," Jonah said, in a very credible Mae West impersonation that actually made McCray grin and shake his head.

While Jonah was in the kitchen pouring the coffee, Jose made a return appearance, rather shamefacedly, McCray thought, and jumped onto the back of the couch. McCray patted the little dog on the head, and the next moment, Jose leaped into McCray's lap, turned around three times, and went to sleep.

Jonah found them like that when he returned with two mugs of coffee in his hands. "That dog has all the luck," he said. He handed one of the mugs to McCray and resettled himself next to the detective on the sofa.

"Let's talk about the first man," McCray said after sipping his coffee and setting the mug on the table before him. "The one the boy left with."

Jonah looked uncomfortable. "Like I told you before, I don't really know anything about him. Only that his name is Harry. He doesn't come in very often."

"So you said. Would you recognize him again if you saw him?"

"Oh, I doubt it. The bar was dark, and like I told you before, it was really busy that night."

McCray tapped the photographs in his pocket. "You didn't have any trouble remembering this guy, and you only saw him once."

Jonah squirmed around in his seat and fiddled with the fold of his bathrobe, pulling it more discreetly over his knees.

"Yes, but that guy sort of made an impression, you know? He looked kind of desperate. And he was handsome."

"Harry isn't handsome?"

"Naw. Harry is just… nondescript."

"But you'd seen him before?"

"Yeah, he comes in occasionally. At least I think he does."

"Suddenly you're not sure? Was there anyone else in the bar that night who might remember Harry? A friend of his, perhaps? Someone you saw him talking to before the boy came in?"

"Not that I remember, no. He just sat quietly drinking his Miller

Lite. Don't recall him talking to anyone."

"Yet you remember what he was drinking."

"I'm a bartender. That's what I do."

McCray studied Jonah's face long enough to make Jonah look away. He made a pretense of sipping his coffee and staring back at the detective with an innocent expression, but he didn't carry it off very well.

"Are you keeping something from me?" McCray asked. "Are you trying to protect someone?"

"Like who?"

"Like Harry. Or maybe the boy."

Jonah felt a trickle of cold sweat dribble down his ribcage inside the robe. To cover his discomfort, he picked up a rubber band from the coffee table and combed his damp hair back with his fingers until he had one thick rope of hair at the back of his head, which he then tied off with the rubber band. With his hair secure, he felt a little more in control of the situation.

"They're only customers, Detective. I don't really know them. Honest. I'm not trying to protect anyone. I agreed to identify the blond man, and I did that. As for the kid, I would probably recognize him again. In fact, I'm sure I would. But I don't *know* him. Just like I don't know Harry. They're just people who come into the bar once in a while to drink. Just like hundreds of other people who come in there to drink. Some I know. Some I don't. These two I don't."

McCray idly ran a hand across the Chihuahua's back. Jose raised his head and licked McCray's fingers.

McCray pulled a business card from his pocket and held it out to Jonah. Jonah looked him in the eye for about three ticks before reaching out and taking the card.

"What's this for?" he asked.

"I want you to call me if you remember anything you haven't told me. You can call any time, day or night."

"This is important, isn't it?"

"Yes."

Jonah read the card. "Does your investigation have anything to do with the murder in Brittany Towers?"

"It might. Did you know Stanley Baker?"

"Once again, I knew of him. He had been in the bar a time or two."

"Have you ever seen him with the hustler?"

"No." It was true.

"Have you ever seen Harry with the hustler before?"

Again, Jonah said no. This time it was a lie. He had seen Harry and Sean chat with each other in the bar three or four times in the past year. He knew, also, that Harry had a thing for the boy. They had talked about it one afternoon when the bar was slow and Harry had had a few too many drinks. But none of this was information he was prepared to share with the detective. Jonah, in fact, had a bit of a thing for Harry himself. It would never go anywhere, Jonah knew, but still it was there. Jonah had no intention of betraying Harry. Harry was an adult. He knew what he was doing. If Harry was finally with the boy, then at least one of them was happy. Jonah was perfectly content to leave it at that. The AIDS virus which coursed through his system, dormant for now, thank God, had seen to it that Jonah would never have another lover. He wouldn't allow himself to endanger anyone he cared for. If Harry was happy, then Jonah was happy *for* him. And that would have to be enough.

"Are they in danger?" he asked. "Harry and the boy?"

"They might very well be," McCray said. "Just on general principles, I'm going to ask you one more time. Do you have any idea where I can find them? Do you know Harry's last name? Do you know where he lives?"

Again, Jonah sipped his coffee, stalling, giving himself time to think. He was torn, now. Torn between betraying a confidence and possibly putting Harry in danger by not answering the detective's questions. He decided to trust Harry's judgment. Harry would know if he were in danger or not. He was with the boy. That much was certain.

But he had also asked Jonah not to help the police any more than he had to. Not to answer any questions if he could get out of it. To give him time to resolve the matter himself. Jonah decided to give Harry that time. It was what he would expect a friend to do for him.

"I've told you everything I know," he said. "If I think of anything else, I'll call you. That's the best I can do."

McCray suspected the man was lying. He wanted to reach out and shake some sense into the guy, but he knew it wouldn't get him anywhere.

"All right," McCray said, "but I want you to do me a favor. If you talk to Harry, if you talk to either of them, I want you to tell them to turn themselves in. Will you do that?"

"Yes," Jonah said. "I'll do that." And he meant it. In fact, he meant to do it about thirty seconds after the detective left.

"Well," McCray said. "Thank you for your time. Tell them what I said."

"If I talk to them."

"Right. If you talk to them."

McCray nudged the Chihuahua off his lap, shook the bartender's hand, and left the carriage house. Hearing the front door snap closed behind him, he felt a sense of lost opportunities. He had his identification, yes, but there were things left unsaid in that interview that bothered him. He was convinced that Jonah knew more than he was saying, but why the man would do that, withhold information, McCray didn't have a clue.

He hoped no more deaths came of it. If they did, he would talk to Jonah again, and the next time, it would not be pleasant.

CHAPTER TEN

AT 9:30 A.M. Harry's cell phone rang. He checked the number on the incoming readout before picking up. It was Jonah.

Harry hit receive and said, "What's happening?"

Jonah sounded tense, but then Jonah *always* sounded tense.

"That homicide detective was just here."

"Did he bring you a picture of the guy that was looking for Sean?"

"Yes. And he bagged the right guy. It was him all right."

"Do the police know his name?"

Jonah hesitated. "I don't know. I got the impression they were more interested in Sean. And you."

"What did the cop say?"

"They want you to give yourselves up. This sounds bad, Harry. Remember that guy who was murdered in Brittany Towers? I think it has something to do with that. The cop asked me if I knew the guy. I told him I didn't. Only that I'd seen him around."

Harry was almost afraid to ask his next question. "Did you give him my last name?"

"No."

Harry closed his eyes in relief. "Thanks, Jonah."

"Is the kid with you?"

"I'm not going to answer that."

"Okay. You don't have to. But the cop said you might be in danger."

Harry rolled his eyes and thought, *no shit*, but didn't say anything.

"Did you hear me, Harry?"

"I heard you."

"Love is grand, Harry, but I think maybe you'd better rethink this relationship you've got brewing. The kid is obviously trouble."

"I'll take my chances."

"I was afraid you'd say that."

In the background, Harry heard Jonah's dog yapping.

"Jose!" Jonah screamed. "Shut the fuck up! It's just the mailman!" To Harry, he said, "Hates the mailman. Unhappy with the service, I guess."

"Jonah," Harry said. "Are they looking for the man in the photograph? Did the detective say?"

"Well, no, I don't remember him saying it in so many words, but I assume they are. I think they're more worried about the kid, though. I think they're more worried about you being in danger from the kid."

So Sean was still the main suspect. Harry knew it. The cops had set their sights on the boy, and they weren't going to change their game plan no matter what other evidence turned up.

"Jonah, the cops have it all wrong. The man you identified is the one they should be looking for, not Sean."

"Are you absolutely sure of that, Harry?"

"Yes, Jonah, I'm sure. Look, I have to go. Thank you, Jonah. I owe you big time for this. I just hope you don't get in trouble over it."

"Don't worry about me. Just worry about yourself."

"You're a true friend," Harry said.

"That's me," Jonah said. "Always the bridesmaid, never the bride. Just be careful."

"I will." Harry disconnected.

AFTER the call, Harry spent the remainder of the morning doing mundane chores, anything he could find to keep himself occupied. He scrubbed the bathrooms and cleaned the kitchen while Sean, feeling guilty for doing nothing, dragged out the upright Hoover he had stumbled across in a back bedroom and vacuumed the house from one end to the other. At one point, as Harry was wiping down the kitchen counter, his hand stopped and he stood statue-still for about thirty seconds, his mind racing with a sudden thought. They should leave. Leave the house. Get out while it was still daylight and it was reasonably safe to do so. They could get a hotel room somewhere, lay low for a few days. Or better yet, get out of town completely. Drive to Vegas or L.A. Put as many miles between themselves and San Diego as they could. Then his hand began to move again, as if of its own volition. Leaving would accomplish nothing. It would only postpone the inevitable. This man would find them sooner or later, and they would have to face him anyway. Better to finish it now.

Harry had given up hope that the police would help. They were after Sean. If he called the cops and told them what he knew, would they believe him? He doubted it. Why should they? The only thing he could give them by way of proof that Sean was innocent was the fact that he had been with the boy at the time of the bombing on the Prado. And that was no proof at all. As for the killing in Brittany Towers, Harry could offer the police nothing in the way of an alibi for the boy.

At noon, while Sean scooped cold ashes from the living room fireplace into an old grocery bag, Harry stood inside the doorway that led to his deck and watched the storm begin. It started with just a few drops of rain against the window pane, but within moments, the rain was a wall of water that lashed across the deck, blown by a whipping wind that knocked over flower pots and rattled the sliding doors. The sound of the storm was like a distant train, roaring along distant tracks, an angry thrumming that muted all other sounds.

Sean stopped what he was doing and moved to Harry's side. Together, they watched the storm's fury increase with every passing minute. Neither of them had ever seen anything like it. Mother Nature seemed to be truly pissed this time, and she was beating on the city with every weapon in her arsenal. A flash of lightning and an instant crack of thunder made them both jump. Eucalyptus trees on the edge of Harry's property whipped about in the gusting wind. They heard another crack of sound, and a huge branch, torn from the trunk of the tallest tree, the one right next to the redwood deck, fell as if in slow motion, barely missing the deck and disappearing down the side of the cliff.

At the sound of the crashing branch, the cats tore out from beneath the Christmas tree and scattered in five different directions, seeking a safer refuge.

"Jesus!" Harry yelped, startled at the sudden stampede.

Unabated, the storm raged on through the afternoon. Lightning, a rare occurrence in Southern California, flashed at ever decreasing intervals until the air was laden with the smell of ozone. Concerned for the safety of his house, Harry pulled on a raincoat and, holding a plastic garbage bag over his head to ward off the rain, rushed to the edge of the deck and looked down, surveying the cliff face—what little he could see of it through the heavy downpour—and ascertaining that it was still stable. The eroded trench down below appeared larger, but up the hillside toward his house, he could see no new washouts. Everything looked the same as it had that morning.

By midafternoon, they could find nothing else to scrub, dust, or vacuum. The house reeked of Pine-Sol and furniture polish. If things went wrong, Harry thought, at least he would die with a clean house.

But he was determined things would not go wrong.

He was convinced the man would come for them. For Sean, at least. The boy, Harry knew, was the man's real target. Aside from being scared and angry, he was also curious. Not for the first time, he wondered just what Sean could have done to make this deranged asshole hate the boy so much.

At 4:30 p.m., Harry's cell phone rang, and once again, he checked the incoming readout before answering. It was Stella, the receptionist at his salon, telling Harry she was closing the salon early due to the weather. They had seen only one customer in the past three hours, and she was afraid the streets would be washed out before she could get out of Hillcrest.

"Kimo is doing a bleach on long hair," she said. "It's going to take a while, and he also has a nine o'clock appointment coming in, so he's going to stay. The rest of us are hightailing it for higher ground while we still can."

Harry, preoccupied with other thoughts, barely listened. He didn't care what the hell was going on at the shop; he had other priorities.

"That's fine, Stella. Just tell Kimo not to forget to lock up when he's through."

"What am I? New on the job?" Stella said and hung up.

After the call, Sean came to Harry and pulled him down onto the sofa where he proceeded to remove Harry's clothing in less than a minute and, with his mouth, brought Harry to orgasm in less than five.

Afterward, when his heart had finally stopped pounding, Harry asked, "What was that? A pity fuck?"

Sean kissed his stomach and smiled up at him. "A pity blowjob. You looked tense."

At six o'clock, they switched on the news and were stunned to learn of the killings outside Sean's apartment building. Two detectives, both family men, were now also dead because of this crazy bastard, and it made Harry furious. The reporter didn't come right out and accuse Sean of the murders, but the implication was there. Where would it end? With all his heart, Harry hoped it would end right here. Tonight. Inside this house.

Shortly after the newscast, with the storm still raging outside and showing no signs of letting up any time in the near future, they heard the huge eucalyptus tree at the side of the house give up its battle against the elements and topple over, its roots torn from the wet ground by the relentless wind. Again, it missed the deck, but they heard a bedroom window shatter as a limb struck it, sending shards of glass flying across the room. Wind and rain swept into the bedroom. As the tree collapsed, it snagged the power line and ripped it from the pole that stood at the edge of the cliff.

Before Harry could react to the sound of the shattered window, the house was plummeted into darkness.

IF THE front desk clerk at the Stevens Hotel had known he was enjoying the last few remaining minutes of his lifetime, he might have chosen to spend them differently. And if he had known the manner of his upcoming death, some twenty minutes hence, he most assuredly would have made different decisions on how to spend his time on this stormy afternoon, the last afternoon he would ever know.

The clerk's name was Amos Smart. His last name could in no way be used as anything but a last name. As an adjective for poor Amos, it would be sorely misapplied. Even his first name was rarely used by those who knew him. To the people on the street, from the addled drunks who sometimes were coerced into sharing their bottles with him, to the reluctant prostitutes who sometimes shared his bed, coerced again, this time by money, he was known as Aimless. And even these people, the ones who lived on the lowest rungs of society's ladder, had little use for him. The drunks resented him for the way he looked down on them, even as he drank their liquor, but it was the prostitutes who feared him. One degrading hour in Aimless's bed was enough to make most of them seek an immediate career change. Only in times of the most dire financial need did they willingly climb into his bed again. Aimless enjoyed the pain of others, and he appraised a prostitute like a painter appraises a blank canvas. It was a place to leave his mark. And he left many. Inside and out. That's what made his tiny prick stand up. That's what made him happy. Hookers might give an inward cluck of pity on first gazing upon the size of poor Aimless's equipment, but by the time he was finished with them, all their pity would be directed toward themselves. It was his words and his fists they would come to fear, not the size of his cock.

Aimless was on the wrong side of forty, bald, and fifty pounds overweight. As he sat behind the front desk, he chewed on a stick of spearmint gum. It made his breath smell sweet and clean, the last thing one would expect from looking at him. Today, his eyes were rheumy and dull from the whiskey he had drunk the night before, his chin was bristly because he didn't trust his trembling hands to shave himself that morning without cutting his own throat, and as always, when hung over, he was in the mood to play. The hangover hots, he called them. He was forty-eight hours away from payday, and the six dollars in his wallet was not enough to buy even the scabbiest of whores. He needed cash, and he thought he might just know where he could lay his hands on some.

The man in room 314 had left the hotel around noon; it was now almost five o'clock, and he had still not returned. Aimless knew he should have checked out the man's room as soon as he left, five hours ago, but there was something about the guy that kept Aimless rooted to the stool behind the front desk for most of the afternoon. That something was fear. The pale man in 314 scared the bejesus out of him. He didn't know what would happen if the man returned to the hotel to find Aimless rummaging through his stuff, but Aimless figured it wouldn't be pretty.

It wasn't the fear of losing his job that kept Aimless nailed to that fucking stool. He didn't think the man in 314 was the type to complain to management. He wasn't the type to fill out a complaint form and meekly submit it to the head office, as if the Stevens Hotel even had such a thing as a complaint form lying about the place. No, Aimless was pretty sure the man in 314 would take the matter of complaints into his own hands. What the man would do, Aimless figured, was simply beat the shit out of him, and though pain was one of Aimless's greatest enjoyments, it was only the pain of others that he craved. Not his own. For, like most cruel people, Aimless was a coward of the highest magnitude.

Still, the growing tingle in his groin and the growing need for sexual release with someone weaker than himself was what finally dragged Aimless's fat ass off that stool and set him on the last poorly chosen path of his life. For Aimless Smart, it was to be his one final mistake in a long line of monumental mistakes. His crowning glory, if you will.

First, he stepped out from behind the front desk and walked across the lobby to the front doors. He pushed his way outside and stood beneath the battered awning that only partially protected him from the rain, which was coming down in buckets. Aside from a homeless woman who sat cowering under a blue tarp like some old Indian woman sitting beneath her tepee, he saw no one. The streets were deserted. No shoppers. No business people. No hookers plying their trade. And best of all, no pale man returning to the hotel after a day of doing who knew what. Aimless stood there in his shirt sleeves long enough for the cold to begin to make him shiver. He watched the corners at the end of the block, expecting the pale man to suddenly pop into view any moment as he wended his way back to the hotel, but the pale man never came.

Aimless returned to the lobby and headed for the stairway. The thought of that expensive-looking Samsonite suitcase, now lying unwatched and unprotected in room 314, drew him forward like a magnet draws metal.

Aimless knew the man was gone, had seen him leave the hotel hours ago, but still he stood outside the door to 314 and pressed his ear to it, listening for sounds from inside the room. And as he knew he would, he heard nothing. The man was not here. But the suitcase was. Aimless had seen the man leave without it.

Aimless pulled a second room key with 314 stenciled on it from his trouser pocket and slipped it into the lock. Easy as pie, he thought, as he quickly stepped through the door and silently pushed it closed behind him. He noticed an open package of Fig Newtons on the dresser and poured a handful of cookies into his palm. As he searched the room, he popped them into his mouth one by one, and before the last cookie was gone, he found the suitcase under the bed.

He tossed the suitcase onto the bed and was momentarily disconcerted to find it locked. But that had never stopped him before. He pulled a tiny piece of wire from another trouser pocket and inserted it into the lock. Pausing every few seconds to listen for footsteps in the hallway, he fiddled with the lock with his trembling hands until the latch snapped open. Aimless was sweating now, fear making his movements erratic. He wanted out of this room, and he wanted out now.

He rummaged through clothing. Shirts. Socks. Underwear. Two pairs of blue jeans. A sweater. He dug to the bottom of the bag and found nothing else. No money. No traveler checks. No expensive watch he could pawn. Nothing.

He checked the lining of the suitcase for hidden spaces where something might be stashed. He found none. Disgusted, he rearranged the clothing as neatly as he could and closed the suitcase. He slid it back under the bed where he had found it and looked about the room. In the small airless bathroom, he saw a shaving kit. He went to it and stirred up the contents, but again, he found nothing of value.

One by one, he opened the dresser drawers. They were as empty as when the man checked in. He flipped up the corners of the bed, checking beneath the mattress for hidden cash. He didn't find so much as a fucking dollar bill.

When he stood up, the pale man was standing in the doorway looking at him with a pleasant smile on his face.

"Find what you're looking for?"

Aimless felt his heart do a somersault inside his chest, and a trickle of sweat slid into his eye, burning him. He brushed it away. The man was leaning casually against the doorframe, his coat wet with rain. A small pool of water was forming at his feet as he patiently stared at Aimless, waiting for an answer.

"There was smoke," Aimless said. "One of the tenants smelled smoke. I thought maybe you were cooking in here."

The pale man's smile grew wider. "Under the bed?"

Before Aimless could formulate a response, the pale man stepped quickly across the room, and only then did Aimless see the knife in his hand.

The shock of seeing the man move so quickly toward him caused Aimless's bladder to let go, and urine suddenly gushed through his tiny penis and down his pant leg. The acrid stench of it was the last thing Aimless would ever smell, and given the life he lived, it might seem fitting that it would be so.

"Wait...," he said.

But the pale man did not wait. He pressed the knife under Aimless's chin and held it there for a moment as he looked deeply into Aimless's frightened eyes.

"Goodbye," the man said, and pushed the knife deep into the stubbly chin, through the tongue and up through the palate. Aimless gasped once as the knife slid into his brain, and after that, Aimless hung dead, impaled upon the blade. As the pale man pulled the knife back out and stepped aside to avoid the spill of blood, Aimless collapsed to the floor at his feet.

Leisurely, the man walked back to the door and closed it. He pulled his suitcase from beneath the bed, opened it with his little key, and began collecting his belongings. He, too, ate a few Fig Newtons as he returned his toothbrush and razor to the shaving kit and then tossed the kit into the suitcase on the bed. He returned to the bathroom, pissed in the toilet, and as it flushed, he reached behind the tank and withdrew the Redhawk pistol and box of cartridges he had taped there that morning. The gun and cartridges, too, he threw into the suitcase.

When he was finished, he closed the bag, locked it, and looked down at the man on the floor beside the bed.

"I'll be checking out now," he said. "Don't get up."

With that, he exited the room, closed the door softly behind him, and walked quickly down the stairwell to the lobby and out of the hotel.

By the time he was back on the street, the desk clerk was all but forgotten. Only thoughts of the night awaiting him filled his mind.

Time for that haircut, he thought, as he walked to where he had parked his rental car on the street two blocks over. That would make him feel better. A haircut always did.

JUDY FORTUNATO phoned Detective Smith in his motel room at 4:30 on Tuesday morning. He wouldn't have been much more surprised if he had awoken to find her sprawled across his bed with her gray head between his legs.

"What's wrong?" he asked, staring dumbly at his travel clock on the nightstand.

Judy sounded chipper and wide awake. Smith could imagine the cigarette dangling from her lips as she spoke.

"Good morning, Hiawatha. Time to haul your brown buns out of bed. Your canoe awaits."

"Say what?"

"*Say what*? What do you mean, *say what*? Aren't you chomping at the bit to get out of here?"

"Well, yeah, but…."

"But nothing. You've got thirty minutes to pack up, don your mittens, and drag your sorry ass outside. Jesse will be there at five to pick you up. Your flight leaves at seven."

Smith rubbed his eyes, scratched his crotch, cleared his throat, and swung his legs out of bed.

"What about the weather?"

"I'm staring at the computer screen right now, and as of fifteen minutes ago, the rain had stopped in San Diego and Lindbergh Field was once again accepting incoming flights. With any luck, it'll hold for another four or five hours and you'll be able to land. If not, they'll reroute you to the nearest city. I'm sure you would find even that preferable to being stranded in Nine Mile. A little closer to the action, don't you think? And you should also know they are predicting snow for us later today. How much and for how long they aren't saying. It would be in your best interest to get out while the getting's good, wouldn't you think?"

"Judy, you're a doll. I could kiss you."

"Don't toy with me, Detective."

"You do realize that it's four thirty in the morning. Don't you ever sleep?"

"Only after sex."

"Ah."

"And I haven't had sex since August of 1983."

"I see."

"I don't sleep much."

"I guess not."

Thirty minutes later, Smith was once again ensconced in Jesse's Jeep Sahara, and miles of frozen Indiana highway were humming along beneath his ass. Once again, Jesse offered coffee and bear claws. After a hasty goodbye and thank you in Indianapolis and a ten minute jog to his gate, Smith found himself taxiing down a runway in a first-class seat, thanks to Judy and her computer skills, on a Boeing 727 bound for Albuquerque, Phoenix, and ultimately, San Diego.

He had not learned a lot on his trip. But he had learned enough. He felt he knew Jackson Andros better now. He still had no idea what made the fucker tick or why he was out to get revenge upon his brother, Sean, but at least he knew now that this was indeed the case. There would probably be hell to pay when he tried to get his travel money reimbursed from the Department, but Smith would worry about that later.

McCray, he knew, had not been idle while Smith was away. He had a definite ID on Jackson Andros. That was a biggie. As for the hustler, it was imperative now that they find the boy. Or find the person who was harboring him. The young man was in danger and needed to be protected. His protector needed protection, as well. Enough people had died already.

Two hours into the flight, as the Boeing was crossing somewhere over Kansas, Smith's luck took a bad bounce when the pilot announced over the intercom that San Diego was once again socked in by rainfall of apparent biblical proportions. As was Los Angeles. Even San Francisco was turning flights away, not because of rain but because of fog. The whole west coast was a clusterfuck of pissed off tourists trying to get out and weary Californians trying to get back in.

His flight was rerouted to Las Vegas. There was nowhere else for it to go, and that was fine with Smith. He would rent a car from there and drive the rest of the way. With any luck at all, and depending, of course, upon the weather, he would still be home by nightfall or shortly after.

Smith had a feeling that events would be coming to a head very quickly now. It wouldn't be long before Jackson Andros knew they were onto him, and he would have to make his move. Smith was determined to be in San Diego when he did.

THE person who occupied Detective Jimmy Smith's mind while he nibbled on stale peanuts, sipped a fairly decent wine, and fidgeted impatiently in his roomy first-class seat some 900 miles east and 12,000 feet up, was currently sitting by the window in a tiny Mexican restaurant on Fourth Avenue, eating a chimichanga. He was idly watching the rain hit the sidewalk outside with all the force of a cow pissing on a flat rock, as his old dad used to say.

Upon careful consideration, the man had decided that as a tourist spot, Southern California just wasn't all it was cracked up to be. The good Lord knew he had met some interesting people, and in some cases, such as with the desk clerk at the Stevens Hotel, he felt he had made a major contribution to the quality of their lives, but gee, it just never seemed to stop raining. Of course, he knew the rain was all part of God's plan to help him with his mission, but it did put a bit of a crimp in his sightseeing.

As he ate, he noticed a spot of blood on the cuff of his shirt, but since there were no other patrons in the restaurant, he didn't bother trying to cover it. Upon closer inspection, he also found dried blood beneath the fingernails of his right hand. His knife hand. He dipped his paper napkin in a glass of water and thoroughly cleaned beneath his nails before once again picking up the chimichanga and taking another bite out of it. He'd have to be more careful in the future. Every child in Bible School knew that cleanliness was next to Godliness. You couldn't be a slob when you were doing God's work. It wouldn't be proper.

The old Mexican couple who ran the place kept casting impatient looks in his direction, but the man ignored them. Yes, he knew it was almost nine o'clock, and yes, he knew they wanted to close, but frankly

he didn't give a shit. Let them wait. He was doing God's work. Surely
to Christ they could hang around a few extra minutes before heading
back to the Barrio and the one-room shack he figured they called home.
So he slowly cleaned his fingernails, and then he *slowly* resumed eating
his chimichanga. He gave the old couple an obtuse smile that must have
set their teeth on edge and slowly turned his head back around to stare
out the window.

Just as he had done for the past twenty minutes, he gazed through
the downpour and studied the business across the street. Harry's for
Hair didn't appear to be a very going concern on this wet winter
evening. Through the glass storefront, he could see all the way to the
back of the salon, and he had spotted only one stylist working. During
all the time he had been sitting in the restaurant, the small man in the
black smock had been toiling away with brush and blow dryer on a
pretty young woman with long blonde hair who was seated in the chair
before him. They seemed to be having a good time. He could see the
young woman turning her head this way and that, admiring her image
in the mirror, obviously pleased with what she saw. Together, they
laughed at something the stylist said, and as he laid the blow dryer in a
tray beside him, the young woman stood and gave him a hug.

After that, the transaction became more businesslike as money
changed hands and the young man helped the woman into her raincoat.
He walked her to the door and opened her umbrella for her before
sending her out into the night.

The stylist was now alone in the salon. Jackson watched him tidy
up his work station and check his watch. It was show time. Jackson
pushed his plate away and pulled on his coat. He laid money on the
table to cover his bill and stepped outside into the rain. As he jogged
across the street, he saw the stylist appraising him through the window,
so he waved a friendly greeting as he sloshed his way to the salon door
and watched the stylist push it open to usher him inside.

KIMO DALISAY, the son of Filipino immigrants, was a petite young
man of twenty-four with the flawless skin of a child and a facial bone

structure that most women would kill for. He had worked with Harry for two years and was a very popular stylist with a large clientele of young professionals, both male and female, who paid him a great deal of money every few weeks in the mostly vain hope that Kimo could make them look as good as he did.

He had been told his entire life that he was too beautiful to be a boy, and this alone, perhaps, was enough to explain why Kimo had chosen also to perform on stage. Every Friday, Saturday, and Sunday night he could be seen at the Show Biz Supper Club on University Avenue in a drag revue under the stage name of Tawny Tann. Dressed as a woman, Kimo was a knockout. Carol Channing, in town with the road show of *Hello, Dolly!* had once come backstage after a late dinner at the club to tell him he was the most gorgeous woman she had ever seen. Kimo's head had floated among the clouds for weeks afterward.

Aside from being an excellent hair stylist and a talented performer, Kimo was also a very nice person. There was no conceit in Kimo. He volunteered at the AIDS Outreach Center on Tuesday nights to cut the hair of patients who were housebound, and every month he sent a sizable sum of money to his aging grandparents in Manila whom he had never met but loved dearly just the same. Kimo's parents adored him and could be seen upon occasion at the Show Biz, enjoying the revue and joking over their sixty-dollar dinners with the waiters who affectionately called them Mom and Dad. If their son's gayness was any sort of issue with them, they chose not to let it show. They loved their son enough to accept him for who he was.

If there was a flaw in Kimo's character, and there is always at least one, it was his penchant for dangerous sex. He had seduced Harry on his second day at the salon, not because he particularly wanted Harry, but just to see if he could do it. Harry had seemed to understand and accept this, and they had never come together in that way again, although they remained on friendly terms.

Many nights would find Kimo cruising the bathrooms in Balboa Park or hitting the dives below Broadway, using his beauty to attract men who appealed to him. Dangerous men. And for the most part, straight men. That was his preference.

He had no desire to be a woman. He liked his body the way it was. And straight men seemed to like it, too. The most homophobic asshole in the world might get a boner just looking at Kimo's luscious lips or rounded ass as he imagined what might be done with them. And in most cases, if the man was clean and handsome and strong, Kimo would be more than willing to oblige.

And the man who now ducked in out of the rain and shook his wet hair out of his eyes, those cold blue eyes that Kimo had spotted from twenty feet away, seemed dangerous indeed. And very appealing.

The man appeared a bit ragged around the edges, as if he had spent a couple of sleepless nights, but that appealed to Kimo too. And the slim hips and sizable bulge in the crotch of the man's well-worn blue jeans did nothing to lessen the appeal.

But the eyes....

"You must be my nine o'clock," Kimo said, feeling that familiar surge of desire rush through him.

"Must be," the man answered.

Kimo helped the man out of his wet coat and hung it on the coat rack by the door. As he did, the man scanned the salon to reassure himself that they were alone. They were.

Kimo turned and stretched out his hand. "I'm Kimo."

"Jackson," the man said, taking the stylist's hand in a firm grip and holding it a beat longer than necessary. Those cold eyes studied Kimo's face as their hands touched, and Kimo felt himself being drawn into the tall man's orbit like the moon draws the tide. The man stood a head taller than Kimo, and it took all of Kimo's will power not to drop to his knees and press his lips to that promising bulge right then and there.

Jesus, those eyes filled Kimo's mind with more erotic thoughts than it had held in a month. And before the night was over, he knew, he would have this man if it was the last thing he ever did.

Little did he know.

"Well," Kimo said, mentally shaking himself. "Let's see what we can do about your hair."

The man smiled like a man who understands his own power, and said, "Okey-doke."

Kimo led him to his styling chair. As he slipped a Sanek strip around Jackson's neck Kimo let his fingers linger a moment on the hot skin at the nape of the man's neck. Then, a bit reluctantly, he covered the lean body with a styling cape.

Kimo ran his fingers through the man's hair. It was as fine as a baby's. And thinning.

"I can make this look thicker," he said.

The man watched him in the mirror but said nothing.

"Any special instructions?" Kimo asked, still enjoying the feel of the man's hair between his fingers but trying to seem professional as he did so. He didn't think the man was fooled.

"Do with me what you will," Jackson said.

Oh, I intend to, Kimo thought. But first let's cut this hair.

WORKING together, Harry and Sean sealed the broken bedroom window by nailing a card table across the opening. It was the only thing Harry could find that was large enough to cover it. They worked by the light of a flashlight because no candle would stay lit in the wind that now poured through the shattered window. When they were finished, Harry again lit candles, more successfully this time, and surveyed the damage. The room was a mess. Sodden eucalyptus leaves were everywhere, and the carpet squished beneath their feet. Shattered mini-blinds hung in a tangle around the broken window. The bed was soaked and would probably have to be discarded.

"Time to remodel," Sean said, appraising the room with his hands on his hips.

Harry was kneeling on the floor, carefully removing the broken picture glass from an oil painting of wildflowers that he had bought for three hundred dollars the year before at an art show in Balboa Park. The painting was undamaged. It would just need to be reframed. He carried the canvas to the hall and left it there to dry.

Nothing else in the spare bedroom was of any importance to Harry. He picked up the candles, shooed Sean out to the hall and closed the bedroom door behind them.

"We'll worry about it later," he said. "Let's get out of these wet clothes. You're shivering."

They changed in the master bedroom. Harry donned clean jeans and a T-shirt while Sean slipped into his new sweat pants and Charger sweatshirt—after he snipped off the sales tags. They didn't appear to fit much better than Harry's pajamas had.

"Maybe they'll shrink," Sean said, looking doubtful.

Harry wrapped his arms around the boy and rested his chin on the top of Sean's head.

"You're having quite a night, aren't you?"

Sean pressed his face into Harry's shirtfront. "We'll get through it. I trust you."

They stood that way for a moment until Harry asked, "Where are the cats?"

"God knows," Sean said, glancing around. "They probably decided this wasn't the safest place to be and hailed a cab. I'm beginning to think the same thing."

They searched the house and finally found the animals huddled together in a utility closet in the small basement where Harry kept his washer and dryer. Down there, the storm sounded far away and less threatening. The cats, with their unerring good sense, had managed to find the safest spot in the house and showed no inclination to leave it, so Harry left them there.

They returned to the living room and Harry set enough candles around to chase away the shadows. "If we weren't waiting for some crazy motherfucker to come and kill us," he said, "this could be quite romantic."

Sean looked out at the night, what little of it he could see through the sheets of rain that washed down the patio window.

"You're an amazing person, Harry. Nothing much seems to rattle you."

"Oh, I'm rattled."

Harry could see Sean smile in the reflection in the glass.

"Well, you don't show it."

"Just keeping up a brave front," Harry said. "You know, for the sake of the cats."

"Right. For the sake of the cats."

Sean turned to look at Harry sitting on the sofa, his face awash with candlelight. He noticed the gun had been taken from on top the desk and was now resting on the coffee table in front of him where it could be reached at a moment's notice.

The two men, one young and one older, studied each other's faces from across the room. Over their heads the storm raged on.

"You've done more for me in the past three days," Sean said, "than anyone else has done in my whole lifetime. You put your life on hold for me, and you've put yourself in danger. Now your house is a mess, your business is probably suffering, and still you look at me the way you do."

"What way is that?" Harry asked.

Sean hesitated, then said, "Like you love me."

Harry brushed his hair from his eyes but said nothing. Thoughts whirled through his head. Memories. More than four-and-a-half decades of experience had molded him into the person he was today. Four-and-a-half decades that had led him on a straight course to this one night. To this one young man who was now gazing at him with such a look of wonder on his innocent face that it made Harry want to cry out with the awe of it. This boy made him feel more like a man, a real man, than anyone else Harry had ever known or cared about. And he loved this boy more deeply than any of the others. More than anything or anyone that had come into his life in all his long years.

Sean came to the sofa, stretched out on it, and rested his head in Harry's lap.

"Talk to me," Sean said.

Harry laid his hand across the boy's cheek and stared out at the storm.

Finally, he spoke, and to his own surprise, the words poured out of him as if they had been waiting a long time to be said.

"I've lived a good life, Sean. I've worked hard and played hard and I've been in three long-term relationships that were very important to me at the time. I've been happy and I've been downright miserable. But mostly I've been happy. My last lover died of leukemia about three years ago, and that was perhaps the saddest time in my life. But I got over it. When something terrible happens, you have to let it wash over you, like a wave. You have to hold your breath until the pain lessens with time, or you'll drown in the misery of it. It took me more than two years to get over Ben's death. And it was the sight of you that finally brought me up for air."

Surprised, Sean looked up into Harry's face. "Me?"

Harry ran his hand over the boy's hair, reveling in the texture of it. He was sorry now that he had colored it. He wanted to see it blond again.

"You," he said. "From the very first night we met, when Biff and the guys presented you to me as a birthday gift. Do you remember?"

Sean smiled. "Of course. The first time we had sex was right here on this sofa."

Harry smiled, too, at the memory. "The way you handled yourself. And the way you handled me. There was no shame in you. And you were the most beautiful thing I'd ever seen. I knew you were being paid. And in the back of my mind I knew you were…."

"A whore," Sean said.

Harry nodded. "Okay. A whore. But still, there was something about you. An innocence. It took my breath away."

"No one can ever accuse me of being innocent, Harry. The things I've done…."

"Yes, but it doesn't matter, see? Somehow those things you've done never reached you. They never changed you. You weren't touched by them. You didn't become hard."

"I became hard plenty of times."

"Very funny. You know what I mean. You didn't become cynical. Through it all you managed somehow to keep that spark of innocence and sweetness that you were born with. I loved you then, that first night, and I love you now. More than anyone I've ever been with. The fact that you love me, too, is an astounding thing to me. The things I've done these past three days, I've done them as much for myself as I've done them for you. I want you with me. I want to change the way you live your life, but I don't want to change *you*. I want you to be happy and I want us to be happy together. I can do things for you, Sean. I have money. We can make you anything you want to be."

Sean snuggled closer, pushing his face into Harry's stomach.

"I just want to be with you, Harry. I just want all this trouble to be over so I can be with you. And I'll be anything you want me to be."

"Just be yourself," Harry said. "Just stay with me and be yourself. I'll make you safe, and I'll try to make you happy."

Sean reached up and traced a finger along Harry's jaw line.

"You already have, Harry. No matter how things end up, you already have."

"Good," Harry said. "Oh, and one more thing."

"What's that?"

"I absolutely insist that you change professions."

Sean giggled. "Well, if you think I should."

"Oh, yeah. I can't afford you otherwise."

"You may not be able to afford me, anyway," Sean said, still laughing. "I require a lot of maintenance."

"I'm beginning to realize that. You don't have any other serial killers after your ass that I should know about, do you?"

"God," Sean said, the smile fading from his lips. "I hope not."

"So do I."

KIMO could cut a head of hair in ten minutes, and do it well, but on this man he would take his time. They were alone in the shop with no other customers waiting and only the long night stretched before them. After work, Kimo had originally intended to go to the club and rehearse his numbers for the new show that would open in a couple of weeks, but that could wait another day. Right now, he had other things on his mind.

As he worked with scissors and comb, he said, "So, you're a friend of Harry's?"

"Why would you think that?" the man asked. His eyes, in the mirror, had not once left Kimo's face.

"The receptionist told me you asked for him."

"Oh."

Strong, silent type, Kimo thought. He liked that.

"I've never seen you in here before. Does Harry usually cut your hair?"

"No, I'm from out of town. Harry and I are old friends, but we lost touch over the years. I was hoping to catch him here, but it seems he's on vacation."

Kimo laughed. "Yeah, a pretty sudden one. Nobody knew he was leaving until he was gone."

"Harry likes whores," the man said, still staring into Kimo's eyes, watching his movements in the mirror. "He probably has a new one he's trying out."

Kimo stopped snipping and looked at the man. "Harry?"

"Yeah, Harry."

Kimo resumed cutting. "Well, apparently you know some things about Harry that I don't."

"I'm sure I do."

Kimo had little interest in pursuing this line of conversation. What Harry did in his own time was his own business. And Kimo liked Harry. He wouldn't be drawn into gossiping about him. His priorities lay elsewhere at the moment.

Kimo turned the chair around until he was standing in front of it. He felt his thighs press against Jackson's knees as he said, "I'm going to shorten the hair in the front. It will make it seem thicker and it will bring out your eyes."

He began to cut.

"My eyes?"

"Yes. They are quite striking. I'm sure people have told you that before. This will make them even more so. Trust me."

Kimo feather cut the front of the man's hair and then paused for a moment to study the effect. Their faces were inches apart. Kimo could feel the man's warm breath on his skin. For a moment, as Kimo straddled the footrest of the chair, he lost his balance, and Jackson reached out both hands to steady him. Kimo felt the man's large hands almost encircle his waist.

Jackson's mind was suddenly filled with the memory of that long-ago night when he stood beside his brother's bed, half naked and hard. He remembered the feel of his brother's mouth as the young boy accepted the gift Jackson offered him. The gift he knew the boy had always wanted. This young man standing before him wanted that gift as well. Jackson could see it on his face, in his eyes. Had sensed it in the sudden intake of breath when his hands had reached out and gripped the young man's waist. And in his body, Jackson felt the stirring of lust. That familiar surge of passion, of sinful longing, that had haunted him his entire life. It angered him as it always had, but he kept the anger hidden deep inside, where this boy could not see it. Not yet.

"I think you'd better lock the door," Jackson said, releasing his grip on Kimo's slim waist. "Do it now."

"Yes," Kimo said, staring deep into those cool blue eyes and trembling now with the sudden tension between them. He, too, felt the lust surging through him. But Kimo's lust was not accompanied by anger. Only want. And thirst. And that thrilling, familiar need.

As Kimo, weak at the knees, pulled away and crossed the salon to flip the lock on the front door, Jackson pulled the cape from around his neck and tossed it to the floor. He sat back in the chair and began unbuttoning his shirt as he watched Kimo draw the blinds on the front window.

"Now take your clothes off," Jackson said as the boy turned to face him. "Take everything off."

"God," Kimo said, smiling. "You don't waste any time." But he did what the man told him to do, and in less than a minute, he stood naked in front of the chair. Jackson reached out and placed his hand, fingers splayed wide, against the firm brown skin of Kimo's stomach, testing the feel of another man's flesh beneath his touch, tenderly, for the first time in his life.

Hands eager and trembling, Kimo spread Jackson's shirt apart. He bent down to press his lips to Jackson's chest, feeling the heat of the man against his face, the taste of the man's perfect skin against his tongue.

"Now take *your* clothes off," Kimo whispered, inhaling the man's scent, sensing the man's passion and need as strongly as he sensed his own.

"You do it," Jackson said.

So Kimo did, first bending down to remove Jackson's shoes and socks and then moving upward to unhook Jackson's belt and the snap of his jeans. Jackson raised his hips from the chair and Kimo grabbed the jeans by the cuffs and stripped them off, flinging them away.

"You're so white," Kimo said, still on his knees in front of the chair. The man's long cock was as hard and warm as sun-washed stone. Kimo gripped the heat of it, pulling back the foreskin. He pressed his lips to the man's thigh, again tasting the hot skin beneath his tongue.

"It's a sign of purity," Jackson said.

"Is it?"

"Yes."

"Purity has never been my long suit," Kimo said softly, running his hands over Jackson's stomach, across his chest. "But I can admire it in someone else."

"You seem to be admiring it now. You're shaking."

"I know. Your body is beautiful."

"I'm glad you like it," Jackson said.

Kimo slid his cheek along the man's thigh, smiling as the mound of crisp pubic hair brushed his face. He looked up into the man's eyes as his hand began to move up and down along the shaft of Jackson's penis.

"I want this inside me," Kimo said. "All of it."

"Do you?"

"Yes."

Jackson studied the young man's eager face, watched the lust burning in those foreign eyes. "Do you always get what you want?"

With his teeth, Kimo gently nipped at the base of Jackson's cock. He grinned. "Usually."

Jackson gave a little cluck of sympathy and said, "I'm afraid this time you're going to be sorely disappointed."

With that, he picked up the scissors from the tray beside the chair and drove them into Kimo's neck as far as they would go. They skittered off bone before sliding deep into the young man's flesh. Releasing the scissors, Jackson gripped Kimo's hair and held that beautiful dying face against his leg until the young man ceased to struggle. Through it all, Kimo made no sound. As hot blood poured out across his thigh, Jackson continued to hold the young man against him as he took his own cock in his bloody hand and masturbated. He came quickly, and when he was finished, he pushed Kimo's lifeless body away from him. It fell, huddled over like a Moslem crouched on his prayer rug at the foot of the chair. Blood continued to seep from the wound at the boy's neck until it all but encircled the slight, naked body.

The death scene had been reflected in a dozen mirrors around the salon, as if simultaneously acted out upon a dozen stages, like a multiplex showing the same performers on every screen going through the same horrible motions.

Jackson took a white towel from a stack on the counter and wiped the blood from his legs. When he was clean, he looked at himself in the mirror. His hair was much shorter now, but it looked good.

"Best haircut I've ever had," he said. "Here's your tip."

With his fingers, he scooped the semen from his stomach and flipped it onto the body.

Jackson retrieved his clothes from where they were scattered across the floor and put them on.

Before leaving the salon, he leafed through the rolodex on Kimo's work station until he found Harry's phone number. He stared at the name on the card. Harry Connors. In his mind's eye, he imagined how that name would look on a gravestone, carved in marble. He could see it clearly.

He tore Harry's card from the rolodex and stuffed it into his pocket. He wasn't sure yet if he would use the number, but it was always wise to be prepared. One never knew what might happen.

Jackson gazed down at the small, still body huddled at his feet, kneeling in the ever-widening pool of blood. Little dead Moslem, praying to Allah.

Yes, one should always be prepared. And circumspect.

It was a pity poor Kimo hadn't known that.

CHAPTER ELEVEN

AT MCCARRON Airport on the outskirts of Las Vegas, with the beep and boop of electronic slot machines clanging away in the background, Jimmy Smith rented a Ford Focus, and a few minutes later, he was barreling down Route 15, well above the speed limit, as if the cavalry was chasing his Indian ass off yet another reservation. The rental car reeked of cigar smoke and drove like a log wagon, but that's what the lady at the Avis counter gave him, so that's what he took.

Two hours later, he stopped to take a whiz and pick up some coffee at a truck stop in Barstow. He was back on the highway in less than ten minutes. Shortly after that, he hit the rain. Or rather, the rain hit him. He drove into it like a man slipping through a curtain, with a visible line drawn across the macadam, going from dry to wet in the space of a second.

He had driven this lonely stretch of highway a few other times in his life, usually on weekend jaunts with his wife to the casinos of Vegas, but he had never driven it alone, and he had never driven it in anything other than desert heat. Tonight the desert air had an unfamiliar chill to it, and the rain seemed out of place, as if someone in programming had screwed up and dumped it in the wrong location. In deference to the hard rain, he slowed down to a suicidal seventy-five and hoped for the best. Thankfully, there wasn't much traffic. Sipping his coffee and blasting the radio to stay awake, he wondered what his partner was up to.

He punched in McCray's number on his cell phone. As he listened to it ring, he steered the car around the carcass of a coyote who had been foolish enough to take his evening constitutional right down the middle of the frigging highway. Someone had nailed the unfortunate creature on the centerline. In his headlights, the body looked wet and pathetic as it lay there in the rain.

McCray answered with his usual, "What's up, Chief?"

"I just left Barstow, my ass is numb from sitting too long, I'm drinking a cup of coffee that tastes like rhinoceros piss, and it's raining like someone should be building another ark."

"Get used to it," McCray answered. "The rain, I mean. I haven't been dry in three days."

"Anything new?"

"Well, I've got some sort of yeast infection on my back. The dermatologist gave me a steroid cream that seems to be clearing it up."

"That's fascinating, Jeff, but I was referring to the investigation."

"Grumpy."

"You bet."

"Well, we haven't found your boy yet. Either one of them, in fact. It's like the hustler just disappeared off the face of the planet, but I think we've got a line on the older brother. A desk clerk at the Stevens Hotel, that fleabag down on Market, was found just a few minutes ago in one of the rooms. We think maybe the killer caught the guy pawing through his stuff and decided to teach him a lesson. Stuck a knife up under his chin and skewered his brains. Sound familiar?"

"Fingerprints in the room?"

"They're working on it."

"It's him," Smith said into the phone. "I'd bet my shield on it."

"I know. Killing the clerk must have spooked him. He took off. Took all his belongings with him. Including the murder weapon. I hate to think what he's up to now. Nobody's safe as long as this asshole is on the street. I've got uniforms checking out all the hotels downtown. He has to stay somewhere. He was at the Grant before he checked into the Stevens. Don't ask me how I know."

McCray was referring to the disjointed statement he had taken from the Mexican mother who lost her young son in front of the U.S. Grant three days before. McCray had a pretty good hunch that the man masturbating in the hotel window was Jackson Andros. He couldn't prove it, of course, but he knew it just the same. Mrs. Esposito had called the man by another name. El Diablo. The devil. McCray didn't figure she was far from wrong.

McCray went on. "They finally finished interviewing as many of the Prado workers as they could find who were in the park on the night of the bombing. Came up with nada. Nobody saw a thing. I already told you I got a definite ID on the guy in the bar. The bartender swears it was Jackson Andros and I believe him. I think he's holding something back, though."

"Like what?"

"Like maybe he knows who the kid left with but for some reason doesn't feel like sharing that information with the police. All we know at this point is that the guy's name is Harry."

"If we find out later that the bartender *did* know Harry's full name and where we could have found him, I want the fucker nailed to the cross when the investigation is over."

McCray did a fair imitation of Margaret Hamilton. "Him and his little dog, too."

"Say what?"

"Forget it. So how was Indiana?"

Smith considered the question for a moment before answering.

"Great food. Lousy weather. Good cops. And I got a free pair of mittens."

"Well, gee. What more could one ask for?"

"This rain is really coming down," Smith said, easing up on the accelerator a tad. "I'm assuming it's doing the same there."

"Oh, yeah. I've never seen anything like it. We've got power outages all over the city. Streets are washed out. Trees are down. Houses are sliding around like they're on wheels, and I think I ruined my suit."

"You sure that's a yeast infection on your back? Might be mildew."

"I wouldn't be surprised. Hold on, Chief, I've got another call."

Smith waited a full two minutes before McCray came back on the line.

"We've got another one."

"Goddammit! Already?" In his anger, Smith booted the car back up to seventy-five.

"Looks like it," McCray said. "Some hair stylist in Hillcrest. Stabbed in the neck and left naked on the salon floor. I'm on my way there now. Maybe it's a robbery gone wrong. Might not be our boy."

"Was the victim's dick intact?"

"I didn't ask."

"It's Andros. I know it is. Another naked, dead gay man. Who else would it be? An unhappy client? Some broad who didn't like her perm?"

"We'll find out soon enough. I'm almost there. I'll call you back."

Smith disconnected and pushed the car up to eighty, then thought better of it and slowed back down to seventy. The rain was just too heavy. He'd like to see his wife and kids again, and he'd like to see them somewhere other than from a hospital bed after paramedics scraped him off this fucking highway. Whatever was happening in San Diego, McCray could handle it. Smith checked his watch. Barring catastrophe, he should be there in an hour and a half.

He wanted this Andros guy more than he'd ever wanted anyone during the course of his career. The man was a walking misery machine. He had left a trail of corpses halfway across the country, including his own parents, and he hadn't even reached his primary target yet, not so far as they knew, anyway. Not for the first time, Smith wondered just what the hell the youngest son of Mr. and Mrs. Andros could have done to set this god-awful chain of events into motion. Or had he done nothing at all? Perhaps Jackson Andros, in his misguided religious zeal, had just decided out of the blue to set himself up as some sort of avenger from God. The guy was obviously nuts. The contents of his trailer told Smith that much. Maybe Jackson Andros had just been a ticking time bomb that finally went off, through no fault of anyone else. Smith felt sure that when all the facts were known, Sean Andros would be proven to be just as innocent as the other victims.

Wherever Sean was hiding, Smith hoped he had covered his tracks well. He didn't want the boy to die. Hustler or not, the young man he and McCray had watched on that security tape from the liquor store looked like someone who deserved a chance to live, and Smith wanted more than anything to be the one to give the boy that chance.

STELLA didn't feel guilty about lying to Harry. Not a lie, really, just a little fib. She had worked as Harry's receptionist for three years, and she knew that he wouldn't have been hanging around the salon when there was nothing to do, either. In fact, old Harry usually beat his last customer out the door. So, when she saw the rain coming down outside the salon window like a waterfall, she knew darn good and well there would be no more customers that day, and it was a perfect opportunity for her to squeeze in a little extra quality time with her boyfriend, Bobby.

Bobby was between jobs. He had, in fact, been between jobs for the entire six months she had been seeing him. But Bobby was also very skilled at making love. If it bothered her that she always paid for their dinners and movie tickets and condoms, and that Bobby was living in her apartment rent free, one flick of his tongue in a critical location and suddenly it would all be forgotten. Bobby knew this, of course. He was no fool. He understood that the piper had to be paid, and Stella was more than happy to fill the role of piper. She figured Bobby was a bargain at any price. Until she tired of footing the bills, at least.

So when she rushed home on this rainy afternoon, she wasn't surprised to find Bobby laid back in the recliner as naked as the day he was born and smiling at her as she walked through the door.

They didn't bother with pleasantries. They rarely did. He merely spread his strong fuzzy legs a little wider, offering her a better view of the merchandise she loved to sample, and just as he knew she would, she came to him, shedding her clothes along the way. By the time she crossed the room, she was as naked as he.

They spent a very enjoyable hour on the recliner and later they dozed.

When they awoke, Bobby was hungry. Stella offered to make dinner, but he insisted on pizza. She didn't particularly want to spend the money—payday was a long way off—but she gave in when he brushed his lips across her nipple and cupped her pelvic bone with his hand. She reached for the phone just as his finger began to do something mystical down there, and he laughed as she gasped while trying to place the order. She felt guilty forcing some poor schmuck out into weather like this to deliver their pizza, but by the time the schmuck rang the doorbell forty minutes later, Bobby's talented tongue had brought her to an orgasm that made her forget all about any discomfort she might have caused the guy while he traipsed around in the rain. She appeased her guilt over the money by scrimping on the schmuck's tip, and this made her feel guilty all over again.

Still naked, they scarfed down pizza and watched the apartment grow dark around them. Later, while Bobby put Lara Croft through her paces on the Playstation, Stella straightened up the place and did the breakfast dishes, which Bobby had managed to ignore throughout the entire course of the day, and as she put the last dish in the cupboard, she remembered that she had forgotten to give Kimo the salon key so he could lock up when he was finished working.

She looked at the clock. It was nine thirty. Kimo's last appointment had been for a haircut at nine. Surely he would still be working. Maybe he hadn't yet realized that he didn't have the key.

She rang the salon and was surprised when the answering machine picked up, her own voice coming back at her, apologizing that no one was in the salon at the moment and to please leave a name and number and someone would be in touch momentarily to return the call, thank you very much, have a nice day. Well, shit! Where the hell was Kimo? Mentally, she told him to pick up the phone, over and over, until the tape automatically disconnected, and then she called back and did the same thing all over again. When the answering machine disconnected for the second time, she faced the obvious, pulled the clothes back on that she had dropped earlier on the living room floor, and headed out the door, telling Bobby she'd be right back. Bobby, lost in the world of *Tomb Raider* and Lara's big boobs, didn't respond.

By the time Stella reached the salon, she was good and angry. At Kimo. At herself. At Bobby. At the rain.

The salon lights were on, but the blinds were drawn. Could Kimo have stepped out for something and missed her call? Maybe even now he was trying to reach her, finally realizing that he didn't have the key.

She ducked under the awning and shook herself off before trying the door. It was unlocked. Of course, it was. She had the key.

Stella stepped inside and immediately saw everything. Kimo's naked body hunched over at the foot of his styling chair. The blood. Kimo's clothes by the door. The thought crossed her mind that this might be a good time to scream, but she didn't. Not yet. He might still be alive, she told herself, but she knew it wasn't true. The blood and the stillness of his small body told her that much. She saw two circles of silver glinting at Kimo's neck. What *was* that? She took two steps closer before she realized what she was seeing. It was the handle of Kimo's chromium scissors. The blades of the scissors had been driven so deep into Kimo's neck that the circular finger grips were now standing up, flush against the skin like a silver bow, catching the light, looking almost festive.

Stella gave a small scream then, like someone startled by a spider, and for a brief moment she thought she might faint, but she didn't give herself the chance. She was back out the door so fast that she caught the sleeve of her raincoat on the doorknob and heard it tear. She fumbled for her keys in the darkness and, not sure why she did it, locked the door behind her before heading for the lights of an all-night diner two blocks down and across the street. It was the only business open at this hour, and there would be people there. She would call the police from the diner, where she would be safe. Where she would not be alone while she waited. Where no one could do to her what had been done to Kimo.

Oddly enough, the diner was busy. It was, of course, only a few days before Christmas. Shoppers had to shop, no matter what the weather was like. And shoppers had to eat.

There was a payphone by the door. With trembling hands, Stella rummaged through her purse until she came up with a handful of change which she promptly dropped all over the floor. A man in the booth next to the payphone stooped down and helped her retrieve the coins.

She dialed 911 and was surprised at how calm her voice sounded as she told the operator she thought there had been a homicide. She answered questions for about a minute and was told to stay where she was until the police came for her. She promised she would.

With that ordeal over, she poked more coins into the phone and dialed Harry's number. It seemed to take forever for someone to pick up at Harry's house, and when someone did finally answer the phone, they didn't say anything, but she thought she heard someone breathing into the receiver.

Stella was in no mood for playing games.

"Harry, is that you? Say something, dammit!"

"Stella?"

Harry didn't seem too thrilled at hearing her voice, but Stella didn't much care. Her nerves had finally caught up to her, and her knees were shaking so badly she thought she might just keel over any second now like a goddamn tree.

"Jesus, Harry, did you ever hear of saying 'hello' when you answer the phone?"

"I'm sorry, but I've got a bit of a situation here, Stella, and I don't want to tie up the line. Can I call you ba—"

"No, Harry, listen to me. We have a situation here too. At the salon. Kimo's been murdered!"

"*What?*"

"You heard me. Kimo's dead. I just called the police. They should be here any minute. I was home when I realized I had forgotten to leave

Kimo the key so he could lock up. When I got back to the shop I... I found him. Oh, God, Harry. It was awful!"

"Where are you now?"

"I'm at the diner up the street. I was afraid to stay in the salon. I told the police where I'd be. You have to come down here."

"I can't."

"What do you mean, you can't? Did you hear what I said, Harry? Kimo's dead! He was lying by his chair. He was... he was naked, Harry. And there was blood everywhere."

Stella took a deep breath and tried to ignore the diners who were beginning to look her way.

She lowered her voice. "His scissors were... his scissors were in his neck. Somebody stabbed him with his scissors. You have to come down here. I can't do this alone."

"Stella, listen very carefully. I can't come down there. The killer is after me too. And I'm going to kill the son of a bitch. But I need time."

"What do you mean he's after you too? Why the hell would anybody want to kill you? Oh, hell, Harry, that's beside the point. The real question is, *are you nuts*? If someone is out to get you, let the police handle it. You're a hairdresser, for Christ's sake! You're not Rambo. What the hell is wrong with you?"

"No. I don't trust the police. I'll handle it myself."

"The killer's a friend of yours, Harry. Kimo's last appointment. He asked for you. When I told him you were on vacation, he took Kimo instead."

"Did he give a name?"

"No. Not that I remember."

"Listen closely, Stella. You have to help me. You have to tell the police I'm gone. You have to tell them I'm out of town somewhere. I don't care where. Just tell them I'm out of town on vacation, like you said."

"I don't believe this! Harry, I'm going to tell the cops exactly where you are. I'll send them over there and they'll put you in protective custody, or whatever the hell they do."

"No! I'm out of town. I'm on vacation. That's all you have to tell them. Do this for me, Stella. You have to. My life depends on it."

"Oh, God, Harry. You want me to lie to the police?"

"Yes. That's exactly what I want you to do."

"But what about Kimo? Don't you care that he's dead?"

Harry's burst of anger shocked her. She had never heard him angry before. "Of course, I care! But I'll cry for Kimo later. I don't have any choice. Will you do it? I'll explain everything to you later. All right?"

"Oh, Jesus. I don't believe any of this. All right, I'll do it. But if you get yourself killed because of me, I don't know what I'll do."

"I won't. I'll be fine. But I have to end this now. There's more than just my life at stake. There's someone else. Someone you don't know about. Just tell them I'm on vacation, and I won't be back until next week. Tell them you don't know where I am. All you know is that I'm out of town. Can you do that?"

"I… I suppose so. I want a raise for this, Harry. A big one."

"You got it. I'm sorry to have to get you involved, but I'll make it up to you. I swear I will."

"Free haircuts for life, Harry."

"Fine."

"Two hour lunch breaks."

"Whatever you want."

"Bail my ass out of jail when they find out I've lied to the police."

"Jesus, Stella! Yes! Whatever you want!"

She pushed her wet hair out of her face and took a deep breath. "Sorry. I got a little carried away."

"It's okay."

"The cops are here. I hear the sirens. Oh, God, Harry, every cop car in the city just pulled up in front of the salon. I have to go."

"All right, Stella. Calm down. Just remember, I'm on vacation. I left the city and you don't know where I am. I don't want them coming here to the house. And don't try to call me back. I'm not going to answer the phone any more tonight in case it's the police. Okay?"

"You're a shitty boss, Harry. A shitty boss and a shitty human being. If you weren't gay, your kids would be shitty, too."

"I know."

"I'm sorry. I didn't mean that."

"I know that too. You're a little tense."

"*Tense?* I'm not fucking *tense!* I'm way beyond *tense*, Harry!" She glared back at the people now openly staring at her in the diner as if daring them to say anything.

"I know, Stella. I'm a little tense myself."

"All right. Just be careful, Harry. If you get yourself killed, I'll never get that raise."

"Cute. Go talk to the police. I really am sorry about Kimo. I never dreamed he'd come after anyone at the shop. Just lie for me, Stella, and we'll all get through this."

"I'll do my best."

"Good girl. And close the shop until this fucker is either dead or in custody. The cops probably won't let you reopen anyway. The salon is a crime scene now."

"A crime scene... poor Kimo."

"I'm sorry, Stella."

"So am I."

Stella replaced the receiver on the hook, automatically checked for change in the coin slot, found none, and decided it was silly to wait for the police to come to her.

If Harry could be brave, so could she. Already, in the back of her mind, she was formulating the best way to keep the cops away from Harry.

The pyramids. The Indian pyramids deep in Mexico. They were sights she had always wanted to see but had never had the money or time to visit. That's where she would send Harry.

If you're going to lie, at least make it interesting.

She girded her proverbial loins and stepped back out into the rain.

JEFFERSON McCRAY steered his Chrysler 300F into the salon parking lot just moments after the black and whites arrived. The uniforms were still arguing over whether or not to break down the locked door, and McCray was on the verge of telling them to go ahead and do it, when a young woman stepped into their midst and offered them the key.

The woman was pretty but looked like she had seen better nights. She was soaking wet, and her eyes had that dull, gut-shot look that he had seen time and again at crime scenes.

McCray took the key from her hand and tossed it to another homicide detective, Blake, who had arrived right after him.

Blake unlocked the door, told the patrolmen to stay the hell out, and entered the salon alone, closing the door firmly behind him.

The young woman watched all this from a distance with the rain beating down on her head, until McCray pulled her under the awning and wrapped an arm around her shoulders.

"Are you all right?" he asked.

She gazed up into his face and tried to smile. "I've been better."

"Are you the one who called it in?"

"Yes."

"You work here?"

"Uh huh. I'm the receptionist. I'm Stella."

She leaned her body into his and he felt her shudder. He figured she was about two minutes from meltdown.

"I have to ask you some questions, Stella. Would that be all right? Are you up to it?"

She nodded.

"Let's go inside," McCray said. "Out of the rain."

He felt her body suddenly go rigid. "No, I can't go back in there."

McCray looked around. "All right," he said. "Come with me. We'll talk in my car. It's right over there."

She followed him to the lot and waited patiently while he fumbled with the key in the rain. He finally got the door open and eased her inside, then jogged around and climbed into the driver side. It was noisy inside the car with the rain pelting the canvas top, but it would have to do.

"Nice car," Stella said.

"Thanks."

"Did you confiscate it from a pimp?"

McCray laughed. "No. It's mine."

"Oh. Sorry."

"Don't be. I get that a lot."

They faced each other across the wide bench seat. He started the engine and turned on the heater.

"Better?"

"Yes. Thank you." She opened her coat to let the warm air reach her body.

"Now then," McCray said. "Tell me what happened."

She told him about leaving work early because of the rain and about forgetting to leave Kimo the key.

"Kimo is the man on the floor?"

"Yes. Kimo Dalisay."

"He was the only one working when you left this afternoon?"

"Yes. Everyone else went home early because of the weather, but Kimo had a late appointment. I booked it for him."

"The appointment was a man?"

"Yes. For a haircut. Nine o'clock."

"Did this man come in to make the appointment?"

"No, he phoned it in."

"Did you get his name?"

"No."

McCray looked out at the rain. Whipped by the wind, it was a swirl of red and blue, reflecting off the flashing lights of a dozen patrol cars. A few of the black and whites were beginning to pull away, but McCray knew the area would be swarming with cops for many hours to come.

"Did Kimo own the salon?"

"No. Harry owns it. You know. Harry's for Hair?"

"Does this Harry have a last name?"

She nodded. "Connors. Harry Connors."

"Did you call him to tell him what's happened here?"

Stella twisted around in the seat to better face the detective. If you're going to lie, look them in the eye. A poetic bit of advice that had never failed her yet.

"I can't call him," she said. "He's out of town."

"Do you know where we can reach him?"

"I don't think you can. He's somewhere down in Mexico, touring the pyramids, doing the tourist thing. He could be anywhere."

"He didn't leave a forwarding number or the name of a hotel where he could be reached?"

"No. He said he'd be moving around a lot."

The woman had seemed eager enough to answer his questions earlier, but now she appeared to be on the verge of another meltdown. He could see her fists clenching and unclenching in her lap. He wondered if she was going into shock.

"Are you sure you're okay?"

"No, I'm not okay. I'm cold. I'm wet. And I just found someone I work with eight hours a day, five days a week, with a pair of goddamn scissors stuck in his neck. Would you be okay?"

"Don't get angry."

"I'm not angry. I'm upset. There's a difference."

"How did you get here?" he asked.

"I drove. That's my car over there. The blue Nissan."

McCray studied her face for a moment. She sensed this and looked back at him. Their eyes locked.

"What?" she asked.

"Are you married?"

A wry smile twisted the corner of her lips. "Why do you ask?"

McCray suddenly felt awkward. "I don't think you should be driving is all. Maybe your husband can come and pick you up."

"Oh. That's sweet, but I'll be fine. And no, I'm not married."

"Then I'll drive you home."

"That won't be necessary. Really."

"I insist. You're in no condition to drive."

For the first time, she looked at this handsome black man as a person and not a cop. She was rather amazed to find that she liked what she saw. His concern for her was a lot different than what she could have expected from Bobby, that much was certain. Bobby, in fact, was probably still twiddling his Playstation controls, playing his stupid game, unaware that she was even gone. And maybe not even *caring* that she was gone. The bastard.

"Well," she said. "If you think you should."

McCray smiled. "I do."

He noticed Forensics' panel truck pulling up to the front of the salon.

"I have to go inside for a few minutes. You wait here. You'll be safe until I get back."

"I'm sure I will," Stella said. "There are a dozen cops per square foot out there." She reached over and touched his hand. "Thank you for being so kind. What's your name?"

He looked down at her small hand resting on his. White on black. Her fingers were cold.

"I'm Detective McCray."

"Is that what I should call you?" she asked.

"No." He rested his other hand on top of hers and gave her a shy smile that Smith, had he witnessed the exchange, would have ragged him about for the rest of his life. "I think you should call me Jeff."

Stella demurely pulled her hand away, although she didn't want to. "All right, Jeff. I'll be right here when you get back."

"Good."

McCray unfolded his long legs from beneath the steering wheel and exited the car. As he trotted across the parking lot, leaping puddles along the way like the linebacker he used to be, and maybe showing off a bit in the process, McCray thought, what the hell am I doing?

The Forensics team had already entered the salon and were unpacking their cases, efficient as always, with no wasted motions. McCray knew they were facing hours of work, and he also knew that this was not their idea of an ideal place for a crime scene. It was a public location with a large human turnover. Fingerprints alone would take days to sift through, the sheer number of them making the task, if not impossible, at least problematic. A full-blown pain in the ass. Analyzing trace evidence would be a nightmare. Hair? Forget it. They could probably open a forensics school with all the different types of hair lying around the place.

Of course, all these problems would be moot if they had a suspect to compare the prints and trace evidence to. Jimmy Smith thought they did. And when Smith had a hunch, McCray had learned to follow it.

He approached the technician in charge, a middle-aged woman he had worked with in the past. He knew her only as Jean.

"Hey, Jean. Were you working the murder at the Stevens Hotel tonight?"

"No. That team is still there. We just started our shift."

As she spoke, she pulled paper booties over her shoes and handed McCray a pair as well. "Put these on," she said.

McCray did.

"When you get back to the lab, I want you to compare what you find here with any evidence they found over there."

Jean popped on a pair of rubber gloves. "You think the crimes are connected?"

"Yes."

"Good. 'Cause we're going to have a whole lot of everything coming out of here."

"I know."

"It will help to have evidence from another crime scene to analyze it against."

"Yes."

"Otherwise, Detective, we'll have a shitload of prints and trace and hair and God knows what else to deal with, and we won't know where to begin sorting it all out."

"I know."

Jean gave the detective a guilty grin. "Have I told you anything you *don't* know?"

"Not so far."

"I didn't think so."

She pointed to an opaque substance splattered across the victim's naked back. "We've got semen, too, unless the killer blew his nose on the guy. Of course, cum and snot are one and the same to us. Doesn't much matter which it is. Did they have cum or snot at the hotel?"

"I don't know," he said, trying not to smile. Gallows humor. You had to love it. And nobody did it like Forensics. The fact that Jean was on the wrong side of fifty and looked like someone's maiden aunt from Fresno made it all the more bizarre.

He touched her shoulder in thanks and knelt beside Blake from Homicide, who was examining the body.

Kimo Dalisay's arms were stretched out in front of him and his face was turned to the side, resting in the pool of blood. His eyes were open.

"A pretty boy," Blake said.

"Was," McCray corrected.

"Yeah, was."

Kimo's knees were under his chest, putting the young man's anus in full view.

"Was he raped?" McCray asked.

"Hard to tell," Blake said. "But he was no stranger to anal intercourse. You can tell just by looking at the skin tissue around his butt. If he had lived many more years, he would have had an ass like a foxhole."

Everyone was a comedian tonight.

"Show a little compassion, Blake."

"Soitainly. Always do."

"Any trauma on the body, other than the stab wound?"

"Not that I can see. And there's no sign of a struggle anywhere. I'd say the guy was getting it on with one of his customers, and the customer offed him."

Blake pointed to a lot of hair on the floor around the chair. Blond hair. "Must have really hated his haircut," he added.

"Is his dick still there?" McCray asked.

Blake all but shoved his head up the victim's rear end to get a better view beneath. "Yep. Still there. A pretty thing, too. Out of operation now, of course."

Smith rolled his eyes. "Smith and I think this is the work of the same guy who killed the man at Brittany Towers and the same guy who later planted the bomb in Balboa Park."

"No shit?"

"We also think it's the same guy who murdered the front desk clerk at the Stevens Hotel not more than three hours ago."

Blake hadn't just fallen off the turnip truck. He'd been around. "You're saying this is the work of the same guy who shot Jamison and Beers?"

"Yes. We think so."

"Son of a bitch!"

"Son of a bitch, indeed. So do this one right. We don't want any evidence lost in the shuffle."

"Don't worry, Jeff. We'll do it right."

McCray had been squatting too long. He stood with an audible groan. Football knees. "Thanks, Blake. I'll be back in a few minutes."

"Where you going?"

"There's a girl in my car who's about to have a nervous breakdown. I'm gonna drive her home."

"Okay. I'm sure I'll still be here when you get back."

"I'm sure you will."

As he headed for the door, the cell phone at McCray's hip broke into a nasal rendition of Jingle Bells. Jean from Forensics said, "How cute," as he grabbed for it, and Blake was reprising the song in full operatic mode by the time McCray could press receive. Blake didn't sound half-bad, for a man with his face less than a foot away from a dead hairdresser's ass. "Echo chamber," McCray heard him say to one of the techs, who looked at Blake in shock, as if the guy had just sprouted a second head. Obviously, the two did not share the same sense of comedy.

"What is it, Chief?' McCray said, after checking the incoming readout.

"Are you there?"

"At the hair salon? Yeah, I'm here."

"Tell me about it."

McCray had only done the most cursory inspection of the crime scene, but he relayed to Smith what he knew.

"Do you think it's our boy?" Smith asked.

"Yes. There's blond hair on the floor beneath the styling chair. Without lab analysis, that doesn't prove it's Andros, but for now, it's an indication. To me, anyway. And the hairdresser was stabbed. Andros likes to stab. We both know that. This guy wasn't mutilated, or at least I don't think he was. We haven't moved the body yet, but his genitals seem to be intact."

"Any witnesses?"

"No."

"Who found the body?"

"The receptionist. She came back to lock up. I've got her in my car. She's too upset to drive. I offered to take her home."

"She must be cute. Otherwise you'd have slapped her on a bus."

McCray didn't dignify that remark with an answer even though he knew his partner was right. He *would* have slapped her on a bus, or pawned her off onto one of the patrolmen to drive home. Or just let her drive herself and hope for the best.

"Thinking with the little head instead of the big one, Jeff. What have I told you about that?"

"Eat me."

"What's the name of the salon?"

"Harry's for Hair. On Fourth."

"I know it. Carol goes there for cuts."

"Well, if she has an appointment coming up with Kimo, tell her she might want to rethink it. He's retired. Permanently."

With the phone still pressed to his ear, McCray pulled the door open for the Medical Examiner, who had just arrived. The M.E. shrugged out of his dripping raincoat at the door and hung it on a hook on the wall. Before proceeding into the salon, he bent over and unlatched the large medical bag he carried, pulled out his own pair of paper booties, and slipped them over his shoes.

"What the hell was Andros doing *there*?" Smith asked through weather-induced static.

"What do you mean?"

"Jeez, Jeff, you don't think he came in there just to get his sideburns raised, do you? With everything else this guy has done, there was a purpose behind it. Or at least it all related in some way to the hustler. Baker was a trick. Childers, like you surmised, obviously fumble-fucked himself into the middle of all this after Andros arranged to meet Sean in the park and kill him there with the bomb. Jamison and Beers were outside the kid's apartment when they were shot. Sledgehammer Willie most likely witnessed Andros trying to dump the Baker murder weapon. And the hotel clerk was found in Andros's room. Maybe he found out something Andros didn't want him to know, or maybe he was just snooping. Either way, it at least makes sense. But what's the sense in this? How does it tie in? You don't really think it's random, do you?"

"Well, no. I sort of figured it was a gay thing. The victim here is obviously homosexual. There's too much homosexuality running through this entire investigation to make it just a happenstance. And now we have another gay victim."

"Yes, Jeff, but why was he chosen? The others were all connected in some way. How is this guy connected? How did this poor innocent hairdresser find himself in the middle of it all?"

On a counter by the door, McCray stared at a stack of business cards by the cash register. Harry's for Hair, they read in mauve print. The apostrophe in "Harry's" was a tiny pair of scissors. Like the murder weapon. As Smith rattled on about something or other on the other end of the line, McCray continued to stare at that logo. Harry's for Hair. Then it hit him. Jesus Christ! What a wooly-pated twit he was.

"Let me call you back, Jimmy. I think I know where the hustler is."

"What? Where? What the hell are you—"

McCray cut his partner off with no small amount of glee and exited the salon, shaking his head in wonder at his own stupidity. He paused for a moment beneath the awning and pulled the paper booties off his feet. He stuffed them into his coat pocket before racing to the Chrysler through the icy rain, which seemed to be falling even more heavily now, if that were possible.

Stella was resting with her head against the back of the seat, her eyes closed. When McCray opened the driver-side door, she jumped about a foot straight up and clutched her heart.

As he slid his ass in and settled himself behind the wheel, she said, "Give a girl some warning next time."

McCray hid his embarrassment by quickly closing the door and turning off the interior light.

He pantomimed shooting himself in the head. "Sorry."

"Are *you*?"

"Am I what? Sorry?"

"No. Married."

"Oh. No, thank God. Not for quite a while."

"That sounds ominous."

McCray laughed and cranked up the engine. "Where do you live?"

"Where do *you* live?"

"Why? Would you rather go there?"

Stella thought that one over. "I'm sorry. Maybe we should go back to a cop/witness footing. I think it's safer."

McCray idled the engine at the exit to the parking lot, unsure of which way to go.

"Are you still scared?" he asked.

"Yes. But this is a whole new scared."

McCray flashed white teeth at her in the darkness, which she acknowledged with a sardonic grin of her own.

"Banker's Hill," she said, pointing to the left. "That-a-way."

Before he pulled out onto Fourth Avenue, he reached across the seat and tucked a finger under her chin, drawing her face toward his. "Are you flirting?"

Stella didn't flinch. "No more than you are."

"Hmm. Okay, from now on you be the witness, and I'll be the cop. You're right. It's safer."

"But not as much fun."

"Not nearly. But I'm working. We don't have time for anything else."

Stella waved her hands in front of her face like a ref calling time-out. "What the hell is going on here? Did I just go into hormone overload? I find a co-worker brutally murdered, and five minutes later, I'm making passes at the detective on duty. What's wrong with me?"

"It's death."

"Pardon?"

"Some people have this reaction to death. A sudden need to procreate."

"You must be joking. With a complete stranger?"

"If that's what's available. It's like when people have feelings of sexual arousal during an earthquake."

"Now I *know* you're joking. The only thing aroused in me during an earthquake is the urge to run like a jackrabbit."

McCray laughed. "Like I said. *Some* people."

Stella stared at his silhouette as he drove.

"You're a homicide detective. You must have the urge to procreate every time you turn around."

"No," he said. "Death doesn't affect me that way."

"What does?"

"A pretty girl."

"*Any* pretty girl?"

He tore his eyes from the road to look at her. "No. Just certain ones."

Stella felt a familiar thrumming down below, like guitar strings, gently plucked. "This conversation is getting out of hand again."

"I know it is."

McCray drove in silence for perhaps a minute, straining to see through the pouring rain, and at the same time enjoying the sexual tension that was shooting back and forth between the two of them like electricity jumping a gap in the wire. He was also wondering how to best frame his next question. He quickly realized there was no "best" way and simply asked it.

"Why did you lie to me about Harry?"

CHAPTER TWELVE

TWENTY miles from downtown San Diego, on a freeway that skirted the suburb of Escondido, Smith was forced to stop due to a traffic accident up ahead involving three cars and a motorcycle. All four lanes were effectively blocked, and Smith knew that even flashing his detective badge at the answering highway patrolmen wouldn't get him through. He impatiently tapped his fingers against the steering wheel, more than a little annoyed at being held up this close to home after traveling almost two thousand miles since sun-up.

With nothing better to do, he tried to figure out what McCray had been talking about. How could he know where the hustler was hiding? What had suddenly led McCray to think he *did* know. Obviously, it was because of information he had acquired at the last crime scene, the hair salon. With that in mind, it didn't take Smith long to figure it out. In fact, the clue was so blatantly obvious he couldn't believe he hadn't thought of it before his partner did.

Harry's for Hair. In red neon. He had seen the sign a thousand times. You couldn't drive through Hillcrest *without* seeing it. Christ. His three-year-old would have picked up on the significance of that sign. And that name. Harry.

Smith grabbed his cell phone and dialed home.

His wife answered on the second ring, sounding sleepy but anxious, just as she always did when the phone rang late at night and her husband was not in the bed beside her. Just as every policeman's wife did. "Yes?"

"Hi, Carol."

"Jimmy! Where are you?"

"Escondido. Stuck in traffic."

"Close enough. I've missed you."

"Me too. Do you still get your hair cut on Fourth Avenue?"

"Uh… is this your idea of an obscene phone call? 'Cause I gotta tell you, it's not doing much for me."

Smith laughed. "We'll do the obscene stuff after I get home. This is police business."

"Ooh…."

"Do you know Harry's last name?"

"You mean Harry the owner of the salon?"

"Yes."

"What's this all about, Jimmy?"

"Just part of an investigation. Do you know it?"

"Let me think. He doesn't cut my hair, but he's always there when I go in. We always speak."

"What's he like?"

"Like?"

"You know. Is he nice?"

"Well, of course he's nice. I wouldn't go there if he wasn't nice."

"Is he gay?"

"I'm not… well, yes, now that you mention it, I suppose he is. Although you wouldn't know it by looking at him. My stylist told me once about him losing his lover to… leukemia, I think it was. So, yes, in answer to your question, yes. He's gay."

"What's your stylist's name?"

"Lily."

"Thank God."

"Do you want to explain to me what you mean by that?"

"Maybe later. And Harry's last name?"

"I'm thinking."

"Think faster."

"Is Harry in trouble? I'm not going to have to start shopping around for another hair salon, am I?"

Smith chuckled. "It's always about you, isn't it? Me, me, me. No, dear. The man is not in trouble. He's a witness."

"Thank God," she said. "I… Connors. His last name is Connors."

"You have a phone book handy?"

"Oh, yes, I always sleep with one under my pillow. Hold on a second."

Still tapping the steering wheel and praying for a break in either the traffic or the rain, he waited for a good two minutes before Carol came back on the line.

"Do you want the number or the address?"

"Both."

He switched on the interior light and pulled his ever-present notepad from the inner pocket of his trench coat.

"Go ahead."

He jotted down the number and address she read to him. 1722 Eagle. It was in Mission Hills. He knew the street.

"Thanks, babe. I love you. Kids okay?"

"They're fine. Hurry home."

"I will."

Barely back in town and he was lying to his wife already. Cop promises, Carol called them. He had no idea when he'd be home and his wife probably knew it too.

"I haven't had sex in three days," he added as an afterthought.

"I should hope not."

"The little Indian is lonely."

Carol giggled. "Tell the little Indian I'll take care of him when he gets here."

"Oh, goody," Smith said and hung up.

THE lights were out over a large area of Mission Hills. With the rain pelting down around his car and obstructing his vision, and with his headlights barely piercing the darkness, Jackson Andros had a hard time finding Harry's house. He was still unfamiliar with the city, and with the power out, he had no reference points to steer by. After thirty minutes of blindly traversing the winding streets and canyons, all but blinded by the driving rain, it was sheer luck that brought him at last to the home with the green Porsche Boxster parked in the driveway.

He drove his rented Taurus a block farther, turned the car around so that it faced outward, and parked in the cul-de-sac that ended Eagle Street. He opened the suitcase that rested on the seat beside him and, in the darkness, felt for the gun. Finding it, he stuffed it in his trouser pocket and pulled a ski mask over his head. This would not be a good time to have the car stolen, so he pocketed the keys as well.

Before stepping out into the storm, he closed his eyes. Among the tiny specks of light that swirled behind his eyelids, he saw the face of God smiling at him. God had sent him here for one purpose. Tonight his sin would be atoned. His one sin. After he finished what he was about to do, he would no longer be ashamed. He would be whole. He had already shown God his power, his commitment, many times over. Tonight, because of him, there were sinners in Hell who might otherwise have waited years to burn there. He had proven his worth to himself and to his God, and now he would end it. The whore would join the others, and it would be finally over.

Jackson removed his coat and stepped from the car. In seconds, he was soaked to the skin, like a newborn baby wet from the womb. The cold he ignored. His anger and his righteousness were enough to warm him.

There was no one on the street. He could see candlelight

flickering through the windows of a few of the houses around him due to the power outage, but most were in darkness.

At the front of the house where the whore was hiding, he could see no lights. He found a walkway by the fence that adjoined the next-door property. Dressed in dark clothing and with the dark ski mask over his head, covering the whiteness of his skin and the blondness of his hair, the man was all but invisible. He entered the narrow space between the house and the fence like a shadow. And, like a shadow, he disappeared.

Behind the house, he found shelter from the rain beneath a terrace that was built out over the hillside. Here the man discovered firewood stacked against the back of the house and lawn furniture stored away for winter. A lawnmower sat beneath a sheet of plastic weighted down at the corners with stones. A short picket fence enclosed this secluded place at the point where the cliff face plummeted down to other homes far below. A narrow wooden stairway led up to the deck above.

In this shadowy grotto, made up of the deck above his head and the rear of the house at his back, he felt safe from prying eyes, even in the brightest flashes of lightning, and he was sheltered from the rain and the wind. It afforded him time to take stock of his surroundings. He spotted the tree that had fallen earlier. It was a large tree, and much of its length now jutted out over the edge of the cliff, its limbs still buffeted by the wind that whipped up the hillside. He could smell the fresh-turned earth where the roots had been torn from the ground. Peering around the corner of the house, he saw the window where the falling tree had smashed through the glass, and he tested the strength of whatever it was the whore had used to seal off the opening. It felt secure, and he knew he would not be able to break through it quietly.

He pulled the gun from his pocket and began to climb the wooden stairs that led to the deck above his head. As his eyes reached the height of the deck's flooring, he saw light at last. Candlelight. Flickering through what looked to be a wide sliding glass door. The curtains were open and he could see into the house, into what appeared to be the living room. On a long sofa that bisected the room, he saw the whore. His hair was a different color, but it was him. And standing behind the whore was the man who was sheltering him.

Jackson wondered if the older man, Harry Connors, had heard about the unfortunate accident that had befallen poor Kimo at work. Judging by appearances, Jackson suspected he had. Old Harry wasn't looking too chipper at the moment. Not pleased at all, really.

Jackson stood there with his head at floor level to the deck and watched the two. The older man and the whore. Anger began to surge through him so that he felt neither the rain or the cold or the wind at his back. He felt only hatred. When the older man reached out and touched the whore's cheek, and the whore responded by pressing his lips into the palm of the older man's hand, Jackson released the safety of the gun and pulled the hammer back.

He had seen enough.

Once again, he began to climb the stairs.

As he did, his eyes never wavered from the face of the young man inside the house.

His brother.

His prey.

His one great weakness.

BY THE time McCray dropped Stella off in front of her apartment, he had extracted the truth from her. Yes, Harry had asked her to lie. And yes, Harry knew the killer was coming for him. Stella couldn't explain how Harry knew this, only that he did. Harry had also told her there was another life at stake. Who this other person was, he didn't say.

But McCray knew. It was the hustler. Sean Andros. McCray didn't have a clue why the older man, a seemingly honest and upstanding businessman, had elected to protect the boy, but it was obvious that Harry Connors was willing to put his own life in jeopardy to do so. McCray suspected that love was the underlying motive for Harry's actions. For what other reason would a man risk himself in such a way?

Stella's tearful confession had put an end to her flirtations, and

McCray felt more troubled by this than by the fact she had lied to him. He liked the girl and he wanted to see her again. Now, he supposed, that would never happen.

These were the thoughts that filled McCray's mind as he parked in front of 1722 Eagle Street and gazed through the Chrysler's side window at the darkened house. He saw no sign of light or movement. He decided not to announce his arrival.

Using a small penlight, McCray found a cobblestoned path that led around to the back of the house. Heavy rain spattered his head and shoulders. He had his gun in his hand by the time he rounded the back of the house and stepped beneath the deck. Afraid to use the penlight now, he let himself be guided by the lightning flashes that were lighting the sky as the storm continued to batter the coast with its fury. The rumble of thunder and the roar of rain slapping the deck above cocooned him in sound so that he could hear nothing else. A cold wind tore at his coat.

He saw the narrow stairway that led up to the deck and he started up it. When he reached the deck he spotted the shape of a man silhouetted against the light coming from inside the house. The man just stood there in the rain, staring in. He had a gun in his hand.

McCray brought his revolver up and rested his shoulder on the railing of the deck, a support against the wind.

He aimed at the man's back and yelled, "Police officer! Drop the gun!"

The silhouette whirled around. There was a flash of light and McCray felt a bullet tear into his chest. His service revolver went off, and he saw the patio door shatter before darkness took him and he stumbled backward down the steps.

HARRY saw movement on the deck just as the man outside spun and fired. A moment later, the table lamp at the end of the sofa burst apart in a spray of ceramic shards and the patio door, weakened by McCray's bullet, gave way to the wind and exploded inward. Blinded by the sudden bombardment of rain and glass that swept into the room, Harry dove for the gun on the coffee table just as Sean leaped to his feet in front of him, blocking his dive and sending them both crashing to the floor. The coffee table upended and sent books, candles, and the gun skittering across the floor.

Harry and Sean both scrambled for Harry's gun but the man in the ski mask reached it first, kicking it out onto the deck.

The room was plunged into darkness when the first blast of wind extinguished the candles, and it took Harry and Sean a moment to realize they were scrambling for a gun that was no longer there.

"Hello, boys," the man said, his voice muffled by the mask across his face. "We meet at last."

Harry pulled Sean to his feet. Together they backed away from the voice and the dim silhouette they could see in front of the strobe-like flashes of lightning that peppered the sky outside the broken patio door. Harry felt Sean trembling beside him. Whether from anger or fear, he didn't know.

"*Who are you?*" Harry screamed into the wind, pushing the boy behind him. *"What do you want with us?"*

"With you, nothing," the shadow said, and raising his gun, Jackson fired twice. The first bullet missed Harry by inches; the second tore into him, and he felt the power of it drive him backward into the wall where he slid to the floor. He felt no pain, only an infinite sadness. He could not protect the boy after all. The man would kill them both and that would be the end of it.

"*No!*" Sean screamed. He ran headlong at the shadow across the room and with his body drove the man out onto the deck, where they both stumbled and fell. Sean landed on top of the man and the breath was driven from both of them. Sean tried to reach the gun in the man's hand, but the man was stronger and quicker than he. He pushed Sean away and rolled over onto his chest, pinning the boy's arms to the deck with his knees.

Sean squinted into the rain that splattered his face and tried to push the man away but couldn't. The man lowered his masked face to within inches of the boy's. His hand came up and brushed Sean's cheek with the barrel of the gun.

"So beautiful," he said.

The man's weight pressed the air from Sean's lungs so that he could barely speak. He could muster only a whisper. "Who... are you?"

The man pressed the gun to Sean's lips. Forcing them open, he pushed the barrel into the boy's mouth and held it there. Sean tasted metal and gun oil, but above it all, he tasted fear.

Somewhere in Sean's mind, a memory stirred. But it was too faint to grasp.

The man leaned over him and put his lips to Sean's ear.

"You remember, don't you? Tell me you remember."

Sean could smell the man's sweat. He tried to pull away from the gun, but the man pushed it deeper into his mouth. The metal sight at the end of the barrel tore the roof of his mouth, and he wailed with the pain of it. He tried to twist his head away from the sharp metal, but the man was too strong. Sean felt impaled by the barrel of the gun, unable to move. Unable to breathe. He tasted his own blood.

Tears stung his eyes. "Please...."

He felt the man's other hand moving across his body. Roughly caressing his chest. Sliding lower to his stomach and slipping under his sweatshirt. The man grasped the waistband of Sean's sweatpants and pushed them down until Sean lay exposed beneath him. Like cold needles, the icy rain pelted the boy's skin, making Sean gasp. Jackson rolled the boy over and pressed a finger to his anus, penetrating the boy with one vicious thrust.

"Please what?" the man hissed. "Please give you this?"

Sean screamed, the pain blinding him to everything else. He felt the ski mask against the side of his face, the man's tongue licking his skin. Sean cried out as the man worked his finger deep inside him. There was no tenderness to the movement. It was meant to cause pain. Sean's face was pressed against the cold redwood deck.

"So beautiful," the man said again, so softly that Sean could barely hear him.

Sean could feel the man who lay over him now fumble with his own clothing. His one free hand releasing his belt buckle, unzipping his trousers, the length of the man's cock now pressing against Sean's back, the man's hot breath against his neck.

"I was your first," he whispered into Sean's ear. "Just as you were mine. And I'll be your last, just as you'll be mine. The circle of sin ends here. Tonight."

The man pulled his finger from the boy and Sean gasped as he felt the hard cock push its way into him." I want to feel you die while I'm buried deep inside you, Sean. I've dreamed of it."

Sean tried to shrink away from that stabbing cock, but he couldn't move. The pain and the humiliation made him yell out. He cursed the man and the man only laughed, pushing harder, sliding deeper into his body, tearing him apart. The pain was intense. Numbing.

"You feel just as I knew you would. Like velvet."

Sean screamed. *"No!"*

He felt a piece of broken glass from the shattered window pressing against his hand. Sean grasped it, and with a strength born of panic, ignoring the pain as the sharp glass cut his palm and fingers, he twisted around and drove the shard of glass deep into the man's hip with all the force he could muster.

The man cried out and rolled off the boy. As Sean tried to run, the man grabbed his shirt and pulled him back to the deck. Once again the man climbed onto the boy, but this time Sean's arms were not pinned. Sean reached up and tore the ski mask away.

"You!" he gasped.

Jackson smiled down at the boy, that cold familiar smile that Sean would forever associate with his brother. And the memories that smile dredged up in the boy flooded his mind and made him weak with fear.

"Whore," Jackson said, bringing the gun up and pressing it to the boy's temple. Sean heard the gun cock.

Before he could either move or think a single thought, Jackson's face suddenly exploded into a mass of blood and froth, and Sean screamed as his brother collapsed on top of him, his hot blood gushing across the boy's face and mixing with the cold rain.

Stunned, Sean felt Jackson's body settle into stillness over him and he knew it was over. He pushed the body away and turned to see a man standing on the stairway at the edge of the deck. A man with dark skin. A man Sean had never seen before. As Sean stared at him, the man slowly lowered the hand that held the gun and stepped all the way up onto the deck.

As if ashamed, Sean pulled his sweatpants up over his nakedness before trying to rise. He fumbled, then gained his feet. Casting a final glance at the man with the gun, he rushed through the broken patio door to Harry's side, wiping Jackson's blood from his face with his sleeve as he went.

Harry looked at Sean with half-closed eyes and tried to smile. "You're still here," he said.

Sean put his arm around Harry and pressed his lips to his forehead. Harry's skin was cold, his body trembling. Sean suspected Harry was going into shock, but at least he was alive. In the darkness, Sean couldn't see how bad Harry's bullet wound was. Hot tears flooded from his eyes as he felt Harry try to lift his arm and pull him closer, but he didn't have the strength. Harry collapsed back against the wall and closed his eyes instead.

Sean wrapped his arms around the older man, trying to protect Harry from the icy wind that tore through the broken window.

"I'm still here," Sean whispered to him. "We both are. And my brother's dead. He won't bother us anymore."

From the deck, he heard the other man, the man who had killed Jackson, calling for an ambulance and more police. It seemed the cops had found them both after all.

Thank God.

JIMMY SMITH'S bullet had entered at the bridge of the killer's nose, and Jackson Andros's head had imploded like a smashed pumpkin, fragments of metal and bone shattering his brain like shrapnel. Smith thought it was a pretty good shot, considering. He felt no regret at having taken this man's life. No regret at all. Smith didn't bother checking for signs of life. He knew there would be none.

He saw the boy turn and look at him before running into the house. Smith let him go. He phoned for an ambulance and squad cars and turned back to the stairway where, moments before, he had found McCray's body sprawled across the bottom steps. He half stumbled back down the stairs and dropped to his knees beside his partner and best friend. He pressed his fingers into McCray's neck and thought he felt a pulse, but he wasn't sure. Looking around for something to protect McCray from the rain, he saw the sheet of plastic that covered the lawn mower. He ripped it out from under the rocks that were holding it down and spread it over McCray's body, tucking it in beneath McCray's chin.

He bent low and whispered into McCray's ear, "Hang on."

He climbed the steps again and entered the house, where he found the boy holding an older man in his arms and knew this must be Harry. He squatted down in front of them, and with his penlight, he looked at the wound in Harry's shoulder. The boy watched his every movement with wide, frightened eyes. Smith could see that Harry had gone into shock, and he figured the kid wasn't far behind. He rushed into one of the bedrooms where he found a blanket and, dragging it back to the living room, draped it around them both.

"He's going to be all right," he told Sean. "Stay with him. There will be an ambulance here any minute."

Smith phoned for a second ambulance and went to the front door, unlocking it and leaving it open.

He recrossed the living room and touched Sean's shoulder.

"My partner is at the foot of the stairs outside. Send one of the ambulance teams down there. All right?"

"Is he alive?" Sean asked.

"I don't know. I hope so." He reached down and ruffled the boy's hair. "Be strong. It's almost over."

Smith left them and stepped back out into the rain, his thoughts not only on McCray, but on the boy as well. Sean Andros would need a lot of strength in the days to come. Smith hoped he wouldn't have to be the one to tell him his parents were also dead, but he suspected he would. And maybe that was as it should be. He felt he knew the boy. And as Harry apparently had, he felt he should protect him in any way he could. The kid had been through enough, and in spite of what he had just told him, it wasn't over yet. The hardest part, the healing, was yet to come.

While Smith was upstairs, a bubble of blood had formed on McCray's lips, and this told Smith for certain that his partner was still alive. He sat on the wet ground and leaned his body over McCray's face, shielding him from the rain. Clutching his partner's hand, he waited for the ambulance.

Minutes later, he heard the wail of sirens in the distance.

CHAPTER THIRTEEN

THE trauma ward of Mercy Hospital at the foot of Fourth Avenue in Hillcrest was a swarm of activity seven days a week, twenty-four hours a day. This morning was no exception.

As Harry slept, Sean sat at the foot of Harry's hospital bed and waited for him to wake. After the surgery performed on him the night before to remove the bullet and repair the damage it had done to Harry's shoulder, the nurse warned Sean that it would be several hours before the anesthetic would wear off and Harry would open his eyes. As Sean waited, he rested his hand on Harry's leg, needing the comfort of touch. He reached over and pushed Harry's hair away from his face and gently felt the bandage that circled Harry's chest. In the past hour, Harry had begun to look less pale, less anaesthetized. His face had softened, and now he seemed merely asleep, his breathing slow and regular.

Sean could not stop thinking about everything that had happened the night before. He still tasted the medicine the doctor had swabbed across the roof of his mouth where the gun sight had torn his skin. He had received a tetanus shot, and the pain of that was still a dull ache in his arm. He was bandaged where the window glass he had used to stab Jackson had slit his hand. The stitches the emergency room doctor had sewn into the wound itched and burned beneath the gauze.

The other pain, the pain where his brother had forced his way into his body, had stopped hours ago. At least, the physical aspect of it. But in his mind, in his memory, the pain was still very much alive. He had not spoken of it to the doctor, too ashamed to mention it, and the doctor had not asked. Perhaps they did not know of the rape, and Sean was not about to tell them about it. With lubricant and a bit of tender handling, Sean had always enjoyed anal sex. But what had taken place the night before on Harry's deck had not been tender. And it had not been an act of sex. Or love. It was an act of humiliation and control that left Sean shaken by the memory of it. He knew he would never speak of it to anyone. Not even to Harry.

As for the death of his parents, the detective, the one named Smith, had sat with Sean for an hour after the emergency room ordeal was over and told him everything. The detective did not tell Sean *how* his parents were murdered, and Sean did not ask. Some day he would, he supposed, but not yet. He did not really want to know. The knowledge that they had died at his brother's hands was enough pain to absorb for now.

When Smith told Sean of the other murders Jackson had committed in his quest to reach him, Sean was stunned. One of Sean's earliest memories was of a nine-year-old Jackson, handsome even then in his blond youth, sitting on the edge of the bathtub back at the farmhouse, soaping down his little brother's back and rinsing the lather from his little brother's hair. Jackson had been gentle then. And tender. Sean closed his eyes. That memory hurt too much.

Sean, who had always cried so freely that even a sappy movie would set him off, could find no tears now for the death of his family. Not yet. He had already mourned their loss. Their refusal to accept his gayness, to accept the way he had to live his life, had taken them from him years ago.

Sean looked again at Harry's sleeping face. This man was his family now. His only family. His lover. And his friend.

Harry was all he had.

And he was more than enough.

THE night before, much to the displeasure of the head floor nurse, Smith had made certain Harry received a double room, and he had also made certain that Sean was given the second bed in that room, even though the boy in no way required hospitalization. Obviously intolerant of homosexuals, the nurse, a nun by the name of Sister Florence, was less than moved by Smith's logic that since the two were lovers they should not be separated. Smith himself had been more swayed by the look of panic that had crossed the boy's face when Sean thought he would have to leave the hospital for the night and might not be there if Harry should happen to wake with no one but strangers around him. It was simply one more way that Smith had found to help the boy. Why it was so important for him to do so, Smith couldn't explain, even to himself.

Now, twelve hours later, Smith stepped back into Harry's hospital room and saw Sean sitting at the foot of Harry's bed staring down at his hands. Once again, Smith was struck by how young the boy looked. He had changed from the filthy, blood-drenched sweats he had been wearing the night before into faded, wash-softened hospital pajamas and a robe. He looked up and smiled when Smith entered the room.

"You look like shit," Sean said.

Smith grinned. "So do you." Smith stepped closer to the bed and stared down at Harry's sleeping face. "How's he doing?"

"Hasn't woke up yet, but they tell me he'll be fine."

"Good."

Sean eased himself gently off the bed and motioned Smith back out into the hall. He quietly closed the door behind them.

"How's your partner?"

Smith glanced down at his feet. "Jeff should be all right. Your brother was packing a Redhawk and that's a powerful gun. I guess it's a miracle Jeff survived. He has some damage to deal with, much more than your friend in there, so he probably has a long vacation ahead of him. But he'll work again. The guy's an ox. I don't think you could kill him with anything short of a nuclear weapon."

"Thank God," Sean said.

"Yes. Thank God."

It was Sean's turn to study his feet. "I don't know how to thank you. Me and Harry, I guess we did everything wrong from the very beginning. I should have gone to the police the night Stanley was killed."

Smith touched the boy's arm. "I can understand why you didn't. But yes, it would have been better."

"I'm sorry, Detective."

"I know you are, son."

They fell into silence, both glancing around at the seeming chaos of activity in the hospital corridor.

Sean cleared his throat. "I'd like to meet him. Your partner. Mr. McCray. I'd like to thank him for what he did. Do you think I could do that?"

Smith took the boy's arm and said, "Let's go see."

McCray was in Intensive Care on another floor. The waiting room outside ICU was packed with McCray's sisters, aunts, uncles, and a handful of off-duty policemen who had stopped in to give moral support.

Smith pointed through a glass partition, and Sean saw the handsome black man being tended by a nurse. His eyes were open and when he spotted Smith through the glass, he gave his partner a feeble thumbs-up. McCray seemed entranced by the sight of the young man at Smith's side. He raised a tentative hand in greeting and Sean mouthed the words "Thank you" through the glass. McCray gave an almost imperceptible nod and turned away, as if embarrassed by his helplessness.

Suddenly overcome by emotion, Sean reached out to the glass to support himself and began to cry. A pretty black woman, whom Smith recognized as McCray's youngest sister, came over and placed her arms around Sean's shoulder. Gently, she led him toward a naugahyde-covered settee in the corner, and a huge black man moved away, without being asked, to give them room to sit.

"I'm Pearl," the young woman said, her arm still around Sean's shoulder. "Do you know my brother?"

Between sobs, Sean managed to say, "He tried to save my life."

Pearl patted his hand and laughed a little laugh that sounded like bells to the boy. "Why, honey, you're still here. It looks like he succeeded."

Sean could only nod, mortally ashamed by his tears and his inability to speak because of them. He wiped his face with the sleeve of his robe and tried to calm himself. Still, the words were hard to get out.

"I've never met him and he tried to save my life. This man, too." He locked eyes with Smith, who didn't know what to say.

Pearl did. "That's what they do. They help people."

Sean could only nod.

"What's your name, honey?"

"Sean."

"Sean, would you like to meet my brother's family?"

"Yes."

"Well, then, let's do it."

She gave Smith a wink and proceeded to introduce Sean to everyone there. With tears still streaming down his cheeks, Sean thanked each of them as they were introduced, and by the time Pearl had made the rounds, there were very few dry eyes in the room, including Pearl's.

She gave Sean a final hug and said, "When Jeff goes home I want you to come and see him. All right? He's the one you should be thanking, you know."

"I know."

She turned to Smith. "You take care of this boy or you'll answer to me."

Smith promised he would.

When they were back in the hall, Sean stopped and held his hand out to the detective. "Thank you again. For everything."

Smith gripped the boy's hand and held it as he said, "You're more than welcome, son. Now let's get you back to Harry. If he's awake he'll be wondering where you are."

"Are all cops like you guys?"

"No, son. We're exceptional."

Sean grinned. "I think you must be."

Smith stopped Sean before they reached the door to his room and pulled him off to the side, away from the bustle of the hospital traffic moving up and down the corridor.

Smith still had questions he wanted answered, and he was running out of opportunities to ask them. First and foremost, was motive.

"Why did he do it, Sean? Why did your brother come after you like that?"

"I don't know."

"I think you do."

Sean watched an orderly pull an empty gurney down the hallway as if it was the most fascinating thing he had ever witnessed. After the orderly passed, Sean closed his eyes.

"What difference does it make now?" he asked.

"None whatsoever," Smith answered. "But I'd like to know, just the same. You owe me that much."

Sean leaned his back against the wall and pulled the hospital robe tight around him. "I suppose I do," he said.

Haltingly, and in a voice so low that Smith had to lean forward to hear the words, Sean told the detective of that long ago night in his farmhouse bedroom when his brother confronted him about his homosexuality.

"How did he find out?" Smith asked.

"He… just did."

"How old were you?"

"Thirteen."

Smith seemed skeptical. "And that's what this is all about? He hated you so much for being gay that ten years later he went on a killing spree that left eight people dead, not counting your own parents? Come on, Sean. There has to be more to it than that. What really happened?"

Sean kept his eyes closed, unable to look at the man who had saved his life. His shame was too deep.

"You… you have to understand my brother. He was very religious. Fanatical. Even as a kid. Somehow… that night I… I tempted him. I made him do something he should never have done."

Smith saw where this was heading. "Did you have sex with your brother, Sean? Is that what this is all about?"

Sean nodded, but still he didn't open his eyes. He would see the same look of disgust on the detective's face that he had seen on his brother's that night so many years ago. He couldn't bear to see that look again, from anyone. It hurt too much.

"I… let it happen. It was my first time. I couldn't stop myself."

"Did you instigate it, Sean? Or did he force himself on you?"

"He… was just suddenly there. Naked in front of me. I made it happen."

"No, Sean. Your *brother* made it happen. Didn't he? Your brother *wanted* it to happen."

Sean opened his eyes and looked into Smith's face. He saw no censure there, only compassion. It shocked him. That look of compassion was the last thing he had expected to see.

"Maybe, but… still. *I let it happen.*"

"Could you have stopped it?"

"No. I tried. But he was so much bigger than me. There was nothing I could do."

Smith smiled at the boy. "Exactly, Sean. There was nothing you could do. He forced himself on you. It was an act of rape, Sean. Instigated by your brother on a thirteen-year-old boy who had no way in the world to prevent it from happening. Isn't that right?"

"I suppose...."

"There's no supposing about it. It might come as a surprise to you to learn that many rape victims feel they were the ones at fault. Did you know that?"

"No."

"It's true. And they are just as wrong as you are now."

A flash of anger and self-loathing crossed Sean's face.

"But I enjoyed it."

"Did he hurt you?"

"Yes. He hit me. Twice."

"Did you enjoy that, too?"

"Of course not."

Smith reached out and grasped the boy's shoulders, giving him a little shake.

"You've felt guilty about this your whole life, haven't you? You felt it was all your fault, didn't you? All this time you've blamed yourself."

"Y-yes."

"And your brother felt guilty about it, too, didn't he? That's what this is all about. Do you think your brother was gay as well?"

"I... don't know. Maybe. To him, it was a sin."

"Yes, Sean. And it was a sin he couldn't control, don't you think? It flew in the face of everything he believed in, but still he couldn't control it. He couldn't control the passion he felt for you, Sean. That's what this is *really* about. He was obsessed with you, and you know it."

"But I let it happen."

"No. You let nothing happen. You were a victim. You were thirteen years old. A child. You had no control over any of it. Your brother had the control and he chose to exercise it. Just like he exercised it last night in the rain. I saw what he did to you, Sean, there on the deck." Smith watched the boy's eyes open wide in surprise before he looked away in shame. Again Smith gripped the boy's shoulders. "You have nothing to be ashamed of. You have to put it all behind you. You have to let it go now and get on with your life. And you have to stop blaming yourself."

"M-maybe you're right."

"No maybes about it."

"But why did he have to kill our parents? What did they ever do?"

"I don't know, Sean. Your brother was ill. Maybe in his mind he thought that, in creating you, they were the source of it all. Of all the longings that were tearing him apart. That's just one hypothesis. There could be many. I don't suppose we'll ever really know."

Smith hesitated for a moment, unsure of exactly what it was he wanted to say to this troubled young man.

Finally the words came. "Son, you've got a second chance now. Try to do something with it, all right? Don't throw your life away. My partner almost lost his life so you could live yours. Make it a good life, okay? Make what he did worthwhile."

"What you both did."

"Yes. What we both did."

Sean took a ragged breath, trying once again to ward off the tears he knew were just below the surface.

"I will," he said. He did not mention that the thought was already in his head even before the detective voiced it.

Smith reached out and tousled the boy's hair, just as he had the night before.

"That's all I ask," he said kindly.

With that, Smith turned and walked away. Sean watched him until he disappeared into the elevator at the end of the hall. The detective had not once looked back.

Sean entered the room and found Harry awake, speaking to a pretty young woman with dark hair. On hearing the door, Harry saw Sean and smiled. Sean smiled back and moved toward the bed.

"This is Stella," Harry said, his voice hoarse from having just awoken. There was no pain in his eyes. Not yet.

Stella held out her hand and Sean took it.

"Harry's been telling me about you," she said.

"Has he?"

Stella stepped up to the boy and kissed him on the cheek.

"Welcome to the family."

Sean did not know what to say.

Harry grinned at his discomfort. "Stella hasn't really come to see me. She's come to see someone named Jeff."

Stella blushed and slapped Harry's foot. "That's not true. I came to see you too. To check on my raise."

Harry laughed. "At some point in the midst of Harry and Sean's excellent adventure, little Stella here has gone and fallen into lust with one of the detectives. A very handsome black man, or so she tells me."

"I just saw him," Sean said. "And she's right. He is handsome."

"Is he all right?" Stella asked.

"You'll find him two floors up. He'll be laid up for a while, but he'll live. Would you like me to show you where he is?"

Stella shook her head. "No. You stay here with Harry. I'll find him. The good detective and I have some unfinished business."

She bent down and pecked Harry on the cheek, gave Sean a quick hug, and said, "Wish me luck." With that, she was gone.

Sean moved to Harry's bed, sat on the edge of it, and laid his hand against Harry's cheek. "Welcome back," he said.

Harry pressed his lips into Sean's palm and Sean thought of the promise he had made to Detective Smith. It was a promise he intended to keep. For the detectives. For his parents. For Harry.

But mostly, Sean knew, for himself.

With Harry's love he knew he could do it. He would not waste the second chance so many people were giving him.

He rested his head on Harry's uninjured shoulder and glanced out the window beside Harry's bed, where he saw the sun shining high in a cloudless California sky.

The storm had ended.

His new life, with Harry at his side, was about to begin. Breathing in Harry's scent, Sean smiled to himself and closed his eyes. This time he would do it right.

JOHN INMAN has been writing fiction since he was old enough to hold a pencil. He and his partner live in beautiful San Diego, California. Together, they share a passion for theater, books, hiking and biking along the trails and canyons of San Diego, or if the mood strikes, simply kicking back with a beer and a movie. John's advice for anyone who wishes to be a writer? "Set time aside to write every day and do it. Don't be afraid to share what you've written. Feedback is important. When a rejection slip comes in, just tear it up and try again. Keep mailing stuff out. Keep writing and rewriting and then rewrite one more time. Every minute of the struggle is worth it in the end, so don't give up. Ever. Remember that publishers are a lot like lovers. Sometimes you have to look a long time to find the one that's right for you."

You can contact John at john492@att.net.

Also from DREAMSPINNER PRESS

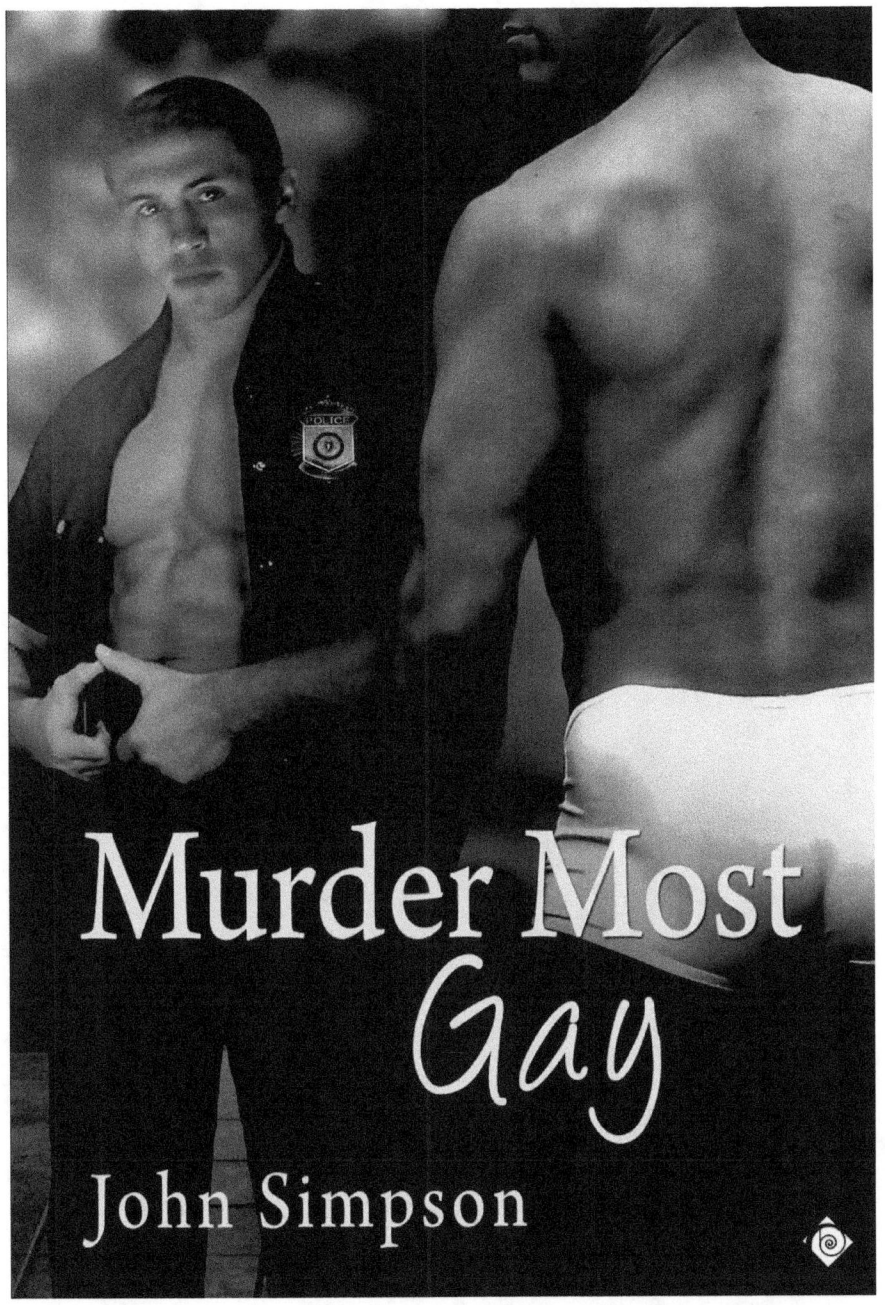

Murder Most *Gay*

John Simpson

http://www.dreamspinnerpress.com

Also from DREAMSPINNER PRESS

SHADES OF
GRAY

Brooke McKinley

http://www.dreamspinnerpress.com

Also from DREAMSPINNER PRESS

CUT
&
RUN

MADELEINE URBAN
ABIGAIL ROUX

http://www.dreamspinnerpress.com

For more of the
best M/M romance,
visit

Dreamspinner Press

www.dreamspinnerpress.com

www.ingramcontent.com/pod-product-compliance
Lightning Source LLC
Chambersburg PA
CBHW070056030726
47506CB00002B/486